About the author

Diane Jackson was born in Carlisle in 1947 where she lives with her husband and three dogs. She has two grown up children. She began writing novels in her late fifties. She loves the Lake District and the Solway Coast and uses her native Cumbria as a backdrop to much of her writing.

_To Sharon_

_Diane_

# THE
# GOLDEN
# DRAGON

## Diane Jackson

DJ 20/10

Published in 2008 by YouWriteOn.com

First Edition

Published by YouWriteOn.com

# PART ONE

## Chapter One

Xi Mei and Jonathan Lee stood side by side in a cramped, shabby office in Hong Sing, southern China, while a minor official pored over their paperwork. No-one had spoken after the man's initial brief demand for it. The small space was unbearably stuffy but Jonathan managed a weak smile at Xi Mei. It did little to reassure her. She wished her husband-to-be would at least take her hand. She stretched her fingers and touched the back of his. He didn't respond to the gentle hint. Hadn't he noticed or did he just not care?

What is he thinking, Xi Mei wondered. He didn't seem as nervous or excited as she was. She realised, with sudden insight, that he didn't seem to care much at all. She felt the first stirrings of doubt begin to grow. She slowed her breathing and tried to relax her shoulders. Think positive thoughts, she told herself.

As he turned each page the official looked up at them, his gaze passing from face to face as if they may have altered during the time he was reading. After each scrutiny he picked up a photograph of the couple from the desk in front of him and stared at it. He filled in forms, stuck the photograph onto a document which he stamped forcefully. When he'd organised the papers into an order important only to himself, he handed them to Jonathan, then without another word or glance he picked up an envelope from an overflowing wire tray and slit it open with a knife, completely ignoring the couple still standing in his office.

Jonathan looked at Xi Mei then leaned over and kissed her on the cheek. She hadn't been expecting it and didn't know how to respond. Should she kiss him back?

"I think that means we're married," he said with a forced laugh that lacked any warmth or emotion and turned away. He folded the certificate, put it into his pocket and walked to the office door; Xi Mei followed as they went to greet the mothers, Lin Yong and Angela Lee, who had waited outside.

"Congratulations to you both." Angela hugged her daughter-in-law much to Xi Mei's embarrassment. Lin Yong quietly echoed the good wishes and Angela bustled them away from the Marriage Registration Office, leading the way back to the Pagoda Hotel for their wedding party.

It was market day in the small town and the street outside was thronged with people. Somehow the news of the marriage of the daughter of one of the stallholders had spread and there was a fair crowd wanting to see the bride and bridegroom. If they were expecting the couple to be dressed in wedding finery, they were disappointed. Jonathan was wearing a plain grey, western-style suit. Xi Mei wore a simple blue cotton dress her mother had made for her to go to university. She wouldn't be going now.

If the marriage itself had been nothing more than the signing of a form, then the walk to the hotel for the wedding feast made up for the lack of occasion. There'd been brisk business that day and the market-folk were in good spirits, calling and jostling, shouting good wishes to Xi Mei and suggestive comments to Jonathan. Xi Mei blushed and looked at her feet. What did Jonathan and his mother think? Perhaps they imagined she somehow invited such coarse expressions. She was mortified until she realised, thankfully, it was highly unlikely they would understand the local dialect. She lifted her head in defiance and tried to smile. No-one must even suspect her true feelings.

Angela was smiling and nodding in acknowledgement of good wishes and Lin Yong's face was carefully bland. Jonathan said something to Xi Mei. She smiled back at him in an automatic response, though she hadn't heard what he'd said. She couldn't even make out whether it was English or Cantonese. Car horns blared and bicycle bells tinkled in a tuneless chorus.

The old spring onion seller from the market, who knew Xi Mei's family well, was loud with her comments. "Eh, do you see that Englishwoman? All them fancy clothes and jewellery. She must be worth a fortune."

Xi Mei winced.

"Her husband's one of us, though. Auntie Yin's his cousin. Good job the boy looks like him, eh?"

That's true, Xi Mei admitted to herself.

The pig-man sniffed noisily. "Lin Yong looked well. Maybe she'll leave her old man to rot in jail and enjoy the money herself. Do you think she'll be back at the market next week?"

Lin Yong had her pride, too – of course she would.

"Never mind that. Let's go and have a beer and drink to the

happy couple. The fellow Xi Mei's married looks a bit miserable. He would be a good looking guy if only he would smile. I bet she'll put a smile on his face tonight."

Oh, God! Xi Mei cringed.

The woman sniggered and elbowed the pig-man in the ribs as they turned towards the beer kiosk. The rest of the well-wishers stopped at the gates to the hotel, letting the bride, bridegroom and their respective mothers enter, still calling for good fortune to smile on the couple, and went on their way gossiping and shouting to one another.

* * * * * * * * *

Back at the Pagoda Jonathan went to change for the party. Xi Mei and the women, now joined by Auntie Yin and the Matchmaker, drank tea and ate sweetmeats, each finding stories to tell about their own and other weddings they'd been to, laughing and joking in an attempt to lighten the atmosphere. Xi Mei felt like an observer, as if she was a peripheral character in a play and not one of the stars. From the bar men's voices drifted out with clouds of cigar and cigarette smoke.

Then it was Xi Mei's turn to get ready for the party. She and Lin Yong were alone in Jonathan's room. No, not *his* room, Xi Mei thought, *our* room. She struggled to imagine sharing the bedroom with him, then struggled even harder not to.

Xi Mei chattered non-stop as she changed her clothes, afraid of what her mother might say if she as much as paused to draw breath. Lin Yong sat on the edge of the bed and looked at her daughter, waiting for her to run out of steam as she must surely do soon. At last Xi Mei stood quiet and still, dressed in a crimson silk dress, modestly high at the neck, with short, cap sleeves and slits up each side of the skirt to mid-thigh. It had been made for her in just a couple of days by the dressmaker whose little shop overlooked the market place. Her husband, who drove a motorcycle-taxi, had delivered it that morning, roaring up to the front door of the hotel in a cloud of noxious smoke.

Xi Mei smoothed the embroidered silk over her slim hips. She'd never worn such a dress. She was, at the same time, dismayed it showed off her figure and revealed far too much leg, and delighted to be wearing such a fabulous dress. I look so wonderfully glamorous, she thought as she looked at herself in the mirror. That should make my husband – husband! – sit up and take notice.

"Well, Ma. How do I look?"

"You look beautiful," Lin Yong replied. "I am very proud of you." She paused. "I'm sorry." The emotion at last broke through her innate reserve. "I never intended this to happen. I'm so afraid for you, going all that way to a foreign country instead of to university in Guangzhou. I'm afraid for me, too. That I'll never see you again once you go away to England." She put her face in her hands and sobbed.

Xi Mei was shocked. She'd hardly ever seen her mother express any emotion and she was at a loss how to deal with it. All she could do was to try to comfort her with words.

"Ma, don't cry. Please don't cry. The Lees are good people, I'm sure." The reassurance didn't seem to be having much affect. "Come on, Ma. I know they'll take care of me. And I'll be able to go to university one day. You'd like that, wouldn't you?" Xi Mei couldn't tell if the couple of strangled words her mother managed were in agreement or not. "And I'll come back to see you, I promise. But Ma, I'll be seeing you a lot before I go. It'll be ages yet. Everyone says it takes a long time to get a visa for England." Xi Mei was crying now. "Oh, I do wish Pa was here. I thought he was coming."

Lin Yong sniffed and blew her nose. "He hasn't been released yet." Xi Mei looked up in surprise at her mother's words. "Don't worry, I paid his fine. I even went personally to Xiao Cheng, the Chief of Police. He said it takes time for these things to be processed. But I know your father could have been out of there in minutes if that man had said the word." Lin Yong's eyes narrowed in hate. "He's always had it in for your father. I've never known what it was between them, but it must have been politics. It always was when they were young." She wiped her eyes on a sleeve and used the other to dry her daughter's tears.

"Before we go down to the party I have something for you." She reached into her pocket. "It is very special. My mother gave it to me on my wedding day, and it was given to her in the same way. Years ago, before the revolution, my family were wealthy."

"You've never told me about any of that."

"I know. It wasn't the correct thing to speak of at one time. And then, later, it didn't seem to matter. It had all gone. The only thing remaining, and it was saved in secret of course, was this." She held out a small package wrapped in shiny red paper tied with fine gold string. Xi Mei took it, looking into her mother's face. The older woman nodded. "Yes. Unwrap it, daughter."

Carefully Xi Mei untied the string and slowly peeled away the wrapping paper. Nestling in a bed of crumpled tissue lay a tiny golden dragon. Every detail was finely wrought, perfect in execution: clearly the work of a master craftsman. The end of the dragon's tail formed a loop with a long, gold chain threaded through. She gasped and looked at her mother in amazement.

"Your father never knew I had this, nor my father, either. They might have felt it was their duty, as obedient comrades of the glorious Chairman Mao, to give it up." She laughed at the look of delighted surprise on her daughter's face, took the chain and slid it over the girl's head. It lay, gleaming in the harsh, electric light, on the red silk. "It is up to you whether to wear it in secret beneath your clothes, in the open in defiance of the old regime, or tuck it away in your belongings as I've done all these years."

Xi Mei walked over to the mirror and looked, eyes wide with enchantment at the golden dragon's reflection. "It's the most wonderful thing I've ever seen. I'll wear it." Before she turned back to her mother she dropped the pendant inside her dress, feeling the cold metal begin to warm against her bare skin. "In secret, for now." The two women embraced for the first and only time in Xi Mei's life. Awkwardly they withdrew from each other and went down to the wedding feast.

* * * * * * * * * *

From the time Xi Mei and Jonathan entered the restaurant to the time they left together, the noise and sheer press of the crowd of invited guests threatened to overwhelm Xi Mei. Even with the luxury of the hotel's air-conditioning it was humidly hot. The mingled smells of perspiration, spicy food and cigar smoke choked the air. Shrill voices competed to be heard above the din. Jonathan, as ever, seemed detached from proceedings. It was hardly surprising as most of the guests gabbled to each other in the local dialect. Friends and family and a good proportion of government officials, included by Angela to ensure goodwill, consumed dish after dish of expensive food washed down with copious amounts of Qing Tao beer. No-one mentioned her father, Fu Gui's, absence. To do so, it was taken for granted, would make the bride's family lose face, and that was not to be done.

To Xi Mei the evening was intolerably long but then it seemed that, too soon, Angela was ushering her and Jonathan from the room. She looked back at her mother and received the barest of nods. Encouragement? Empathy? Xi Mei couldn't judge. Great cheers and raucous comments followed them up the stairs. Xi Mei felt embarrassed by her innocence. She'd lived all her life in a farming community and witnessed the mating of animals many times. Often she'd heard the women gossiping, relating the most intimate and salacious details about this person or that. She knew, in theory, what to expect on her wedding night but it was an experience she'd been trying to avoid thinking about. At the same time she couldn't help her curiosity. What will it be like, she wondered. She didn't expect romance, but it would be nice if Jonathan was at least kind and understanding. She realised how little she knew about him.

## Chapter Two

Was it only ten days since Xi Mei and her mother, Lin Yong, had waited in Hong Sing market place? Xi Mei had jumped when a high pitched voice called out their names. It was the woman everyone knew as the Matchmaker. She was a round ball of a woman and her tightly drawn-back hair pulled her features into a smooth mask. She looked Xi Mei up and down, apparently approving of what she saw: tall and straight, face a perfect oval with an ivory complexion, eyes as obsidian black as her hair, lips full and slightly turned up at the corners. The girl was willow slim. She wore a black skirt and black flat shoes; her light cotton blouse was plain white.

Lin Yong was an older version of her daughter with the story of her life, labouring in the fields in all weathers, written in the lines of her face. She was dressed, as befitting her age and her purpose here today, in sober grey. It seemed to her the future she had planned for her daughter was flowing away like a river into the sea. It would have been hard to have afforded to send Xi Mei away to university, but it was impossible, now. The carefully saved, hard earned money had gone. She must never let anyone see how devastated she was by this turn of events. It would not do to lose face so badly. At least this way Xi Mei would have the possibility of an easier life as the wife of a rich man. But it would mean her daughter would be far away, in England – lost to her, for all intents and purposes.

Xi Mei's feelings could not be guessed at. Her calm exterior hid a sick nervousness that she was fighting to control. How has it come to this, she asked herself. Only last week I was young and happy. I could hardly wait to go away to college. The future was waiting like a new book, full of blank pages to be filled with exploding thoughts, exciting ideas. She could almost laugh at the fanciful thoughts she'd had of adventures to be drawn in and painted in glowing colours; dreams arching over everything like bright rainbows. Now it seemed that book was to be put away, back on the shelf. The dreams of a poor village girl – how naïve. In her mind she continued with what seemed now like a rather immature analogy: I can start another book. I'll fill it with new people and places. I'll have new dreams. It'll be different, but maybe just as exciting. Xi Mei forced herself to be optimistic. It was all she had left to cling to.

As the three women made their way out of the market place they were followed by the eyes of shopkeepers, customers and on-lookers alike. What the Matchmaker was up to was always an endless source of fascination and gossip. She was leading the way to the hotel, moving surprisingly swiftly for someone of her weight, and kept glancing behind, obviously impatient that Xi Mei was lagging behind so. They went through the gates into the hotel garden. A marble path led them past flowering shrubs and shade trees. Above, the hotel rose majestically, with tiers of ornately decorated balconies.

As they entered the reception area Xi Mei looked around, impressed by the grandeur despite herself. The ceilings were high with electric fans stirring the air with their rattan paddles. The walls were covered with rich red fabric which was echoed in the upholstery of the sofas set around low tables. In one corner a group of prosperous-looking men dressed in western-style suits sat in a miasma of cigarette smoke in deep discussion. A middle aged woman rose from a chair nearby and hurried across the white marble floor towards them. The Matchmaker greeted her and introduced her as Auntie Yin, a relation of the man Xi Mei had come to meet. She ushered them to a lift whose sliding doors whispered open at the press of a button. Xi Mei was intrigued, looking around curiously. She had never been in a lift before. I wouldn't mind riding up and down like this all day, she thought. Actually I would rather do that than go where I'm being taken. But, as they stepped out, she could see her mother was thankful to set foot on the firm, carpeted floor of the hotel restaurant.

The scents of food wafted enticingly across the room, but Xi Mei was so nervous she scarcely noticed. In front of them the large space was nearly full of diners and along one wall were several doors with brass name plaques. Through one or two open doors she could see private rooms set with dining tables. Waitresses glided in with steaming dishes and out again, laden with used plates and glasses. Auntie Yin led them past Water Lily and Double Happiness to one named Instant Success. Xi Mei wondered what that portended. Her father had taught her that instant success was not to be trusted; only by hard work and perseverance, he insisted, could success be achieved. Thinking of him almost brought tears to her eyes. Her mother had worked so hard to earn the money to send her to university, all to come to nothing. Her father wasn't really to blame but she did wish he wouldn't be so outspoken against the wrong people. It was ironic that his misplaced idealism would now be the cause of turning her from a promising student into the bought-bride of a rich man. Would this be better than the life her mother had known? She couldn't tell. She only knew she couldn't let her mother, nor her father, down. She squared her shoulders and walked determinedly into the room. It contained a large dining table surrounded by seven chairs and set out for a sumptuous meal – and three people.

Rising clumsily to his feet was a large man with a weatherbeaten face. Although dressed in a western-style suit his untidy hair and large, calloused hands betrayed him as a typical local man. Another man sat with his back to them. A woman, already standing, commanded Xi Mei's attention.

She's European! Xi Mei's eyes widened in amazement. Why hadn't anyone told her? They'd said the family was from England, so it seemed likely that this woman was English. Who is she? Why do an English family want a Chinese wife for their son?

The woman appeared to be in her mid-fifties and was elegantly dressed in a well-cut light fawn suit over a green silk shirt. Her blonde hair was short and stylishly cut to emphasise her best features and revealed heavy jade earrings hanging from small ears. Her face, with its creamy-pink complexion, betrayed too strong a personality to be called beautiful, but handsome she certainly was. Auntie Yin performed the introductions.

"This is my husband," she indicated the large man, now standing awkwardly beside the table. Xi Mei dragged her eyes away from the Englishwoman. The man nodded and smiled at the three new arrivals.

"Everyone calls me Uncle Jin," he smiled showing crooked teeth.

"And this is my cousin's wife from England," Auntie Yin continued.

Oh, she's married to Auntie Yin's cousin. So the son's obviously half-Chinese, Xi Mei reasoned.

The woman came forward and shook hands, "Hello, I'm Angela Lee." Her eyes hardly left Xi Mei as she politely greeted the other two women. Her Cantonese was good, and she spoke with a marked accent which Xi Mei found rather endearing. Angela Lee drew Xi Mei forward. "This is my son, Jonathan." Xi Mei's eyes now went to the man whose back had been towards her since she entered the room.

Here goes, she thought, her heart pounding uncomfortably. But what's the matter with him? Is he deaf? Hasn't he heard us come into the room? Oh, God! Is he going to be some sort of idiot that his mother has to buy him a wife? Or is he being rude? This is definitely not a good beginning.

He was staring into a teacup, apparently unmindful of the new arrivals. She let her eyes travel over him; more than would have been seemly if he had been looking up. His suit, like his mother's, looked expensive. His white cotton shirt was freshly pressed and his striped blue tie was knotted fashionably loose. As far as she could see he was physically well-favoured and, judging by his profile, good looking enough. Jonathan didn't seem interested in looking at his proposed bride. His eyes remained fixed on his cup. "Jonathan," Angela Lee said sharply, causing her son to jump and knock the table, sending tea slopping into the saucer. He stood up as she said his name again. Xi Mei felt her breath release in a rush, not realising she had been holding it in, when she looked full into Jonathan's face.

Well, she thought with relief, he's certainly handsome. He looks pure Chinese. But does he have to look so miserable? Why can't he smile? He obviously doesn't want to be here, either. The realisation lit a spark of defiance in her: who does he think he is to humiliate us in this way?

His mouth was turned down in an ill-tempered pout and his eyes refused to meet either hers or his mother's. Xi Mei judged him to be about thirty – much older than she had imagined and a good ten years or more older than herself.

Remembering her manners and what this marriage would mean to her family, Xi Mei inclined her head and said in a soft, pleasant voice that cost her no little effort to keep from trembling, "It's a pleasure to meet you."

"Say hello to Xi Mei, Jonathan."

"Hello," Jonathan obeyed his mother's command, his eyes flicking over Xi Mei. She felt more insulted by the casual glance than if he hadn't looked at her at all. He sat down again and resumed his study of the teacup in front of him. There was little enough in that one word for Xi Mei to judge what his voice was like.

"Please, do sit down," Angela invited. "I'll ring for our lunch to be served." Xi Mei seriously doubted she would be able to eat anything. Her throat was tight with suppressed anger at Jonathan's rudeness and her stomach felt like a clenched fist.

Conversation over the meal was cordial, however, for both Xi Mei and her mother wanted to make a good impression; their pride would not let them do otherwise. Xi Mei watched Jonathan, trying not to be too obvious about it. She was still amazed that he looked so completely Chinese.

He really doesn't want to be here, she thought again. But why? He must want to get married or else he surely would never have consented to come here to meet me, his prospective bride. What sort of relationship does he expect? She mentally shrugged. Never mind, I'll cross whatever bridge I come to, and make the best of it.

Jonathan continued to show little interest in what was going on around him nor in anyone at the table. He ate sparsely and played with the rest of the food put before him. When anyone spoke do him his replies were monosyllabic.

Angela talked about their home and their life in Newcastle-upon-Tyne in northern England. Her husband was ill, too ill to make this journey, she said, but his dearest wish was for their son to be married to a traditional Chinese girl, so they had come to his cousin's home in China to find a suitable bride. She was pleased that such a lovely young woman – she smiled graciously at Xi Mei – had agreed to meet them and she would so much like to welcome her into their family.

There's more to it than that, Xi Mei thought, but said nothing.

Everyone had finished eating. Although there was plenty of food left on the table, Angela had stopped offering tasty morsels to Xi Mei and her mother. Jonathan pushed his chair back and stood up. "Excuse me. I must go to my room. I need....." His voice trailed off and his face reddened.

"Very well, Jonathan." A sharpness had crept into Angela's voice as she excused him. After a moment she rose from her seat saying, "I know he's very tired from the journey and it's so hot here. And he's not used to the food. I'd better go and see if he's all right." Angela left the room, followed by Auntie Yin.

What was all that about, Xi Mei wondered. It sounded as though she was talking about a child, not a grown man.

The women could hardly discuss Jonathan in front of Uncle Jin, so the stilted conversation was confined to the weather and prices in the market. It was an uncomfortable half hour before Auntie Yin came back.

They all looked up expectantly as she settled into her chair. She made small-talk for some minutes before embarking upon the purpose of the visit.

"My cousin has made a good offer for Xi Mei."

The Matchmaker and Lin Yong studied the figures written on a card Auntie Yin laid on the table between them. They exchanged glances that Xi Mei couldn't interpret and Lin Yong spoke.

"Thank your cousin for her interest, but I cannot give you an immediate answer. I must discuss this with my husband and his parents," she said. Her voice had taken on an edge of cold formality. What on earth is written on the card, Xi Mei wondered. Whatever, it can't be good. Lin Yong rose to leave but the Matchmaker put a restraining hand on her arm, apparently sensing the beginning of what might be a long negotiation.

"Please. Let me order some tea for you," Auntie Yin quickly offered.

"Thank you," the Matchmaker hurriedly accepted the suggestion of refreshments for them before Lin Yong could refuse. "Tea would be very acceptable. Did I mention that Xi Mei would be going to university this year? Such a talented student – very clever and a good artist and she writes beautifully. Sadly she would have to give all that up if she were to marry." Xi Mei was embarrassed her meagre accomplishments were being laid out as a bargaining point, but realised this was part of the game.

Auntie Yin nodded at the hint. "I will talk with my cousin and see if we can come to some arrangement. Please excuse me."

Xi Mei knew it was vital she made a good marriage. Her father was a kind man really, and he had done his best for his family. His trouble was he had such high ideals. "Anyone can get on these days," he would say in his thin sing-song voice. "But the right palms have to be greased, appropriate presents given to those in authority. I don't see why I should spend hard-earned money for permits for me to work somewhere else, or just for them to look the other way when necessary."

Xi Mei could picture him standing up, hands folded behind his back, rocking on the balls of his feet as he spoke in that lecturing way.

"Honest work should bring its own rewards. I cannot accept the corruption that is everywhere these days. You have to bow before it or suffer. Nothing will make me compromise my principles." She could almost recite the often repeated the words along with him.

If only he'd kept his mouth shut when Xiao Cheng was appointed Police Chief. Why didn't Pa know better than to criticise the man so publicly? But he didn't, and now it seems I have to pay the price, she thought, or rather the fine imposed on him. They have to sell their only asset: me. She wondered at her calm acceptance of the situation but she knew it was her duty to her parents. I can't let Pa go to jail, and this way the family honour will be intact: I'll marry into a rich and powerful family and Ma will pay Pa's extortionate fine. She thought her father would probably rather stay in prison, but her mother's pride wouldn't allow such a demeaning thing.

Xi Mei sighed. I have to do this and forget my own ambitions. Jonathan Lee seems all right, even though he's gone out of his way to ignore me. But maybe he's not feeling well, she thought, trying to find an excuse for his behaviour. He's reasonably young and good looking. He's wealthy. Surely, somehow, I can make a success of it.

Yes, Xi Mei was resigned to the marriage she was sure would be arranged.

It seemed an age before Auntie Yin returned with Angela. "I will be direct with you, Xi Mei," Angela said, despite the looks on the faces of her cousin and the Matchmaker. They all knew Angela should have taken little part in the discussions and the two women shook their heads at the typically English way she had of coming straight to the point without going round and round to approach it discreetly. "My husband is ill; you know that. His dearest wish is to hold a grandchild in his arms before he dies."

A grandchild? Xi Mei began to realise what this was all about.

"I know you would be giving up a place at university to marry my son and come to England. But what if you didn't have to give it up entirely?" She looked at Xi Mei intently. "What I am proposing, my dear, is that as soon as a child is born you are free to continue your studies. There are good colleges, universities and specialist schools in Newcastle. You could take your pick. Study whatever you wish. I will even employ someone to help with the child."

She smiled into the astonished face of the girl then turned to her mother. "Well, what do you say?" she asked Lin Yong. Auntie Yin placed another card face down on the table. The Matchmaker turned the card and showed what was written upon it to Lin Yong.

Lin Yong looked into her daughter's face. Xi Mei looked back, trusting her mother's judgement in this matter. Does Ma really have a choice, Xi Mei asked herself. It might be months before another suitable offer comes along and I doubt Pa will survive that long in prison.

"Very well," Lin Yong said. "We are pleased to accept. You may arrange for the wedding to take place."

\* \* \* \* \* \* \* \* \* \*

Jonathan opened the bedroom door and let Xi Mei enter first. She could still hear the distant clamour of the wedding reception coming from the hotel restaurant. The closing of the door cut the sounds off. The sudden silence was unnerving.

They stood in the middle of the room, facing each other in the dark – virtual strangers. Carefully, Jonathan undid the silk-covered buttons that fastened Xi Mei's dress at the shoulder, then drew down the zipper at the side. The silky fabric caressed her skin as it slid down to pool around her feet. Her underclothes followed as she stood there unresisting. She wasn't ashamed of her body – there'd been little chance of modesty in the close confines of her upbringing – but this was different. She shivered slightly, even though the night was humidly, uncomfortably, warm. The little golden dragon glowed softly in the moonlight that filtered through the leaves of the trees, casting dappled shadows around the room. She wondered what Jonathan was thinking and feeling.

Jonathan was remembering his promise to his father before he left on this trip to China: to provide an heir to the Lees' fortune. It was Jonathan's duty and he must keep that promise. If he had to marry it was as well to have a submissive young wife rather than any of the over-assertive western-raised women he already knew. He didn't know Xi Mei – he didn't need to. It was a business transaction, engineered by his mother in accordance with his father's wishes. All he had to do was consummate the agreement which was complicated by neither love nor passion. He dropped his clothes on the floor and led Xi Mei to the bed.

\* \* \* \* \* \* \* \* \* \*

The honeymoon lasted barely a week. Jonathan hired a car and a guide the day after the wedding and each day the newlyweds embarked on sightseeing trips. He began to call Xi Mei, May.

"It'll be much easier for you," Jonathan explained. "May isn't an uncommon name in England, and it suits you, anyway," he added with a rare smile. "You're May Lee now." She was happy enough with that, pleased he was at last taking an interest in her.

May was amazed and fascinated by everywhere they went – she'd hardly been further from her village than the local market town. Much to her delight Jonathan gave her a camera and showed her how to use it and through the lens she began to see the scenery as though through another person's eyes. Hesitantly at first, she translated for Jonathan what the guide was telling them about the places they visited.

There were times, during those few days, May felt that at last they were getting to know one another a little. They spoke in English, even though she struggled with the language. Jonathan, patient for the most part, corrected her pronunciation and grammar. Then at times, suddenly, as though a light went out from behind his eyes, he would became the remote Jonathan of their wedding day. May was at a loss to understand him.

Every night, in the darkness of their room, they made love. No, she thought in the quiet hours when she lay awake, that would assume she took an equal part in the physical act. There were times when she felt herself responding, could feel something – something that might be delightful – beginning to happen, but then it was over and she was left to wonder what it might have been.

\* \* \* \* \* \* \* \* \* \*

May was already dressed and Jonathan was in the shower when Angela knocked at the door the fifth day after the wedding. Her mother-in-law kissed her on the cheek as May let her in. Angela seemed upset.

"Where's Jonathan?"

"He's having a shower. Is there something the matter?"

Angela threw open the bathroom door, calling to her son. Jonathan came out, still dripping and pink from the hot shower, a towel wrapped around his waist. He raised a questioning eyebrow.

"We must go home. Your father is ill again."

"Mother, please calm down. He's got the best care money can buy."

"But I want to be with him. If… If he died and I wasn't there I'd never forgive myself."

May looked from one to another as they spoke, understanding little of the swift exchange of words.

"Is he that bad? Is he dying?" Jonathan asked, his voice taking on that hard, edgy tone May had begun to recognise.

"Jonathan, don't be stupid. You know as well as I do it can only be a matter of time."

"But the doctors think he has months yet."

"Huh. Doctors!" Angela paced up and down the room. "They haven't been much good to him, have they? What do they know? We must go to him. Today."

"What? Now?"

"Yes. Now." Angela turned to her daughter-in-law. "May, I'm sorry." Her voice softened a little as she looked at the girl they would have to leave behind for who knew how long. "We must go but you have to stay till your visa comes through. I'll take you to Auntie Yin's on the way to the airport. She'll tell you about the arrangements I've made for you. I'll telephone you at her house and give you what news I can about Adam – your father-in-law. Please understand, my dear. I must be with my husband and our son must come too."

May had always known she'd have to stay behind. It would take months to get a passport and then a visa from the British Embassy. It was a time she planned she would use to learn English and gain some sort of understanding of the English way of life. Auntie Yin knew of a woman who had lived in England for many years and was willing to take on the task of teaching May.

Angela was becoming impatient with her son. "Jonathan, get packed. We have to leave in two hours."

## *Chapter Three*

The aircraft banked sharply and began its descent. The shuddering alarmed May as it penetrated the thick, grey clouds. She felt her stomach heave. Please don't let me be sick, she prayed. Trying to quell the feelings of nausea she looked out of the window, curious to see something of the countryside she would soon call home. She'd seen nothing of the land beneath the small plane as she travelled the last leg of the long journey from China. Then the fields were suddenly there, frighteningly close, sodden from all the rain which pooled in corners reminding her, unexpectedly, of flooded rice paddies. A prickle of homesickness threatened. She took a deep breath as the tarmac rushed upwards, and at the solid jerk of landing and roar of the engines the man in the seat next to her let out an audible sigh. So, he's as relieved as I am to be on solid ground again, she thought.

The announcement came over the PA system: "Welcome to Newcastle Airport. The outside temperature is eight degrees with rain forecast for the rest of the day. We hope you have enjoyed the flight. Captain Matthews and the crew wish you a pleasant stay. Thank you for travelling with us."

May found it hard to understand the electronically distorted words but gradually her English was getting better, more fluent. Another thing she'd have to get used to was her new name: May Lee. Just as she'd been getting accustomed to Jonathan and Angela calling her May, they'd gone and once more she was Xi Mei. But she'd left that behind, now.

She gathered her belongings and joined the queue shuffling towards the exit doors then down the aircraft steps and onto the wet tarmac. She shivered as the cold wind blew sharp pinpricks of icy rain into her face and flung her long, black hair around. Disembarking passengers pushed past eager to get into shelter. The smell of kerosene and exhaust fumes tainted the air as vehicles jockeyed to tend to their many duties around the plane. Hurrying as fast as she was able, May followed the other passengers into the airport building. She found her luggage and passed through

Immigration and Customs without a hitch. She'd been afraid she'd lose something, or that she'd be denied entry to England at the last minute.

To May, everyone seemed to know where they were going. She had managed the long journey alone, even negotiating the crowds and clamour of Guangzhou and London. A sense of adventure and a new beginning had carried her through. But here she was at journey's end and she felt her aloneness keenly; she'd left her old life and family behind and she was standing in the no-man's-land between them and her new life and family. Had she done the right thing? Was it too late to go back?

May looked around anxiously. She already knew that none of the family would be meeting her. Jonathan had phoned her at Auntie Yin's just before she left.

"I'm sorry, May. I probably won't be at the airport. Father's in hospital again." His voice was distant and the line crackled.

May's English had improved considerably in the intervening months but she wished Jonathan wouldn't speak so quickly. He paused, obviously expecting a response. She didn't quite know what to say.

"May? Are you still there? God! This is an awful line."

"Yes, Jonathan. I'm here."

"Father wants to be at home to welcome you, but I don't know. It all depends on what his doctor says."

"But how will I..." Surely Jonathan didn't expect her to find her own way in a foreign country, did he?

"Listen." He sounded impatient.

May could picture his face. She was certain he would be wearing that sullen expression again. She could hear it in his voice. "Yes, Jonathan," she replied.

"If I can't get to the airport I'll send Armstrong with the car. You'll be all right. He'll bring you home."

Arm...? Was that a name? Why couldn't Jonathan come himself? Why did he have to be with his father? May realised she was being unreasonable. It was a son's duty, after all, to take care of his parents.

"Look, May. I've got to go." His voice cut through her self-doubts. "Do you understand?"

"Yes, Jonathan." But she didn't, really.

"Goodbye, May. See you soon."

"Goodbye, Jonathan."

The line went dead. She felt tears of disappointment well up. She fought them back. I'll manage, she thought. I'm not stupid.

And here she was. Jonathan had said someone would be there to bring her home, though. But how would she find that person? That Arm-somebody.

"Mrs Lee?"

May, either failing to hear or not recognising her new name, continued looking around wondering who would be here to meet her.

"Mrs Lee?" A dark-suited middle-aged man with the peaked cap of a chauffeur and a piece of card with her name printed on it was coming towards her.

"Mrs May Lee?" he asked again.

"Yes, I'm May Lee," she said, at last realising someone was speaking to her. The announcement still felt strange, though she'd practised it many times in the last few months. In the mirror she'd looked at herself. "I'm May Lee," with a smile. "I'm May Lee," with hand extended to shake. "I'm May Lee," trying to convince herself who she was now.

The man smiled, "Welcome to Newcastle, Miss. Are these your bags?" His accent was strange, not quite what she was used to hearing from her teacher, but his tone was warm and his face friendly.

May nodded, smiling back.

"I'm Armstrong, Miss. Mr Lee's driver and general dogsbody." At her look of puzzlement he explained, "That means I not only drive the car, but I tend the garden, keep the house running smoothly and see to anything else the family might need. Just follow me, please Miss. The car's not far." He led the way towards a large grey car where he deposited May's case and cabin bag in the capacious boot. Coming back round he opened the rear door for her and May slid inside. As she relaxed into the luxury of the leather seat she felt the child within her kick vigorously.

* * * * * * * * * *

"We're here, Miss." Armstrong's voice woke May; she could

hardly believe she'd fallen asleep. She'd been eager to see where she was to live, the countryside and the city streets and she'd missed it all. Armstrong opened the car door and reached in to take May's hand to help her out. He produced a large, black umbrella which opened magically as he pressed a button on the handle, sheltering May from the rain which still fell, puddling in the road and on the pavement.

May saw they were in a tree-lined avenue with rows of tall, pale grey-brick houses down either side. Four wide steps led up to each imposing front door, flanked by stone pillars she thought looked more than a little forbidding..

"Let's get you inside. I'm sure you're more than ready for a nice, hot cup of tea, and perhaps a scone to go with it." May smiled gratefully at Armstrong, but wasn't sure exactly what it was he was offering.

He slipped a key into the lock on the door and opened it, then motioned May to enter first. Space and light – that was her first impression of her new home. The floor was tiled in chequer-board black and white. No, not white, she could see now: cream. The walls were cream, too, and a chest of drawers in honey-coloured wood stood to one side where a huge bowl of flowers perfumed the air. Several doors led off the hall. Armstrong pointed, "That's the drawing room and this is the dining room, but come on into the kitchen and I'll make you that cup of tea."

May was overwhelmed at the size and the unfamiliarity of her surroundings. Her teacher back in Hong Sing had given her piles of books and magazines to show her what English houses looked like but, still, she felt completely stunned by this huge house that was now her home.

"Here now, Miss. Sit yourself down while I put the kettle on." Armstrong pulled a chair out from the table that stood in front of a tall window through which May could see a small garden. He busied himself brewing tea, pottering about the kitchen, taking the milk out of the fridge then putting in back again once he'd filled a jug. She watched his square, capable hands as they buttered scones and arranged them carefully on a flower-sprigged plate. He has kind eyes, May decided; they were a sort of greyish blue. His hair was grey and crinkled but thick and strong. He might have been an anonymous, unnoticeable man: medium height, medium build, grey hair, had it not been for his ruddy complexion and ready smile which lit up his whole face.

May was learning that the English take milk in their tea and was determined to get used to it that way. Obediently she ate and drank what was put before her, hardly responding to Armstrong's friendly conversation, shy in her unfamiliarity with the language. He didn't seem to mind, though, as he talked on, not saying much but filling what might have been an awkward time.

"If you're ready, Miss, I'll take you upstairs to your room, then I'll bring your cases up." May followed him up the wide curving staircase that led out of the hall to the upper reaches of the house. She looked around, trying to take everything in. Would she ever be able to find her way around such an enormous place? It was nearly as big as the Pagoda Hotel. She was impressed and just a bit intimidated. "Mr Jonathan will want to show you around properly, I expect." Armstrong pointed to the doors leading off the first spacious landing. "Here's Mr Adam and Miss Angela's rooms." He must mean Father-in-law and Mother-in-law, May thought. "Yours and Mr Jonathan's are on the next floor." He led the way slowly, considerate of the late stage of her pregnancy. On this landing there was, like the one on the previous floor, a tall arched window glazed with coloured glass set in geometric shapes. May guessed that when the sun shone, as it surely would eventually, the whole area would be a patchwork of bright colours. Armstrong indicated the door to the right. "This is Mr Jonathan's room." He opened the door to the left. "And this is your room, Miss." He stood back to let May enter. Again the window was tall and the ceiling high. The soft carpet was a pale, minty green and the walls painted ivory. The double bed had ivory and green covers, with a touch of pink here and there. Armstrong walked across and opened a door, one of several lining one side of the room, to reveal more wardrobes and drawers than May doubted she'd ever have clothes to fill. This one room is bigger than our entire house in China, she thought in amazement. There was even a pink-veined marble fireplace in front of which was placed an ivory covered *chaise longue*.

"Oh. How beautiful," she exclaimed, forgetting her shyness. "Is this really all for me?"

"Yes, all yours, Miss." Armstrong pressed a button to the side of the fireplace and it immediately sprang to life, blue and orange flames flickering from the real-looking logs. How on earth had he done that? "It's gas," he explained seeing the question on her face. "Much easier than carrying coals or logs up all these stairs. It's not really necessary with the central heating, but it makes the room cheery, don't you think?" He smiled at May's genuine pleasure. "And here is your bathroom."

"A bathroom? Just for me?" May couldn't believe it. It was too wonderful to be true. Yes, she had seen pictures of houses very much like this, but this was real and it seemed it was to be hers.

"I'll be back with your cases in a few minutes, Miss." May sat on the seat in front of the fire and looked around; her very own room. She'd never imagined such a thing. She was used to sharing; she'd always had to. That man, Armstrong, had said Jonathan's room was across the hall. Aren't we going to sleep together, she wondered.

Armstrong was soon back. She had only two bags and if he thought it wasn't much to contain all her worldly possessions he didn't say so. "Can I help you with anything else, Miss."

"No, thank you. I will unpack my things, now."

"Very well, Miss. I'll leave you in peace, then. I have to go to pick Miss Angela and Mr Jonathan up from the hospital. We'll be back in about an hour."

"Thank you, Armstrong," May attempted to say the unfamiliar name.

"Thank you, Miss."

* * * * * * * * * *

For the second time that day a man's voice woke her. "May. May. Can I come in?" It was Jonathan. For a moment May didn't know what to do. Why does he want to come into my room, she thought, still half-asleep. Jonathan was virtually a stranger. But he's your husband, she told herself. You need to remember that.

"Yes. Come in, please." May sat up, swinging her feet to the floor. Jonathan opened the door and stepped inside. May thought he looked tired, older than when she'd last seen him. He came over and kissed her on the cheek, awkwardly, as if not quite sure if it was the right thing to do.

"I'm sorry I wasn't there to meet you. But Father..."

"Yes, I know. Armstrong took good care of me. But how is

Father-in-law?"

"Much better, thank you."

"He stays in hospital?"

"Yes, for a few more days, then they say he will be well enough to come back home."

"That will be good."

A silence grew between them. They had so much to say but neither seemed to know how to begin. It hadn't been so difficult during most of their several phone conversations over the last months, but now they were face to face it felt different.

"You look well, May. Are you all right?" Jonathan broke the ice. "And the baby?"

"We are both doing well. Oh!" May gasped as the baby kicked, as if knowing it was the subject under discussion.

"What? Is something wrong?"

"No, no. It's the baby. He's just kicking." She laughed at Jonathan's expression. A mixture of surprise and curiosity. "Here. Feel." May took Jonathan's hand and placed it on the mound of her belly. At first she felt his resistance then he relented and grinned.

"That's amazing. He's so strong." In that moment May felt connected to her husband, intimately joined. For the first time in their short acquaintance, for that's all they had even though they were married and about to have a child, she felt comfortable in his company. Jonathan seemed like a different person: warm and relaxed. Well, he's in his own home in his own country. Maybe, just maybe, ours will be a real marriage or at least a friendship. May began to feel some of the tension and apprehensions begin to drain away.

"Come on," Jonathan took May's hand and helped her up from the *chaise longue*. "Let's go and see Mother, then I'll show you around the house."

Angela Lee was sitting on a brown leather sofa sipping a glass of white wine. She jumped to her feet and hurried across the room as May entered. She took her daughter-in-law's hands in hers and smiled at the young woman.

"How well you look, my dear. I'm so sorry we weren't here when you arrived. Adam was so poorly, and I was afraid."

"That is no trouble. I see he is weller." May faltered, suddenly painfully conscious that she was a stranger here and being a

29

nuisance. "Forgive me my English. I.... I...."

"Oh my dear. It is you who must forgive me. I was very selfish, but now I must make amends. Come, sit down and tell me all your news. Are you well? How is the baby? And your parents? I can't tell you how thrilled we were when we heard the news you were expecting a child. Adam has been so impatient for you to arrive. Every month we had to wait seemed like a year. And you, my dear, you must have thought you would never get here. And what a greeting when you did. Only poor old Armstrong."

"He was very kind to me."

At that moment Armstrong appeared at the door and announced the meal was ready. Angela tucked May's arm into hers and led her into the dining room. The food was strange to May. Armstrong had excelled himself in the kitchen preparing a traditional English meal: roast beef, Yorkshire pudding, potatoes and vegetables, steaming hot and delicious. May had never seen a meal anything like it, but she enjoyed the new experience and relaxed as both Angela and Jonathan talked about everything from the state of the weather to a concert Angela wanted to go to. The house and their lives seem to be entirely westernised, May observed. There was very little here to reveal their ethnic origins.

"This house belonged to my family," Angela explained as if reading May's thoughts. "They were in shipping and my great-grandfather bought the house when the business prospered. I was born here and so was Jonathan." May tried unsuccessfully to stifle a yawn. "But that's enough family history for now. I'm sure you would like an early night, my dear," Angela said. "You've had a long day. I've made an appointment for you at the maternity clinic tomorrow. Jonathan will take you." Angela patted May's hand. "Off to bed with you now. Sleep well."

May might have felt as though every aspect of her life was being controlled by others, even when to eat and sleep, but she felt strangely comforted that her wellbeing was thought to be important. To have her mother-in-law taking care of her was the complete opposite of what would have been expected at home. No, not 'at home' she reminded herself, this was home now. Back in China several of her friends had become hardly more than maids to their mothers-in-law. At least she had escaped that fate.

Jonathan paused at the top of the stairs. "I hope you like your room. I thought you would prefer your own. I'm just over the way in case you need anything." He kissed her gently on the cheek. "Goodnight, May. We'll be a happy family. Just wait and see."

As May undressed she caught sight of the golden dragon glowing between her breasts in the soft light cast by the bedside lamp. "May you always attract good fortune to me and my family," she told it before slipping into bed to spend the first night of her new life in her new home in England.

# Chapter Four

May lay on the examining table while Dr Erica Simmons gently felt her rounded tummy, pressing a stethoscope to the bare flesh to hear the baby's heartbeat. Then she listened to May's chest, took blood from her arm, her blood pressure and asked all manner of questions about the progress of her pregnancy. She seemed satisfied with the answers.

"You're a healthy young woman, May. I don't expect any problems. Everything seems quite normal and the baby is a good size. I don't want to disturb either of you with any more tests but I do want you to come in every week to see me until the baby is born – that's just over a month away. If you have any worries or concerns just ring my nurse and I'm sure she'll be able to answer any questions. Is there anything you want to ask me now?"

"No, thank you. I am feeling very well." May had immediately liked both women and instinctively trusted them to take care of her and the baby – when it decided to arrive.

The nurse smiled at May reassuringly. A badge saying, 'Barbara – Midwife' was pinned to her white uniform dress. She turned to Jonathan who had sat to one side during the examination. "Would you like to be present at the birth, Mr Lee?"

Jonathan jumped, startled at being addressed. "Um… er… well… I…"

Nurse Barbara laughed. "No need to worry. Many fathers-to-be have that reaction. Discuss it together and we'll see how you both feel on the day."

"I'll see you next week, May. And maybe you too, Jonathan?" Dr Simmons raised her eyebrows with a smile.

"Yes, of course. Thank you, Doctor." He rose and helped May down from the examining table. He waited with apparent patience as she adjusted her clothes then led her out of the room.

The private maternity clinic had once been a large house, a mansion, and still felt very unhospital-like. It was set back from the road in well tended gardens surrounded by a low wall topped by black-painted iron railings. Yellow trumpet-heads of daffodils clustered under the trees and the grass sweeping down to the front entry was studded with the purple, yellow and white of crocus. The trees were still bare but several showed signs of buds about to burst. Only a small signboard by the side of the gateway gave away the fact it was not still a grand private house.

"Whew, I'm glad that's over," Jonathan admitted. May always felt surprised when he spoke, his accent was so purely English.

"It wasn't too bad. My doctor back home..." she paused, "...in China was always pleased with me. He said I was carrying a strong son."

Jonathan looked at her keenly. "How could he tell? That it will be a boy, that is?"

"I don't know." May laughed. "I think he was just telling me what he thought I wanted to hear. You know how highly boys are prized. I expect he wanted to make sure he got a good fee." She looked up into a sky as clear and blue as yesterday's had been cloudy and grey. "Can we walk a little way, please? It's such a lovely morning and I feel so well."

Jonathan had brought her in his own car this morning, a shiny, dark green Mini Cooper. May had had a little trouble getting into the low-slung vehicle. It was only a few streets from home, but Angela had insisted that he drove her. May had told them she walked everywhere in Hong Sing: to and from her English lessons, the hospital appointments, shopping in the market, but Angela was insistent. However, Jonathan relented and as they walked Jonathan took her arm and threaded it through his own. It felt comfortable and comforting to May..

"Look, there's a café across the road," he pointed. "How about we get a coffee? You'll have to start picking up English habits, you know." Without waiting for a reply he led her across the street to a parade of small shops: a florist with a profusion of flowers that spilled out of the door and onto the pavement; a travel agent, the window full of this week's special offers printed in eye catching colours; a hairdresser's where a handful of stylish-looking women were undergoing various cuttings, colourings and blow-dryings. There was a shop stuffed with bric-a-brac that proclaimed 'Antiques' on the panel above the plate-glass window. Tucked between this and 'Beryl's Blooms' was a shop-front, the surround painted red – red as the pillar-box standing at the street corner. Black lettering proclaimed 'The Scarlet Parakeet Café'. Inside there were tables of all shapes and sizes, some with wooden benches others with assorted chairs, even a couple of old sofas with the stuffing showing through the worn covers. It should have been scruffy and seedy but it had a welcoming charm that drew the late morning refreshment seekers in from the street. Most of the tables were taken but, as luck would have it, a couple rose from a table in front of the window just as May and Jonathan entered.

"I'll be with you in a minute," the waitress called over as she put the cash from the departing couple into the till. May and Jonathan had hardly settled themselves in their seats when she came over. "Mornin'. D'you know what you want, or should I give you a few more minutes to decide?" Her clothes were an unexpected Bohemian mix that few people could have carried off. She seemed to fit exactly the ambience of the whole place: a conglomeration of styles that shouldn't have met but which, here at least, looked right.

"I'll have coffee, Colombian please." He looked across at May. "How about you, May?"

"I'll have the same, thank you." May hadn't the slightest idea what she'd be getting. She'd had coffee a couple of times with her English teacher, but it was a taste she had yet to acquire. Still, she was determined to fit in here and she was going to take a lead from her husband.

"Anythin' to eat? We've some canny lardy cake this mornin'. Just fresh made by me own fair hands."

"No thanks. It sounds very nice, but just the coffee for now." Jonathan smiled coolly at the girl. May looked at him in puzzlement.

"What did she say? I didn't understand a word. Was she speaking English?"

Jonathan laughed. "No, not as you've ever heard it. It's the local accent – Geordie. You'll soon get used to it." He laughed again as May frowned. "She wanted to know if we'd like a piece of cake with our coffee. I hope you didn't. I said, no."

"That's all right. I'm fat enough as it is without eating cake."

"You're not fat. You look lovely to me." It was the first time that Jonathan had paid her a compliment and May blushed, looking out of the window to hide the sudden flush of pleasure. She couldn't get over how different this Jonathan was from the one she'd married in Hong Sing eight months ago. That one had been withdrawn, morose almost, and certainly not friendly. This one was relaxed and was making an effort to help her feel at home. She was saved from trying to reply by the arrival of the waitress with their coffee.

"Thank you," May smiled at her as she placed the cups and saucers on the table. There was something about her that May found intriguing. Perhaps it was her brightly coloured clothes and open, cheerful face. Perhaps it was only that she'd never met anyone quite like her.

"You're welcome," she replied.

May watched as the girl stopped by another table and said something to the two women who sat there, then picked up a steaming jug of coffee and refilled their cups, saying something else that made them laugh. May felt a pang of envy at her easy, friendly manner. She took a sip from her own cup and couldn't help but grimace.

"Some sugar might help," Jonathan suggested. May, grateful for him noticing, added a spoonful of the brown granules in the glass bowl on the table and stirred until she thought it would be dissolved. She took another tentative sip.

"Better?" asked Jonathan.

"Much better, thank you." May took another sip. "I think I quite like it, now."

"I'm going to have to leave you to your own devices this afternoon," Jonathan told her.

"Devices?"

"Sorry. I meant leave you by yourself at home. I have to go with Ma to see Father."

"Of course. I will just rest in my room." It felt odd to say 'my room' and know it was hers alone. At home – I must stop thinking of China as home, she reminded herself – she never had anywhere of her own. In the apartment she had shared with Auntie Yin and Uncle Jin she slept on a pull-out bed in the main room. In her parents' home she and Grandmother shared a bed. Now, she had not only that huge bedroom but the unheard-of luxury of a bathroom.

The waitress was back at their table. "Would you like your cups refilled?"

"No, thanks. We must be going. Can you just bring the bill, please?" Jonathan replied without consulting May.

"Right you are, sir."

Not quite understanding the words, May picked up something in the girl's tone that Jonathan didn't seem to notice: a certain cheeky lilt at the 'sir'. As they left the café the waitress grinned at May. May couldn't help responding.

Outside, Jonathan took May's arm again and they strolled slowly back to the car. Angela was waiting for them when they arrived home, eager to hear what the doctor had said.

"Everything's fine, Ma. Due in about a month. Dr Simmons is pleased at the baby's progress. She says May's in the best of health, too."

Angela smiled at May. "That's good news. I hope there'll be good news this afternoon, too. I'm hoping his doctors will let Adam come home tomorrow. You'll be all right here on your own, won't you, dear?"

"Of course she will, Ma. She's going to have a bit of a lie down, aren't you May?"

"Jonathan," Angela chided her son. "You really must let May speak for herself. She's got a mind of her own and besides, she's got to practice her English. Anyway, lunch is ready now and then we've got to be on our way to see Adam. Come along both of you."

\* \* \* \* \* \* \* \* \* \*

The room was getting dark when May awoke to hear loud voices close by. She sat up and listened. "Be careful, Jonathan. No, let Armstrong do it. Here, I'll get the door." She heard both men reply to Angela's commands then the hoarse growl of another male voice. May knew immediately her father-in-law had come home. She'd thought it would be tomorrow at the earliest. Up until now he had seemed unreal, a hidden presence that influenced others, but that must be his voice. May was suddenly fearful. It was at his bidding that Jonathan married me, she thought. His will that rules our lives. What's he like? Will I like him? But, more important, will he like me? There was a tap at her door and Angela poked her head round.

"Can I come in?"

"Of course, Angela."

"Oh dear. I hope we didn't disturb you."

"No, you didn't." May told the polite white lie.

"Adam is home. He insisted. He'd intended to be here to

welcome you when you arrived and wouldn't hear of waiting another day." Angela sat down beside May and immediately got up again. May had never seen her less than calm and composed, except that morning when she'd ordered Jonathan back to England. It made May wonder about her in-laws' relationship. Was Angela afraid of her husband? "I must get back to Adam. Jonathan and Armstrong have helped him upstairs, but he's so impatient – he hates to be dependent on anyone. It's left him in a foul mood."

Jonathan appeared in the doorway as his mother was about to leave. "Oh good, May. You're awake. Father wants to meet you."

"No. He must rest. The doctor made him promise," Angela protested. "Besides, May has just woken up."

"You know what he's like," Jonathan put in. "If he doesn't get his own way he won't rest. It's easier all round just to give in to him."

May realised then, that this was how her husband lived his life. Was this how her life was going to be, too? What was it about Adam Lee that made everyone dance to his tune? Daring, for the first time, to make her own decision, May said, "First I must have a bath and change my clothes. I will be ready to see Father-in-law in one hour."

## Chapter Five

She knocked firmly on the door and at his command May entered the room to meet Adam Lee. She walked, as firmly as her pregnancy would allow, across the room towards the man sitting in a large armchair by the fire. She'd expected him to be weak – diminished by his illness. What she saw surprised her. His face bore a tracery of lines, like a piece of tissue paper that has been crumpled then carefully smoothed out again; his hair iron-grey and thick. How like Jonathan he is, she thought immediately. But Jonathan's moodiness isn't there; there's an air of determination about him. It shows in his eyes and in his mouth. She stood in front of the man, head up, refusing to look as intimidated as she felt, waiting for him to speak. It seemed an age, as he looked her up and down: from her long, black hair, fastened back from her face by a clip, to the tips of her low, patent leather court shoes.

"By the looks of it I've got my money's worth and Jonathan's obviously done his duty well, judging by the size of your belly." He spoke in English. May was appalled by the coarse, rudeness of the man. She didn't reply. "What's the matter? Got nothing to say for yourself? Don't you understand English." He said the same thing again, in Cantonese. Still, May stood there, saying nothing.

"What's the matter with you, girl? Scared of me like that useless excuse for a son?" he sneered.

"No, Father-in-law, I am not frightened of you. I am sorry for you if you think that you have to bully people to get your own way. As my husband's father I must show you respect, but it is hard to respect one who speaks as you do." May didn't know where she got the temerity to say such things but there was something about the man that made her stiffen her spine and, for the first time in her life, stand up and speak out. Somehow she knew she must not show any signs of weakness or she'd be under his thumb for ever.

Adam Lee made a hoarse sound. May could not tell whether it was a laugh or a cough. "Well, well, well. Got a bit of spirit, have we? I never expected that. Pour yourself a cup of tea and sit down. While you're about it you may as well fill my cup, too. They won't allow me anything stronger." May sat in the chair opposite Adam

38

and sipped silently at her tea as he slurped noisily at his. He's doing it on purpose, trying to shock me, she realised. I wonder if he'd do it if Angela was here.

As she waited for him to speak again she looked around the room, curious to see part of the house she hadn't yet visited. Like her own room there was a marble fireplace. Flames licked round real-looking logs but no ashes had fallen so she assumed they were artificial and the fire was gas, like hers. The chair in which she was sitting was similar to Adam's own, covered in flowery chintz echoed in the curtains drawn across the windows to keep out the cold evening. There were two double-sized beds beside which were low tables with lamps emitting a soft glow. The colour of the room was predominantly blue and even though the man May sat opposite seemed far from welcoming, the room's ambience was just that. Despite everything she felt calm and interested to hear what the old man was going to say next.

"My wife says you went to the clinic today. I'm pleased that everything seems well. Do you feel well?" His concern for her wellbeing surprised May.

"Yes, thank you, though the baby is getting so big he makes me feel a bit uncomfortable at times."

"He? You said, 'he'. Are you sure it's a boy? What makes you think it's a boy?" Adam asked sharply.

"I don't know. It's just a feeling I've had ever since he first moved." May found herself telling her father-in-law details she'd never mentioned to anyone, even her mother. "Jonathan and I were only together a few days," she had the grace to blush a little. "I somehow never thought... never expected..." May looked down at her hands still holding the teacup above the swell of her belly. She put the cup on the table and raised her eyes to her father-in-law's. "Expecting a baby seemed to make it easier for me to get a visa to come here. I was told it could be many more months."

Adam laughed. She was sure of it this time. "That and more than a little of my influence in political circles. A lucrative shipping contract swung things just in time for you to get here for the birth."

May found herself responding with a smile. "I'm grateful for that. I wouldn't have liked to travel all that way with a young baby."

Adam yawned behind a hand. "Sorry, I seem to be tired all of a sudden." Immediately May rose to leave. "You will come to see me again in the morning. I'll send for you. Goodnight."

Despite herself May was intrigued by her father-in-law. In turns rude, forthright, warm and humorous with a dash of imperiousness thrown in for good measure.

"Goodnight, Father-in-law."

"Adam. You must call me Adam."

"Goodnight, Adam."

Over the next days it became the established routine for May to go to Adam's room with his morning coffee and then, later, spend an hour with him before the rest of the family had dinner downstairs. He seemed to have got over his rudeness; May suspected it had just been for effect, to see what she was made of. I'm glad I stood up to him that first time, she thought. I don't know what made me do it, but it must have been the correct thing. I think he likes me.

At first Adam told her very little about himself, "There's plenty of time to hear all about that. It's you and your family I'm interested in. What about your parents? Tell me about them. How did they meet? In halting English, peppered with Cantonese words she couldn't yet translate, May told him the story her father had told her many times. She could hear the echo of Fu Gui's voice.

\* \* \* \* \* \* \* \* \* \*

It was in the early years of the Cultural Revolution. Fu Gui, at thirty years old, still wasn't married. His parents, despairing he ever would be, took matters into their own hands and called on the services of a Matchmaker.

"Don't worry," the Matchmaker told them. "I know a girl – strong, a good worker – who would be very suitable."

A week later she led Fu Gui and his mother to a house on the outskirts of the village where the girl and her family lived. She introduced Fu Gui and his mother to the girl's parents. "And this is Lin Yong," she eventually said, bringing a young woman forward. She was dressed, as they all were, in dowdy, shapeless trousers and jacket.

Why on earth does this lovely girl have to depend on a Matchmaker, Fu Gui wondered as she smiled, ever so slightly, before lowering her gaze: the respectful, prospective bride.

Before long the Matchmaker was at his elbow, steering him to the door. "They have asked for a visit to your home," she told him delightedly. "They will come one week from today and, if the family approve, the marriage will go ahead."

Lin Yong was accompanied by her mother and two sisters to Fu Gui's village, tucked away behind high, blue-tinged mountains, six hundred kilometres south of Guangzhou. The women had not travelled this deep into the hills before. What they saw when they trudged along the road was a settlement of several dozen houses set round a bare patch of earth which served as the village square. Each house was built of clay with tiny, high windows, the roofs thatched with reeds. Narrow alleys ran between the houses. The Matchmaker was there to meet them and guided the women round a group of villagers who were clustered together having their midday meal, rice bowls in their hands and trouser legs rolled up to ease the heat of the summer's day.

The authorities, then, did not permit wedding parties and so the couple were married without a ceremony and gained permission for Lin Yong to leave her village to live with Fu Gui. He arrived, to fetch her, riding on the back of a tractor that was going in his direction, on its way to the fertiliser factory to pick up supplies. The bride and bridegroom helped load the trailer with sacks of fertiliser then rode back home perched on top. Fu Gui paid the driver with a packet of cigarettes that cost him a week's wages. He thought it was worth it.

All that marred their lives was the death of their baby sons. Their firstborn died at only five months. Their next son lived for little more. Almost a year after the death of his second child Fu Gui was waiting impatiently for the birth of a third. Lin Yong had sent him off that morning with an impatient sigh. "Your mother will get the Barefoot Doctor for me in plenty of time. Please, you'll be in trouble if you don't go out with the others." He couldn't refuse and he knew Lin Yong was strong, but two babies had already died; how would this one fare?

He had hurried along the alleyway towards the village square wishing he was free to be himself. Mao Tse Tung's Cultural Revolution and had bitten deep into the fabric of Chinese life. He supposed that he was lucky to be a humble 'poor peasant' in an insignificant village. He had never gone to high school and, though he loved to read books and prided himself in having a greater knowledge than others in his position, he could never be classed as an intellectual. He'd had his dreams but knew they would never come true. Just as well or he might have found himself beaten and imprisoned, maybe transported to work in a coal mine or as forced labour anywhere in the vast country. As it was he already lived in a remote spot where his family worked the land, growing as much rice as they could possibly coax out of the fields, striving to meet the unrealistic targets the authorities set.

Conventional education had become a thing of the past throughout the country as the struggle to eradicate old ideas, old culture, old customs and old habits was brutally enforced. Fu Gui took his part in the endless sessions of criticising self and others for having incorrect thoughts and read the 'Thoughts of Chairman Mao' aloud from the Red Book, then set out for the fields to join other villagers in a day's labour.

That day it was rice planting. They waded ankle-deep plunging clump after clump of the grass-like plants into the rich mud. Fu Gui was scarcely aware of what he was doing; his mind was on what was happening at home. Only the conditioning of years, doing the same task, saw him safely through the morning. It would not do if any of the student Red Guards suspected him of not pulling his weight. If they did, tomorrow he would find big-character posters stuck to the school walls denouncing him as thinking more about his family than about his work. He barely took time to wash the mud from his feet before starting back to the village for the midday meal. He was thankful everyone else was eager to be back, to get out of the hot sun and even have a sleep before the afternoon stint began.

So Fu Gui was at home when his daughter was born. He had crept quietly into the house and sat, fearful, in the gloom. He was pretending to mend a broken hoe his father had put aside to see to later, so he could not be accused of laziness. Instead of sitting in the living room where his father usually did this sort of job, he stayed in the kitchen perched on a small stool beside the table where the family ate their meals so that he was as close as he could decently be to the bedroom where his wife was. The door remained closed but he could still hear sounds he would rather not.

One of the great innovations of Chairman Mao was to provide each village with its own medical practitioner now that qualified doctors were relegated as dangerous academics. The uneducated peasants who had taken their place had barely enough training to apply a bandage to a cut and Fu Gui despised the lot of them and what they represented, but he held his own counsel and permitted the Barefoot Doctor to attend to the family's medical requirements.

So, despite the attentions of the Barefoot Doctor, Lin Yong was safely delivered of the daughter that was to be their only child. They named her Happy Flower – Xi Mei.

\* \* \* \* \* \* \* \* \* \*

Adam Lee listened avidly, May's story giving him pangs of an unexpected homesickness as well as relief that his own father's flight had saved them from years of persecution under the heel of the Communist revolutionaries.

## Chapter Six

May's days now had an established pattern. Armstrong brought breakfast up to her room on a tray; Jonathan went to the office; Angela went out – May didn't ask and Angela didn't say where. May enjoyed morning coffee with Adam, sometimes they talked, sometimes they sat quietly. Then it was time for lunch. She had felt ill at ease sitting at the large table in the dining room all alone, so now she sat in the kitchen with Armstrong. She'd felt awkward asking him, but he had smiled and said, "It'll be a pleasure, Miss."

At this late stage of her pregnancy May felt very tired so usually took an early afternoon nap. She lay on her bed and listened to the radio. She liked to hear the voices and every day her English improved. She didn't understand everything that was said and often she felt herself lulled into a doze by the talk. Refreshed, the afternoon seemed to stretch endlessly ahead of her before either Jonathan or Angela returned home, and May began exploring the neighbourhood.

The streets were wide and tree-lined. The houses, townhouses May learnt they were called, were tall and imposing with bay windows on the ground and first floors. Nearby was Jesmond Dene, its parkland in a deep valley with meandering walkways, and a pond where waterbirds of all sorts gathered. The Scarlet Parakeet Café wasn't far away and she became a regular customer. May remembered the first time she had gone alone. The same waitress that had been there the day she'd gone with Jonathan had come to take her order.

"Do you have green tea, please?" May had asked.

"Aye, we do. Would you like a pot?"

"Yes, please."

"Anythin' to eat?"

"No, thank you."

"Right you are."

May found she could understand most of what the girl said and liked the way she almost sang the words. She enjoyed sitting at the window watching the passers-by on the street and the comings and goings in the café. I like it here, May thought, and she seems nice –

the waitress appeared to have something to say to everyone.

"Have you just been or are you goin'?" the girl asked as May paid the bill.

"Sorry, I don't understand," May said at a loss.

"To the clinic." She nodded her head towards the building across the road.

"No, not today," May replied.

"You must come back next time you go. We're open every day."

"Yes, I'd like that." May smiled her thanks to the girl.

"OK. See ya, then. Me name's Jenny. It's Janet really but I hate it, so everyone calls us Jenny."

"Goodbye, Jenny."

The next week Jonathan took May to the clinic. When they came out she suggested, "Shall we go to that café and have coffee?"

Jonathan looked at her as though she'd suggested going into a bar and ordering double gins. "I don't think so," he said. "I thought it was a bit down-market, didn't you?"

May had no idea what he meant but his voice dripped disapproval. What have I done wrong, she thought miserably, imagining that somehow she'd overstepped a mark that, to her, was invisible. She didn't ask him again. Next time she went back on her own. Jenny's cheery greeting was friendly and welcoming.

"When are you due? It doesn't look like you've long to wait," Jenny asked one day as May was leaving.

"Next month." May was finding she enjoyed these brief exchanges.

"Oh, April. That's a canny time to be born, with spring and all that. Aye, well. I'd best be gettin' on. Can't stand here talkin' all day. Bye, then."

"Goodbye, Jenny," May had said, smiling as she left.

Today, May had felt uneasy all day. She'd annoyed Adam by not giving him her full attention. She didn't feel like taking her usual nap so instead she went out for a walk thinking the fresh air would do her some good. It was a lovely spring day and she was sure the sunshine would improve her mood. She found it didn't. Is it worth it, she wondered. My feet hurt when I walk and my back hurts when I sit down. I feel hungry but I don't want to eat. I wish Jonathan was here to talk to.

After a promising start when May had first arrived, Jonathan had, of late, grown somewhat distant. What have I done, she asked herself. Have I said something to annoy him? She decided he was bored with her as she caught him gazing out of the window instead of listening to what she was saying. Then, suddenly, he would be all solicitous attention again and everything would be all right. She sighed and wondered whether she would ever understand her husband.

May was sitting alone in the Scarlet Parakeet with a coffee, which she quite liked now, on the table in front of her, untouched. She shifted in her seat, trying to get comfortable.

"What's the matter, pet? Are you all right?" Jenny asked. "Is the baby kickin'?" She'd obviously noticed May had been fidgeting about ever since she came in.

"No. He's been fairly quiet for the last couple of days. My legs and back ache today."

"Not to worry. Won't be long to wait, now. Shall I bring you a bit of chocolate cake? Nothin' like chocolate if you're feelin' down."

Jenny seemed to have appointed herself as May's guardian angel and May felt herself enjoying the attention. On days where there was no-one else in the café, Jenny would sit at the table and the two would chat and now she knew May's name and where she lived. In her turn May learned Jenny and her mother lived in the flat above the café.

"Thank you, Jenny, but no. I don't think I have room for any food. Armstrong told me off for not eating any lunch."

"Then you definitely need somethin'. You can't go around carryin' that great lump without eatin'. Go on, have a bit of cake."

"Just to make you happy, then. But only a very small piece, please."

Jenny soon returned with the cake. "You're lookin' very pale." May was trying, in vain, to hide that she was now in some discomfort. "Here, you're not havin' pains are you?"

"No. No. I just feel a bit uncomfortable. I think I'll go home."

"Not on your own, you're not. Shall I phone your husband to come for you?"

"No. He's gone out to a business lunch with his mother today. They won't be back for ages yet." Unaccountably May had felt abandoned and now she thought Jenny was making a fuss about nothing.

Jenny shouted over her shoulder to her mother in the kitchen, "Mam, see to the café for me. I'm goin' to walk May home. She just lives round the corner so I won't be long."

They were hardly out of the door before May put her hand in the small of her back and groaned. She leaned over, gasping with the pain. What was the matter with her?

"You *are* havin' pains, aren't you?"

"No. It must be the baby lying awkwardly." May tried hard to convince herself. "The midwife at the clinic said it was normal. Anyway, it feels better now," May reassured Jenny. Jenny eyed her sceptically.

"Well, if you say so...," trailing off as May groaned again. "I don't care what you say, I think you're havin' contractions. Not that I'm any expert, but it seems pretty obvious to me. Come on. I'm takin' you to the clinic, and no argument."

May protested. There was no need, she'd only been for her check-up a couple of days ago. Jenny prevailed and May let her lead her across the road. She gritted her teeth but another moan escaped as the two passed through the wrought-iron gates.

"Them's pains and they're comin' regular. You sit here and I'll get someone to help."

Jenny sat May down on a wooden bench, placed so that strollers in the garden could rest and take in its delights, and ran into the clinic, her long vivid skirt flapping as she went. May felt like crying. What am I doing sitting here alone? I want to be at home, safe in my own room. I'll feel better there.

But she found she could no longer deny the pain that gripped her.

* * * * * * * * * *

Dozens of red Chinese lanterns lit the street and banners stretched across the narrow gaps between buildings. Fire-crackers exploding outside competed with the popping of champagne corks inside the glittering restaurant. Jonathan Lee stood smiling as a toast was proposed in his honour.

"Ladies and gentlemen, raise your glasses to Jonathan Lee," a red-jacketed Master of Ceremonies announced. "Chinese Businessman of the Year." Cheers erupted and voices echoed the toast. Glasses clinked and Jonathan was acknowledged as running one of the most successful businesses in the city. His mother sat smiling at his side, though she knew it should have been Adam receiving the honour. Jonathan didn't deserve it – he was riding on the back of his father's farsightedness and the good management team he had put together before illness stopped him taking an active part.

* * * * * * * * * *

As Jonathan was accepting his award May lay in the delivery room of the private maternity clinic. One contraction had barely abated before another gripped her. A young student nurse held her hand and murmured encouragement as a midwife pressed a stethoscope to the distended belly. May watched, feeling strangely divorced from reality. Where was Nurse Barbara? Where was Dr Simmons?

"You're doing well, May. It won't be long now." The midwife reassured. "The doctor is here to check you over."

May, expecting to see her own doctor, almost recoiled as large man with a white coat and a red face loomed over her. He said something she didn't understand. He repeated it several decibels louder but still May had no idea what he was saying. Was he speaking a foreign language? Another contraction twisted like a knife. How can he expect me to understand anything when it hurts so much? She shook her head and moaned.

He muttered something else and went to sit on the stool at the end of the bed, between May's splayed legs. As he spoke to the midwife May began to pick out the odd word. He was speaking English but with such a strong accent it was almost impossible for her to understand.

It wasn't supposed to happen like this, May thought with increasing panic. Where's Dr Simmons? She said she'd be here. I don't want this strange man. I don't like him. And where's Nurse Barbara? May felt very alone and frightened.

Where's Jonathan? Why hasn't he come? Hasn't Jenny phoned him?

May was drowning in a haze of pain. Voices were unreal: sometimes loud and booming; sometimes gentle and soothing.

Metal clanged against metal and bright lights bounced off shiny white tiles. She felt a sharp, stabbing pain then agonising pressure before a wet, slipperyness between her legs brought immediate relief from the torment she knew she could stand no longer.

"Your baby's born," the young nurse said in her ear. "You have a son."

A son! Oh, a son. How wonderful. May felt herself bathed in a wave of euphoria. I have a son. She kept repeating it to herself, not quite able to comprehend the fact.

Something was still going on at the end of the bed. May looked up. The midwife was holding a swathed bundle and May could just see a tiny foot peeping out. My son, she thought. My little boy. The baby wailed.

A sudden sharp pain attacked May's most intimate parts. The doctor bellowed something as she cried out in shock.

"You need a few stitches," the nurse beside her explained. Tears of self pity misted May's eyes. She had thought it was over but she was being forced to submit to yet more indignities. Would it never end? Then at last the doctor had finished. He said something else she couldn't understand. He shrugged his shoulders and left. The student nurse reassured May it really was all over now. May's eyes closed in relief. Suddenly they sprang open again. Where had the midwife gone? What was she doing? Where was the baby?

"My baby? Where's my baby?" The midwife had returned, alone.

"Your baby is fine, May. You mustn't worry."

"Is he all right? What's happened? Where's my son?" May could hear her voice rising shrilly.

"He's fine. Really, he's fine. He's nine pounds two ounces and he has lots of dark hair. He's a lovely little boy."

May leaned back against the pillows, allowing herself to be reassured.

"His birth was a little difficult for you," the midwife smiled and patted May's hand. "We'll keep an eye on him for a few hours while you get some rest. How about a nice cup of tea? And I'm sure you could eat a slice of toast." May didn't care about cups of tea and slices of toast, but she did want to rest. She wanted to sleep for a hundred years. But first she wanted her baby and her husband. Where was Jonathan? Oh yes, she remembered now, he was out at that business lunch with his mother, but surely that had finished hours ago. It couldn't be lasting this long. Hadn't anyone contacted them? Why didn't they come? She felt foolish tears trickle down her face and onto the pillow.

\* \* \* \* \* \* \* \* \*

The atmosphere was hazy with smoke; empty cigarette packs lay crumpled on the table amid a clutter of glasses containing dregs of wine and beer. Talk and laughter filled the room with noise. A waiter came over and spoke to Jonathan. Angela grabbed the waiter's arm as Jonathan rushed to the phone.

"What's going on? What did you say to my son?"

"It was a message from your house, madam. Mr Lee's wife is having a baby," the young man stammered.

"Of course she's having a baby. Everyone knows that," Angela snapped, impatient with the waiter."

"Yes, madam. She's having the baby now."

Jonathan arrived back at the table, his face a mixture of disbelief, shock and joy. "It's May," he told his speechless mother. "She's had the baby. This afternoon. A boy." His face stretched into a wide grin. "I've got a son, Ma."

The others at the table overheard Jonathan's news and roared their approval.

"It's a boy," he shouted over the din. "He's to be called Robert, to honour my grandfather."

Adam had already chosen the name. None had been considered for a girl; he'd refused to acknowledge such an eventuality. Everything depended on his having a grandson.

More champagne, more food, more cigarettes, more noise and congratulations. Jonathan Lee was a contented man. He stood among the milling group of well-wishers patting his shoulders or shaking his hand. He was a father. Father to a son, and what a life they would have. His – Jonathan's – future was secured and his own father, as always, had got what he wanted, what he had paid such a lot for.

At that moment Jonathan resolved to try to change. He knew he hadn't been fair with May. He'd been moody and, he had to admit, difficult at times. And May – she'd been patient and uncomplaining. There'd been a subtle change in the atmosphere at home since she arrived. He wasn't sure what it was – a sort of calmness, perhaps. She was pleasant, if undemanding, to be with. Surely, if he really tried, they could make something of their life together.

* * * * * * * * * *

Jonathan sat at his wife's side and took her hand. Angela stood beside the bed and smiled at the couple.

"You mustn't stay long, Mr Lee. Mother and baby are just fine but they are both tired. Your wife needs a good sleep. You can come back in the morning and spend more time with them then." Jonathan smiled gratefully at Nurse Barbara as she reassured him all would be well. "I've just come on duty. I must say I got a surprise to find her here and that she'd already had the baby."

"You're not the only one who got a surprise today," Jonathan replied ruefully. He turned and smiled at his wife. "How are you May? I came as soon as I could. What happened? You weren't due for another fortnight. And where's Dr Simmons?"

"I'm well," May answered moving her head slightly to avoid Jonathan's rank breath. It was obvious he'd been drinking – the smell of alcohol and cigarettes still clung to him

"Mother and I saw the baby – little Robert – before we came in to you. He looks very well. He's got lots of black hair. I don't know what colour his eyes are, he was asleep, but they are bound to be black, aren't they?"

"I wish I could see him." Tears threatened as she looked pleadingly at Jonathan. He'd never realised how beautiful she was with her ivory skin and coal-black eyes. Oh yes, he had seen she was attractive enough. He wondered idly if he would have still married her if she had been plain. Probably. He was tired of his father chipping away at his dignity and self-respect. His friends and business acquaintances all saw him as a strong man successfully running the business his father had inherited. What a laugh! He had neither power nor talent. All he had was his father always telling him what to do.

"Look, the nurse said you have to rest. I'll come back in the morning and we can count Robert's fingers and toes together. Ma's already gone. She'll be waiting for me. I must go and tell Father. He'll be so pleased. It's everything he's wanted for so long."

Jonathan kissed her on the brow. "Goodnight May. See you in the morning. Sleep well."

## Chapter Seven

May didn't expect to sleep, but she did – deep and long. She woke, gradually becoming aware of a soreness between her legs and a heaviness in her breasts. Suddenly she remembered and tried to sit up, falling back with a gasp as the stitches caught. Slowly and carefully this time, she sat up in bed and gingerly swung her legs out and her feet to the floor. She wasn't going to wait one more minute to see her baby – she was going to find him. At that moment Nurse Barbara came into the room to wake May for her routine checks.

"May, what are you doing? Please don't try to get up yet. I'll help you, but just sit there for a minute. We can't have you leaping out of bed and fainting, can we?"

"Where is my baby? Is he well? What have you done with him?"

"He's in the nursery and he's doing fine. He was slightly jaundiced but…"

"What!" Fear for her baby caught at May. She knew she'd had two brothers who had died in infancy. The midwife hurried to reassure her.

"No. He's not ill and it's not uncommon. We've kept a good eye on him all through the night and, I must tell you, he is now demanding to be fed in a very loud voice." She paused. "Do you feel up to feeding him?" May could say nothing, her emotions threatened to overcome her if she tried. Barbara seemed to understand. "Come on, now. Take my arm and I'll walk you to the bathroom, then when you're done and settled I'll bring young Robert to you."

May couldn't take her eyes off her sleeping son. He was beautiful, with no sign of the yellow taint of jaundice. Carefully she unfolded the blanket he was wrapped in. She held him close and kissed his eyelids then laid him on the bed. Gently, and with fingers that felt like thumbs, she undressed him. Oh, she thought, he's so perfect. She kissed his clenched hands and marvelled as the fingers uncurled, showing exquisite little nails on each finger. His feet were long and straight. She kissed his toes. When she looked back at his face, his eyes were open. They were the darkest shade of chocolate.

His hair was soft against her lips.

"You are the most wonderful thing I've ever seen," she told her son. "I was so afraid – why did they keep you from me? But I'm here now, my darling. I'm here now."

With her baby at last in her arms, cradled to her breast, sucking lustily, May experienced such an incredible surge of loving contentment that she felt as though she wanted stay like this forever. This is a moment I'll never forget, she thought. The baby sucked contentedly then one little hand closed firmly around the golden dragon that hung so close to him. May thought about her mother. How she wished Lin Yong was here to share this moment.

She was so wrapped up in the wonder of her son and thoughts of her mother that at first she didn't hear Jonathan enter. He stood there for almost a minute watching the girl who was his wife and mother to his son. May looked up, smiling when she saw him.

"Come and see our son. Our little Robert." She had some difficulty pronouncing the name. Jonathan laughed.

"Why don't we call him Bobby – it's short for Robert."

"Bobby," May said, stroking the shock of black hair that stood up from the baby's head, making him look startled. "Yes, I like that. Bobby."

\* \* \* \* \* \* \* \* \* \*

May's only other visitor was Jenny who came that afternoon, carrying a huge bunch of spring flowers and a box of gingerbread.

"Mam baked it for you specially," she told May.

"Please say thank you to her. She is very kind." May was touch by the thoughtfulness of a woman she didn't know. May also thanked Jenny for helping her the day before. She didn't know what she would have done if she'd been on her own without the kindness of the girl who seemed now to be firmly established as May's first English friend.

"You gave me a real fright yesterday, though. I thought you might be playin' an April Fool trick on me," Jenny said half joking, half serious.

"A what?" May was puzzled.

"Yesterday was the first of April. In England we call it April Fool's Day when you try to trick someone. It's just a bit of fun." May shook her head, not understanding what her friend was talking about. "I think that this young man played a good trick on you, though. Arrivin' like that." Jenny peered into the cot which was now placed beside May's bed. "God, he's got a lot of hair. Do all Ch..." she trailed off, blushing.

"Were you going to say, do all Chinese babies have a lot of hair?"

"I'm that sorry. I didn't mean to be... I didn't think that..."

"Jenny, don't worry. We are Chinese. How could I mind you mentioning the fact?"

"I just don't want you to think..."

"Think what? That you're interested?"

"Well, yes I am, but we'll talk another time I hope. Now I've got to get back or else Mam will think I've gone AWOL."

"Gone where?"

"Absent without leave. It was one of me Dad's expressions. He died a few years ago and it's just me and me Mam now."

"Oh, I see."

Jenny raced on, talkative as ever, determined not to let any awkward silence fall between the two of them. "It's nice workin' together, though, me and Mam, when I'm not at uni."

"You go to university?" May asked.

"Art College actually. Workin' part-time at the café means I can afford to study art." Jenny's face was animated with the passion she felt about her painting.

"So you're a student. I was going to be a student but here I am instead – a wife and mother."

"You hardly look old enough to have left school, to me."

"I'm nearly twenty-one."

"Oh. That old, eh?" Jenny laughed and impulsively hugged her new friend. "Anyway, it's time I was off."

"Will you come and see me again? Can I ring you when I get home?"

"Of course. Here, let me write my number on the back of this card." With a few swift strokes Jenny sketched a cartoon version of herself holding a phone to her ear then jotted the number underneath and handed it to May who laughed delightedly.

"Goodbye for now, Jenny."

"See ya soon, then May." The room seemed empty after she left.

\* \* \* \* \* \* \* \* \* \*

The next day Jonathan took May and Bobby home. Armstrong came bustling into the hall as he heard them arrive, fussing over May and marvelling that Bobby was such a strong, handsome chap. The baby lay cradled in his father's arms, with Angela overseeing the whole operation.

"Mr Adam wants to see you both – you and the baby – straight away," Armstrong told May. "You'd better go up. He's that excited it can't be good for him. Best not stay too long, Miss," Armstrong warned.

"But you must come too, Jonathan," May said.

"It would seem he just wants the two of you." Jonathan handed Bobby over to May with a slightly petulant expression.

Unwrapping the baby from the exquisite shawl Angela had bought, May introduced the old man to his first grandchild. Adam's lined face lit up with pleasure.

"Robert Adam Lee," he said with satisfaction. "You've done a good job, girl. Well done. Here, come and sit beside me and let me look at the boy for a while." May was about to protest, say that he had to rest, that Armstrong had told her not to tire the old man, but he pre-empted her. "Just for a little while. I want to see as much as I can of him while I'm still here. He's the future, you know. The future of this family and the company. Jonathan's no good. Worse than useless…" Adam trailed off. May looked at him, surprised he was saying such things to her about her husband. "That's enough for now," Adam dismissed her. "Bring him back in the morning. We'll talk some more then. Send Jonathan in."

She was glad he wanted to see Jonathan but it puzzled her why the three of them hadn't gone in together. And what had caused Adam's outburst?

\* \* \* \* \* \* \* \* \* \*

May laid the still sleeping baby in the crib which she'd set next to her bed. She gazed at him, examining each feature in minute detail. Almost all the time she was pregnant it somehow hadn't seemed real to her. Didn't seem possible that she was really going to have a baby, that it was growing inside her. Not even when Angela took her shopping for all the things a new baby would need had it seemed real. It wasn't until she was folding the tiny vests and putting them in a drawer that it finally dawned on her that she was carrying a real baby and these were the clothes it was going to wear. She'd sat down on the edge of the bed and wrapped her arms around the bump, tears springing to her eyes with emotions she didn't understand. The tears ran down her cheeks unchecked and dripped from her chin onto the front of her dress where she watched them make little dark spots on the fine fabric, growing and merging with one another. She hadn't known why she was crying as the deep emotions welled up inside and made their escape in tears.

She sighed in contentment at the sleeping child. Her room was full of flowers and cards from well-wishers she didn't know. Only the cards from Jenny and Nurse Barbara meant anything to her, and Jonathan's and Angela's of course.

* * * * * * * * *

Everything now revolved around Bobby and his requirements: bathing, feeding, sleeping; times for a walk out in the pram, times to see Grandfather. The days were filled to capacity. How could one little baby take up so much time in the lives of the other members of the household?

Then there came the time for Bobby's baptism. May would have liked to ask Jenny to be a godmother but she wasn't even consulted. She found she didn't really mind all that much. She was fascinated by her son and took little interest in anything else. No-one interfered in how she was caring for him and she didn't bother to interfere in the plans Angela made.

Godparents were chosen from business and family friends, people that May had hardly met. She knew they had been chosen carefully, Jonathan had explained who they were, but, to May, it seemed it was not for their loving concern for the welfare of the child, more for what advantages could be gained for him. Their presents to the little boy were lavish. Angela organised everything and, of course, the whole event went off with military precision, and was about as friendly, in May's opinion.

May felt herself being carried along like a log in a flooded river, being swept this way and that but having nothing to say about where she was being taken and knew it wouldn't have made any difference if she'd tried.

It was the day of Bobby's baptism and high summer. The doors and windows were wide open, people came and went, stood in groups in the drawing room, in the garden, round the table that held enough food for an army. May stood to one side, a glass of champagne in her hand almost untouched after the toasts, with Jenny beside her.

"Do you realise Jenny, you're the only person here that I know?"

"Give it time, May," she said. She seemed to be enjoying watching the guests. She'd had more champagne than was good for her, May thought, but it was such a novelty she was obviously making the most of it.

"Angela said it is a sort of delayed wedding reception as well as a Christening. All hers and Adam's friends and business acquaintances have been invited to meet me. Even so, I still feel left out of it all."

"But you were introduced to everyone, and Jonathan gave that speech sayin' you and the bairn were the best things since sliced bread."

May laughed. "You say such funny things, Jenny. I don't know what I'd do without you."

"Well, I'd say it's about time you got out and had a bit of fun."

"Oh no. Bobby's too little for me to leave him."

"Don't be daft. But if that's how you really feel, I'll leave it for now. But don't think I'm givin' up, it's not that long till your twenty-first, is it, and you've got to do somethin' for that."

May grimaced. Her family had never celebrated birthdays. She'd always thought it probably had something to do with the brothers who had died before she was born. Whatever the reason, it was best forgotten. "We'll see."

Jenny laughed at her friend's grim expression. "Anyway, I fancy another bit of that cake and another glass of champers to wash it down with." Jenny wove her way across the room, looking like an explosion in a paint shop. May loved her friend's eclectic choice of clothes, but it was clear from some of the looks that followed her progress not everyone felt the same.

May could see Jonathan in the garden, looking bored as an older Chinese man talked to him. He was wearing his sulky expression again. May sighed. If only he could always be as amusing and happy as he had seemed earlier.

She didn't know what to make of him: her husband, Bobby's father. He hadn't really taken that much notice of the child after the first excitement of his arrival. Jonathan hadn't ignored him – he always asked how the boy was and was delighted at the appearance of his first smile – but he never seemed to want to hold him for very long. Maybe it will be better when Bobby starts to walk and talk, she thought, there's not much they can do together just now while Bobby's so little.

It was his attitude to her that May found most confusing. She longed for the friendship and intimacy of marriage. She'd felt a growing closer in the days when they'd waited for their baby's birth and in the few weeks after. She hadn't imagined it. Love? Well, that was another matter. Perhaps it would come, perhaps not, she thought, and what you've never had you never miss so they say. It didn't worry her, they'd never professed to love one another, it was a marriage of convenience, but surely there should be something between them. Jonathan often put his arm around her, kissed her goodnight on the cheek or brow, but it felt more like casual brotherly affection than anything else. Their few nights together in China had left May feeling that there could be so much more; should be more. There had to be more to it than the act that had left her feeling as if someone had started telling her an exciting story and stopped before the end.

Then there had been the embarrassment of the night she had invited Jonathan to share her bed again. They had gone upstairs together and were about to go to their own rooms.

"Dr Simmons says I have recovered from Bobby's birth."

"Good. That's good to hear." Jonathan had his own bedroom door half open.

"She says that we can... That it's all right to..." She looked helplessly at Jonathan, willing him to understand.

"I don't think so." His look at her was cold, almost scornful.

"But I thought..."

"Well you thought wrong. Goodnight."

May watched, wretched with humiliation, as Jonathan closed his bedroom door behind him. She didn't understand. What have I done wrong, she thought, to make him so angry.

\* \* \* \* \* \* \* \* \*

May's twenty-first birthday would have passed without comment or acknowledgement if it hadn't been for Jenny. She'd had no success in getting her friend to indulge in a night out in Newcastle.

"All right then, if you don't want a knees up let's go and get some retail therapy."

"Jenny, I have no idea what you're talking about."

Jenny laughed. "Let's go on a shoppin' spree. It's time you had some new clothes, it'll be winter before you know it. And I'm sure we'll be able to find somethin' canny for Bobby." She held out the carrot she was sure her friend would take.

"Very well. I'll ask Angela to look after him for a little while and we'll go shopping. How about the day after tomorrow?"

"You're on."

"Are you and Jonathan doing anythin' special for your birthday?" Jenny was curious about the apparently casual relationship between May and Jonathan.

"No. I don't think he knows it's my birthday."

"You're jokin'!" Jenny was incredulous. "Haven't you told him? How can he not know?"

"I don't think it's important. It's only a birthday."

"Well, I don't know about you," Jenny said. "If it was me I'd be expectin' a big present and at least a champagne supper somewhere candlelit and romantic."

"I don't really like champagne."

"Oh you. You're impossible." Jenny wasn't about to give up, though, and phoned Armstrong when her friend had left.

\* \* \* \* \* \* \* \* \*

It was the twenty-fourth of September, a glowing early autumn day when it seemed that summer hadn't been beaten yet. As usual Jonathan had left for the office and Angela was nowhere to be seen. May went into the kitchen to get her breakfast, carrying Bobby in her arms. She was startled when Armstrong burst into song.

"Happy birthday to you. Happy birthday to you. Happy birthday Miss May. Happy birthday to you."

May burst into delighted laughter at the extraordinary sound that emerged from Armstrong. If she'd ever been asked, if she'd ever even thought about such a thing, she would have expected Armstrong to have a deep scratchy voice, not quite in tune. What emerged was a beautifully modulated tenor. He presented her with a bouquet of sweet smelling flowers.

"Thank you. You are very kind. But how did you know?" May immediately realised. "Did Jenny tell you?"

"Yes she did, Miss. And very glad I am that she did, if I may say so. You can't let your twenty-first birthday go by without at least a bunch of flowers."

"You haven't told my husband or my mother-in-law have you?" May asked. She didn't want to be the centre of any fuss made.

"No, Miss. That's not my place."

"Good. Please don't. I really don't want to trouble them."

"Very well, Miss. Would you like me to put these in water for you?"

"No, Armstrong. I'd like to do it myself if you would take Bobby for me for a minute or two." She was touched by the simple gift and wanted to arrange the flowers herself.

"Of course, Miss. Come here, young man. Give Armstrong a cuddle, then."

May arranged the lovely flowers in a large crystal vase and placed it in the centre of the table.

"I'll take them up to your room later on, Miss, if you'd like."

"That would be very kind. I think you are a very kind man, Armstrong." She wanted to hug him but felt it wouldn't be at all the correct thing to do.

Armstrong blushed and smiled and put the kettle on to make a pot of tea. He was true to his word not to tell Jonathan and Angela but he hadn't made any promises about Adam.

When May knocked on Adam's door later that morning he bade her enter in his usual gruff manner. Once she'd poured his cup of not-too-strong, milky coffee and sat down beside him, he poked a box at her.

"Here. Take this."

"What? What is this?" Adam had never given her anything, other than a generous allowance, never a present of any sort and May didn't expect anything.

"Are you stupid, girl? It's a present. Open it." Adam became brusque and sometimes rude when he felt emotional. May had come to realise this as she'd got to know him and she wasn't offended. She took the box. It was obviously not new and embossed on the lid, in silver, was the name of a jeweller in New York. May opened it and caught her breath. Inside was a pair of pearl earrings. Each huge, glowing pearl was shaped like a teardrop and mounted in gold. She didn't know what to say to such a wonderful gift. Instead she kissed Adam on the cheek. "Well, aren't you going to put them on?"

"I can't," May was almost in tears as she held the lovely earrings in her hand.

"What do you mean? Don't you like them?"

"It's... I... I haven't..." she stumbled over the right words.

"Spit it out, girl," he growled.

"My ears. They haven't the holes in them." May was defeated.

Adam burst out laughing. "Well, I'm relieved it's so small a problem," he said. "I think you mean your ears aren't pierced. You're bound to have holes in them or you wouldn't be able to hear me." He laughed even harder at the joke.

May left him to his coffee and his mirth, taking the blue leather box with her. She was moved and delighted that Adam cared enough about her to present her with such a gift. Back in her room she opened the box and looked at the earrings again. She couldn't help wondering who they had belonged to.

The next morning May arrived, as usual, with Adam's coffee tray. She sat demurely beside her father-in-law and passed him his cup. Her ears looked red and sore but dangling from them were the pearl earrings. Adam smiled and said nothing.

## Chapter Eight

Adam grew to trust and love May, if such a man could love anyone. Every day May and Bobby spent time with the old man and he began to reveal how he had arrived in England and come to run one of the most successful shipping companies in the north-east. His story intrigued May.

\* \* \* \* \* \* \* \* \* \*

Adam's family had fled to Taiwan when the Communists took power. His older brother had chosen to stay behind and disappeared during one of the many purges instigated by Mao Tse Tung.

Adam was in his twenties by then and he took a job as a clerk in a shipping office in Chi-lung. He was ambitious and went out of his way to learn as much about the business as he could. In the mid fifties he left Taiwan for his firm's Hong Kong office, changing his name from Li An Dong to Adam Lee. Then, with China's Liberation Army massing across the border, ready to strike and rid Hong Kong of its imperial rulers, Adam Lee fled to England.

Standing in the jam-packed crowd of refugees at Victoria Harbour, jostling to get aboard the ship, Adam stood firm as they pushed and shoved. He resolved never to find himself at the mercy of others again. To achieve this he required money – a serious amount of money – and he was determined to make a fortune, whatever he had to do. Within hours of boarding the ship Adam had begun to fulfil his promises to himself: he'd found a job and signed on as crew. The galley became Adam's refuge from the crowded cabin he shared with several others. By the time the ship docked Adam was well on the way to becoming an accomplished cook and had earned a tidy sum of money, too.

The next major decision in his life had been made when he was at a loose end. His shift in the galley had finished and he wandered aimlessly on deck. He met the pair of brothers who shared his cabin: David and Terry Wang, who were on their way to join family in north-east England.

Terry asked what Adam was going to do when he got to England. Adam told him he hadn't really decided. "I expect I'll look for a job like everyone else."

"Why don't you come with us to Newcastle?" David suggested. "We've heard there's plenty of work to be had."

So Adam Lee arrived in Newcastle-upon-Tyne, and found a single room above a Chinese restaurant. The jobs open to new Chinese immigrants were scarce and the Wang brothers, along with many others, found it hard to make ends meet. Adam recognised an opportunity. He was relatively well off, thanks to his job on the ship, and began lending the odd pound or two.

Adam prospered. But he wanted to do better than be a money-lender. However lucrative that might be, he knew there was much more he could achieve. He went back to the trade he knew best: shipping.

Sir Robert Forster took to him immediately, seeing great potential in his new clerk. Adam proved his worth as he assumed more and more responsibility. In less than two years he was managing the company.

He was in Sir Robert's office when a young woman breezed in. She was blond haired and fair skinned and, though not conventionally pretty, had a presence that made her the centre of attention. She smiled at Adam and looked at her father, expecting an introduction.

Adam knew a good business proposition when he saw one – marrying the only child of the owner of the shipping company – but realised he had to play this very carefully. For months he courted Angela, trying not to appear too eager, not taking things as far as she made obvious she wanted. He sensed that if he proposed to her too soon, Sir Robert may well forbid the marriage and he may even be out of a job.

\* \* \* \* \* \* \* \* \* \*

"My patience won: Angela married me for love. I married her for money." Adam smiled ruefully when he told May this as she sat nursing her sleeping child. "It wasn't as cold-blooded as I make it sound," he said as May frowned. "I liked Angela, liked her a great deal. We've had a good marriage all these years."

Bobby stirred in May's arms and woke, starting to grizzle. Adam broke off the telling, looking deep into the logs in the glowing gas fire, sighing at his memories.

"You go and see to the baby," he told May. "I'm tired." Adam closed his eyes and seemed to forget she was there. May rose and left, hushing Bobby so as not to disturb his grandfather's rest. She was surprised and a bit shocked at Adam telling her such intimate details and wondered why, though she had heard that people sometimes tell strangers the most extraordinary things about themselves. Perhaps it's a sort of therapy, she thought. Almost a confession as he neared the end of his life. She shivered at the thought it might be a premonition.

## Chapter Nine

"Have you thought any more about going to college?" Angela asked one evening when Jonathan was out yet again. Bobby was more than a year old now. He was a good child and slept each night through. At six months old May had reluctantly moved him into a cot in his own room. She'd missed him but accepted it was the way it had to be – she knew he couldn't stay with her forever. May enjoyed adding her own touches to the nursery Angela had prepared before she'd arrived from China.

"Well, yes," she admitted, now. "Jenny has offered to get me the prospectus for her college. I'm seeing her tomorrow and I said that I'd look at it with her."

"Any thoughts on what you'd like to do?"

"Not really. I don't suppose I'll have that much free time."

"You do remember our conversation before you agreed to marry Jonathan, don't you? I'm ready to keep my part of the bargain: to employ a nanny to look after Bobby."

"Oh, Angela. I'm sure you are. But I don't think I can give him up." May was torn between caring for her son and doing something interesting: something just for herself. I can't be bored, can I, she'd asked herself. Not with a lovely little boy like Bobby. It was easy to coax a gurgling laugh out of him and his baby chatter delighted her so. And there were all the things he was learning, that she was teaching him. But if I don't do something else now, perhaps I never will, she reasoned. The teasing thought that there might be something exciting out there waiting for her intrigued May. But she had Bobby, and the rest of the family, too, of course. May was in a dilemma.

"No," she said at last. "I don't think it would be a good idea."

"Why don't you talk to your friend, see what she has to suggest? Then we can discuss it again," Angela said. "I know we can work something out."

\* \* \* \* \* \* \* \* \* \*

It was fun, May couldn't deny, sitting in the Scarlet Parakeet with

Jenny, considering the courses on offer.

"What were your best subjects at school?" Jenny asked, curious about her friend's education.

"I liked maths, I hated history."

"Did you ever think about what sort of career you wanted?"

"No. I never thought I'd have a career. I never thought I'd be able to afford to go to college, let alone be accepted." May remembered how excited she'd been when she'd passed her entrance exams. "But my parents couldn't afford to send me. Then I married Jonathan and here I am." May skated over the full story.

"Anythin' else?"

"My art teacher said I was quite good, and I loved drawing." May didn't like to feel she was bragging and didn't tell how highly praised her drawings had been. She certainly didn't mention that both her parents and her teachers had been trying to steer her towards an engineering degree. Suddenly she was almost overcome with an unexpected attack of homesickness as she remembered sitting with her sketchbook open on her knee drawing the great water-buffaloes as they ploughed the mud of the paddy fields, or the pigs in their pens behind the house, snuffling at the sweet-potato stalks they were fed. She would never forget one particular day when she was sent to the sweet-potato fields.

* * * * * * * * *

Her mother was busy with other tasks about the house so she sent Xi Mei to dig some sweet-potatoes for their evening meal. Her friend, Ying Kui, went along too. They took baskets balanced either end of carrying poles her grandfather had made especially for them. Chattering happily they soon covered the half mile to the field where the vegetables grew in long earthed-up rows.

Xi Mei was daydreaming as she absentmindedly rubbed off any soil clinging to the sweet-potatoes before dropping them into a basket. She was startled by shrieks coming from the far side of the field where the other girl was. Xi Mei ran across to see what on earth was the matter. What she saw almost made her shriek in fright too: a green snake was coiled around Ying Kui's ankle. Without stopping to think, Xi Mei grabbed it and wrenched it off her friend. Revolted by the creature she flung it as far away as she could.

Ying Kui was sobbing noisily and, though she was shaking in fright herself, Xi Mei did her best to comfort her friend as they hurried home, forgetting their baskets. All the family, except Fu Gui her father, were there when the girls got back.

Xi Mei and Ying Kui tried to tell the tale both at the same time and at the tops of their voices. As Xi Mei showed how she'd wrestled the snake off her friend, Grandmother grabbed her. "Her hand. She's been bitten," she yelled.

In the heat of the moment of catching the snake, Xi Mei had not felt its deadly bite. Now her hand was swelling rapidly and was turning an angry, dark blue. Lin Yong realised she needed help, and fast. She grabbed her daughter by her uninjured arm and dragged her out of the house, across the alley, squeezed between the opposite houses and into the next alley where Snake Uncle lived. Ying Kui and the grandparents followed.

Snake Uncle was renowned for his remedies to cure snake-bite and all sorts of poisonings. He took one look at Xi Mei's hand and then, using a little knife with a needle-sharp point, stabbed it into the swollen skin where the snake fangs had punctured. Xi Mei didn't even utter as much as a moan.

"See the colour of the blood," he asked, dramatically, raising the girl's hand so all could see the dark blood dripping from the wound. "This snake had a very powerful venom." He looked around as everyone watched, fascinated and horrified at the same time. "If you'd waited another minute to bring her to me..." He rolled his eyes and shook his head in theatrical horror at what might have been. He then applied a poultice of herbs and bound up the hand. "As it is, she will recover. Bring her back in two days." He looked solemnly at Xi Mei. "This must be your lucky day."

Lin Yong was not convinced that her only child getting bitten by a venomous snake was good luck. It was a long time before she let her go to the potato field again.

* * * * * * * * * *

May looked down at the star-shaped scar on the side of her hand, shuddering at the memory. She remembered how she'd been too frightened even to cry at the time. She pushed it to the back of her mind and concentrated on what Jenny was saying.

"You've never said you could draw. Even when you knew I was at Art School." Jenny was indignant.

"It didn't seem important and compared to the paintings you've done mine seem so poor. Anyway, I left all that behind in China."

"What about doin' the same course as me, then? We've got some brilliant teachers. There's this one that's so drop-dead gorgeous I could eat him for dinner." May laughed at her friend who held her hands up. "I know, I know. That isn't the point, is it? Anyway, what about it?"

"I don't think so." May was tempted by Jenny's enthusiasm but she wanted to be independent, even of her best friend.

"What about Art History? No, you said you didn't like history."

"It would be a lot different from the history we were taught at school, but I don't know. What else is there?" May picked up another brochure. And so the discussion went on. May was beginning to feel overwhelmed by the choices.

"Isn't there anythin' you'd like to do?" Jenny asked.

"I've always had a small thought at the back of my mind that I'd like to be a doctor."

Jenny whistled in amazement. "That'd be quite an undertakin'. It takes years you know and you'd have to do A-Levels first, I'd imagine, then a degree and then medical school. What would Jonathan say and would you be happy away from Bobby for so much of the time?"

"I wasn't thinking of Western Medicine. I would be more interested in Chinese Traditional Medicine."

"Oh, I see. Would there be anywhere local you could go?" Jenny thought the idea a novel one, but she didn't know the first thing about it. "And what about patients, or are they clients?"

"I have read a lot of people are now seeking alternative health care." May thought for a moment. "I'll ask Adam if he knows where I could study. He's bound to know of someone who could teach me." She was becoming excited at the idea and could hardly wait to get home. Suddenly she felt guilty – she'd have to agree to Angela's offer to employ a nanny for Bobby. Could she really do it?

Adam was resting when she got home so May decided to tell Jonathan and Angela what she was considering. She'd wait until tomorrow before talking to her father-in-law, in the meantime it would do no harm to sound out her husband and mother-in-law.

May hoped Angela might know something about Chinese Medicine. Perhaps even know someone who would teach her and she wouldn't have to bother Adam with it at all. May looked expectantly from one to the other, waiting for their reaction. They're bound to be amazed, she thought, and they won't be able to help being proud at having a doctor in the family. Come on, say something.

"I wouldn't hear of such a thing," Jonathan almost shouted. May was shocked. She hadn't thought he'd mind what she did. "I'm not having my wife putting her hands all over some… some… sick person's body," he spat the words out. Why he would feel so strongly about that May couldn't imagine. He certainly doesn't want my hands on *his* body, she thought.

"But Jonathan, surely it wouldn't be like that," she protested.

"And God knows what diseases you would bring home to infect my son. No, you must find something more fitting to your family's position in this city."

May wanted to yell back at Jonathan, tell him she could do what she wanted; it was part of their marriage agreement. But that wasn't her way. She didn't understand what he could possibly have against it. And Angela. Why didn't she say anything? It had been her idea in the first place. No, May thought, this is what I get for being ambitious, for being selfish. Perhaps Jonathan is right.

"Very well," May told Jonathan in a quiet voice. "I will consider something else. I will let you know what I decide and hope that you will approve." She swallowed her disappointment. "I must go and say goodnight to Bobby then I will go to bed myself. Goodnight Jonathan. Goodnight Angela." May left the room quietly, closing the door with a gentle click behind her.

"How could you, Jonathan?" Angela burst out as soon as May had left. "Why were you being so unreasonable? You must realise May is free to study whatever she wishes. It was a promise I made that I fully intended be kept."

"She can study something else if she must study at all." Jonathan was unrepentant. He poured himself a Scotch then sat down to read the newspaper as if his outburst had never occurred.

\* \* \* \* \* \* \* \* \* \*

May settled on English and Business Studies. She never

mentioned to Adam what had been her first choice, though she felt that through his intervention she could have got her own way. No, that would have been dishonourable and she knew Adam would have seen it that way, too, and he approved of her eventual choice. So in her quiet way she committed herself to whatever the road open to her would bring. Jenny, of course, was delighted that May would be studying in the city.

"When you're a fully qualified business-woman you could open a gallery and sell my work then I'll become a famous artist. You could say you discovered me and everyone'd think you were a brilliant judge of character and modern art." Jenny laughed, delighted with the picture of their meteoric rise to fame and fortune.

Angela, true to her word, found a nanny for Bobby. Carol Hughes was calm and efficient and, best of all, kind and loving with Bobby. She was in her late thirties but seemed, to May, much younger. May had to admit she didn't like the woman very much. Perhaps I'm jealous, she thought. But May was happy to be free to go to college. Jonathan accepted her choice without comment.

That was more than a year ago and May knew she'd made the right decision. She'd written to tell her mother, full of excitement at doing something for herself. Lin Yong had replied, urging caution. "Never forget that the Lees could take everything away just as quickly as they gave it," she wrote. "Make sure you keep some of your allowance secure. You never know what might happen."

From the first, May had received a generous allowance from Adam Lee, paid into her own bank account. He also undertook to pay her fees for college and paid for Bobby's nanny. She never thought to question why Adam paid for everything and not Jonathan. May spent only a fraction of her money and regularly sent her parents sums to help them out. As for herself, her life couldn't have been more comfortable. Her comings and goings weren't questioned and there was never anything domestic for her to worry about. Armstrong saw to that.

Adam was growing more frail with each passing month. Angela had confided that the doctors didn't know what kept him going.

"But I think it's Bobby, of course," she said. "The boy means everything to him."

* * * * * * * * *

November dusk closed round the city. Mist rose from the river in wisps, obscuring the stars. May sat on the top deck of a bus crowded with commuters as it crawled along in the evening traffic. She was crushed against the window by a large man in dirty jeans who fiddled with the ear-piece of his Walkman. It emitted an irritating buzz, too loud to ignore and too muted to hear properly. She clutched a bag stuffed with files and books and thought about that afternoon's lecture but she couldn't concentrate. She gave it up as a bad job and peered out of the window. It was steamed up and offered no respite from her neighbour who had begun a tuneless humming.

The bus stopped and started, letting people on and off. The man with the Walkman got off at an early stop. May let out a sigh of premature relief as his place was quickly taken by an elderly man who smelled of cough mixture and moth balls. He sneezed into a none-too-clean handkerchief. May hoped he'd trapped all his germs, she didn't want to take a cold home to Bobby, or Adam. Bobby – she was late and he'd already be in his pyjamas and ready for bed.

The bus drew to a halt at the end of the road where May lived. She pushed and squeezed her way off, breathing in deeply the damp air, relieved that the journey was over. She knew she should have left college earlier and guilt mixed with the discomfort of the bus ride combined to make her feel on edge. She walked quickly down the avenue, the yellow street-lights, haloed by the mist, doing little to light the way.

Armstrong met May in the hall as she came in. His face looked the colour of old ashes, his eyes bloodshot.

"Oh, Miss. He's gone."

"What? Is it Bobby? Is he all right? Where is he? Where's he gone?" Panic struck May as she thought of all the things that might have gone wrong while she was out. She shouldn't have been late. It was her punishment for being selfish.

"It's Mr Adam. He's passed away," Armstrong almost sobbed.

The English idiom still occasionally mystified May. "Armstrong, what is it? For goodness sake, just tell me."

"He's dead. Mr Adam is dead."

Relief that nothing had happened to Bobby almost made May laugh aloud. She put a hand over her mouth, shocked at herself. Then distress at the awful news hit her. "Oh, Armstrong," she said, gripping his arm. "What are we going to do?"

"Miss Angela and Mr Jonathan are in the drawing room." Armstrong was visibly fighting to maintain his composure, his voice tight with suppressed grief.

"I'll go in and see them, shall I?"

"Yes, Miss. That would be best."

Adam. Oh, Adam. May was on the verge of tears, too. How had it happened? When? And I didn't even say goodbye, she thought miserably.

Angela was sitting, perched on the very edge of the sofa with a cup of tea in her hands, her eyes staring blankly into the distance. She seemed to have aged ten years in less than ten hours. Jonathan stood in front of the fire, smoking a cigarette, an unheard of thing in this house: his mother abhorred smoking. Angela's eyes focused on May.

"Have you heard? Has Armstrong told you? Adam..."

"Yes. It's such a shock." May stood in the doorway, at a loss what to do or how to act. "I know he hasn't been well for a long time, but somehow I expected him to be here forever." May had grown very fond of her domineering father-in-law. She couldn't believe he was dead. She stepped into the room and went to sit beside Angela.

"It was this afternoon. Armstrong took tea up to him as usual. He thought Adam was asleep, sitting in the chair in front of the fire. But he wasn't. He was, he was..." Angela blinked quickly and blew her nose. "He had died, quietly and without any fuss. Alone. If only I'd been with him. Why couldn't I have been with him?" Tears were falling now, unstoppable. May took the teacup out of Angela's shaking hand and folded her mother-in-law in her arms, trying to comfort her. Why isn't Jonathan doing this, she thought, glancing up at him. Jonathan continued smoking, gazing into the fire. Suddenly he turned and ground the cigarette butt into his mother's saucer.

"I'm going out." May couldn't believe he was leaving his mother at a time like this.

"Jonathan, please don't," May pleaded.

"Don't tell me what to do. Nobody can tell me what to do now. It's finished. I can do what I bloody well want, and I want to go out." He left without a backward glance.

May was shocked. Angela didn't seem to notice.

## Chapter Ten

The days before the funeral were an ordeal. May had no idea what she should do, struggling to come to terms with the changes that Adam's absence forced on them and the unexpected intensity of her grief. Jonathan was out, no-one knew where, most of the time and Angela seemed to have shrunk into herself; become a woman old long before her time. Armstrong was the mainstay of the family. Carol was a tower of strength, too, taking care of Bobby. The funeral director was helpfulness itself, talking gently to Angela, guiding her through the thousand and one things that had to be done.

The morning of the funeral was bright and crisp, sunshine soon melting the light dusting of frost that rimed the trees and grass. Many of the trees still had leaves clinging on, faded russet, the yews in the cemetery so dark a green they seemed almost black.

The family plot where Adam was to be buried was atop a slight rise in the graveyard, edged with low metal railings, painted shiny black. The service had been in the small chapel and now the great black limousines crawled their way along the narrow roadway that wound between the graves. The ornate coffin was lifted onto the shoulders of six men. The minister, clad in black gown and white, starched surplice, led the way towards the open grave. Angela, leaning heavily on Jonathan's arm followed the coffin, May behind with Armstrong. Dozens of dark-clad strangers drifted towards the burial party with sober, funeral faces.

The priest intoned the timeless words, as slowly Adam's coffin was lowered into the ground. The sun shouldn't be shining, May thought as the golden light streamed out of a clear blue sky. Among the crow-black mourners May stood out. She wore a crimson silk Chinese jacket. She remembered Adam giving it to her.

"Here, put this on," he'd said, thrusting the tissue wrapped garment into her hands. May wondered where on earth it had come from. She knew he wouldn't tell, so she didn't ask. She unfolded the jacket.

"Put it on," Adam repeated.

May slipped her arms into the sleeves, the silk smooth and cool on her skin. The jacket was quilted with embroidery: flowers and

74

dragons, beautifully detailed. "It's lovely," she said, smoothing the padded fabric. She smiled at the old man.

"Wear it at my funeral." He studied her face, as if watching for her reaction. It clouded with sorrow.

"But Adam…"

"Don't 'but Adam' me, young woman." His voice was harsh. "Just wear it." Then he seemed to relent. "Please," he added softly.

So May wore it, and she doubted Angela even noticed. Though she had expected some comment from Jonathan when he saw what she was wearing, he had said nothing. She listened to the priest's voice as he read the committal.

"Earth to earth, ashes to ashes, dust to dust; in sure and certain hope of the resurrection to eternal life, through our Lord Jesus Christ…"

May wondered whether Adam had been a Christian; they had never discussed religion among the many things they had talked about. May herself had been brought up in a household, a whole country, devoid of any sort of religious observance – by order of the government. Having a ceremony like this, she realised as she stood at the graveside, gave a focus, a time to say a final farewell.

The funeral tea was at the house and gradually the hushed tones became louder and more animated, even some low laughter, but kept subdued for decency's sake. Angela received condolences with a calm dignity, Jonathan still at her side. May knew her mother-in-law had loved Adam deeply and couldn't imagine what she must be feeling. She thought knew how she'd feel if she lost Bobby, but that was different. Adam had been ill for years, fading visibly in the past few months. Surely Angela had been prepared. But perhaps no-one is prepared, even for the inevitable, she thought. May knew the shock she had felt when Armstrong told her Adam had died. How bereaved she felt, how she missed the gruff old man who drew out of her memories of her childhood and her parents, who told her his own story and went some way to explain the mystery that was Jonathan. Again, his frankness had surprised May.

* * * * * * * * * *

Sir Robert had been overjoyed when Angela told him he was to be a grandfather. Nothing was too good for her: the best doctors and an even more extravagant allowance to buy all the new clothes she would need as her pregnancy progressed and to supply the thousand and one things a new baby would need.

When Jonathan was born the old man was beside himself. How could his blond, blue-eyed, peaches and cream-skinned daughter give birth to a black-haired, black-eyed, olive-skinned child? He had never stopped to consider that Adam and Angela's child may take after its father in looks.

All during Jonathan's childhood years his grandfather had treated him with a distant restraint. Adam admitted he was scarcely ever home during the boy's waking hours. Angela spoilt him unmercifully and, when Sir Robert insisted Jonathan be sent to public school as a boarder, she was inconsolable. She cried and raged but, in this, her father was implacable. Adam was in agreement with his father-in-law, as he seemed to be in all things. Contrary to expectations Jonathan did well at his new school and acquired the polish to his manners and demeanour his grandfather had planned.

Adam had paused at this point, leaning forward to say to May, "It's my fault that Jonathan is the way he is."

"What do you mean?" May had asked, puzzled.

"That school changed him."

"But that's what you and his grandfather wanted, wasn't it?"

"Yes. I suppose it was. But not in the way it worked out. I thought he would acquire the bearing and values of a gentleman."

"But he has. Jonathan is very charming and I know he loves Bobby. And I care for him, very much." May was determined to care a great deal about Jonathan, even though it seemed he couldn't love her in return. She had to, if only for the sake of their son.

"Oh, he's charming enough, when he wants to be. But he's weak. Haven't you seen that?" May had to admit she hadn't and told Adam about Jonathan's insistence she not study Chinese Medicine.

"He didn't seem very weak, then," she added.

"He's pig-headed, not strong. Not in the way a good father, a good son, a good businessman needs to be strong. His public school career left him with certain, um, interests that aren't compatible with a stable family life."

May didn't know what her father-in-law was talking about. "What do you mean? What sort of interests?"

"Have you never wondered about his friends? What he does when he goes out night after night?"

"Well... yes. I have."

"He's a gambler, May. And worse. There are places that cater for all his dubious requirements and those of his so-called friends." The old man started to cough and May poured him a glass of water from the jug on the table. He sipped it slowly and gradually the coughing fit passed. She wanted to ask what Adam meant but he was clearly exhausted.

"Adam, you must rest. Please don't upset yourself further. Jonathan is kind to me and I am sure he will be a good father to Bobby. Isn't that all that matters?"

"Far from it, my dear." Adam reached out and grabbed May's hand and squeezed it so hard she had to bite her lip to stop herself from crying out. "It's all for Bobby. There'll be nothing for Jonathan that he doesn't work for." He dropped her hand and started to cough again.

"I'm going to get Armstrong. I know he has some medication to give you if you need it. And I think you need it now. Please, Adam, you really must rest."

May sat for a long time in her room thinking about what Adam had said. Gambling? What's so bad or surprising about that? Don't all – well, most – Chinese men gamble? I've heard them myself: laying wagers on everything from the weight of a pig to when the rain would come.

She knew Jonathan stayed out late. She'd often heard him coming home in the small hours. Is that why he still doesn't share a room with me, she wondered. Does he not want me to know, or is it that he doesn't want to disturb me, coming in late?

And what of their non-existent physical relationship? It was a topic that May had agonised about over and over again. Suddenly it dawned on her: he's got a mistress! That's where he goes, that's why he doesn't want me. But who are his friends? He never mentions anyone. The questions without answers went round and round in her head. May was at a loss to understand. But perhaps she was misjudging Jonathan. She needed to forget what Adam had said, and tried to imply, as well as her own wild imaginings. She reached up to her neck and held the little golden dragon which was her amulet to ward off evil spirits.

* * * * * * * * * *

May went back to college the day after the funeral.

"Life goes on May," Angela told her. "You must live it to the full, be happy. Little Bobby deserves a happy mother, doesn't he? It's what Adam would expect."

"Are you sure, Angela? I feel bad leaving you alone."

"I managed before so I expect I'll manage now. Go on with you. I need to learn to be without Adam. But of course I won't be alone. I have Bobby and Carol here, as well as Armstrong, and Jonathan will be in from the office in time for dinner." May left with misgivings.

It was several days before she noticed the man following her. She'd been dimly aware of someone on the periphery of her sight for some time as she and Jenny walked along the street talking loudly in amicable argument about an exhibition they'd been to at the Art Gallery.

Jenny was gesturing wildly as she spoke dismissively of the Pre-Raphaelite paintings they'd just seen and May wondered if her friend really felt that way or if she just wanted to take the opposite view to spark a discussion. She could hardly be unaware that she looked like the model for a Pre-Raphaelite painting herself with her dark auburn curls that fell past her shoulders and long, green velvet skirt. The striped many-hued jumper jarred the effect, though. Jenny stopped, and struck a comical pose, lifting her skirt to reveal unlovely heavy-soled, lace-up boots. May turned, laughing and looked straight at a thick-set Chinese man with a shaved head and dark glasses, turning the corner maybe twenty yards behind them. He stopped when he saw May looking at him, then looked back at her defiantly. He didn't threaten her in any way, but May felt a cold drift of fear that he was following her.

"What's the matter with you? Seen a ghost?" Jenny laughed at the expression on May's face. "Or seen the light? Decided that Hockney is better than Burne-Jones?"

May dismissed her feelings as fanciful; it wasn't at all unusual to see a Chinese man on the streets of Newcastle. And, besides, why should she be important enough for anyone to follow? "No, you just reminded me of that painting. What's the one?"

"Mona Lisa? More like Mona Freeza! I'm perished. Come on, let's get into the warm. Mam'll have some scones on and I for one would kill for one or even two with a nice hot cuppa." She strode off, pulling May with her, towards the Scarlet Parakeet.

May spotted him the next afternoon as she and Bobby fed the ducks in the park and yet again the following day as she came out of the library. She shook her head and told herself not to be so stupid. It was just a co-incidence, that's all. Why would anyone want to follow her? Still, she couldn't help but wonder.

* * * * * * * * * *

May and Jonathan were alone one evening later in the week. Angela had acquiesced to a friend's insistent invitation to play bridge. Carol had gone to see her parents for an extended weekend. May had long since tucked Bobby into bed. At two and a half he was talking well and babbled sleepily as May bent down to kiss his soft, round cheek. The golden dragon charm fell forward as she leaned over and Bobby caught it, hanging onto it tightly so his mother couldn't pull away. This was a game he loved.

"Dwagon, Mummy. Tell 'bout dwagon."

His pleading always won May over so she re-told him the story her mother had told her on her wedding day, with a few embellishments of her own, just to make it interesting and exciting for a child. It was one of his favourites, and hers, too. He soon drifted off to sleep, lulled by the sound of her soft voice. She went down to join Jonathan.

"Jonathan, there's something I need to tell you," May began, uncertain whether she should tell him what was bothering her. Jonathan looked up from the paper.

"Well, fire away. I'm all ears." He seemed willing to listen so May told him about the man she thought was following her. He dismissed her concerns with a laugh. "Aren't you over-reacting a bit? It's probably just some poor sod that fancies you or something." He didn't quite say she was imagining things, but she felt he thought it. She'd wanted reassurance and she supposed she'd got it – in a way. Jonathan went back to his newspaper and May picked up a book but before she had the chance to find her place she heard the sound of the doorbell in the distance then Armstrong's footsteps crossing the tiled hall. A moment later the sitting-room door opened.

"There's a gentleman to see you, Mr Jonathan." Jonathan raised his eyes in surprise. It was a rare thing indeed for a visitor to come calling. "It's Mr David Wang."

"Oh no. Not another of Father's old friends looking for a handout." From his annoyed tone May expected him to tell Armstrong to say he was out. "I suppose I'd better see him, Armstrong. Show him in."

"Very well, Mr Jonathan."

"May, why don't you go up to bed," Jonathan said, more an instruction than a suggestion. "I'm sure you don't want to be bored by another tiresome old man talking about the good old, bad old days."

Though May wouldn't have minded meeting Adam's old friend, she didn't press the point, and she did have plenty of reading to do. But once she was in her room she couldn't concentrate. She eventually switched on the television, looking for something to take her mind off the man with dark glasses and wondering what David Wang wanted to see Jonathan about. She found she didn't like being dismissed in that peremptory fashion but she shrugged her shoulders. It was just Jonathan's way.

* * * * * * * * * *

Jonathan stood up as David Wang entered the room and waited until Armstrong shut the door behind him before speaking.

"Uncle David. How are you?"

"I am an old man. My bones ache."

"I'm surprised you come visiting, then," Jonathan remarked.

"You disappoint me, Xaio Li."

"Uncle, please do not disrespect me by addressing me as 'Little Lee'. I would prefer it if you called me Jonathan, but if you must use the old form, you might call me 'Lao Li'. I am the oldest now my father is gone."

David Wang laughed, dry and dusty as old leaves. "Have pity on an old man. At least ask me to sit down." Jonathan nodded slightly and the visitor settled himself into the leather armchair close to the fire. He looked pointedly at the tumbler of whisky on the light oak table. Jonathan picked it up and took it to an open drinks cabinet, splashing more of the liquid into the glass.

"Would you care for a drink, Uncle?"

"Thank you. It would warm my bones." Jonathan poured a small measure into another glass. He didn't want to give the old man cause to stay too long.

"Your father and I came to this country together."

"Yes, I know."

"With my brother, Terry."

"Yes, Father told me."

"I'm the last one left." David Wang sipped his drink and looked into the flames flickering in the gas fire. "There's no-one left who remembers how it was then."

"No, I don't suppose there is." Jonathan was getting fed up with this rambling conversation.

"Your wife is a very unusual girl." He changed the subject. Jonathan was surprised, not knowing where this was leading. "First Son tells me she goes to college. Maybe she should stay at home and look after her husband and child."

"It's kind of you to take an interest, but you don't need to concern yourself."

"First Son also tells me she has unsuitable friends."

"And how, exactly, would he know?" Suspicion began to seep into Jonathan's mind. He'd thought it might be First Son Wang from May's description earlier but couldn't imagine why he'd want to follow her. What did she have to do with anything? "Has he been watching her, following her?"

"Just keeping a friendly look-out. There are some bad people about, these days." David Wang drained his glass and rattled it onto the table. Jonathan ignored the implied suggestion that a refill would be welcome. He took another gulp from his own glass. Was the old devil threatening May? He didn't understand.

"What sort of bad people would they be?"

"Oh, I don't know," the old man scratched his chin. "Perhaps the sort of people you would not want to have close to your wife."

"And you think it's your son's duty to protect her?"

"A friend likes to lend a helping hand, Lao Li."

"Would this friend expect some recompense for his trouble?"

The old man shook his head ruefully. "You misunderstand." He appeared to be considering how to resolve the problem. He smiled coldly as if an idea had just occurred to him. "It is possible this is a friend who would like to land a cargo without interference from the authorities."

"What sort of cargo?"

"Oh, I wouldn't know. I don't interfere in other people's business. Perhaps it might be a container from Hong Kong or a package from Taiwan. Something like that maybe."

"I don't see what I could do about it." Jonathan was becoming increasingly uncomfortable at the direction this conversation was taking.

"Maybe you should have a meeting with Second Son. He can be very helpful in these matters. He's a businessman, just like you. I have no doubt you could be of assistance to each other. I understand it could be very lucrative," David added slyly.

"I don't need that sort of money, thank you."

"My information is that you do. Your preference for, shall we say, exotic entertainment doesn't come cheaply. Nor does the discretion required to keep your family in ignorance of your gambling debts."

Jonathan was stunned. What did this man know? How could he know anything? Maybe he was trying to trade on a rumour. If he took the bait that was being offered, he'd be hooked. The rumour would be confirmed.

"I really don't know what you mean, but if you think I could possibly be of help to your son or his business associates, perhaps you might arrange a meeting," he said casually. "Most likely it will come to nothing, but I'm willing to see what I can do." Jonathan felt he hadn't committed himself; hadn't admitted anything. "For the sake of your friendship with my father."

"Very well." The old man struggled to his feet. "Second Son will be in touch."

"By the way," Jonathan said. "Tell your First Son to stay away from my wife. I won't have her worried by this." David Wang inclined his head and stepped to the door.

After he had gone Jonathan slumped in his chair. He pressed his thumbs into his eyes, trying to stem the tears of self-pity and fright that threatened to overflow. How had it come to this? What exactly was David Wang suggesting? Drugs, most likely. Or illegal immigrants, maybe. Whatever it was, he couldn't be part of it, even though he was strapped for cash. What he spent his money on wasn't illegal – ill advised, perhaps. The gambling debts were something else, though. Now he thought about it, it seemed likely it was David Wang, indirectly through the gaming club, to whom he owed a great deal of money. But there'd be plenty coming from his father's will before long. More than enough to repay what he owed. As for the other, though the thought of his family finding out gave him a sickly feeling in his chest, he couldn't, wouldn't let himself be blackmailed. He would go to the police, if the worst came to the worst.

Why couldn't he have kept his promise to himself and made his marriage work? But May was so... boring.

He didn't understand her reserve was a protective barrier she hid behind. He didn't see the warm and loving person it concealed.

## Chapter Eleven

It was nearly Christmas. Jonathan was home more often these days and they seemed more like a family than they had since the first weeks following Bobby's birth. They took walks in the park, well wrapped up against the crisp cold. Jonathan was patient with Bobby's attempts to kick a ball and laughingly praised him when he succeeded. May felt a gladness lighten her heart. But then came a letter from Adam's solicitor.

May and Jonathan were invited to his office to discuss Adam's will. Jonathan had snapped that he didn't know what it had to do with May, but the request for her to accompany him had been an insistent one. Jonathan's attitude puzzled her, but that was nothing new. Just when she thought all was going to be well, the old, sullen Jonathan would put in an appearance.

The firm's offices were in the city centre, through an imposing panelled wooden door in a stone archway flanked by solid stone pillars which were resplendent with a well-polished brass plaque announcing the firm's name. Uncarpeted stairs led to the first floor. May and Jonathan were ushered into the inner sanctum where the senior partner, Arthur Mawson, sat behind an enormous desk. As they were shown in he rose slowly and shook hands with both before seating them in worn chairs set in front of his desk. May's eyes roamed the room, taking in its old fashioned clutter.

"Come in, both of you. Sit down, won't you. How are you, Jonathan? Delighted to meet you May. I feel I can call you May. Adam told me so much about you." His kind face darkened with sorrow, the wrinkles lining his brow deepening. "I was sorry I couldn't be at his funeral. I liked him very much and I'll miss him."

He folded his long frame into his chair where he proceeded to rifle through the towers of files and papers on the desk. He obviously found what he'd been searching for and pulled a file out, threatening to topple the already unstable pile. He opened the manila folder and peered at the contents.

"I've already spoken with your mother, Jonathan," he said glancing up. "She was aware of the contents of your father's will." Mr Mawson continued in a dry, emotionless voice as if he had long realised it was the only way to deal with situations where the news wasn't quite as good as expected.

"The family home, I'm sure you know, already belongs to your mother; her father left it to her. There are several personal bequests: James Armstrong receives an annuity as do you, May. Yours is, in effect, a continuance of the allowance you have been receiving. This is free and clear, no matter what future circumstances may seem to dictate." May looked down at her hands clasped in her lap, then raised her head to look at Mr Mawson.

"That is very generous. Adam was very kind."

Mr Mawson continued, "The residue of his personal wealth is bequeathed to Angela." He looked over the top of his glasses which threatened to slip off the end of his nose. "His shares in the firm of Forster Shipping Company Limited, which amount to eighty percent of the stock, are to be held in trust for his grandson, Robert Adam Lee, until such time as his trustees are confident he can manage his own affairs. Angela, of course, owns the remaining twenty percent."

Jonathan wasn't surprised; how could he be. His father had already said as much when he told Jonathan to marry and produce an heir. But, all the same, he had expected, hoped for, something. He had banked on it. "And where, exactly, do I come into the equation?" he asked.

Mr Mawson continued steadily. "Bobby's trustees are yourself, along with your mother, May and myself."

"May? What does anything have to do with May?" Jonathan's voice rose in disbelief.

"Your father placed great faith in May. He was convinced she has great potential." Mr Mawson had been expecting some reaction from his friend's son. It wasn't every day he had to tell a man he was disinherited.

Jonathan turned on May. "So, that's what you were doing every afternoon, was it? Weaseling your way into my father's good graces. How did you manage it? What did you do for him? What did he tell you?"

"Jonathan, please. I don't know what you mean. I don't know what any of this means." May looked helplessly at Mr Mawson, appalled at her husband's outburst, begging for some sort of explanation. He held up his hands in a placatory gesture.

"Jonathan, please sit down and we can discuss this further. I know it will have been a shock. Let's have a cup of tea, shall we?" Mr Mawson pressed a button on his desk and the woman who had shown them in appeared at the door. "Will you be so kind as to bring us some tea please, Jane? And biscuits if there are any?"

The three sat in an uncomfortable silence until Jane returned with a tray set, in old fashioned preciseness, with a silver teapot, cream jug and sugar bowl with tongs. The cups and saucers were fine china patterned with pink and yellow flowers. A plate of carefully arranged biscuits was placed to one side. Jane poured the tea, adding milk and offering sugar, then the biscuits. Jonathan declined but May accepted one out of politeness even though she thought she might choke on it, her throat felt so tight with suppressed emotion. What's this all about, she wondered. Why is Jonathan so angry?

"I was your father's friend as well as his lawyer," Mr Mawson eventually continued, speaking to Jonathan. "He confided in me certain, er..." He searched for a suitable word. "...misgivings about placing the business entirely in your hands."

"I'm not exactly sure what you mean," Jonathan said in the public school drawl he knew could intimidate. The old solicitor was made of stern stuff, though, and ignored the tone Jonathan had adopted.

"Let us just say he was aware of some of the expenses your lifestyle incurred and took steps to ensure the future of the business." Mr Mawson took some pains not to let the distaste for Jonathan's conduct show. He hadn't been shocked when Adam had shared his worries; he was pretty well unshockable. He was more upset his friend had to resort to the tactics he had used to ensure the future of the old established company.

"What I spend my money on is no concern of yours," Jonathan snapped back.

"Of course, it isn't, and I have no desire whatsoever to interfere in your private life as long, that is, as it does not interfere with the finances of Forster Shipping Company." Mr Mawson paused and, under May's fascinated gaze, dipped his biscuit into his tea and sucked the soggy mess into his mouth with every indication of deep satisfaction. He took a final sup of tea and set his cup carefully on the tray.

"Your position as Managing Director will continue, with a rise in salary. The day to day running of the company will be accomplished by the managers your father put in place; you cannot replace them without permission of your son's board of trustees. You may not make any policy changes, sell assets or take on commitments of a financial nature or of any sort which may have an negative impact on the company."

"What am I supposed to do, then? Sit in that fancy office and twiddle my thumbs all day?"

"Your father wasn't an unreasonable man…"

Jonathan snorted in derision.

"Your father wasn't an unreasonable man. You are entitled to a large share of any profits accrued from your own efforts. He wanted you to play an active part in the company's success and to be well rewarded."

"And how am I supposed to do that if I'm to be under the thumb of the managers?" Jonathan asked sarcastically.

"I'm sure you'll find a way. What you cannot do is imperil the company's standing by using it to underwrite your personal debts – should you incur any," he added blandly.

"Thank you Mr Mawson. You have made my position quite clear." Jonathan rose from his seat. "Come along, May. Mother will be wondering where we've got to."

"Just a moment before you go, May. I will be in touch with you about a meeting to discuss your position in all this. I'm sure you'll have lots of questions that will need to be addressed. Perhaps next week?"

"Yes, of course." She pulled her elbow from Jonathan's grip and turned back to the solicitor. "I don't really understand what all this means. I hope you will be able to explain it to me. Goodbye for now."

Mr Mawson shook his head as the door closed behind Jonathan and May Lee. He felt sorry for the girl. How could she have known what agreeing to marry Jonathan would mean for her? At the time Adam had put forward his proposals to his friend, Arthur Mawson had had grave misgivings. Luring so young a girl into what could only be a mockery of a marriage had seemed unfair at best. But once Adam had met May he had told Arthur she would be a force to be reckoned with when she found her feet. She may appear meek and mild but underneath the submissive mask, he was sure, was a woman of spirit. Arthur Mawson wondered how long it would take her to discover what Adam had been convinced was her true self.

* * * * * * * * * *

As they regained the street Jonathan tucked May's arm into his as they walked along. "What a fuddy-duddy old Mawson is." His mood seemed to have changed for the better, to May's profound relief.

"He's a what?" May didn't understand.

"He's old fashioned. Old fashioned and out of touch. Never mind, let him worry his bald head off." Jonathan laughed in what seemed genuine relief to have got a necessary but unpleasant job over and done with.

The street was lively with Christmas shoppers and up and down the road cascades of bright lights were hung from building to building, cheering up the grey December day. Garlanded fir trees were everywhere, bringing a cosiness into the winter streets that would be gone come January. All the shops were decked with sparkling, coloured decorations and there was a buzz of expectation in the air. This was May's third Christmas in England and she still hadn't become cynical about the commercial event that was the Festive Season. The pair stopped and gazed at the magical display in the windows of Fenwick's department store. They agreed Bobby was old enough this year to enjoy a visit.

"We'll bring him next week but now let's go and have some lunch and then what do you say to doing a bit of shopping for Bobby's and Mother's Christmas presents?" Jonathan had apparently regained his good humour and May knew he was the most charming and pleasant companion when he was in this mood. "Where would you like to go? There's a dim-sum house just round the corner. Would you like that?"

As they drank glasses of jasmine tea they ate a selection of delicious dumplings from a bamboo steamer and sticky rice wrapped up into parcels with leaves. May chatted with the young waitress in rapid Chinese, feeling it at first strange on her tongue then with almost a sense of relief that she could speak and understand without conscious effort. She saw Jonathan's slight frown and disapproving tightening of his lips. She thanked the girl in English declining the offer of yet more delicacies from the trolley.

May enjoyed the rest of the afternoon. The surly, arrogant Jonathan who had been with her in the solicitor's office had vanished. They wandered through the bustling streets. May had learned a little about the history and architecture of the city at college and she loved the impressive red-stone buildings, so different from anything she had ever known or imagined. If only it could always be like this, she thought, and pushed away any worries or uncertainties the visit to Arthur Mawson had raised.

* * * * * * * * * *

Christmas itself was a fairly quiet time. They all missed Adam but little Bobby brought the joy back into the house. It was purely for him that Armstrong brought in a Christmas tree. It was the day before Christmas Eve and he set it up in the bay window of the drawing room. Bobby stared in wonder which became excitement as Armstrong began to hang the decorations, hopping from foot to foot and shouting that he wanted to hang some, too. Armstrong, of course, let him help, lifting the little boy up to carefully place the shiny baubles. May watched, laughing at the joy in her son's face. She never ceased to be amazed at Armstrong's patience and kindness. When, at last, the star had been placed right at the top Armstrong made a great show of switching on the fairy lights. May could have sworn she saw tears of emotion sparkling in the man's eyes as the little boy squealed and danced with delight. Bobby dashed off to fetch his grandmother to see the marvellous tree and even Jonathan, when he came home, agreed that at last it really felt like Christmas. May thanked Armstrong for his thoughtfulness.

"Well, you've got to make an effort for the bairn, haven't you?" he said. "The little lad makes it all worthwhile." And, smiling, he hurried off back to the kitchen.

Carol was to be away for the holidays and May had seen her off with a sense of anticipation that Bobby was to be hers alone for a whole month. Angela viewed her excitement at looking after the little boy with a wry humour. Most mothers of two-year-olds would give their eye-teeth to have someone take over. Bobby was a pleasure to have around, but there was no getting away from the fact he was quite a handful and a strong-willed one at that.

James Armstrong was a comforting presence in the background, keeping the household running on an even keel. May often visited him in the kitchen and listened as he reminisced about Adam.

\* \* \* \* \* \* \* \* \* \*

The phone interrupted May's conversation with Armstrong one afternoon in the week after New Year. Bobby was having a nap; Carol was still away. Armstrong picked up a cloth to wipe his hands but May forestalled him.

"I'll answer it. You're busy with the vegetables." She picked up the phone extension in the kitchen, mounted on the wall behind the door. "Hello. May Lee speaking." A voice she didn't recognise spoke.

"This is David Wang."

"Good afternoon, Uncle," May recognised the name, though, and replied using the honorary Chinese title. "I'm afraid that Jonathan is not home yet."

"Is that May I'm speaking to?"

"Yes," she repeated. "This is May."

"Well, isn't that lucky. It was you I wanted." May was puzzled. What on earth would an old friend of her father-in-law want with her?

"How may I help you, Uncle?" May asked politely.

"I'm just an old man. One who misses a dear friend. Adam Li," he used the old pronunciation, "came to this country with my brother and me. We shared a cabin, you know."

May did know. Adam had told her all about his journey from Hong Kong to England and the Wang brothers.

"I have two sons of my own now and several grandchildren. First Son's first son is celebrating his birthday next Saturday. He will be three."

"That is very nice. My own son will be three soon, too." May sighed, wondering where this was leading. Be patient, she told herself, he's an old man.

"I would deem it a great favour, to an old family friend, if you and your son and your dear mother-in-law would come to the birthday party."

May hesitated. "I don't know what Jonathan is doing that day."

"Don't worry about your husband. He and First Son have never got on well with each other. I would not want him to lose face having to be polite to First Son. Please, do my daughter-in-law the honour of meeting you. Maybe the little boys will be friends even though their fathers are not."

May felt she was trapped by good manners. But it might be nice to go to the party and meet another Chinese woman. And, surely, Angela would agree to go with her. "Thank you, Uncle. I am the one being honoured."

"I will send you a card with the address. Goodbye, Xi Mei."

May replaced the receiver on its cradle, puzzled over his use of her Chinese name. No-one here ever used it; she hadn't thought anyone even knew it. She shrugged and put it down to the eccentricities of the old man.

## Chapter Twelve

Jonathan was on the way to his meeting with David Wang's 'Second Son', Freddy. He barely concentrated on his driving as he agonised over what he was going to say. He'd suggested a venue outside the city; he didn't want to be seen meeting this man. The Wangs had a questionable reputation.

There was a lot of traffic on the A1 going north, the lorries throwing great clouds of spray from their tyres, obscuring the road ahead. Jonathan was relieved when he turned off onto a minor road and slowly drove the few miles, almost traffic-free, into Ponteland. Just beyond the village he pulled into the car park of the hotel where he had arranged to meet Freddy Wang. The car tyres crunched the well-raked gravel as Jonathan parked his green Mini Cooper close to the entrance. There was only one other car: a red Jaguar. It was still raining heavily, an icy wind blowing from the east. Jonathan shivered as he got out of the car and dashed into the hotel.

The place was quiet; in the doldrums after the frenzy of Christmas parties. A porter in a white jacket and black trousers who, Jonathan thought, ought to have retired a dozen or more years ago, showed him into the lounge.

"Can I get you a drink, sir?" The voice was as feeble a croak as Jonathan had ever heard.

"I'll have a Scotch and soda. No ice."

"Very well, sir."

Freddy Wang sat nursing a drink. His well-cut navy pinstripe suit tried, but failed, to disguise his bulk. His blue-black hair was as well-cut as his suit. Narrow black eyes narrowed still further as Jonathan joined him at the low, dark wood coffee table. It was flanked by easy chairs covered in an extraordinarily garish chintz. A huge grate held a fire of logs which sparked and shifted as if by his presence Jonathan had disturbed them. He was grateful for the warmth that radiated into the room. The porter returned, remarkably quickly for one of his years, bearing a silver tray with Jonathan's drink. He placed the heavy crystal glass on the polished table in front of Jonathan and an bottle of soda water which gave a hiss as he opened it.

"Will you be taking luncheon with us, gentlemen?"

"No." Freddy Wang replied before Jonathan had a chance to open his mouth. The old man floated away, ghostlike, into the far reaches of the hotel, leaving Jonathan and Freddy alone.

Jonathan sat in silence, waiting for the other man to speak. Freddy said nothing. The fire plopped and flared, rain tapped against the windows, from somewhere out in the hall came the slow measured tick-tock of a long-case clock. The ice in Freddy's glass tinkled as he drained the last of the liquor. He put the glass down, drew in a deep breath and told Jonathan what he wanted of him.

* * * * * * * * * *

Jonathan sat alone. Freddy had left more than an hour earlier, Jonathan standing by the window watching as the other man showily skidded his car around in a tight circle, sending up a spray of gravel as he went. The two sons of David Wang were similar in appearance but, while the elder presented a sober demeanour along with his shaven head, the younger effected a more flamboyant style. The porter appeared silently at Jonathan's side in response to a ring on the brass bell which stood on the mantelpiece. Jonathan was tempted to have another Scotch but the thought of being breathalysed on the way home stopped him.

"A pot of coffee, please. Strong. And if you can rustle up some chocolate biscuits I'd be grateful." Jonathan needed comfort food. He'd made it clear to Freddy Wang that he wasn't going to get involved in the smuggling racket his family was running. But Jonathan now had a dilemma: did he go home and forget all about it – pretend nothing had happened, or talk to the police? He drained the coffee pot and polished off the biscuits down to the last crumb as he debated the problem in his head. He had been brought up to respect the law, and he still did.

The realisation that the Wangs were trying to blackmail him made Jonathan angry rather than frightened. The thought of how his mother would feel when the whole sordid story came out made him queasy but he knew she would support him, see him through. How May would feel didn't come into the equation. She would have to accept the situation; she didn't have much choice. What about family friends and business acquaintances? How would they treat him when they learned of his hitherto hidden homosexuality? Well, he'd *thought* it was hidden, but if the Wangs knew about it, how many others did, too? If he'd always been open about it no-one would have turned a hair. It didn't seem to matter too much these days. Even now, being forced into the open, he supposed it would be a nine day wonder. But it was the gambling, the huge debts he'd run up as he threw good money after bad trying to recoup his losses, that might prove his downfall. He'd been living on his expectations but his father's extraordinary will had put paid to the hope that he'd be able to repay his debts. But perhaps it didn't all have to come out. Perhaps if he went to the police somehow he might keep a lid on it.

The police – Jonathan quailed at the thought. Perhaps he should just keep it all to himself. Maybe he could get through this without involving them. But the thought of illegal drugs, and the sort of people that dealt in them, frightened and sickened him. For all his failings, drugs had never been a temptation. He just couldn't see his way through this alone. OK then, Jonathan decided: the police it is.

\* \* \* \* \* \* \* \* \* \*

Detective Inspector Sam Castle listened carefully. He asked a few questions as Jonathan outlined what Freddy Wang wanted from him.

"One of my ships is due in Taiwan next week. I was asked to ensure that a certain firm is given the contract to supply workers to clean and paint the accommodation."

"Is that unusual?"

"Not really. The crew have their own jobs to do. It's cheaper to get a specialist team in to do the work while the ship is on passage to Teesport," Jonathan explained.

"Just out of interest, what cargo is she carrying?" The detective wanted all and any information that might be useful.

"Cars."

"What did you think was the point of such a request? Why did you think there was something illegal involved?"

"If it was a reputable firm they wouldn't need me to instruct the Captain to employ them. It just feels wrong. I hardly know Freddy Wang. My father wouldn't have much to do with his father once they'd arrived in this country together. I'm sure drugs must be involved somewhere, but I don't know how." Jonathan spread his hands in a helpless gesture.

"You've done the right thing, sir. I appreciate it can't have been an easy decision for you to make. There are some aspects of Mr Wang's business dealings we have been taking an interest in for some time and it's just possible you have given us the key. What I'd like to do is discuss this with my colleagues and come up with a plan of how to use what you've told me. If it wouldn't be too much trouble, could you come back in the morning? I have an inkling how you could help further, if you'd be willing, of course."

"Yes, naturally. I'll do whatever I can." Jonathan was relieved to have laid his problem on another's shoulders.

"Shall we say eleven o'clock?"

\* \* \* \* \* \* \* \* \* \*

The interview room Jonathan was shown into the next morning was different from the one he'd occupied the previous afternoon only in that the window was larger. The furnishings were identical: a plain table topped in wood-effect plastic, four moulded plastic chairs in various un-matching shades, a large double-cassette tape recorder which wasn't running and a scratched metal wastepaper bin. The air was stale and over-heated. DI Castle greeted Jonathan and introduced his colleagues: DCI Marie White, a tall, athletic brunette who looked to be in her mid-forties and DS Mike Atkinson whose red hair and pale freckled face made him look boyish. Pleasantries completed they settled into the chairs around the table and the Chief Inspector spoke.

"Mr Lee, I'd like to take you into my confidence and put you in the picture as to the nature of our interest in Freddy Wang and his family. I would impress upon you, however, that this is to go no further than these four walls." Her voice had a soft Scottish lilt and her clear blue eyes looked deep into Jonathan's as if they could see right into his mind. It made him slightly uncomfortable. He agreed to keep everything he was told to himself.

"Are you well acquainted with Chinatown?" she asked.

"Well... " Jonathan hesitated.

"I'll take that as a yes, shall I?" She continued, "The Wangs have several restaurants, also gaming establishments, legal as well as illegal."

"I don't know anything about any illegal ones," Jonathan put in quickly, looking around the three faces.

"It's not the gambling we're particularly interested in, though closing down their illegal operations would be a bonus," DI Castle said.

"I'd better come to the point," continued Marie White. "It's their smuggling operation that most concerns me." She turned to the Detective Sergeant. "Mike, would you please give Mr Lee the outline we agreed on.

Unexpected in a detective sergeant Mike Atkinson's pale face flushed a deep red, clashing vividly with his ginger hair, but his voice was steady as he read from a paper on the table in front of him. "There have always been illegal immigrants entering the country but there is now a worrying increase in organised people-smuggling. Families pay extortionate sums for, say, a son to come into the UK to work, to send home much needed cash to keep the family going. Once here they are used and abused, oppressed and cheated of much of the money they earn. They cannot do anything about it." He looked up at Jonathan. "They can hardly go to the police can they?"

Jonathan's eyes opened wide as the realisation hit him. It seemed so obvious now.

"We know Mr David Wang runs such an operation, but knowing isn't enough. We've got to find how they work it first, then obtain proof." The DS had obviously finished as he sat back in his seat, folded his arms and looked towards his boss. Sam Castle continued.

"We have a way into their operation now. We'll be able to see who and how. Right from beginning to end. You can help, Mr Lee." He leaned forward, arms on the table. "Will you?"

Jonathan hadn't expected this. He'd been so sure it was illegal drugs not illegal immigrants. How could such a thing exist in this day and age? Surely the people who took the risk of entering the country illegally realised they'd be at the mercy of what amounted to gangsters?

As if Jonathan had asked the questions aloud, Sam said, "They're desperate. They've got no money, no future, no hope. They believe they'll be the family's saviour. People beg, borrow or steal to get together enough money to pay for their passage. They think it's the only way to a better life. They're so wrong."

"I don't see how I can help you," Jonathan said, shrugging his shoulders helplessly.

"If you let us know who the extra workers are and who supplied them, you'll provide the key to this operation," Marie White put in.

"But I've already told Freddy Wang I won't be involved in his racket."

"Ring him and tell him you've changed your mind. We'll see you're not put into danger and we'll cover this so deep that neither the Wangs nor their associates will ever know where the information came from." The soft Scottish tones were persuasive, but Jonathan wasn't so sure. He said so. It took Marie White the best part of two hours to convince him.

"Are you sure no-one will ever find out the truth?"

"Positive. I can guarantee it."

"All right, then. I'll do it," Jonathan said sounding more positive than he felt.

* * * * * * * * * *

Freddy Wang faced his father. "I'm sorry, Father. I have failed you. Lee would not consent to be of help to us."

"Is that true?" David Wang sat behind his antique, heavily carved desk in the office behind his New Dynasty restaurant. "Were you persuasive?"

"I pointed out what he would have to gain from being of assistance to his father's old friend. And what he might lose if he was not."

"He needs further persuasion." The older man ran his hand over his thin grey hair as though it helped him think." I happen to know where his family will be tomorrow. Perhaps a little fright would convince him to co-operate. Your brother will see to it then you can arrange another, more productive meeting with Lee."

## Chapter Thirteen

May was reading a storybook to Bobby when Jonathan got home that evening. The boy was already in his pyjamas and rosy from his bath. Jonathan sat on the sofa beside them. May smiled and continued to read as Bobby reached out his arms to his father then climbed onto his lap. Before she reached the end of the story Bobby had fallen asleep. It could always be like this, May thought, if only Jonathan would make the effort. What could she do to make him realise it?

"I'll take him up to bed and then get you a drink, if you like," she offered.

"No. Just leave him for a while." Jonathan looked down at his sleeping son. "He's such a beautiful boy. I'm very lucky to have him. And you too," he added.

"I think I'm the lucky one." May gently rubbed the golden dragon between her fingers. "I have been granted great good fortune." The charm swung on its chain as she let it go. "You look tired tonight, Jonathan."

"I am a bit. I've had a busy day."

"Are you hungry? I'm sure Armstrong has set something aside for you. Shall I ask him?"

"No, leave it. I'm all right. Tell me what you did today."

May was surprised. Jonathan hardly ever asked what she had been doing. "Nothing much – it's been too wet to go out, so Bobby and I stayed around the house. We played some games and he had his nap." May hesitated, "And I did some sketching."

"I didn't know you could draw. *Can* you draw?"

"A bit, but I'm not as good as Jenny. I think she's very talented."

Jonathan snorted. May had long since realised he didn't like her friend and now she wished she'd never mentioned her. To divert his threatened ill humour she continued, "I did some drawings of Bobby while he was sleeping."

"Of Bobby? Would you let me see them?" Jonathan now seemed genuinely interested in what she'd been doing and May hurried to fetch her sketchbook. Bobby slept on in his father's arms. When she came back Jonathan had his eyes shut. May thought he had fallen asleep and she took the opportunity to do a quick sketch of father and son. Until now she hadn't realised how alike in looks they were with both their faces relaxed, eyes closed, dark lashes fanning their cheeks. Jonathan opened his eyes.

"What are you doing?"

"Oh, I thought you were asleep."

"Were you drawing me?" Jonathan raised his eyebrows curiously. "Let me see," he asked rather than demanded. May turned the book round to let him look. Jonathan contemplated the pencil drawing.

"Are there any more?"

"None of you, but quite a few of Bobby." The sketchbook and a box of drawing pencils had been May's Christmas present from Jenny and she had been doing little sketches ever since, practising skills she hadn't used for some years and which had now grown very rusty.

Jonathan took the book from her, careful not to disturb the little boy. He turned the pages and saw most of the drawings were of Bobby: sleeping in his cot; kneeling on the floor playing with his favourite toy, a furry black and white cat; at the pond feeding the ducks. One or two were tinted with a gentle colourwash. May hadn't been able to resist buying a small box of watercolours.

"Some of these are very good," said Jonathan.

"I'm glad you like them." May felt pleased by Jonathan's unexpected approval.

"Have you been drawing and painting for long?" he asked.

"I've just taken it up again. I used to do a lot when I was still at school. I haven't done any since we were married."

"Why did you give it up? You shouldn't have given it up. You have a real talent if these are anything to go by."

"Oh, I never seemed to have time." May hesitated, unsure whether to continue, but she felt closer to Jonathan than she had for a long time and wanted him to see her in a new light. Perhaps.... Oh, please, she prayed, stay like this. Just for one night. Don't let that horrible, moody Jonathan take over.

"The very first time I saw you I wanted to paint you. I thought you were very handsome," she told him softly. A faint blush coloured May's cheeks and Jonathan lifted a hand to trace the delicate bones that shaped her face.

Shyly May raised her eyes to his, hardly daring to hope that this might be the beginning of a new understanding, a new closeness. Suddenly Bobby's cry destroyed the moment. She tore her gaze away from Jonathan and took the child from him.

"Shh. Don't cry, baby. Shh." Gently she rocked the child. "I'll take him to bed and stay with him till he settles. I shouldn't be long, then I'll make us a drink. Would you like tea?"

"Yes, all right. Tea would be nice."

But Bobby didn't want to be settled into bed quickly. As May rose from kissing his downy cheek he grabbed the golden dragon so she couldn't escape, demanding the story from her.

Jonathan wasn't in the drawing room when May came back down. Perhaps he's in the kitchen, she thought; maybe he was hungry after all. He wasn't in the kitchen. May's imagination began to run away with her. Maybe he's upstairs waiting for me. Maybe tonight... With shaking hands she made a pot of tea and began to set a tray as prettily as she could. If he sees how much care I've taken, she thought, he'll be pleased. May reached into the fridge for milk to fill the little milk jug. She noticed a plate of sandwiches and put them on the tray too. There was a bowl of prawns there; big and juicy. Her favourite. Normally she didn't raid the fridge, it was Armstrong's territory, but tonight she had no qualms about taking a couple. There were plenty so she doubted Armstrong would even notice any missing. Delicious. May felt very bold as if, for once, she'd taken charge rather than fitting in with everyone else. She carried the tray upstairs hardly daring to hope.

She began to smile as she opened the door. Will he be sitting on the chaise longue in front of the fire? Or, perhaps, already in bed, waiting. There was no sign of Jonathan. She looked around the room. Where was he? The bathroom. May blushed slightly as she glanced in, but the bathroom was empty. He's not there, she realised. Disappointed, May put the tray down on the bedside table. She paused and considered. Perhaps he was waiting for her in his own room. Jonathan had never invited her into his bedroom. She'd seen inside a couple of times when the door was open and Armstrong was vacuuming so she knew it was similar to her own, but the colours were sombre and dark. Not realising she was holding her breath May walked across the small expanse of carpet that lay between Jonathan's door and her own. His door was closed.

She listened: silence. She knocked.

"Jonathan," she called his name softly: silence. She knocked and called again – a little louder, sure he must hear her thumping heart. She waited: nothing. Remembering her earlier feeling of daring, she reached out and took hold of the door handle. Slowly she turned it, then met a hard resistance. She tried again. It was locked. Locked? He'd locked her out. Or did he always lock his door?

She hesitated a moment then crept back inside her own room. She leant against the door as it clicked shut. She felt rejected yet again, shamed beyond imagining. But she didn't recognise it had all been just her imagination; a desperate need for love and affection that had fooled her into thinking Jonathan had begun to feel the same way. May laid on the bed and sobbed. Why can't he love me? Why can't he want me? What's wrong with me? The questions went round and round inside her head, unanswered. She cried harder and longer than she ever had before, tears of self-pity overflowed and soaked into the quilt making a patch of wetness that felt cold against her burning cheeks.

She must have undressed and crept under the bedcovers for when May woke the sheet beneath her was wrinkled in disarray, the quilt crumpled as if it had been flung around in the night. Her head throbbed and her stomach was clenched in a painful knot. She crawled out of bed and stood unsteadily under a hot shower hoping it would wash away enough of her misery to allow her to get through the day. Anyway she had Bobby to attend to. Then May remembered: it was the Wangs' birthday party for their grandson today. She groaned in dismay as much as misery. She really didn't want to go, but she had promised. Angela was coming too and Armstrong was to drive them. She had to go; she hated to think she might inconvenience anyone.

May lifted Bobby from his bed. His happy smile did much to raise her spirits, but when she carried him into the kitchen for his breakfast Armstrong took one look at her pale face and red eyes and sat her down, lifting Bobby into his highchair.

"Have yourself a cup of tea before you make the lad's breakfast, Miss. If you don't mind me asking, Miss, are you feeling all right?" Armstrong sounded concerned.

"Thank you, Armstrong, I'd love a cup of tea. Can I have lemon in it, please? I do have a headache this morning. Have you any aspirin?"

"I've a bottle of paracetamol. Would a couple of those do?"

"Yes. Thank you." May swallowed the tablets with her tea and nibbled on a piece of toast Armstrong had put in front of her. She started to feel better. Armstrong had already given Bobby his breakfast and she thanked him for his thoughtfulness.

By lunchtime the headache had returned with a vengeance. Angela looked at May worriedly as she pushed her plate of salad to one side, untouched "What is it, my dear? You haven't looked well all morning."

"I'll be fine. We have the party to go to this afternoon." May felt distinctly queasy at the thought of the elaborate display of food the Wangs were bound to put on.

"We don't have to go. Not if you feel as bad as you look."

"I don't want to lose face by refusing the Wangs' invitation. I must go." A wave of nausea hit May. She rushed from the table and made it to her bathroom just in time to be violently sick.

Angela followed not believing May was, indeed as 'fine' as she'd insisted. She looked at her daughter-in-law's pale face as she lay on the bed recovering. She picked up May's hand. It was cold and clammy. "May, you really cannot go out like this. Where's Jonathan? Has he gone out? I haven't seen him this morning." Before May could reply Angela marched out of May's room and knocked on Jonathan's door, not waiting for an answer before going in. May wondered when he'd unlocked it. She could hear raised voices then Angela came back.

"I've told Jonathan you're sick. He's agreed to go in your place."

"Oh, I don't want to bother him. Please, Angela, I'll be all right in a minute." Another dash to the bathroom proved her wrong.

"Get into bed and rest. I'll get Bobby ready. I'll put him in his blue dungarees and the little red jumper I got him for Christmas." May's only reply was a moan.

* * * * * * * * * *

Jonathan was furious and he told his mother so in no uncertain terms as the big grey car slid through the city streets, Armstrong impassively at the wheel.

"It was underhanded of old man Wang to go behind my back.

And what did May think she was doing not telling me?"

"She probably didn't think it was important enough. Or maybe she knew you'd kick up a fuss and wanted to keep the peace. Or perhaps she just wants another Chinese woman as a friend and for Bobby to meet with other children." Angela tried to calm Jonathan.

"And the Wangs of all people. She knew Father would have nothing to do with them." Jonathan wasn't to be mollified.

"How would she know that? David Wang came to the funeral. He was treated cordially," Angela reasoned.

"Well, don't get comfortable there. We're leaving as soon as we can politely escape. I may not want to mix with them but I won't be seen to insult them by not accepting their hospitality. If we ever get there," he added, looking out of the window to see what the hold up was.

They were heading towards the New Dynasty restaurant where the party was being held. Ahead, the street was in pandemonium. A delivery van was parked carelessly and the driver was unloading cartons, carrying them leisurely, one by one, into one of the many restaurants in the narrow street. There was just enough room to squeeze past but the traffic was building up, waiting while each vehicle edged its way carefully past the van. Car horns blared and there was a hail of insults flung at the delivery driver who blissfully ignored everything going on around him. Across the road a gang of workmen hung from scaffolding around a building being renovated, adding their comments to both sides of the disturbance. Bobby was standing on his father's knee regarding the proceedings outside with childish interest. Armstrong sat patiently, waiting for his turn to pass, idly watching a battered blue Ford Transit revving impatiently trying to get out of a side lane between two buildings. A cloud of blue-grey fumes was blowing out of the noisy exhaust. It was obvious to all, except the Transit's driver it appeared, that he could get nowhere fast. Perhaps his foot slipped off the clutch because suddenly the van leapt forwards.

It hit the limousine beam on, crushing the side door into Angela. She died never knowing what had happened. The force of the impact pushed the big car towards the other side of the street. It caught the base of the scaffolding which folded, like a house of cards, and collapsed. The heavy metal poles clanged like untuned bells, planking and workmen crashed to the ground. One of the poles punctured the car roof and impaled Jonathan. He died unaware his mother had preceded him.

The world seemed suspended. After the clashing and tearing of metal came silence, but only for a second. Then the screaming began as the injured in their pain and fright, called for help. Others were quiet, softly whimpering in shock. People from the restaurants, shops and flats flooded into the roadway. Soon the hee-hawing of emergency vehicles filled the air, adding their raucous voices to the din.

Gently the injured were extricated from the muddled jigsaw of wreckage and ferried to the Accident and Emergency Department at the nearest hospital. One workman had serious, but not life-threatening, injuries and two others had minor abrasions. Five pedestrians were treated at the scene for shock. Four people died at the scene: Angela, Jonathan, a pedestrian in the wrong place at the wrong time, and a young builder who, only seconds before, had been leaning on the scaffolding watching the free show in the traffic-jam filled the street. Armstrong and Bobby were in critical condition. Of the Transit driver there was no sign.

## Chapter Fourteen

The police car drove slowly along the street, the WPC in the front passenger seat peering at the house numbers.

"OK, Alan, we're here. It's the one with the green door. There's room to park right in front. Jesus! I bloody hate this."

PC Alan Moss executed a perfect piece of parallel parking and the pair got out of the car.

"Let's see if there's any neighbours in first." He didn't like breaking this sort of news to someone on their own. He looked at the array of buttons on the house next door to the Lees'. "Looks like these are flats." He pushed the top button, waiting a few seconds for any response. There was none. He pressed the other two buttons, again waiting for an intercom to burst into life. None did. "Doesn't seem to be anyone in. We'll have to try the other side." The response to his ring on the old-fashioned brass bell pull was almost immediate. The occupant must have been watching from the window. The door opened a crack, held by a robust-looking chain. Eyes filled the gap, looking the two police officers up and down. They didn't seem reassured by the uniforms.

"What do you want? There's nothing for you here." The voice was scratchy, sounding as though it hadn't been used in some time.

"There's nothing to be alarmed about, madam." The policeman tried to sound reassuring.

"Do you have a search warrant, or a warrant for my arrest?"

"Er… no."

The door was slammed firmly in PC Moss's face.

"Bloody hell. What's bitten her?" The WPC was as startled as her colleague.

"No help there, then" Alan said shrugging his shoulders. "It's just you and me then, kid. Better get it over with. Come on."

Loud banging woke May, dragging her from a deep sleep. At first she couldn't tell whether the noise was inside her head or somewhere else. She groaned and closed her eyes again. The light hurt them. She tried again. It was a bit better, but not much. She pushed the quilt back with a shaking hand and sat on the edge of the bed. Her head reeled and her stomach felt sore, as if she'd been punched. Again the banging. It wasn't inside her head she eventually realised: it was someone knocking loudly and persistently at the front door. Why wasn't Armstrong answering? Still the banging. Why didn't they just go away and leave her in peace? She sighed and stood up, steadying herself with a hand on the bedside table. She supposed she'd better go and see who was there; they were being very persistent. She dragged on a jumper and trousers, crumpled from being dumped on the floor.

May opened the door to see two police officers, a man and a woman, standing on the step, the man with his hand raised into a fist, ready to knock again. Beyond them the winter afternoon light was already fading and one or two street lights had begun to glow orange. A car was reversing into a vacant parking place across the way; two boys on skateboards rattled noisily past, the wheels click-clacking on the dry pavement. The police-woman spoke.

"Mrs Lee?"

"I'm May Lee, but I expect it's my mother-in-law you want: Angela Lee."

"We're police officers, Mrs Lee. I'm Jackie Spencer this is Alan Moss." They showed cards, holding them out so May could take them if she wished. "I wonder if we could come in for a moment. Please?"

"Sorry, how rude of me to keep you standing here. Please, do come in. But my mother-in-law is out. Or is it my husband you want? He's out too. I don't think they'll be long, if you care to wait." Even through the strange disorientation the sickness had left her with, May's innate politeness asserted itself. She led them inside and opened the door into the drawing room. She flicked the switch by the door, flooding the darkening room with light. There was a slight chill in the air and May shivered. Her head throbbed as she leaned over to press the button to light the gas fire. The blue and yellow flames sprang instantly to life.

"Mrs Lee, can I call you May? It's you we've come to see. Can we sit down, do you think?"

May was puzzled but indicated the leather chairs. The pair sat down and May positioned herself on the sofa opposite, thankful to be able to sit; her legs still felt wobbly. The man spoke.

"I'm afraid we have some bad news for you. There has been an accident involving the car your family was travelling in."

"I don't understand. I'm expecting them back soon." May looked at the square brass carriage clock that stood in the centre of the mantelpiece above the now warmly glowing fire. It was nearly half past four.

"They sustained some serious injuries, May," the woman told her gently.

"Injuries?" She shook her head causing a brief stab of pain behind her eyes.

"Yes. They've been taken to hospital."

"Who…"

"All of them, May."

"Bobby?" Sudden comprehension hit hard. "My Bobby! He's hurt?" The nausea returned. May pressed a hand to her mouth.

"I'm afraid so. The man driving the car, James Armstrong, is badly hurt too." Jackie Spencer paused gauging the moment. "Do you have a friend, someone you would like to be with you?"

"What?"

"Can I call someone? A friend, perhaps, who could be with you." Jackie reiterated.

A friend? What friend? Why? May wondered what on earth they were talking about. One minute they were telling her about an accident and now they wanted to know about her friends.

As if reading May's mind Jackie said, "Someone to come to the hospital with you."

"There's Jenny," she finally offered.

"Jenny?"

"Jenny MacLeod. She lives just round the corner. At the Scarlet Parakeet Café."

"Do you have her phone number? I'll ring her," Alan Moss offered.

May reeled off Jenny's number, picturing, with sudden clarity, the little sketch her friend had done along with her phone number on the card she'd given May when she'd had Bobby.

Jackie cleared her throat, regaining May's attention. "I'm afraid there's more bad news, May."

"Jonathan and Angela. Are they hurt too?"

"I'm sorry, I'm afraid they died in the accident." Jackie delivered the devastating news as gently as she could but without mincing her words. She did not want to be misunderstood. May looked back at her blankly.

"The friend's on her way," Alan told Jackie quietly. To May he said, "When Jenny gets here we'll take you to the hospital to see Bobby."

"Yes, thank you. That would be very kind." A sort of calm had descended on May after the initial panic. "If you'll excuse me I must get changed."

Jackie stood up as if to go with May. Her glance at her colleague said she didn't trust this calmness to last. "Are you OK on your own or would you like me to come with you?"

"No thank you. I will be fine."

"Well, if you're sure?"

Somehow May got herself ready and was seated, with Jenny, in the back of the police car. Why doesn't the driver go faster, she thought; why is he going so slowly? She shifted impatiently in the seat feeling the seatbelt restraining her. Then, illogically, she wanted him to slow down; she didn't want to get to the hospital yet. She was too afraid of what she might find there. Outside, car headlights glared in the early evening gloom. Red brake lights brightened and dimmed as the traffic stopped and started. Orange indicators flashed as the cars in front turned this way and that. People walked along the pavements chatting, going in and out of shops; some waited at bus stops others dawdled or strode along eager for home. Why did everything look so normal?

Arriving at the hospital, Alan Moss drove up to the glass doors of the Accident and Emergency Department, a white board with black lettering pointing the way. He looked meaningfully at his colleague as she was getting out of the car. May missed the look of pity and probably wouldn't have recognised it as such, anyway. As Jackie, Jenny and May walked towards them the doors opened, sliding wide with a soft swish. Inside, Jackie spoke with a blue-uniformed man behind a desk. He, in turn, spoke into a phone summoning a nurse from the inner reaches of the department.

"Where's Bobby?" May asked the nurse, increasingly desperate to see her son.

"Mrs Lee? Please come this way. I'll bring the doctor who's treating him. He'll have a few words with you then take you to see Bobby." The nurse showed the three women into a vacant family room and asked them to wait. The room was painted a soft blue with framed prints of landscapes on the walls. Four blue-upholstered chairs surrounded a glass-topped coffee table. In the corner was a hot-plate where a jug of coffee was keeping warm. There was a kettle and teabags as well as mugs, milk and sugar. There was even a packet of biscuits.

"But I want to see Bobby now." May had begun to sob. Jenny put an arm round her shoulders to comfort her. In less than a minute a sober-faced middle aged man entered the room and sat in front of May. He introduced himself as Dr Cameron Reid. In a soft, calm voice he told May what had happened: Jonathan and Angela were dead, killed instantly. Bobby and James Armstrong were in a critical condition.

Dead? Husband and mother-in-law dead? Realisation hit May: the police-woman's words had merely skimmed her understanding. But how can it be, she asked herself. They've only gone out to the Wang boy's birthday party. How can they be dead? She put thoughts of Jonathan and Angela to the back of her mind.

"Please may I see my son?" she asked. "I need to see him." May's voice rose a tone.

"Mrs Lee, you must prepare yourself first. Bobby is unconscious and he is being helped to breathe through a tube in his throat," the doctor explained in simple terms. "He is surrounded by and connected to several machines to monitor his condition. You shouldn't be alarmed by all the hisses and bleeps you'll hear. Do you understand? Are you ready?"

Bobby was hardly visible beneath the confusion of tubes and wires surrounding him. He looked so tiny and frail. It's not him, May thought, just for a second. She could feel her heart pounding, hear her blood rushing. The smallest flicker of hope that it had all been a dreadful mistake flared briefly and died. She took a deep breath.

"Can I touch him?" she asked the nurse who stood beside the bed.

"Of course. Would you like to hold his hand?"

Bobby's hand, still plump with baby fat, was cool and dry. May raised it to her lips and kissed his fingers. "How is he injured? I can't see. Is he in pain? Does he hurt?" Dr Reid stood on the opposite side of Bobby's bed and looked down at him.

"He isn't in any pain. He suffered a blow low on the back of his head."

May's tear-filled eyes looked at the doctor, willing him to give her good news. Please tell me Bobby will soon wake up. Dr Reid continued.

"The damage is inside his head."

"How long will it take for him to get better?"

"At this stage I cannot say anything definite. We're monitoring his condition and doing tests to ascertain the extent of his injuries. Other doctors will be examining him shortly. You can stay with Bobby as long as you wish. I'll be back again soon." Dr Reid patted May on the shoulder and left. May hardly noticed.

The nurse, dressed in green trousers and top, studied the print-out that was emerging from one of the machines connected to Bobby. She tore it off and clipped it to a board. "Can I get you anything, Mrs Lee?" she asked May. "A drink of something?" May shook her head and the nurse moved away.

May again took Bobby's hand, careful not to disturb the lines attached to him. How tiny his hand is, she thought. She gazed at his face, what she could see of it; his eyelashes – miniature fans of black against his pale face; small ears set flat against his head; dishevelled hair that needed to be cut. As soon as he's better I'll take him to have a proper haircut, she decided. So far she had managed to cut it herself with a lot of help from Armstrong to persuade the wriggling little boy to sit still. May smiled at the memory and gently stroked her child's hand.

The nurse came back every few minutes and looked at Bobby then at the monitors that inscribed wavy lines across their screens. She murmured something soothing to May. Then May was asked to step outside for a few minutes while a man and two women – doctors, May was told – examined Bobby as Dr Reid had said they would. May went to the family room where Jenny was waiting.

"How is the little lad?" Jenny asked.

"He's unconscious. The doctors are looking at him again, now." May stifled a sob. "He looks so little and helpless lying there. Why can't I do something to help him, Jenny?"

"You can just be there for him, I guess. Talk to him and that."

A young woman in a white coat stuck her head around the door and spoke to May.

"You can go back in now, Mrs Lee. We've finished examining

Bobby. Dr Reid will come back to talk with you soon."

The door whispered shut as the doctor left. May got up to follow her.

"I'll be waitin' for when you want me," Jenny told May.

She looked back at her friend, nodded her head and left the room.

May sat with Bobby, holding his hand and talking to him, for hours, or was it just minutes? She didn't know. Time seemed to have no meaning for her. She became aware someone was standing beside her. It wasn't the nurse who came and went at regular intervals; May could recognise her soft footfalls on the scrubbed rubber flooring. She looked up to see Dr Reid.

"We need to talk, Mrs Lee. Do you want to come along to my office?"

"Can't we stay here?" May asked, not wanting to be apart from her son even for the shortest time.

"Of course we can." Dr Reid found another chair and sat beside May. She turned in her seat to face him.

"When will Bobby wake up?" she asked.

Dr Reid took a deep breath, almost a sigh, before speaking. "I'm sorry. He won't get better. Bobby won't wake up." The doctor tried to break the devastating news as gently as he could.

"I don't understand. Why not? What are you talking about?" May's voice had taken on a sharp edge.

"Bobby has damaged part of his brain that can't mend. The part that makes his body function, that keeps him alive, that makes him who he is."

"Are you sure? How can you tell? He's breathing. He's living. I can see he's alive." What's this man saying? May shook her head in denial. He's wrong; I know he is. He has to be. But maybe I've got it wrong. Maybe I've misunderstood. May looked at the doctor. Her eyes pleaded with him to explain.

"This machine is keeping Bobby alive, breathing for him." The doctor pointed to one of the monitors where a light flashed rhythmically. Then to another where lines traced patterns across a screen. "These show his heart rate, the amount of oxygen in his blood, his blood pressure. This one would show the electrical activity of his brain. I'm afraid it shows none." He hesitated to say the words but, in the end, they had to be said. "I'm very sorry, Mrs

Lee. Bobby is dead, brain dead."

May felt hot, then cold. She tried to take a breath but something was stopping her. Her head was too heavy to hold up. Her insides were empty. Please – no – please – no.

"Mrs Lee. May." The doctor's voice penetrated the fog that seemed to be gradually enveloping May. She at last took a ragged, painful breath.

"He's not. He's alive. I can see he's alive."

"It's just the machines. They make it seem that he's alive but, truly, he's dead. His brain is dead. We've done many tests, myself and other doctors, and there can be no mistake, I'm afraid." He paused a moment letting the dreadful truth sink in. "Let's go and sit down with your friend and talk some more."

May grabbed hold of the rails at the side of Bobby's bed as if she would fight to remain with her son.

"Just for a few minutes, Then you can come back." Gently Dr Reid took May's arm and she let him lead her into the little room off to the side. She sat down heavily on one of the blue-covered chairs and cried as though she would never stop. Jenny could do nothing but hold her and let the tears flow.

After some time Dr Reid said softly, "We – you and I – have next to make the decision about the life support system that's keeping Bobby breathing. Do you understand what I'm saying, Mrs Lee?"

May nodded. It's not real, she told herself. It's all a bad dream. It'll stop soon. She felt outside it all, watching from afar as a strange doctor in a strange hospital talked to a strange woman that was somehow herself and told her things she didn't want to hear.

"When you tell me you are ready we will take away the tubes and machines. Gradually Bobby's heart will stop beating. You can be with him, even hold him if you wish."

Again, time became an unknown dimension as May sat with her son, struggling to come to terms with the truth. Then she heard someone with her voice saying the words no-one ever wants to say. Then one by one, with Dr Reid telling May what was happening, the tubes were removed and the machines and monitors gradually fell silent.

With Jenny at her side, Dr Reid and the nurse standing in the background, May held her little son as his life quietly slipped away.

\* \* \* \* \* \* \* \* \* \*

May and Jenny had been at the hospital all night as well as the following day and night. The chapel had been a place of refuge: a halfway house for May, between being a wife and mother, and a woman on her own. The atmosphere was tranquil, the lighting subdued. A dais held a simple table upon which stood a plain, brass cross. There were a dozen or more chairs. The walls were white, the floor polished wood. The two sat side by side in silent thought.

"I don't know what to do." May felt totally helpless. The first torrent of grief had passed and now she was empty, nothing more than a shell. Sometime, in the morning's early hours, she had accepted all that had happened with an innate fatalism. Her child, her life with him at its centre, had gone forever. The acceptance had brought a sort of calmness.

"I don't know what to tell you. Why don't you come home with me first, have some breakfast and see what Mam says? She'll know what to do, what with Dad an' all that."

May looked gratefully at her friend. "Thank you Jenny, but I don't want to impose on your mother."

"Don't be daft. It's no imposition. Come on. Are you ready?"

"Yes, suppose so."

Jenny linked her friend's arm through her own and led her from the chapel towards the big glass doors through which the great, empty world lay. As they walked through the foyer, a tall man who had been standing beside the reception desk, stepped towards them and spoke to May.

"Are you May Lee?" May nodded. "I'm Detective Inspector Sam Castle. I'd be very grateful for a word with you."

"Can't you see she's in no fit state? It'll have to wait, whatever it is."

"And you are...?" Sam Castle asked, a look of irritation at the interruption marring his otherwise good looking face.

"Me name's Jenny MacLeod. I'm May's friend and she's comin' home with me."

"The address, please."

Jenny was tempted to tell this arrogant man what to do with himself in words of one syllable but managed to limit herself to: "The flat above the Scarlet Parakeet Café in Gosforth High Street."

"It is important, Miss MacLeod. I really do need to speak with Mrs Lee as soon as possible." Sam Castle was insistent.

"It'll have to be later, but ring first. We're in the book." Jenny turned her back on the detective and led May, who went along like an obedient child, out of the hospital and into the colourless winter morning.

* * * * * * * * * *

"Aw, yer poor lass. Come on in and get yersel warm." Kate MacLeod drew May into the big sitting room where a fire blazed, chasing the dank coldness of the day. Turning to Jenny, "Put the kettle on and make us a hot drink, there's a good girl. And you'd better get some toast on, too. I bet you haven't eaten or even thought about it."

May let herself be seated on the sofa in front of the fire, drank the tea and even ate the hot, buttered toast Kate gave her.

"Good lass. Put your feet up here and rest a bit." May put her feet up onto the sofa as she was told and rested her head against the soft cushion. "That's grand. I'll be back in a minute." Even though she had thought she never would again, May fell into a deep, healing sleep. Jenny sat opposite, gazing into the fire.

## Chapter Fifteen

May awoke with a start, not knowing where she was. She opened her eyes to find herself lying on the big, comfy sofa in Jenny's flat. What on earth was she doing here? Why wasn't she at home? What time was it? She looked at the big clock hanging on the wall: twenty past two. It was daylight so it must be afternoon. What day? She remembered. A sick dread hit her low in the stomach. She wrapped her arms around herself, drew her knees up and moaned. Ah, no. Please don't let it be true. The sound woke Jenny from a fitful doze. She went to her friend, comforting her while sympathetic tears of sorrow spilled down her own cheeks. The phone's shrill ring made them both jump. Jenny snatched up the receiver.

"Yes?" she snapped, impatient to be rid of the unwelcome caller.

"May I speak to Miss Jenny MacLeod, please?" The man's voice held a false tone of politeness.

"Who's callin'?" Jenny had recognised the detective's voice immediately.

"Detective Inspector Sam Castle." He enunciated his title and name carefully as if to a slow child.

"It's Jenny MacLeod speakin'." Jenny couldn't help but think Sam Castle had known it from the first.

"Would it be convenient for me to come round to speak with May Lee now?" The irritation in Sam Castle's voice was barely concealed.

"Not really but I suppose the quicker you get your business over with the quicker we'll be rid of you."

"Thank you for your understanding. I'll be there in five minutes."

He was there in five and a half. As Jenny let him in she hissed in his ear, "If you go upsettin' her I'll have you out of here before you can say Jack Robinson."

"Miss MacLeod, this is police business and I'll get on better without your interference," he said quietly so only Jenny would hear. Dismissively, he turned his back on her and stepped towards May. "Thank you for seeing me May. I realise this is a very difficult time for you."

A snort came from behind him, "Oh, aye. To say the least."

He ignored it. "I'm very sorry for your loss. I can't begin to understand what you must be feeling." He paused as if trying to gauge May's present state of mind. She seemed composed enough even though a little red-eyed so he continued. "I very much regret having to ask you to officially identify the bodies of your husband and mother-in-law."

May stiffened but nodded. It had to be done.

"When you're ready I'll take you to see them. If you wish you may have a friend to accompany you."

"Yes, of course. I'll come with you now. I've got nothing else to do."

May sounded so lost that Sam almost put a comforting arm around her. Jenny beat him to it and glared back at him.

"You don't have to, you know. I can do it for you," Jenny offered.

"I must. For myself and for them, I must."

"I'll come with you, then."

"No Jenny. I'll do it by myself. I have to."

Jenny began to protest but Sam cut in, "I won't leave her alone. I'll be there all the time and I'll take her home afterwards."

"You can bring her back here," Jenny demanded, a bit hurt that May would go without her.

"I think I need to be at home, Jenny. I'll ring when I'm back, I need to thank your mother for her kindness. Please understand?"

It was with a look of contempt for Sam Castle and pity for May that Jenny saw them out of the flat.

\* \* \* \* \* \* \* \* \*

Sam handled the formal identification process with an unexpected sensitivity. May looked at the bodies with detachment: she had never known Jonathan, he hadn't let her; Angela had been kind and thoughtful, but somewhat distant.

"While you're here at the hospital would you like to visit James Armstrong? I'll be happy to wait for you," Sam Castle offered.

May felt guilty. She'd hardly given the man a thought. "Yes, but you really don't have to wait."

"I'd feel better if I did, if you don't mind. I'll wait there." Sam pointed to the coffee shop in the main atrium of the hospital. "He's on the first floor, turn to the left and it's the third door on the right."

May climbed the stairs, joining the stream of hospital workers and visitors about their own business. She spoke to one of the nurses at the desk as she entered the ward. "I've come to see James Armstrong. I'm May Lee."

"Are you a relative, Ms Lee?" If ethnic origin was anything to go by it was clear that May wasn't, but she supposed it had to be asked.

"No. I... You could say I'm a friend. He works... worked for my family. He was driving the car..." May couldn't go on.

"Oh, I see. If you come with me I'll show you where he is. He's conscious now and he's had a good night but please don't stay too long." The nurse led the way and showed May into a small single-bedded room that was cluttered with various pieces of equipment some of which Armstrong was attached to, others standing idle.

The figure in the bed looked so unlike the man May knew, she glanced back at the nurse, wondering if she'd been taken into the wrong room. The nurse nodded as if reassuring May she was in the right place.

"Try not to disturb him too much. He's still pretty groggy from the anaesthetic." She left, the squeak of her shoes on the shiny floor receding as she walked away down the corridor.

May saw that Armstrong's right arm was in plaster and hung suspended in a frame. His right leg was pierced by metal rods which were also strung up on a frame. His face seemed held together by fine black stitches. One eye was swollen closed and bruises bloomed everywhere. His good eye opened as May walked across the room; he wasn't asleep as she'd first thought. May stepped up to the bed and laid her hand on his as it lay on top of the blanket.

"Are you all right, James?" It was a foolish question, she knew, but she couldn't help asking. She was barely aware she'd called him by his given name for the first time. Until then he'd been 'Armstrong' but this was too intimate a moment to be formal.

"They've gone, lass. They've all gone and it's my fault. I'm that sorry. The van came too fast. I couldn't avoid it. I just couldn't." His voice was anguished.

"I know. James, oh James, what are we to do?"

"I don't know, lass. I don't know."

"Bobby..." Her voice trailed off, uncertain how, or if, to tell him.

"Aye," he said. A tear slid down his cheek and caught in the stitches. "Aye, they told me. Ah, the poor little lad."

The pair sat in silence, May still resting her hand on Armstrong's. There were no words that could be said between them, no words that need be said. At last May sighed and rose, placing a kiss on Armstrong's forehead. It seemed the natural thing to do.

"I'll come back tomorrow, James."

"That'll be nice."

* * * * * * * * * *

Sam Castle, sitting at the polished aluminium table in front of an almost untouched mug of now cold coffee, watched May approach. She seemed composed. He got to his feet. "Let me get you a drink. Coffee? Tea?"

"Tea would be welcome." May sat down while Sam went up to the counter, returning with a pot of tea, jug of milk and two cups balanced on a tray. "No milk, thank you," she said as he began to pour. She sat staring into the cup as if looking for an answer.

"You don't really want that, do you?" Sam said gently, nodding at the untouched cup.

"No. Not really."

"Come on then, I'll take you home."

May was surprised to find it was dark outside. "What time is it?"

Sam consulted his watch, a tough-looking stainless steel one. "Twenty past five."

"This time yesterday…"

"I know. Look, do you want to go back to that friend's? What's her name? Jenny?"

"No. I want to go home, please."

Sam had to double park at the house. "Shall I come in with you?"

"That won't be necessary. I'm all right."

He looked at May sceptically. "Are you sure?"

"I'm sure."

Sam got out of the car, went round to open the passenger door and helped May out. "I'll be in touch with you tomorrow, to see how you are."

"It's really not necessary," May said.

"I'm afraid it is." He watched as she climbed the few steps leading to the front door. She slipped the key in the lock, opened the door and went in. He heard it close behind her with a crisp click. He sighed and got back into the car, pausing for a few moments before driving off.

* * * * * * * * *

May entered the vestibule. The soft glow of lights from inside the house welcomed her. Someone's here, she realised suddenly. Her heart leapt in joy at the thought that it had all been some horrible nightmare that was now over. But reality flooded back and a worm of fear wriggled inside her. Someone's here. Someone has put the lights on. She stopped breathing and listened. Just the creaks and whispers of an old house. Then she remembered: It was me. I must have left the lights on myself when I went out with the police officers. Was it last night? Or perhaps longer. I don't know. It seems like a lifetime ago. It was a lifetime; three lifetimes. The sense of acceptance she'd felt, wavered. A surge of nausea hit her, sending her rushing to the cloakroom. She wretched dryly. Throat aching May made her way into the kitchen for a drink.

Jenny – I promised to phone her.

"Are you all right?" Jenny asked when she heard May's voice. "Shall I come round. I can stay the night if you want."

"I'm managing, Jenny. Thank you."

"Are you really?"

"Yes. Really."

"You'll call me if you need me?"

"I'll call."

"Well, then."

"Goodnight, Jenny."

"Goodnight, May."

Working on automatic, May brewed a mug of Earl Grey and carried it up to her bedroom. She looked at the bed. The last time I laid down on that bed Bobby was alive and running around in excitement at going to a party.

May wanted nothing more, at that moment, than to sink into the bed and find oblivion. Instead she wearily shed her clothes and made for the bathroom. A long soak in a hot bath might soothe some of the tensions that made her body ache. She leant over the bath and turned the taps on, watching as clouds of steam rose into the room.

She looked into the mirror expecting to see someone entirely different from the last time she'd looked at herself. She felt different. She saw the same smooth ivory-tinted skin, pink full lips, eyes a dark, unfathomable black, fine black eyebrows arching above, black hair that still held a sheen and fell to her shoulders, breasts more rounded and fuller than before she had her child. But there was no glint of gold between them. No golden dragon nestling there. Involuntarily, her hand went up and met only flesh. Where? Her eyes scanned the floor, then the bath, expecting to see the golden dragon on its chain resting underneath the water. It wasn't there. Where are you, her thought called out silently. There was no response, no psychic link as she'd expected. Was it in her clothes? Perhaps she'd pulled it off when she undressed. A worm of unease insinuated itself within her already jangling emotions as she searched her discarded clothes, finding nothing.

Panic threatened to overwhelm May as she searched frantically. She steeled herself to go into Bobby's room, perhaps the golden dragon was there. Maybe he'd pulled it off as he'd pleaded for another telling of its story. The sight of his empty bed was almost more than May could bear. No Bobby. No golden dragon to be found, either. She'd lost it. The talisman that had brought good fortune had gone.

The sound of running water sent May rushing back to her bathroom to find the water had overflowed and was pooling on the floor. She turned the gushing taps off and grabbed a handful of towels from the cupboard to mop up as best she could. She left the sodden mess in a heap on the bathroom floor, crawled miserably into bed and cried herself to sleep.

Her dreams were full of twisted images, shattered glass, dazzling lights and impossible, frustrating tasks she could never accomplish. She woke several times in the night panic-stricken that she had brought all the misfortunes down on herself and her family by losing the golden dragon. Where? How could she have lost it? It was her fault that Jonathan, Angela and little Bobby were dead and Armstrong badly injured. Dawn was lightening the sky before May fell into a restful sleep.

It was late morning when she awoke. Somewhere, somehow, a balm had soothed her bruised spirit. She cleared up her bathroom and this time managed to have a bath. The warm water, scented with a refreshing bath essence, managed to restore May a little. She dressed warmly and went down to the kitchen, lunching on breakfast cereal before setting out for the hospital to see Armstrong.

He seemed stronger today and was even sitting up as much as his arm and leg would allow. The doctors were pleased, he told her. His progress in the short time since the accident was very good. They didn't expect him to be in hospital for too long. Then, as long as he had someone to care for him, he could go home.

"You must go and see the solicitor, May." Suddenly they had become 'May' and 'James' to each other, dropping the formality of 'Miss' and 'Armstrong' by tacit agreement. "There'll be a lot of things to see to and he'll know what to do. With the best will in the world, you aren't really up to it yourself. Are you?"

"You're right. I'm very useless. Worse than useless." May told him about the loss of the golden dragon and that the accident had been her fault.

"That's daft," Armstrong told her. "Just plain daft. If anyone's responsible for the accident it was me. I was driving. I should have seen it coming. Anyway, us blaming ourselves isn't going to help anyone."

"I'll take your advice and go to see Mr Mawson this afternoon. Oh!" May put her hand over her mouth in horror. "I haven't told Carol. I forgot all about her."

"Poor Carol. She thought the world of the little lad." Armstrong had forgotten, too.

"And I'll have to write to my mother."

"Does she still not have a phone?"

"No. Auntie Yin does but I really can't phone her and let her know before my mother. She's such a gossip it'll be all over Hong Sing market before my mother ever hears."

May could just imagine the relish with which Ying Kui, the spring onion seller who claimed to be her mother's oldest friend, would spread the news. "Hey, have you heard the latest?" she'd ask anyone close enough to hear her rough voice. There'd always be someone eager to hear a titbit of news, the gossipier the better.

"You remember Xi Mei, Lin Yong's daughter?"

"Wasn't she the one that married that fancy Englishwoman's son?"

"That's the one. She turned out to be real bad luck for that family."

May could imagine the pig man spitting into the dust. "How do you mean?" he'd ask, straining his ears to hear anything about Lin Yong or her family.

"Her kid's died." May could just imagine the satisfaction in the woman's voice as she'd say the words. Then she'd pretend that was all she had to say, picking up a bunch of her wilted onions and calling to the crowds to buy. Of course, someone would have to ask, "What happened? What did the husband say?"

"Husband?" Ying Kui would snort. "He's dead too."

There'd be much shaking of heads and tutting before the old woman would come out with, "And the mother, too."

The pig man would be sympathetic. "Poor Lin Yong. How will she hold her head up with the shame of it, having a daughter like that? She must take after her father. His side of the family were cursed from the start. Him an only child and then all those boy babies dead and only a girl to show for it all. Lin Yong should have married me while she had the chance. I'd have given her plenty of good strong kids." He'd make one of his obscene gestures which would set Ying Kui cackling in delight.

May couldn't bear it for her mother to be the brunt of more gossip. If she wrote to her, maybe the news wouldn't get around. May's mind came back to the present.

"I'll write to my mother soon. Bad news like this will keep for a little longer. And there's so much I have to do. I need to go and see Jenny and her mother, and that policeman, Mr Castle, said he wants to talk to me some more."

"Aye. He's been to see me already. I didn't like the way his questions were going. It sounded like he didn't think it was an accident. I dunno." Armstrong shook his head. "You go off now, May. You shouldn't be spending your time with me."

"You're all I've got left, James."

\* \* \* \* \* \* \* \* \* \*

Though she didn't have an appointment Arthur Mawson saw May immediately. He came out of his office and took her hands in his, expressing his deep sympathy. He drew her into the shabby old room and seated her in one of the worn chairs that stood in front of his desk, taking the one beside her. He talked her through the huge amount of things to be done.

"I'm so confused. I don't know where to begin." May struggled to draw herself back from the verge of self pity.

"Let me see to it all for you. I would gladly take as much of the burden from you as possible. What about the funerals?"

May felt almost detached from the deaths now. She had said goodbye to Bobby when he died in her arms and to Jonathan and Angela in the mortuary viewing room. They had gone. It was the way forward, through the maze of complications that daunted her.

"What do you think?" she asked Arthur Mawson.

"Shall we have just the one funeral for the three, then burial in the family plot alongside Adam?"

"Yes. I think that would be fitting." Truthfully, May didn't care much. Her family were dead. It was her fault.

Mr Mawson was continuing. "Then there's the question of the wills. There will be a lot of paperwork to sort out, too. The future of the company must be considered. And there's the house. Your allowance will continue, of course. And also, there will be extra expenses to be met. I will be able to organise funds to cover everything. Yes, my dear, you must leave everything to me."

May wasn't really listening. The solicitor's offer to organise the funeral was kind. A task she knew she wasn't up to.

"I will phone to let you know what I have arranged," Arthur Mawson continued. "Are you staying at the house?"

"Yes. I expect so." May couldn't think of where else she could go. Jenny and her mother didn't have the room for a guest though they had both assured her they wanted her to stay with them if only for a few days.

"If you need me, please don't hesitate to ring." Mr Mawson walked to the door into the street with May, watching her thoughtfully as she walked away.

## Chapter Sixteen

May sat in the kitchen which felt empty and lifeless without Bobby toddling around, playing with his toys or asking a stream of questions about everything he came in contact with. She could almost see him, hear him. She sighed. And Armstrong, who would chat while he prepared the meal with deft efficiency.

May was beginning to realise just how useless she was as she looked for something to eat. She'd never, in her whole life, made a meal, gone shopping for food, cleaned the house. Back in China her grandmother had run the home and May had done no more than the chores set her. At school she hadn't, at the start, worked towards going to university, it had just come her way by doing well and being pushed forward by her teachers. She had married because it was required; there'd been no other way to get her father out of the trouble he'd landed himself in. She hadn't chosen to have a child. It had been the unexpected outcome of her short honeymoon's passionless sex. She'd never planned one aspect of her own life. If she hadn't met Jenny by chance she probably would never even have bothered to go to college. May realised she was adrift in a sea she was unable to navigate.

The doorbell dragged May from her brooding thoughts and she found Jenny standing on the step with a bulging plastic carrier bag.

"God. It's freezin' out here. Are you not goin' to let me in, then?" May stepped aside and Jenny marched in. Her man-sized boots clumped on the tiled floor of the hall as she made her way to the kitchen. She plonked the bag on a counter-top and proceeded to empty it. When a stack of covered foil trays was arranged and May still hadn't moved from where she stood in the doorway watching her friend, Jenny said, "Get the plates, then. I don't know about you, but I'm starvin'. I've been to the Indian take-away. There's prawn korma, lamb passanda, chicken jalfrezi, basmati rice, poppadums and naan bread. Come on, before it gets cold. I didn't think you'd want to be bothered cookin'."

May was ashamed of it but had to admit she couldn't cook. Jenny was amazed. She had learned to cook and bake at her mother's side from when she was tiny. She couldn't imagine anyone not being able, at least, to know how to put together a basic meal. As they ate May told her a little about her life growing up in a small rural village in post-Cultural Revolution China.

* * * * * * * * * *

She'd grown up alongside the other village children, as close as though they were one family. From the time they could walk they would follow the adults to the fields, their little bare feet padding along the dirt track leading from the village into the valley where the rice, sugar-cane and vegetables grew. The distant misty mountains, the hot blue sky, the yellow, swaying grasses on the hillsides, the rice fields full of sparkling water dotted with fresh green rice plants formed a back-cloth to their hard lives.

The children who were too young to work in the fields amused themselves with simple games. The terrace where they played was a concrete platform built a little way above the rice field. Here the villagers spread the crops to dry, but it made a perfect playground. The children would range about the hillsides when they had tired of their games on the concrete terrace. There they found delicious little red fruits: a wild version of the cultivated guava. They ate their fill then stuffed their pockets to take home.

The family now kept pigs; the draconian days of Mao's regime were passing and a little free enterprise was allowed. For weeks Fu Gui had worked hard making mud bricks in his spare time to build a pigsty behind the house, and soon it was home to two grunting, snuffling pigs. He would lean in over the walls to scratch their hairy, black backs. Xi Mei kept her distance, though.

"Don't be scared," her father told her, smiling at her reluctance to come too near.

"I'm not scared." She eyed the pigs suspiciously. "I just don't like the way they look at me. It's as if they want to eat me rather than the other way round."

Fu Gui laughed at the foolishness of his little daughter.

Labour in the fields, at this time, was still compulsory. Lin Yong had to rise as early as five o'clock in the mornings to help her mother-in-law prepare the day's food and other household tasks before going out to work. All the food they grew went to the co-operative and the labourers received their allowance which was scarcely enough to sustain them. Rice was the staple diet supplemented by cabbage leaves and perhaps the odd egg. If a wild bird was careless enough to stray close, it also went in the pot. So they survived the years of what was close to famine.

\* \* \* \* \* \* \* \* \* \*

Jenny was always fascinated to hear about May's life in China.

"Do you think you'll go back, now?" Jenny asked after May had finished her story.

"I've been thinking about it a lot, but no, I don't think so. I'm not ashamed of my heritage, but I can't go back. It's a different world, a different life I've left behind. Besides…"

"Besides what?"

"I'd be an outcast. No-one would want me. You see, they'd think I had brought bad luck to my family and anyone who associated with me would have bad luck, too."

"That's stupid! None of this was your fault." Jenny was indignant.

"I'm afraid it was. I lost my golden dragon necklace."

Jenny snorted in denial and changed the subject to how they would overcome May's shortcomings in the kitchen.

"I think it would be best if you got in a good stock of ready-made meals," Jenny advised. "Don't tell me Mam I said such a thing, though. She'd be horrified."

May agreed. She couldn't think what else she'd do, and Jenny said she'd call in the morning to go shopping at the supermarket.

May told her friend she'd been to see the solicitor, Mr Mawson, and he had taken on the task of arranging the funerals.

"I'm glad you have someone like that to take it out of your hands. I remember all the worry me Mam had when me Dad died. I was too young to be able to help her much and anyway, I was too full of me own misery that I didn't think about her and how she felt. I was that selfish. I should have done more for her." Jenny sighed, May's bereavements seeming to bring back unwelcome memories of her own.

The phone rang. "Do you want me to get that?" Jenny offered.

"No. It's all right. But I can't think who would be ringing at this time of the evening."

"If it's that bloody copper again tell him where to go."

May picked up the phone. "Hello?"

"This is David Wang."

"Hello, Uncle. What can I do for you?" May answered politely.

"I was very sorry to hear about the accident. It was a terrible thing to happen. Terrible."

"Yes. It was."

"In a way I feel responsible. They were coming to my restaurant at my invitation."

"No. No. It was an accident. No-one's fault," May reassured the old man though she believed it was her own fault.

"As an old family friend, can I be of assistance to you?"

"That is very thoughtful of you, Uncle." May didn't know what the old Chinaman could do. She didn't want him to do anything.

"Have the police discovered how the accident happened?" David Wang was all caring interest.

"They said a van came out of a side street without stopping and crashed into the car."

"Terrible. Terrible," he repeated. "And what of the van driver? What did he have to say for himself? Was he injured?"

"I'm sorry. I don't know. I haven't been told."

"I see. A terrible thing." He paused, then asked, "About the funerals. Can I help in any way?"

"Thank you, but our solicitor is seeing to everything." May didn't want David Wang to be involved.

"What about afterwards? Have you thought about where to hold the meal after the funeral?"

"No. No, I hadn't even considered."

"You must be seen to be honouring the memory of your family. You would lose face badly if you did not offer the mourners your hospitality. As it is, your great misfortune will reflect badly on you. You must let me help you." May began to protest but he persisted. "I feel very badly about all this. After all, they were on their way to my grandson's birthday party. I feel responsible. You must let me welcome your guests to the New Dynasty Restaurant. I insist." His voice was quiet but May sensed a hint of steel behind it. She felt powerless to refuse.

"Thank you, Uncle. You are very generous. I will let Mr Mawson know about your very kind offer."

"That is well. I will say goodnight, child."

May put the phone down slowly, wondering how she had got into this position. She told Jenny.

"I think it's very kind of him. He's only tryin' to help the daughter-in-law of an old friend in a difficult situation."

"Oh, if you put it like that. You must think I'm very ungrateful."

"No. Just hurt and confused. Look, I'm off now. Try and get some sleep. See you in the mornin'." Jenny left, taking the remnants of the meal with her. She didn't trust May to even think about putting the debris into the bin.

* * * * * * * * * *

DI Sam Castle was worried. There had been no sign of the driver of the van that had caused the fatal crash. The vehicle had been reported missing, assumed stolen. There were no fingerprints; nothing to suggest any culprit, but the hazy descriptions of the driver, given by bystanders, had fitted both sons of David Wang and, he had to be honest with himself, a lot of other men, too. But he didn't believe in co-incidences and there were too many suggesting themselves in this case.

Jonathan Lee had come to him with his story of a conspiracy to smuggle illegal immigrants. The Wang family were involved. Jonathan had refused to help them. Then suddenly the Wangs were all pally: inviting his mother, wife and child to a party. The accident occurred on the way to that party. The driver responsible had disappeared.

But what would they gain by Jonathan's death? Sam considered the problem. It didn't make sense. They needed Jonathan for their plans to work. Maybe it *was* an accident? No. He couldn't believe it. Then he realised: Jonathan wasn't meant to be in the car. It should have been his wife but she had been sick, or something. Sam Castle slapped the side of his head. *She* had been the target. The equivalent of a beating-up, a powerful persuasion for Jonathan to go along with the Wangs or suffer the consequences. But it had gone too far. It *had* been a bloody accident after all. They hadn't been meant to die, just a bit shaken up, cuts and bruises maybe. But how to prove it?

Sam felt a tremor of worry for the girl but he doubted she'd be in any danger. It was too late now for the Wangs to use the Forster

Shipping Company. They'd killed the goose they'd hoped would lay the golden eggs. There'd be no sting operation. He groaned in frustration, drained the cold dregs of coffee and left the office.

## Chapter Seventeen

The limousine stopped outside the Lees' house. The dark-uniformed chauffeur got out and opened the rear door. Arthur Mawson stepped out and stood on the pavement smoothing his black coat and composing himself. He looked up at the sky, wondering if it would snow – the clouds had that look about them. He put his hat on and climbed the steps to the front door. He rang the bell. The door opened and he stepped inside, taking his hat off again. Carol Hughes, Bobby's nanny, led the way into the drawing room. May was dressed, as she had been for Adam's funeral, in a plain black skirt and the scarlet, embroidered silk jacket. The colour, today, did not suit her. It made her skin seem sallow. But her eyes were dry and her face calm.

"Are you ready, May?" the man asked.

She nodded. Arthur Mawson took May's arm and led her out to the waiting car, Carol following behind, her eyes red and swollen. The limousine drove them to the funeral parlour where the undertakers had laid the bodies of Bobby, Jonathan and Angela in their coffins. May had not visited; she didn't want to see them lying in boxes ready to be closed away forever; their bodies empty shells, now. Three hearses carried the three coffins and the limousine drove slowly, crawling along the road at a snail's pace, behind them. The drive to the cemetery was completed in silence save for the soft purring of the car's engine. As the cortege drew up at the porticoed entry to the chapel in the heart of the cemetery, May saw there were dozens of people waiting for them. She blew her nose once and got out of the car. Jenny and Kate MacLeod, who had been travelling in the car behind, flanked May as she followed the coffins as they were borne inside. Mr Mawson took Carol's arm and they fell in step behind.

The chapel was filled to overflowing but May noticed no-one, her attention fixed on the three coffins: two of them large and ornate flanking a pitifully small one, simple but lacquered bright red. There were no flowers. May heard someone speaking but it meant nothing. After the short service she followed as the minister led the procession out into the graveyard.

As he said the words for Bobby, Jonathan and Angela he'd said for Adam less than two months ago, it began to snow from a low, leaden sky. The flakes drifted slowly, lazily down, soft and ethereal. They covered the ground and blanketed the coffins as they were slowly lowered, one by one, into the cold earth.

\* \* \* \* \* \* \* \* \* \*

The New Dynasty restaurant was rapidly filling to capacity as the mourners shuffled their way inside, extending their sympathies to May who stood alongside Arthur Mawson in the lobby. Jenny, for once in her life dressed in conservative black, was hovering in the background, on hand in case May found it all too much.

The display of food verged on the vulgarly ostentatious and Arthur Mawson tutted to himself as he watched how swiftly it vanished as the friends and associates of Jonathan and Angela Lee descended on it. Not all of them were free-loaders, though, there was genuine grief as well as crocodile tears. May sat watching but not seeing. She started as Jenny poked her in the elbow.

"I don't believe it," she said, drawing May's attention to the tall figure that was talking to Mr Mawson. "It's that so-called detective. Couldn't detect his own ..." She stopped herself. It wasn't the time or the place to let her antipathy towards the man show. Sam Castle approached them.

"I'm very sorry for your loss, May. How are you?"

"Thank you. I'm getting by. One day at a time is what Jenny's mother said, and that's how I'm taking it."

"Miss MacLeod." He nodded curtly to Jenny. She frowned back. Sam returned his attention to May. "Aren't you having anything to eat? The buffet looks as though it was magnificent. Why don't you have something before it's all finished?"

"No. I don't want anything."

"Miss MacLeod, why don't you come with me and help me choose something for May to eat?"

"Don't you understand English or somethin'? She said she doesn't want anythin'."

"I'd be very grateful for your help, nonetheless," Sam insisted and May missed the compelling look he gave her friend.

"All right, then. I'll be back in a minute, May." Jenny allowed the detective to steer her to the buffet table before snatching her arm away from him. "What in hell do you think you're doin'?"

"I'll come directly to the point so we don't have to spend any more time than is absolutely necessary in each other's company." Sam spoke quietly but firmly. "Whose idea was it to come to this restaurant?"

"What's that got to do with you?" Jenny glanced back at May, assuring herself that her friend was all right.

"Please, just tell me."

"If I tell you will you leave us alone?"

"Just tell me." Sam's voice was showing a growing impatience.

"If you must know, Mr Big-Shot-Detective, it was the owner of the restaurant himself. He was a good friend of old Mr Lee. Does that satisfy you?"

"What has May got to do with him?" Sam asked.

"What the bloody hell has that got to do with the price of chips?"

"Jenny, you're really trying my patience."

Jenny looked in surprise at Sam; it was the first time he had called her by her given name. He sounded exasperated. She answered. "May has nothin' to do with him. She's talked to him on the phone a couple of times, that's all. I was there when he offered to do all this. She didn't want it, but Mr Wang insisted. He apparently said it was the last service he could do for his old friend."

"Is that true?"

"Are you sayin' I'm a liar?" Jenny stepped back so she could look up into Sam's face.

"No, of course not. Calm down."

"Don't you tell me to calm down. Sod off and don't come back." Jenny whirled away leaving Sam staring thoughtfully after her.

\* \* \* \* \* \* \* \* \* \*

In the shadows at the back of the restaurant David Wang had watched the exchange. He saw Jenny go back to sit at May's side and the detective speak a word to May then leave. He wondered whether this had been a good idea after all. His pride had perhaps got the better of him in arranging this feast. He cursed his son's bungling of a simple job. A little persuasion had been all that was required, now the entire scheme was in jeopardy.

David Wang thought of ways he could rescue the situation. May was the obvious target, now. He needed to befriend her; find a way into her confidence. He would naturally offer to help her in whatever way he could. Then he would suggest he could do her a service and take over the shipping business – done as a favour by an old friend of the family, of course. Somehow or other he would find a way to get what he wanted.

\* \* \* \* \* \* \* \* \* \*

Jenny was speaking with Arthur Mawson. The pair had liked each other from the first, as unlikely as it seemed: the staid old solicitor and the colourful, outspoken girl. They had a mutual interest in the wellbeing of May Lee.

"I think she'd had enough for today, don't you, Mr Mawson?" Jenny asked.

"She's done remarkably well, but I think you're right. I understand a little about the importance to the Chinese to save face by always doing the correct thing, but I really think she's done enough." Arthur Mawson admired the way the bereaved young woman had conducted herself.

"Will you take her home, then? I'll phone her later on just to make sure she's managin'."

"It's very kind of both you and your mother to take such good care of May."

"She's my friend. What else would I do?"

"Quite so. Quite so."

On the drive back to the house Mr Mawson told May he would need to talk with her about her future, but first he suggested she take a few days to herself. Think about what she might want to do. "But there's no need to rush into anything," he said. "Just take your time. I'll be there for you to talk to whenever you need me. Ring me when you're ready."

"You've been very kind to me. I will ring in a few days."

The car, for the second time that day, pulled to a stop in front of the house. Arthur Mawson got out with May and walked her to the door.

"Goodbye, my dear."

"Goodbye, Mr Mawson, and thank you."

\* \* \* \* \* \* \* \* \* \*

May thought she'd never get used to the emptiness of the big house. She sometimes found herself listening for a child's laugh and pattering steps; for the front door slam as her husband came home; for the click of her mother-in-law's high heels on the tiled floor. Just as emotions threatened to overwhelm her, she would firmly push her thoughts away, promising herself she'd think about all this some other time. But the house seemed to echo as she walked through it as it never had before. She walked slowly, tiredly up the stairs and took off the beautiful red jacket, uncharacteristically bundling it into an untidy clump and pushing it into the back of a wardrobe. She never wanted to see it again. Unconsciously, her hand went to where the golden dragon should have been. She still couldn't believe she'd lost it. She drew in a deep breath and let it out slowly, squaring her shoulders, then dressed herself in grey trousers and a blue woollen sweater. Downstairs in the cloakroom she found a coat. Once more dressed to face the world she slipped out of the house.

The initial influx of visitors had slowed to a few stragglers. May joined their ranks and made her way up the stairs and along the corridor to Armstrong's room in the hospital. He was sitting awkwardly in a chair at the side of his bed, leg propped up on a stool and his arm resting on a pillow. He smiled at May as she entered the room. She smiled a wavering smile back and kissed his cheek.

"Well, James, they've gone. It's over," she sighed despite her attempt at cheerfulness.

"I'm that sorry to miss the funeral, May, but they're still holding me prisoner here. How are you? Should I ask how it went?"

"I think it went well. Mr Mawson had kindly arranged everything and Mr Wang was very generous providing hospitality at the New Dynasty."

Armstrong drew in his lips thoughtfully. "I'm not sure Mr Adam would have altogether approved of that. I always had the impression he didn't trust Mr Wang, or his sons."

"Well, it's done now and it's finished. I don't expect to see him again and I don't want to. And you're right. There's something about him that I don't trust, either. I don't know why. He's always been very civil and pleasant."

"All right. Let's forget him and talk about you." With his uninjured hand Armstrong took May's cold hand, chafing it with his thumb to encourage some warmth into it.

"And you, too, James. Are you coming home soon?"

"Next week, if I keep up the good progress, the doctors say." He paused. "I don't want to desert you, lass, but you can't look after me, can you? You can hardly look after yourself. And I'll need a lot of looking after until I'm on my feet again." Armstrong let out a forced laugh, "I'm well aware of your shortcomings in the housekeeping department." He saw her hurt expression and hurried to reassure May. "I'm not blaming you that you've never learnt. It's not your fault." May had told him, like she'd told Jenny, about her life growing up in China. "I'm going to my sister's in Cumbria," Armstrong blurted out eventually.

"Oh. That's… that's nice." May felt a wrench as though he'd left her already. He was all she had left of her life in the big house in Gosforth. Her last link with the Lees. He's my family, now, she realised, and I don't want him to go away.

"No, lass, it's not nice, but it's the only sensible solution. I'm worried about you in that great barn of a place on your own, though."

"You mustn't worry. I'll be just fine. And, don't forget, I've got Jenny and her mother to keep an eye on me. They've been looking after me very well."

"I know they have. They're good sorts, they are. But I can't help it. I'd feel much better if I could look after you like I've done from when you first came."

"Well, I'm going have to learn to do things for myself." May tried to sound positive. She didn't want Armstrong worrying about her. He had to concentrate on getting better. "I'm going to see if I can get some cookery lessons for a start." The idea came to her suddenly.

"I hope you find as good a teacher as I had. Maggie, my sister, somehow managed to instil the art of cookery and good housekeeping into my thick head all those years ago," Armstrong remembered.

"I'm sure I will." Suddenly May could feel she had something to work towards; something to achieve to help her go forward into a new phase of her life. She looked at Armstrong to see him staring intently at her. "What? What's the matter?"

"*I'm* going to find you a teacher and, God and herself willing, it'll be the very self-same one as me." Armstrong smiled his first genuine smile since the accident. "She's coming to see me this weekend, our Maggie is, and I'll ask her. I can't see her turning me down. Once she's taken you on she won't give up till you've learnt everything she knows."

May felt a surge of mixed emotion: elation, misgivings, hope, fear. "I couldn't possibly. She doesn't know me. Why should she?"

"Because she's a glutton for punishment, that one. You'll see, lass, it'll be just what you need. A break; time to get used to the way things are now. Are you up for it?"

"Well..." May hesitated.

"So that's a 'yes' then. Grand, it's settled. You're coming to the Lake District with me."

# PART TWO

## Chapter Eighteen

The Range Rover showed signs of its farmyard habitat even though someone had obviously tried to clean it. Armstrong stared at the mud that still smeared the side of the large white vehicle but didn't comment. With May at one side and a nurse at the other, he managed to haul himself into the back seat. His leg was still encased in plaster with a considerable amount of metalwork protruding from it. His arm, too, was still in plaster. He muttered and groaned as he was made comfortable. It had been touch and go whether he would be released from hospital this week, but with a sheaf of notes, x-rays and instructions his doctors had finally allowed him to be taken into his sister's custody.

"Are you sure you've got everything I asked you to bring?" he asked May and Maggie suspiciously.

"Yes, everything," said Maggie. "Stop fussing."

"You haven't forgotten anything, have you?"

"Don't worry, James. We packed everything on the list." May added her assurances. "Your bag is in the back along with mine."

"Well, then," said Maggie. "We're ready for the off. Are you comfy back there?"

"I will be if you drive carefully."

"I'll be careful. I couldn't stand seventy-odd miles of your moaning if I wasn't."

May settled herself into the front seat alongside Armstrong's sister, fastened her seat-belt and folded her hands in her lap with a sigh. The older woman looked at her. "You OK, lass?"

"Yes thank you, Mrs B." May had felt calling the woman 'Maggie' was too familiar. Margaret was out – May still had some difficulty with pronunciation. Mrs Bell was too formal, so they had settled on 'Mrs B'. There was no mistaking she was Armstrong's sister, even though she was several years older. Her hair was white with a strong tendency to curl whereas his was grizzled, but their eyes were the same deep-set blue. Her face was lined and, though it told of many hours spent outdoors in all weathers, had a lively expression that belied her years.

The city's roads were as busy as ever with cars, buses and lorries.

Motorcycles wove in and out, seeming to defy space as they squeezed between vehicles. Maggie drove confidently and steadily through the mid-morning traffic. She negotiated the huge roundabout that crossed over the A1 Great North Road and soon they were heading west towards Cumbria.

Though only February, the day held a promise of spring. The sun had dispelled an overnight frost and the sky was a crystal blue. Snowdrops grew alongside the road and catkins hung from hazel bushes. The traffic had thinned considerably and only the occasional car overtook them. They passed through a couple of small market towns and then it was open fields bounded by hedgerows again. May hadn't been very far from Newcastle since her arrival three years ago. Jonathan had taken her and Bobby to the coast once or twice, but that was all. She began to feel an immense sense of release as the countryside opened around her; a letting go, as the life she had known, and had ended so tragically, fell behind her. Armstrong was dozing and Mrs B, seeming to know May needed this time to herself, had tuned the car radio into a classical music station which played in the background as they travelled.

In a little over an hour they were approaching Carlisle. They skirted the city and veered to the south-west, now climbing as the fells of the Lake District rose before them. Then suddenly a panorama opened up and May caught her first view of a lake: Bassenthwaite with its snow-covered wooded slopes rising sharply behind and the sun glittering on the water as a breeze ruffled the reflections on its surface.

"Oh. How beautiful it is," May exclaimed.

"Aye, it's beautiful right enough," Mrs B agreed. "And it's putting on a good show for you today. I remember when I first came here nearly fifty years ago. I fell in love with it then and I still love it today. I couldn't imagine living anywhere else." She patted May's knee. "Not far to go now."

The road wound around the lake, leading them towards Keswick, which sat comfortably in the fold of land between two lakes: Bassenthwaite and Derwentwater. With each turn of the car away from the main road, the track became narrower and narrower until the wing mirrors were almost touching the dry-stone walls that lined both sides. Then they were driving through a gate where a cattle-grid rattled as they crossed it. Sheep looked up curiously as the Range Rover drove past.

Ravendale Farm looked as if it had grown out of the earth, so perfectly did it sit in the landscape. The farmhouse was built from slate and limewashed a sparkling white. In front of the house a small garden was enclosed by a low wall. Ranged behind and to the side were the farm buildings: stone-built and slate roofed. An old dutch-barn, its corrugated iron roof rusted to a gentle copper-brown, housed bales of hay. Behind, planted countless generations ago, stood a shelter-belt of magnificent oak trees, winter-bare. Mrs B drove round the buildings and into the yard which was cobbled in intricate patterns and sloped slightly to a drain in the centre.

A mud-caked tractor stood beside the house's back door, a dog lying underneath. As the car drove into the yard the dog jumped up wagging its tail in recognition of the vehicle and barking a welcome. Mrs B got out of the car and the dog came bounding towards her. It jumped up, putting its muddy paws on her smart woollen trousers. She laughed, unmindful of the mess. "Down, Tess. Down, there's a good girl." The black and white collie sat at Mrs B's feet, looking up eagerly, waiting to see what was required of her next.

Then it seemed the yard was full of people. John Bell, Mrs B's husband was first, followed by his two sons, their wives and assorted children. There were shouts of, "Grandma," "Uncle Jim," "Get down, Tess," and somehow Armstrong was manhandled into the big kitchen and May welcomed with hugs that threatened to lift her off her feet. It seemed there was no standing on ceremony here.

The sons were Robin and Tom, their wives Kath and Sally. May was ashamed not to be able to remember the names of the five children, and who was whose she wasn't to work out for quite some time. It transpired that the sons lived in the hamlet of half a dozen cottages less than quarter of a mile away. May was thankful they did. She didn't think she wanted to cope with such a lively lot around the house all the time. The youngest was eight, Mrs B had told her, and the oldest twelve.

As soon as the family welcoming committee dispersed for their jobs and other exploits, Mrs B warmed up a pan of home-made soup for the three of them along with bread, sliced thickly from a crusty loaf. The others had eaten already and the big kitchen was now peaceful. May had the unexpected feeling of being completely at home, though, of course, she had never been anywhere like this before in her life.

Until he could manage the stairs Armstrong was to sleep in the parlour – a 'best' sitting room that was only used on high days and holidays – and May was taken to a bedroom. It was as different from her own as could be imagined. There was only space for a single bed, an easy chair, a small wardrobe and a bedside cabinet, none of which matched, all in dark wood. The walls were painted white which reflected the small amount of light that came through the tiny window set in the thick walls. There was only one bathroom in the house which was just along the passage.

May unpacked the few things she had brought with her. Mrs B had warned her to bring warm clothing – nothing fancy – and strong shoes, wellies if she had them. It seemed that most of her city clothes would be useless here. Still, she didn't expect to be going out much so it didn't matter. She was here to learn how to look after herself, not have a social life. The small chair was squeezed in at the foot of the bed. May sat on it and looked out of the window, over the farmyard to the fells beyond. She thought how different her life was going to be from what she had expected when she came to England three years ago.

She'd written to her mother only last week. She'd dreaded it and had put it off for as long as possible. It would be a month or more before she could expect a reply. She would probably be back in Newcastle again by then. What am I going to do with herself when I go back, she wondered. She thought could manage on the annuity she received from Adam to finish her courses at college. But then what? She'd have to get herself a job, she knew. What that would be, May had no idea. Perhaps Jenny would have some suggestions, or James. Would he want to come back to Newcastle with her? The questions were never-ending and she could find no answers. She sighed and went back downstairs.

Mrs B was standing at the long wooden table in the kitchen preparing their evening meal. She beckoned May over.

"Come on, then. Might as well get you started. There's a pinny in the drawer by the Aga."

May stood where she was, not altogether sure what she was supposed to do.

"I can see you're going to need lessons in more than cooking. The Aga is the big blue stove over there. It's not like an ordinary cooker;

it stays on all the time and runs the central heating and hot water as well. Do you know what a pinny is?"

May shook her head. Mrs B pointed to the apron she had tied round her waist. May smiled in understanding. Then, clothes protected in the correct manner, she returned to the table.

"I'll take it you know nowt – nothing. Now then, this is what we're having for our supper tonight..." Mrs B started May's introduction to the art of cookery.

May was a fast learner and within a few days she could anticipate much of what Mrs B would ask for in the way of vegetable preparation. She had a notebook by her side all the time and jotted down notes, sometimes with little drawings to illustrate the instructions. Armstrong sat by the Aga, his leg up on a footstool, watching and listening and nodding approvingly of May's quick grasp of what was required.

Armstrong's visit to the Cumberland Infirmary in Carlisle was May's first trip out, if it could be called that. Mrs B dropped them off and went to do some shopping, leaving May in charge of James. He was having the plaster casts removed, but the metal pins had to stay in his leg for a little longer. The physiotherapist showed them some exercises he had to do religiously every day if he was to regain full use of his leg. May was there to help and encourage him – another thing she had to learn.

The drive back to Ravendale Farm was far more comfortable for Armstrong than the drive into the city had been. Being free of the restricting casts put him in a more cheerful frame of mind. The x-rays showed the bones were knitting together well, and, with care, he could now get around under his own steam. The first thing he was going to do was have a long, hot bath he told May and Mrs B as he scratched at the wizened, flaking skin of his arm and leg.

Then came the day, at the end of May's third week at the farm, that Mrs B said, "I'm having a day out in Kendal tomorrow. I'm meeting a friend and we're going to do some shopping and have a spot of lunch. I won't be back till gone four. Think you can manage to make our supper, May?" Supper, May had learned, was what they called their main evening meal in these parts.

"Yes, if it's something simple. I'll have James to rescue me if I go wrong." May's reply was given with more confidence than she felt, but there had to come a first time and this was a good an occasion as any.

"What are you going to make? Any ideas?" Mrs B was giving May the chance to ask her advice without seeming to interfere. May thought about it.

"How about braised steak? I think I saw some in the freezer. And I can do creamed potatoes and vegetables. Does that sound good? You showed me how last week."

"And pudding? John likes a good pudding, you know."

"Apple crumble and ice-cream." May had made that before.

"That sounds grand, lass. Just take your time and remember to use the proper oven. Don't want it burning do you?" Mrs B smiled at May's eager suggestions. "Sound OK to you, Jim?"

Armstrong was fiddling with the knobs on the radio, trying to get better reception. Here, in the fells, it wasn't always very good. "Aye. It'll be right."

"That's settled, then." Mrs B put her arm around May shoulders and gave her a hug. "You'll be fine, lass. Just fine. Now then, let's get some tea brewed, John and the lad'll be in soon. There's some fruit cake in the tin. Get it out for them, May. They always say tea is too wet without a bit of something to go with it." She laughed and filled the large kettle that sat on the Aga, never far from the boil.

It wasn't just cooking that May learned at the farm: cleaning the house, washing and ironing, shopping for groceries and, it seemed, a thousand and one other things that seemed necessary to run a home. May found solace in the work and gradually began to gain in confidence. Warmly dressed in borrowed clothes, each afternoon she and Armstrong, using a walking stick, took a stroll down the lane, taking care he didn't overdo things. They were easy, comfortable with each other, chatting or walking in companionable silence. They never discussed the future. Neither was ready to face it.

May had packed her sketchbook in her bag and one day she took it out in the refuge of her own little room. Seeing her drawings of Bobby and the single one of Jonathan, she cried in sadness and loss. There were still times when grief took her by surprise and there wasn't time for her to shut it away in a remote corner of her heart. Sitting on the chair at the window she made little sketches of the yard beneath and the fellsides beyond. She found she loved drawing trees, fascinated by the sturdy shape of the old oaks. She habitually drew a little boy somewhere in the picture. She felt comforted as though his presence was still there, but just out of reach.

\* \* \* \* \* \* \* \* \* \*

May was standing at the stove stirring a pan of broth one morning in late March when John Bell burst into the kitchen, mud-caked boots still on.

"Get the vet on the phone, Maggie. There's been a bloody dog on the loose and it's had one of the ewes." Not waiting for a reply he went to a locked cupboard in the pantry where he kept his shotgun. He pocketed a box of cartridges and, holding the gun under his arm, strode out again. "It's in the field by the beck," he shouted over his shoulder.

May was unsure what was going on but knew it was something unusual, something serious, to have let John leave great clods of mud on the kitchen floor without a tongue-lashing from his wife.

Armstrong began to get dressed for the outside, pulling on wellies and an old waxed jacket that had seen better days. "I'm going to see what I can do to help. If he sees yon dog I wouldn't give tuppence for its chances, though." Grim-faced, he followed in his brother-in-law's wake, slamming the door behind him.

Mrs B was already on the phone, talking in precise, measured words, wasting no time on the usual pleasantries she would have enjoyed. Call over she turned to May who hadn't moved from the stove. "The vet'll be here soon," she said. "It's the lass, which won't please John. Thinks it's a man's job: vetnary. But she's out this way and it'll save time. He'll have to make do."

An hour later May heard John drive the farm's quad-bike into the yard. She looked out of the window to see him towing a trailer containing the injured sheep. Someone in green overalls stood in the trailer, holding firmly on as it bounced across the cobbles. She watched as the pair manhandled the sheep into a byre and went in with it. Soon after, Armstrong appeared, limping heavily. In the heat of the moment he'd forgotten to take his walking stick. May hoped he hadn't done himself any harm. He came into the kitchen and sank stiffly into the chair by the Aga, rubbing his bad leg.

"Are you all right, James?" May was concerned.

"Here, get this down you, you daft beggar." Mrs B handed

Armstrong a mug of tea. "Chasing off like that. I don't know." She frowned at her brother's foolhardiness. "How's the ewe? And the others?"

"I think it'll live. John and the vet have brought it in and she's going to stitch it up where the dog got at it. It'll lose the lamb, she says." Armstrong shook his head. "John shot the dog. The bugger was coming in for another go."

"Did he recognise the dog? Whose it was?" Mrs B asked.

"No, he didn't know. It had a collar on and the vet lass it going to take its body back to the surgery and see if it's got a micro-chip. Seems that lots of folk get one put into the dog's neck and if it gets lost it can be identified," Armstrong told her. "The things they can do these days."

John brought the vet in for a mug of tea and to get washed. Mrs B introduced her to May. "This is Fiona Wrightson, one of the vets from town. She was at school with my lads."

Fiona dried her hands on a towel then shook May's hand with a firm grip. She would be in her early thirties, May guessed. Of medium height, about the same as May. Curly, light brown hair, green eyes that crinkled at the corners as she smiled, and rough, weatherbeaten hands. Neither pretty nor plain, she had a friendly, open face. May liked her immediately.

"Pleased to meet you, May. I've heard to were staying here for a while." She smiled at May's look of surprise that anyone knew, or cared, she was at the farm. "The local grapevine is very efficient." Fiona gulped the tea down and managed to do justice to the plate of buttered scones May had made earlier.

"Mmmm. Up to your usual standard, Maggie," Fiona said picking at the crumbs left on the plate.

Mrs B made no reply but smiled over Fiona's head at May, giving her a nod of approval. May felt a deep sense of achievement.

"I'll have to be on my way. I've still got a few more calls to make," Fiona said, getting up. She turned to John Bell, "I'll come back tomorrow, John, and take a look at that ewe. Keep an eye on the others and give me a call if you need me to come back before then." Fiona slipped her boots back on as she went out of the door. "Thanks for the tea, Maggie. See you tomorrow, May. Bye, everyone."

"She didn't do a bad job," John Bell said as he waved her off.

"For a lass."

## Chapter Nineteen

True to her word Fiona Wrightson appeared on the doorstep of Ravendale Farm the next morning. She shouted in through the open door, "I'll go and check on that ewe then I'll come in. Any chance of a coffee?" She was off about her business without waiting for a reply.

The morning was bright and clear. The snow on the fells was beginning to melt, swelling the beck that ran through the field below the farmhouse. Above the oak trees the rooks called to each other as they ferried twigs and mosses to build their nests high in the branches. May stood in the yard, drinking in the sights and sounds and enjoying a breath of fresh air before calling to Fiona that coffee was ready.

"Be there in a minute." She appeared at the byre door. "This old girl's doing well. The stitches look good and clean. I'll give her another injection of antibiotics to keep it that way and I'll be right in."

Mrs B welcomed Fiona into the kitchen and, as the vet washed her hands, asked about her father, where she'd been that morning and where she was going afterwards. "Any word on that dog?"

"Yes. It didn't have a micro-chip but the police had had a dog reported missing from Keswick yesterday morning. Seems it was a bit of a nervous type and it ran off when a low-flying jet went over."

As the three women settled down round the big table for coffee and homemade biscuits Mrs B told May and Fiona just what she'd do with noisy aircraft and people who couldn't control their animals.

"How's John today?" Fiona asked. "And where's James?"

"John's fine. Got over his upset from yesterday, but he's still mad as a hornet about it. He's taking a look at the rest of the ewes and Jim's gone with him."

"Are you enjoying your holiday, May? Have you seen much of the countryside?"

May didn't quite know what to say. "It's not really a holiday."

Mrs B cut in, "May's been giving me a hand round the place. That brother of mine is too much to deal with at times. We haven't had much chance to get out and about and the weather hasn't been up to much, either." She turned to May. "I've been thinking you must be ready for an outing. See something of the place while you're here."

"I know," Fiona said. "Would you like to come with me today? I've got two more calls this morning and then I've got the afternoon off. What about it?"

"Oh, I don't know… It's very kind of you but…"

"Now then. You need some time off. Get the cobwebs blown out. You should go, May. I'll manage without you," Mrs B said encouragingly.

"Well, if you're sure." May looked down at her clothes. "I'd better get changed."

"You're fine as you are," Fiona said. "Jeans and a warm sweater are just what you need. Bring a pair of wellies and you'll be right." Her good-natured enthusiasm was infectious and May smiled in return. Her heart lightened at the thought of going out with Fiona.

The vet's car was a clutter of papers and cardboard boxes overflowing with the accoutrements of an on-call veterinary surgeon in a predominantly rural practice. She pushed the ones that had invaded the front seat into the back of the car, making room for May. She chatted easily, telling May where they were going and about the people she would meet.

The first call was in the next village: a pet cat had been in a fight. The old chap who owned it wasn't able to drive any more so Fiona was going to visit him. It turned out the cat wasn't badly hurt, just feeling sorry for itself. Fiona reassured the owner and they went on to her last call of the day.

This time they drove down the valley, fields green now the snow had gone. The house they came to had once been a farm but now had only the few fields adjoining it. The outbuildings had been converted to stables and out of three of them horses heads appeared in curiosity as Fiona drove into the yard.

"Come on and I'll introduce you." Fiona didn't say whether it was to the horses or the yet-to-appear owner. "Better put your wellies on, it's a bit mucky."

It was a longer job than Fiona had expected. One of the mares had cut herself badly on barbed wire and needed stitching. The distraught owner didn't think of inviting May into the house while the job was in hand. To keep out of the way May got back into the car and, to occupy herself, began to sketch the stables and horses on the back of an old envelope she found, with a ball-point pen she picked up off the floor. She was so engrossed in the task she didn't hear Fiona come back. She jumped when the vet got into the car and slammed the door behind her.

"That's really good," Fiona remarked, peering over May's shoulder.

"Oh, it's not much," May said, folding the paper and trying to put it away. Fiona took it and smoothed it out.

"No. It's very good. And you've captured the horses beautifully. You're quite an artist, May."

"You are very kind. I haven't done much drawing recently. Apart from…"

"Apart from what?" Fiona was interested and didn't notice as tears appeared in May's eyes.

"Apart from my little boy."

"I didn't know you had a son. He isn't here with you, is he? I haven't seen him."

May told her: the full story, as far as she knew it, as they drove through the fells and down to a pretty lakeside village.

"Well," Fiona said at last. "You've had quite a time of it, these last four years, haven't you?" Realising May didn't need mawkish sympathy, Fiona said, "Come on, I'll treat you to lunch. I, for one, need some comfort food after hearing all that. Are you up to it?"

"Yes. I think I am. Do you know, you're the first person I've told the full story to? Mrs B knows, but I didn't have to tell her."

"I'm very flattered you feel you could tell me. I'll keep it to myself, of course."

Fiona led the way into the pub. It was cosy inside with a bright fire burning in a huge fireplace. The ceiling was low and polished brasses hung from its blackened beams. The bar glowed with polish and behind it bottles sparkled with reflected light. The man behind the bar greeted Fiona.

"And who's this you've brought with you today?"

"Not known for minding your own business are you, Uncle Fred?" Fiona laughed. "This is my friend, May Lee. She's staying at Ravendale Farm with Maggie and John Bell. May, this is my Uncle Fred: my father's cousin, Fred Swales. And he's a right nosey parker but serves the best steak and ale pie and chips this side of Windermere."

May smiled at the banter between the two, sensing the deep regard the pair had for each other. They got their drinks, decided that steak and ale pie would be just the job, and went to sit near the fire. There were one or two people already enjoying meals and several locals sat at the bar having their lunchtime pints.

Fiona told May about growing up in Keswick as the only daughter of the local vet, then following in his footsteps. "It hasn't been easy. Traditions run deep here and a lot of farmers think it isn't right for a woman; in their opinion, being a vet is a man's job. But they know my father and they're starting to trust me, but it's hard work sometimes, convincing them I know what I'm talking about." Fiona grinned mischievously. "Still, it wouldn't feel half so good when they tell me, or my Dad, that I'd done a good job if they'd accepted me from the first."

"What about your mother?" May asked. "Does she mind you being a vet?"

"Mum died when I was little," Fiona replied.

"I'm sorry," May said, concerned she may have upset her new friend.

"Don't worry. It was a long time ago. I don't really remember her."

"That's sad for you."

"I suppose so, but Dad more than made up for it and I often went to stay with my aunt and uncle and played with my cousins. I had a happy childhood." Fiona smiled, her face lighting up with the memory.

The sun was dipping below the fells before Fiona dropped May off at Ravendale Farm with the promise to speak on the phone soon and arrange another day out. May couldn't wait. Then she felt guilty – she'd spent the best part of the day enjoying herself. But there'd been some sort of release, she realised, telling Fiona about herself and her previous life.

* * * * * * * * * *

It was during the following week, after breakfast one morning when they were alone, Mrs B took May's hand in hers. "I know what day it is today, lass."

May nodded, realising James must have told his sister. She hadn't been going to say anything. "It's Bobby's birthday," May said quietly. "He would have been three today." Her throat hurt with suppressed emotion. She determinedly held the tears at bay.

"I want to take you somewhere I think might be a comfort. Will you come?"

May nodded, not trusting herself to speak, and soon they were in the Range Rover driving out and clattering over the cattle-grid. "It's not far," Mrs B said and, sure enough, had gone only a very few miles before stopping in a small car park that was little more than a clearing at the side of the road. "Come on. We'll walk."

They walked down a tree-lined drive and skirted a large house before heading through fields and down towards a lake. There, standing on the lake shore, was a tiny church.

"To me, this is a magical place," Maggie sighed. "I used to come here on my own quite often when my first baby was stillborn. The comfort it gave me made me feel it was worth carrying on. The atmosphere of peace is so strong, here. Then, again, when I miscarried the second baby."

May sighed. "I never knew, never thought…"

"Oh aye, lass. I know what you're going through. And going through it is just what you've got to do. You'll come out the other side eventually. You'll never forget the little lad, of course you won't. But, I promise you, you'll be stronger. You may even find someone else to love one day."

"You mean a man?" May looked across the lake to the far shore in silent contemplation. "I didn't love Jonathan, you know," she confessed. "He didn't love me either: I didn't deserve it." Suddenly she turned to Mrs B. "It was my fault they died. I lost the golden dragon. I didn't take care of my good fortune and it was all taken from me." May turned her head away in despair. "There can never be anyone else. I would never bring bad fortune like that to anyone. Not to anyone I cared for. I wouldn't do it."

"Surely you don't believe that?"

"I do. I can't help it."

Mrs B shook her head and sighed. "Go on. Have a walk into the church. Then, when you're ready, you'll find me by the waterside. Take as long as you want. I'll wait."

May walked slowly into the church. She sat in one of the wooden pews and gazed at the pictures on the stained glass window. She thought about how she was feeling today: Bobby's birthday. Three years ago I gave birth to him. Barely three months ago I saw him die. It seems like two different lives: then and now. I'm not the same person as the one who was Jonathan's wife and Bobby's mother. That person was compliant, always falling in with other people's plans. I never needed any of my own. I'm adrift, now, she thought. Without purpose or direction. May sighed and looked round the little church. It was true what Mrs B had said: there was a sense of peace about the place. She closed her eyes and let the atmosphere wash over her.

As she sat there May decided it was time she took control of her own life. She had to learn to make decisions. Always she'd gone along with the plans and suggestions of others. Day by day she was becoming more able to look after herself and her home, wherever that would be. Mr Mawson had assured her everything in Newcastle was being looked after, but she would have to go back before long and take her things from the house. She realised she didn't even know whose house it was now.

Where did she want to be? Not China, that was certain. Newcastle? Jenny was there. Mr Mawson and Kate MacLeod were there, too, but May couldn't build a life around them. Here, in the Lake District? Did she want to stay here? In just a few short weeks she had made as many friends, maybe more, than she had in the previous three years: Mrs B and John and their family, Fiona Wrightson, too. May hardly knew her, but she felt that, already, they were friends, good friends. And where did James Armstrong come into the picture? He was of both places: her connection to the past and perhaps her link to the future.

May shivered, realising she'd sat in the church until she was cold. How long have I been here? And Mrs B will be waiting. May hurried outside to find her walking by the shore.

"Have I been too long?" May asked apologetically. "I didn't think about the time."

"No, that's all right. I've enjoyed a walk, I haven't been here for ages." Mrs B looked at May. "And you, lass. Did it help?"

May linked her arm through Mrs B's. If the woman was surprised at the Chinese girl's sudden affection she didn't show it.

"Yes, thank you, Mrs B. It did help. I seemed to see things more clearly than I have for a long time."

"Good. I hoped it would." As they walked companionably back to the car Mrs B said, "Feel up to a trip into Cockermouth? I don't think you've been yet, have you?"

"No, I haven't. And yes, I would like to go. I don't want to be sad today."

"Good girl. Jim will see to his and John's lunch. He's nicely on the mend and it'll be good for him, having something to do. Come on, then, and we might even find a new jacket for you. That old one of mine you've got on is falling to pieces."

* * * * * * * * * *

May felt changed by her visit to the church by the lake. Day by day she began to gain in self-confidence. She'd had long phone conversations with Jenny who told her all the goings in her life. The Scarlet Parakeet was as busy as ever, more so even. Kate was going to take on a new girl who could help in the kitchen and serve in the café. Jenny confessed she'd gone out with a lad from college and had made a fool of herself by drinking too much. May laughed at her friend's antics, cheered by her chatter.

Again, May went out with Fiona on her rounds. As she got into the car, waving Mrs B goodbye, Fiona presented her with a rather crumpled paper bag that had been lying on the back seat. "Just in case you get bored," she told May. Inside was a small sketchbook and a propelling pencil with an eraser on the end.

"Oh, Fiona. That is so kind of you."

"Not really." Fiona grinned. "There's method in my madness, you know. The surgery walls could do with some brightening up and I hoped you'd oblige with a couple of drawings. Maybe even paintings?"

"I'll do my best," said May. She was going to say that her drawings wouldn't be good enough but her new, positive self emerged. "I'll enjoy it. Where are we going?"

Farmhouses and barns, sheep-dotted fells, lakes and becks soon filled May's new sketchbook. She began to enjoy meeting the people on the farms; hardy types, mostly, who had been born and bred here. She didn't mind showing her drawings if they were curious enough to ask to see.

Back at Ravendale Farm she told Mrs B what she'd been doing that day. "Where's the nearest art shop?" May asked. "I'd like to get some watercolours. I don't think a couple of pencil sketches will brighten up Fiona's walls."

"I think there's one in town," Mrs B said, pausing in her pastry-making. "I won't be going in for a few days, but you can come with me and have a look around."

"I don't want to put you to any trouble."

"No trouble, lass. But it's a pity you can't drive. You could have taken the Range Rover yourself."

As the spoons were scraping the last of Mrs B's apple pie and custard from the dishes at that evening's supper table, May said, "James, do you think you could teach me to drive?"

"What? What did you say?" Armstrong leant back in his chair certain he hadn't heard right.

"Could you teach me to drive?" May repeated.

"Teach you to drive?"

"Yes."

"What the hell for?"

"So I can go places. Be independent."

"I'll soon be able to take you wherever you want to go. The leg's just about right again."

"That's not the point. I know you would, but I want to do it myself."

"Why?"

"Jim, behave yourself." Mrs B intervened. Seeing May asserting herself for the very first time almost brought tears of pride to the old woman's eyes.

"Well…" Armstrong prevaricated. "That Range Rover is no use for a learner."

"She can borrow our Sally's Fiesta. She doesn't use it all the time. I'm sure she could spare it for the odd hour here and there."

"Well…" Still Armstrong wasn't convinced.

"I'll take you into Keswick tomorrow, after all, lass. We'll get you a licence and L-plates. Then you'll be up and off before you can say Jack Robinson." Mrs B was adamant.

"You'll teach me, will you James? Please?" May was beginning to feel a sense of excitement at doing something different, something positive.

"I'll have to, won't I? Two women against one poor, helpless man isn't fair. You've won." Armstrong laughed, happy to see a spark of life ignited in May. "If you've got to learn to drive you may as well learn properly and I'm the right man for that job."

John Bell drained the last of the beer from his glass, smacking his lips in relish. As usual, he said nothing.

\* \* \* \* \* \* \* \* \* \*

The bright red Fiesta with L-plates soon became well known on the roads around Ravendale Farm. The first few times had seen May no further than the farm gate as she learned to change gear and steer the car up and down the track. For her first time on the road Armstrong took her to a quiet, straight road beyond Cockermouth. With infinite patience he took May through the intricacies of handling a car and being a good, considerate driver. May enjoyed it, eager for her daily lesson. She plagued Armstrong with questions. She became an almost impossible passenger, trying everyone's patience with instructions and pointing out where they were going wrong.

"The sooner you get your own car, the better," Fiona said one day. "That's the umpteenth time you've told me to slow down because there's a bend coming up. I know there is. I've lived here all my life. I've been driving these roads for fifteen years." Exasperation tinged her normally calm voice.

"I hadn't thought about that," May said, immediately contrite.

"What? That I know these roads?"

"No. About getting my own car."

"If you aim to be independent you'll need one. You won't be living with the Bells forever, will you?"

"No, I don't suppose I will." May thought about it. "I wonder if I could use Jonathan's car. I expect it's sitting in the garage, unused. I'll have to ask Mr Mawson."

"Why do you think you need to ask for permission. It'll be your car now, won't it?"

"I don't know. If it isn't, I'll have to see if I have enough money to buy one. I haven't been spending much of my allowance recently."

May fell silent. Perhaps it was time she took steps to find out what her own position was; see how much money she would have to live on. The allowance from Adam had been generous and she remembered it would continue, no matter what. Maybe there would be enough to rent a little cottage or a house. May realised that the Lake District was where she wanted to live for the foreseeable future.

## Chapter Twenty

The Scarlet Parakeet Café was quiet. It was the new girl's day off and Jenny was on her own. Her mother was upstairs doing the book-keeping. The only customers were a couple of oldies sitting over a pot of tea. The bell on the door jingled and Jenny looked up to see an old Chinaman come in. He looked at her seeming to expect immediate attention.

"A table for one, is it, sir?" she asked. He nodded. She indicated a table near the window. He sat. As he did so he took his hat off and laid it on a chair. Jenny handed him a menu and left him to read it for a few minutes. She was almost certain, no, absolutely certain, that it was Mr David Wang. She recognised him from the Lees' funeral. She wondered what he was doing here.

Jenny glanced at the elderly couple sitting beside the old-fashioned radiator, soaking up its comforting warmth. "Can I get you anythin' else?" she asked them.

"A refill would be nice, please dear." Jenny suppressed a sigh and took the teapot to add some hot water. Oh, what the hell, she thought and brewed them a fresh pot, picking up a plate of biscuits on the way back to their table.

"Oh, we don't… we can't…" the man began.

"Compliments of the management," Jenny whispered and stepped over to the other table. "What can I get you, sir?" She didn't acknowledge she recognised him.

"A pot of China tea." He considered the array of cakes and biscuits arranged inside the glass display counter. "And a slice of fruit cake."

Nice manners, Jenny thought to herself sarcastically as she laid out the tray to take it back to Mr Wang. She adopted an excessively servile attitude as she placed it on the table in front of him.

"Is there anythin' else I can get you, sir?"

"No."

"Very good, sir." She glanced at the old couple and winked. The man shook his head slightly as if in sympathy at the other's brusque attitude, then frowned as David Wang slurped noisily at his tea. Jenny was hard put not to laugh outright.

He finished his tea and cake then came to the counter and paid – the exact amount – and left without another word. I wonder what that was all about, Jenny thought to herself. The old couple stayed for another half hour before paying their bill and leaving.

A cold wind that seemed to have blown straight in from Siberia was cutting through the city, chilling the day and chasing the clouds about when, a week to the day since his first visit, David Wang came back. He ordered the same tea and cake as he'd had the week before. There was no-one else in the café. When Jenny brought him his tea and fruit cake he smiled, showing crooked, yellowing teeth. It wasn't a pleasant smile and Jenny thought she'd rather he kept to his previous demeanour.

"I'm David Wang, a friend of May Lee," he said.

"Yes, I recognise you from the New Dynasty restaurant." Who does he think he is claiming to be May's friend? May doesn't even know the man and she doesn't want to, either.

"How is May? I haven't seen her for a little while."

"She's on holiday." Jenny wished he'd go away.

"Oh, yes. Quite so. I remember her telling me she was going away for a while. But an old man's memory is not as it was. I can't remember where she said she was going."

"She travellin' around." Jenny felt uneasy about the direction this conversation was taking.

"Of course. So she said."

You lying old bugger, Jenny thought.

"Please give her my best wishes when you next speak with her," David Wang said.

"I don't hear from her very often. The last thing was a postcard from Edinburgh," Jenny lied as blandly as the old man.

"And when will she be back? I will call on her. Out of respect for my old friend Adam Lee."

"I'm sorry, I don't know." Jenny wasn't going to tell him anything. She was becoming increasingly suspicious of his motives.

"Here is my telephone number." David Wang handed her a business card with just his name and a number printed on it. "You would be doing an old man a great favour if you would let me know when May is to return."

Jenny took the card and said nothing.

David Wang drank his tea and ate the cake. This time, when he paid his bill he left a large tip for Jenny.

Jenny felt like scrubbing the entire place out with disinfectant after he'd gone. There was something unwholesome about the man.

The next week he called again. Same table, same order of China tea and fruit cake. Again, he asked after May. Jenny told him she hadn't heard. As he was leaving he said quietly, "I admire your loyalty to your friend but I am losing patience. You will let me know where she is." David Wang looked around the café as if sizing it up to quote for a painting job. "This is a nice place. Your mother does well here. I hope her good fortune continues."

The words themselves held no threat, but it was lurking there, nonetheless. This time he left without paying. Jenny closed the café, locking the door behind him, and pulled down the blinds. She found the phone book and, with a deep breath of trepidation, dialled. A man's voice answered. She asked to speak to DI Sam Castle.

"DI Castle," he answered after a wait of only a few seconds. Jenny found herself irritated but at the same time strangely comforted to hear his voice.

"It's Jenny MacLeod."

"Miss MacLeod," he drawled. Jenny almost put the phone down. "How may I help you?"

"You know at the funeral you were talkin' about Mr Wang and May?"

"Yes, I remember."

"He's been askin' about her."

"Has he really?"

"Yes, he has. Really. He's been into the café three times now. I don't know why he comes in here. He's got his own restaurant. I don't like him."

"You'd be out of business if you only catered for people you like."

"That's not the point." Jenny was becoming annoyed. Not just at him, but at her own inability to put into words the unease – no it was stronger than that – the fear that David Wang had left her with.

"There's obviously something wrong, or you think there is, or you wouldn't have called me. Would you prefer it if I came round and we had a talk? I could come now."

"Yes. That would be better. Come to the café. You'll have to knock at the door cos I shut up shop after Mr Wang left. I'll make you a coffee, though."

"That sounds like an offer I can't refuse. See you soon, Jenny."

She felt foolish when she put the phone down, then embarrassed. How could she have let herself get so rattled by some stupid old man? Rattled enough to phone the one person she didn't want to have anything more to do with – apart from Mr Wang himself, of course.

Jenny and Sam sat, a pot of coffee between them, while she told him of Mr Wang's three visits: how he'd lied about May telling him she was going on holiday; how he seemed over-eager to know where she was and when she'd be coming back; and finally the perceived threat in his parting words that afternoon.

"I'm sorry. You must think I'm bein' pathetic. He's probably just a lonely old bloke that's goin' a bit doolally." Jenny lifted her eyes from her cup to Sam's face and saw he was staring intently at her. She blushed. Jenny could not believe she was blushing. She never blushed. She poured herself some more coffee to hide her confusion.

"You're not being pathetic, Jenny. I think you're very perceptive. Enough to feel that something is very wrong. I'm not sure how, but I think it may be linked with the accident."

"How d'you mean?" Jenny had got over her embarrassment.

"We have our suspicions about the Wangs." Sam said quietly as if he knew he shouldn't be saying this.

"Bloody hell! But what does he want May for? She's as honest as the day's long. I'd stake me life on it." Jenny forgot any constraint between herself and Sam. "Are you tryin' to say that it wasn't an accident?" Jenny's mind was racing. "Did Mr Wang kill Jonathan?"

"Jenny, Jenny. Hold your horses. I'm not saying anything of the sort."

"But you think it, don't you?"

"What I think is beside the point. There is no proof, no shred of evidence that connects the Wangs to the accident. And I don't want you repeating any of this to anyone. Do you understand?" Sam's voice took on a firm note. "Understand?"

"Yes. But May? Is she safe?"

"I'm sure there's no immediate danger – no danger to her at all," Sam amended as Jenny took in a sharp breath. "Look, why don't you phone her and ask her if she knows why David Wang is so desperate to get in touch with her? I'll be right here. We'll talk some more afterwards."

Jenny spoke with Mrs B. May was out with Armstrong, having a driving lesson.

"All right, then. Just tell her I called. Bye, Mrs B." Jenny turned to Sam. "I expect you heard – she's out. Learnin' to drive, would you believe?" Jenny laughed in delight. "She told me she was goin' to. Our May drivin'. What do you think of that?"

Sam grinned. "Good luck to her, is what I think. Anyway, Jenny, that doesn't answer any questions, does it? We'll leave it as it is for now. Yes?" Jenny nodded. "And you say Mr Wang has come here at the same time on the same day for the last three weeks?" Jenny nodded again. "Well, next week I'm going to be in the back, waiting for him. All right?"

"Yes. Sure."

"Till next week, then. But you will call me in the meantime if anything worries you, won't you?"

"I will. Thank you for coming DI Castle."

"I think we can dispense with titles, don't you?"

"OK then, Sam. See ya next week. Ta-ra." Jenny gave him a mischievous smile and let him out.

* * * * * * * * * *

Jenny's hand shook as she punched the numbers into the dial. She hardly waited for the answer before asking for DI Castle.

"DI Castle. How can I help you?"

"It's Jenny."

"Jenny. Is anything wrong?"

"We've been burgled."

"When?"

"Now, I think."

"Is there anyone there with you?" Sam was concerned.

"Yes. Me Mam."

"Are you sure the intruder isn't still there?"

"No there's no-one here. It's a small flat. There's nowhere to hide."

"Are you all right?"

"Yes, just bloody mad."

"I'll be straight there. Don't touch anything, just sit tight." Sam slammed the phone down and shouted to Mike Atkinson. The sergeant quickly made the necessary arrangements for a formal back-up team and followed his inspector out of the office.

At the flat nothing seemed to have been taken. There were drawers open and a few things scattered around. The door had been expertly forced.

"Not your opportunist, then?" Mike Atkinson said.

"I wouldn't think so. And I've a feeling the stuff was thrown around a bit just for effect. I think somebody knew exactly what they were doing."

"I don't believe it!" Jenny burst out. "May's paintin'. It's gone."

"May's painting? You mean a painting she owns?" Sam asked.

"No. A paintin' she did. She only sent it last week."

"What was it a painting of?" Sam already suspected the answer.

"It's the farm she's stayin' at."

"And I suppose she wrote the name of the farm at the bottom."

"Yes. But what of it? It's not valuable. Not to anyone else, anyway."

"Right. Maybe the thief thought it was. The lads will check for fingerprints and see if there are any that aren't yours or your mother's. But I'm sorry, Jenny. The likelihood of getting anyone for this is very remote. I'm not going to patronise you by saying anything else."

"Yeah. I suppose I know that. Ah well. I guess it could have been worse. And I won't have to spend me whole day off tomorrow cleanin' up. This stuff won't take long to put away again." Jenny sounded defeated after the initial fright of finding her home broken into.

"It's my day off too," Sam said.

"That's nice," said Jenny.

"Yes, it is." Sam seemed as if he was about to leave it at that. "I've got an idea. You might like it or you might not. How would you like a lift over to see May tomorrow? I'm not doing anything better. Are you?"

"No. I mean, no I'm not. Doin' anythin' better, that is. It would be grand to see May. I haven't been over to the Lake District for ages. You sure you don't mind?"

"Don't mind at all. It's ages since I've been, too. See you tomorrow then. Tenish?"

"That'll be fine. See ya."

"I didn't know you had the day off tomorrow?" said Mike as they got into the car.

"I haven't. What I do have is a horrible suspicion that the Wangs now know where May Lee is."

"Do you think they'd harm her?"

"I don't think so, not yet anyway. But I do think that somehow they're going to try to get their hands on the shipping company. What else could they want?"

\* \* \* \* \* \* \* \* \* \*

Jenny felt a surge of excitement at the thought of having a day out with Sam. It couldn't be the fact of being with Sam, she told herself. It was just that it would be lovely seeing May again. She smiled in anticipation. Jenny couldn't help herself looking out of the window to watch as Sam and Mike walked over the road to their car. He might not be such a bad bloke, after all, she told herself.

## Chapter Twenty One

Supper was over and the dishes were washed and put away when the phone rang. Mrs B was napping in front of the fire and John was out taking a last look at the stock. May answered.

"Hello. Ravendale Farm."

"May. It's Jenny."

"Jenny. How are you? And your mother?"

"Aye. We're canny. Are you OK?"

"Yes. I'm very well, thank you."

"Are you doin' anythin' tomorrow?"

"Nothing special. Why?"

"I'm comin' to see you, if that's all right. I've got someone to give me a lift over."

"Jenny, that's fantastic. What time will you be here?"

"Oh, about half eleven, twelve or thereabouts."

"It'll be wonderful to see you. Who's bringing you?" May was curious. Jenny had never mentioned anyone who would be willing to drive her over to Cumbria. She could always have got the train or even a bus to Carlisle, but getting over to Keswick wouldn't have been so easy.

"Just a friend. No-one special," Jenny replied casually. Casual enough to raise May's suspicions that her friend was being a bit too cagey.

"I'll look forward to seeing you both." May gave Jenny detailed directions how to find Ravendale Farm and rang off.

At quarter to twelve the next day a silver Renault estate car bumped up the track and pulled into the farmyard. The driver tooted the horn and Jenny tumbled out of the front seat in a dazzling mix of colourful scarves and brightly patterned Indian skirt. May hardly had time to open the door before Jenny flung herself into her friend's arms, hugging her and telling her how well she looked. May laughed and looked into Jenny's flushed face.

"You look good, too. I'm so pleased to see you. I've missed you a lot." May looked past Jenny curious to see if the friend was getting out of the car. "Isn't your friend coming in?" The light was reflecting on the windscreen and May couldn't see who it was.

"I expect so. He probably wants to give us a minute to say hello." Jenny beckoned to the driver. The door opened and Sam Castle followed his long legs out of the car. He smiled at May's look of amazement.

"Hello, May. By the look on your face I take it Jenny didn't tell you who was bringing her." Sam smiled and stepped forward and, placing his hands on May's shoulders kissed her once on each cheek.

"Inspector Castle!" May managed to find her voice. "It's very, er good, to see you again." May wasn't sure it was so good. He brought with him memories she didn't welcome.

"Sam. Please will you call me Sam?"

He looked very different from the detective she'd met in Newcastle, May thought. He was wearing jeans and trainers with a fleece jacket over a greenish plaid shirt. Instead of being combed neatly flat, his sandy hair stuck up in odd spikes as if he'd just run his hand through it. He looked much younger – boyish almost. While she'd been greeting Jenny and Sam, Mrs B and Armstrong had come into the yard. Sam and Armstrong had already met but Mrs B didn't know either of the visitors. Introductions were made and they were soon all sitting round the big kitchen table drinking coffee and chatting like old friends.

"I'd be very interested in having a look around. Would you mind giving me a guided tour, Mr Armstrong?" Sam asked.

"Aye, of course. Ready to go now?" If Armstrong was surprised at the request he showed no sign.

"No time like the present. Lead on, Mr Armstrong." Sam followed Armstrong into the farmyard. "Glad to see the leg is well on the mend."

"Aye, I'm doing just grand." Armstrong laughed as he patted his healing leg. Once they were out of earshot of the house he turned to Sam. "Now then, lad. Something tells me it's not the farm you want to talk about."

"No, Mr Armstrong. Actually, it's not a social visit, as far as I'm concerned. Mind, Jenny doesn't know. She thinks it's my day off."

As the two men walked around the outbuildings and down the fields towards the beck, Sam told Armstrong of his suspicions about the Wang family. Armstrong sighed heavily.

"What you say doesn't really surprise me. I got the impression Mr Lee didn't trust them. I never realised that David Wang might be taking an interest in May. And to threaten poor Jenny. Well!"

"I don't think May is in any danger, Mr Armstrong."

"I think you can drop the 'Mister', Sam. I'm either 'James', 'Jim' or just plain 'Armstrong' to everyone." Armstrong had warmed to the detective.

"How about 'Jim'?"

"That'll do."

"Right then, Jim, I think David Wang is likely to try to make contact with May. If he does, give him a bit of space to talk to her. Don't leave her with him, though."

"I'm not daft, lad."

"Do you think she'll tell you what he wants? Assuming he does make contact."

"Aye. I think she will."

"Will you let me know?" Sam handed Armstrong a business card.

"Aye, I will." Armstrong pocketed the card and the pair headed back to the house.

Inside, as soon as the men had left, May had turned to Jenny. "What's going on? I thought you hated Sam?"

"I don't think I ever said that," Jenny replied.

"You said he was an arrogant, useless bas..."

Jenny cut her friend off, looking apologetically at Mrs B who smiled back serenely. "I don't remember sayin' quite that."

"Oh, you did. And quite a bit more besides," May reminded her.

"Well, anyone can be wrong. I've changed me mind." Jenny smiled, showing dimples that May had never noticed before. May smiled back.

"He's quite good-looking when he's off duty, isn't he?" May remarked with a grin.

"Is he? I never noticed." Jenny feigned indifference and took a too large bite of scone and nearly choked. She was red and coughing when Armstrong and Sam came back in. Sam thumped her on the back, trying to get rid of the crumbs that had caught in her throat. "Gerroff. You'll have me black and blue."

Sam stood back while Jenny recovered. He held his hands up in mock surrender. "Only trying to help." He smiled.

"Well, that's the sort of help I can well do without."

"How about I buy you lunch to say sorry? If we go into Keswick you and May can do a bit of shopping, if you'd like, and I'll have a walk around. Sound like a good idea?"

"I think it's an excellent idea," Mrs B cut in. "Me and Jim will put our feet up till John comes in for his lunch."

May gave Sam directions and they were soon settled in a small café where Mrs B had said the food was good. The place had the atmosphere of a Mediterranean patio with plants hanging down the walls in cascades of greenery. True to his word, after their meal he told the two friends he was going to take a walk down to the Derwentwater lakeshore. They made arrangements for meeting up again and went their separate ways.

May felt lighthearted and a great sense of freedom as she and Jenny wandered around window-shopping. Jenny laughed in amazement when May told her about the driving lessons.

"Armstrong says I've to apply for a test soon. If I pass I might be able to buy a little car," she said proudly.

"You'll pass with flyin' colours, mark my words. Come on, though. We've been ages. We'd better get a move on or we'll be late meetin' Sam."

Sam was sitting in the car, watching the comings and goings in the street. As he gazed around idly, he noticed May and Jenny, talking animatedly, coming towards him. As he watched, a dark blue car pulled up beside them. He stiffened as he saw the driver was an Oriental. The passenger, a much older man – Sam was sure he recognised David Wang – said something to the driver and the car pulled back into the stream of traffic and drove off. Sam took a notebook from his pocket and jotted down the blue car's number. He'd regained his composure by the time May and Jenny got into the car. They'd been so engrossed in their conversation it was obvious they hadn't noticed anything out of the ordinary.

"Righto. Where next? Any more lakes around here?" he asked.

"Buttermere is lovely. Fiona, my friend the vet, has taken me there a few times," May suggested.

"Would you like that, Jenny?" Sam asked. Jenny said she thought it would be 'canny' and they set off, driving along sinuous fellside roads, busy with sightseers already, even though it was still early in the year.

\* \* \* \* \* \* \* \* \* \*

They were laughing at a story Sam was telling as they got back home. "I don't believe a word of it," Jenny told him.

"It's true. Scout's honour."

"You were never a Boy Scout."

"I can show you the photos to prove it."

"Huh!" Jenny snorted.

"Thank you for a lovely day out," May said as they got out of the car, ignoring the exchange between Sam and Jenny. "Mrs B will expect you to stay to supper. You will, won't you?" She was reluctant to let her friends go. She was intrigued by their new relationship.

Mrs B appeared at the door. "Of course they will. I won't take 'no' for an answer."

The evening was a lively one with Jenny in good form. Even the usually monosyllabic John Bell joined in the conversation. Sam managed to get a quick word with Armstrong before he and Jenny left. Sam told him about seeing David Wang in Keswick.

"Don't worry. I'll keep an eye open. I'll let you know if I see anyone suspicious."

* * * * * * * * *

The red post-van bumped to a halt in the farmyard. The postman climbed out and shouted a good morning to John Bell who was cleaning out the byre where the injured ewe had been housed. She was now well enough to have been turned out with the others. Bill the Postman, as he was known to one and all in the district, was a cheery sort and would have finished his job in half the time if he didn't like to stop and pass the time of day with everyone. He poked his head round the kitchen door and called out a greeting.

"Come in, Bill," said Mrs B.

"I can't be stopping. Must get on. The daughter and the new bairn are coming today and I've strict instructions to get home early. The wife'll be on the warpath otherwise."

"Haven't you even time for a cuppa?" offered Mrs B.

"Not today, thanks. But it's tempting. Them cakes look good enough to eat." He laughed. It was one of his favourite jokes. He put a pile of letters on the table. "Just a load of bills, the usual junk, a postcard from Robin and Kath and the kids from Torquay. Her mother lives there now, don't she? And there's one from Newcastle for young May. How's she getting on with her driving? I've seen her all over the spot with that brother of yours in Sally's car. Blasted great blue Merc almost ran me off the road at the bottom of the hill. She'd better watch out she doesn't end in a ditch like I nearly did." He was still talking as he went out, not bothering to wait for any answer or comment.

Mrs B laughed and shook her head. "Talk the hind leg off a donkey, that one." She raised her voice and called, "Letter for you, May." May took the envelope Mrs B handed her, turning it over to see who it was from. There was no indication so she tore it open, curious to see who was writing to her.

"It's from Mr Mawson, the solicitor," she told Mrs B who was trying not to seem too interested in the other's correspondence.

"Oh aye. What does he say for himself?"

May sat at the table and spread the sheet of paper out. Arthur Mawson had written to say that he'd now had enough time to sort through the wills and relevant documents dealing with Adam Lee's estate. It had been quite convoluted because of the subsequent deaths of his wife, son and grandson. He needed to explain to May what it all meant and get her signature on some documents. "I don't want to drag you back over here, so I have sent everything to my nephew, Thomas Watson, who is a partner in a firm of solicitors in Carlisle. He will telephone you to make arrangements."

"He's got some papers for me to sign. His nephew is going to contact me about it." May had been expecting she would have some legal obligations. After all, there had been that business of being one of Bobby's trustees after Adam had died.

"I wonder what the papers are? I hope I'll be able to understand what I'm signing. I'm afraid I won't understand." May turned concerned eyes up to Mrs B.

"If he's got anything about him, he'll explain it to you so you *do* understand. Anyway, lass, you do yourself down. You're bright enough to cotton on to most things and if you don't I'm sure you'll make it your business to find out." Mrs B was as proud as a mother hen over May's emerging from the shell of sorrow she'd been encased in when she first arrived at the farm. May knew it; Mrs B told her often enough. It was wonderful to be praised. For someone to notice her achievements, however small, and tell her she was doing well, was a new experience for May. She felt her confidence growing and a quiet contentment she'd never before experienced.

\* \* \* \* \* \* \* \* \* \*

The phone call came sooner than May had expected. It had been raining heavily for the last day or so and when the sun came out after lunch May had pressed Armstrong into taking her out driving. When they got back Mrs B said there'd been a phone call from 'that solicitor fellow'. He hoped May would go into the Carlisle office to sign the papers that had been sent over from Newcastle. He'd suggested half past ten the next morning.

"But I'm supposed to be going out with Fiona," May protested unwilling to be reminded of what she'd lost. Some sixth sense warned her there would be things said that she didn't want to face.

"Fiona can wait. Sounds like he can't. He was very insistent. And you know these things are better tackled straight away." Mrs B put her hands on her hips. When she did this May had learned there was no arguing with her.

"I can't go. There's no bus to get me there by that time." May suddenly saw a way out of the appointment. Mrs B had other ideas.

"Jim can take you in the Range Rover, can't you Jim?" She took her brother's assent for granted and changed the subject. "Get them spuds scrubbed, there's a good lass, and stick them in the oven to bake." It was settled, then. Carlisle tomorrow to see Thomas Watson, and no excuses.

\* \* \* \* \* \* \* \* \* \*

The offices were in a newly built business park on the city's perimeter. There were already several cars in the small car park and Armstrong had to manoeuvre the big vehicle carefully to slot it into the space left.

"Would you please come in with me, James? I'm afraid I won't understand everything." Armstrong looked at her with raised eyebrows but he got out of the car with her and they pushed through the heavy glass doors into the spacious reception area. Inside it was clean and efficient, everything new and streamlined. The receptionist smiled apologetically. "Mr Watson is terribly sorry.

He's had to fit in an urgent appointment. Would you like to take a seat? He shouldn't be too long." She gestured towards a comfortable seating area.

"But he said it was urgent for me to meet with him," May said, unaccountably annoyed to have to wait. She really didn't want to have to stretch her mind round the complexities of Adam Lee's estate. It was part of a different life. Could this be a valid excuse not to see him today? Armstrong, standing a little behind May, seemed to sense she was ready to walk away. He touched her elbow.

"Sit down, May. We don't have anything else to do, now do we?"

May was about to protest but, seeing his determined look, sat. She picked up a copy of *Country Life* and began to flick through its pages, not reading.

"Would you like something to drink?" The receptionist had come round from behind her desk. "Coffee or tea? Or there's hot chocolate if you prefer."

"No, I don't want anything," May replied. She caught Armstrong's disapproving look at her rudeness. She added, "Thank you."

May was surprised at her own lack of good manners. This wasn't like her. There was no reason at all for her to feel so annoyed at being kept waiting for a little while. What's making me act like this, she wondered. Uneasily, she turned her thoughts inwards, where she'd shut away things she didn't want to think about. I'm frightened, she realised. Frightened what the solicitor might tell me. She wasn't afraid of being left pennyless when the estate was settled. No, she finally admitted to herself, what I'm afraid of is that I will inherit too much.

A discreet cough startled her out of her introspection. She looked up into the face of a tall man standing in front of her. He smiled and held out his hand.

"Mrs Lee. I'm so sorry to have kept you waiting. I'm Tom Watson."

May stood and automatically accepted his handshake. Then she snatched her own away quickly: too quickly for politeness. She felt as though she wanted to run away from a hidden danger, sensed but not seen. She reached up to her chest as if to touch the golden dragon for reassurance. It was a renewed shock to find it wasn't there. A sudden overwhelming sense of loss threatened to overcome her, but Armstrong was there, strong and sure. Again he appeared to sense May's turmoil and took quiet control.

"Pleased to meet you, Mr Watson. I'm May's friend, James Armstrong. I'm acting in *loco parentis*, as it were. Is that the right expression?

Tom Watson took stock of the older man, seeing a quietly determined individual: one who had an air of dependability about him. "If you mean you have Mrs Lee's best interests at heart, then indeed it is. Come into my office, won't you." He led the way into a large airy room whose window looked over an inner courtyard where a pond reflected the sky in its unruffled surface under which carp swam lazily.

It seemed to May that it took hours for Tom Watson to lay out the terms of the wills. She tried not to listen. She watched the fish in the pond; the branches of a weeping willow swaying lazily above the water; the birds hopping around the secluded garden. She noticed the texture of the table; how the chairs were made of matching wood; the pale grey of the walls. She gazed in fascination at Tom Watson's hands as he turned over paper after paper: long fingers with clean, well-clipped nails, a wedding ring on his left hand, an almost healed scratch on his right. It was as if by not hearing it, it wouldn't be true. But still the words penetrated. It was what she had dreaded: the entire estate was hers. Everything belonged to her – house, money, antiques, jewellery and much more. But most frightening of all to May, the shipping company was hers too.

"But what am I supposed to do with it?" she asked Tom in bewilderment.

"Live in the house, or sell it and buy another one. Do you have a knowledge of the business? Do you want to run the company yourself?"

"No. Of course I don't. I couldn't."

"You could sell that, too. You own it outright; there are no shareholders to take into account."

"But who would buy a shipping company? What would they do with it?"

Tom Watson considered the questions a moment. "It's unlikely it would be taken over and run as your father-in-law did. Most likely the ships the company owns would be bought to add to an already established fleet. Any lucrative charters could be taken over by other companies. The property: offices, warehousing and such, would be sold off as separate lots. It would all realise a respectable sum." Tom paused as if doing some mental arithmetic. "I don't know the business myself, but I don't think it would be any less than eight million pounds, perhaps considerably more. Uncle Arthur would be able to give you a better idea than myself." He placed a page of figures on the desk in front of May. "The rest of your inheritance will realise a similar amount."

May looked as if she was going to be sick. Armstrong took the initiative. "What about the staff? The people in the offices, on the ships?"

"They'd get other jobs soon enough I suppose."

Armstrong pursed his lips. "Perhaps not, though."

Tom agreed. "Perhaps not."

"Any other alternatives?" Armstrong asked.

"Mrs Lee could employ a general manager to run it for her."

May collected her scattered wits. "It's too big a question to deal with now. I need some time to think things over. Mr Mawson has been seeing things run smoothly since Adam died. Do you think he would be willing to continue for a little while?"

"I can't speak for him but, knowing Uncle Arthur, I'm sure he would do everything in his power to be of assistance to you. I'll discuss it with him and then make an appointment with you to talk on the subject again. Now, there's the question of the house in Newcastle. Have you any thoughts on that?"

May sighed. "It's far too big for one person, even for two." She smiled weakly at Armstrong. "Neither of us wants to live there. Can it be sold?"

"Of course, Mrs Lee. But are you sure?" Tom Watson asked.

"Very sure."

"Would you like my uncle to arrange to put it on the market for you?"

"If he would be so kind. Yes." May was relieved.

"And the contents. Would you see to them yourself?"

May looked distressed at the thought of going back to that rambling great house and sorting through it. Armstrong said, "I'm sure May would be grateful if a firm of packers and shippers could be employed to clear it."

"That wouldn't be a problem." Tom Watson sounded grateful that at least something positive would be achieved from this meeting. "Are there any pieces: furniture, antiques, paintings, that you would wish to keep?"

"There's nothing I want," May said. "James, what about you?"

"Just the personal stuff from my flat. And there's Mr Jonathan's car – a Mini – I think May would find it useful to have it here."

"Certainly, Mr Armstrong. I'll have it seen to immediately. All personal items: jewellery, clothing, papers and so on will be packed and despatched to you at Ravendale Farm. Is that in order?"

"That's our address for now. I'll let you know if it changes."

"Righto. Will do. Now, Mrs Lee, Uncle Arthur sent some papers for you to sign if you would be so kind." Tom Watson outlined the contents of the documents for May. She signed them in relief that the meeting was nearly over.

"All that will be set in motion for you. Please think about the company, though. If you have any more questions please get in touch with me, or with Uncle Arthur."

"Yes, Mr Watson, I will."

May couldn't get out of the office and into the car quickly enough. She sat breathing raggedly, trying to stem the tears that threatened to fall.

"I don't understand you, lass," Armstrong said, surprised at May's reaction. "Most folk would be over the moon to be left a fortune like that."

"It's too much, James. Far too much. But it's the company's future that is worrying me. All those people, families, depend on it for their jobs. I can't run it – I don't know the first thing about business."

"You've been taking that Business Studies course, though."

"That's not enough. It only shows me that I cannot deal with it. And I cannot sell it. I would feel I was betraying a trust Adam placed in me." May shook her head. The problem weighed heavily on her and she couldn't see a way through.

"Let it be for a while then. Mr Lee put in some good managers. They'll keep it running for as long as you need."

"Yes. You're right. Thank you, James. What would I do without you?" May leaned over and kissed his cheek.

"Get away with you! You'd manage just fine. Now, I, for one, could do with a pie and a pint. How about you? There's a pub I know just down the road."

# Chapter Twenty Two

May's driving test was in Kendal; the roads were busy and unfamiliar. She negotiated the traffic-clogged streets carefully but with the confidence that comes from being well-schooled. Armstrong had done his job well. He was waiting for her when she finished. She carefully composed herself and walked towards him with a disappointed look on her face. Armstrong frowned his own disappointment when he saw her.

"Never mind, lass. You'll make it next time," he tried to comfort her.

May couldn't keep up the pretence any longer. "I've passed! I've passed!" she burst out. Armstrong spun her around, laughing at her successful attempt to fool him, before setting her down again. Ceremoniously, he untied the L-plates and dumped them in a bin.

"I knew you would pass. Had to, with the best teacher in the world, hadn't you?"

It was nearly summer. The days were lengthening and the sun held a real warmth. The last of the snow hiding in the shadows behind the dry stone walls on the fells had melted. Delicate-looking leaves clothed the trees and blossom decked the hedgerows. Alongside the Rowan Beck the alders dipped down towards the water and Ravendale Farm's sheltering oaks were covered with their new bronzy-green leaves.

At the farm lambing was underway. Already the lambs on the lowland farms were well grown and fat but high in the fells the lambs were still arriving. May watched the miracle of new life when she took flasks of tea and hot bacon sandwiches to John Bell and his sons as they spent hour after hour in the lambing shed. Armstrong was still not, even after all these years, comfortable in dealing with animals, he told May. At least there were no cattle now; the farm concentrated on sheep. But he helped out where he could.

Sheep were a new and fascinating experience for May. At home, in China, there had been pigs and the great water buffalo they used in the fields. The chickens that pecked around her village were little different from the ones here – a bit more scrawny than the sleek grey-speckled fowl that strutted round the Bells' farmyard.

One night John Bell brought an almost lifeless lamb into the kitchen and wrapped it in an old towel before putting it into a cardboard box beside the Aga. He told May its mother had rejected it. "But the warmth from the stove and a bit of TLC from the wife will keep the little mite alive, you'll see." Soon the lamb was wandering around bleating for the bottle of milk that Mrs B, and then May, fed it on.

The days passed quickly. Jenny hadn't been back but they spoke frequently on the phone. Fiona often took May out on her rounds with her. May was amassing quite a bundle of drawings from the places they went and one day she was looking through them when Fiona called for her. She leant over May's shoulder as she collected them together, marvelling at her friend's talent at capturing the people and animals.

"Who's this? I don't remember a child at the Evans's when we went," Fiona asked picking up a drawing May had tinted with watercolour. She touched the paper where a little boy stood, dressed in blue dungarees and a red jumper, looking at a collie pup trying to round up some ducks.

"No, there wasn't," May said.

"Who is it, then?" Fiona persisted.

"Bobby," May said quietly, lightly touching the paper with her fingertips.

"Oh. Oh, May. I'm sorry. I didn't mean..." Fiona stammered. "Oh, I could kick myself. I always manage to blurt out the wrong thing."

"No, don't be sorry. Putting Bobby into pictures makes me feel happy. Look." May spread some of the coloured drawings out. "Here he is again. And again." In each of the drawings there was a little boy dressed in blue dungarees and red jumper. Sometimes he was splashing in puddles, sometimes playing with toys, other times just standing watching.

"These are so good. Why don't you have them mounted and framed then you can hang them up in your room?"

"I don't think so."

"But it's such a waste to leave them here just stuffed into a folder. Look, I know someone who does framing. Why don't you bring just one and we can go and see him and see what he thinks? Yes? Please say 'yes'."

"Oh, I don't know." May hesitated. Fiona gave her a comic, pleading look. May laughed. "Very well. Yes. Are you happy now?"

"Ecstatic! Come on, we'll go now."

Fiona pulled the car into the car park of the gallery in the middle of Beckthwaite. There were several cars already there. May didn't know it then, but it was quite a famous place, noted for its support of local artists and craftsmen, and not least for its generous Lakeland Afternoon Tea. A green slate-flagged path led up to the entrance, bordered by flower beds resplendent with early bedding. A scruffy-looking man was pottering around, weeding and trimming, humming as he went. He straightened up, put his hands into the small of his back and groaned.

"Don't tell me old age is creeping up, Alex. I've some horse liniment in the car. Want me to rub some on for you?" Fiona called to him.

"I'm the same age as you, Fee, so you can keep it to yourself. Don't you know that weeding is backbreaking work?" The man ambled over and enfolded Fiona in a huge hug. She hugged him back.

"Come and meet my friend." Fiona dragged him over to May. "Alex, this is May Lee. May, this is Alexander Martin." The two shook hands after Alex had wiped his, with a rueful grin, on the seat of his mud-streaked trousers.

"Go inside and have a look around. I'll get cleaned up and we can catch up on the latest," Alex said then disappeared through a door at the top of a metal staircase that, May thought, looked as though it served as a fire escape. May and Fiona stepped into the gallery.

Three walls were painted white, though very little showed as just about every inch of space was taken up by pictures: drawings, paintings, photographs, all depicting some aspect of the Lake District. The fourth wall was bare stone. On it hung handwoven rugs, rich-coloured tapestries and two patchwork quilts. Then there were display stands with jewellery, pottery, carving. The friends wandered around, occasionally exclaiming over the delights they saw and calling each other over to see something that particularly caught their eye.

Alex appeared at the door and beckoned. He must have had a quick shower as his blond hair was plastered wetly to his scalp and his fair skin glowed. He had changed into a bright blue shirt and chinos. May felt an instant attraction to him – he was very good-looking and his smile lit up his whole face. Deliberately she put the feeling aside. There was no point in harbouring romantic notions about any man, let alone one who was so obviously a close friend of Fiona's. He led them up a flight of stone stairs May hadn't noticed earlier to an enormous room which seemed to be where he lived. Sliding glass doors opened onto a balcony which afforded wonderful views across the valley over the rooftops of Beckthwaite. May walked over and looked out, then pointed to where a cluster of buildings sat at the edge of small, stone-walled fields.

"Is that Ravendale Farm?"

"It certainly is," Alex replied coming to stand beside her. He put an arm round her shoulders and pointed. She felt the warmth of his body against her side and her breath caught in her chest. His voice cut through the strange feeling. "And you can see through the trees over there the sun reflecting off the waters of Bassenthwaite Lake. If you climb onto the roof you can even see Keswick and Derwentwater."

Fiona laughed, coming over to admire the view. "We'll pass on that one for the time being, thank you. Actually, Alex, we can't stay long. I've got evening surgery today and I've to get back in decent time or Dad gets his knickers in a twist thinking he's going to have to do it himself. You know how he is."

"Yes, I do know how he is. He used to terrify the life out of me when I was younger." Alex dropped his arm and straightened up, turning back to Fiona.

May felt strangely abandoned. Pull yourself together, she told herself sternly. What sort of person are you that reacts to the first man who shows you a bit of kindness? And that's all it was, May realised. Kindness. Besides, he's obviously very close to Fiona – are they lovers? The question raised a welter of unwanted emotions. She looked sideways at the pair, trying not to be seen obviously studying them. They seemed so happy and relaxed with each other. Why hasn't Fiona mentioned him before, May wondered.

"So, Fee," Alex was saying. "You've obviously not come just for the pleasure of my company, more's the pity. What can I do for you?"

"Picture framing. I've got a drawing I'd like you to do, if you've got the time." Deliberately Fiona didn't let on it was May's. She laid it on the cluttered table, on top of the spread of newspapers and magazines. "What do you think?"

"This is lovely. Where did you get it? Who did it?" Alex picked up the drawing.

"From a friend," Fiona looked at May with a grin.

"Lucky you. Come down to the workshop and we'll look at some mounts and frames. See what suits. I think I know just the thing." Alex picked up the drawing and strode out of the room, down the stairs, through the gallery and into a small back room that was full with the paraphernalia of picture-framing. He never even glanced back to see if May and Fiona were following.

Fiona agreed with Alex's suggestions, glancing surreptitiously at May for her wordless agreement. They arranged to come back in a week's time and left Alex in the workshop.

"Why didn't you tell him it was mine?" May wanted to know when they got outside.

"I thought you ought to see his unbiased reaction. He was impressed, wasn't he? He genuinely loved it. He wasn't just saying so to please you, though that's not Alex's style, anyway. He wouldn't say anything was good if he really didn't think so." They got into the car and drove off. "We'll tell him when we collect it. It'll be a laugh to see his face."

"Tell me, though, how is it that a gardener also does picture-framing?"

"The two things don't seem to go together, do they? But that's Alex all over – never wants to settle to one thing."

"Oh. Have you known him a long time?" May tried to sound casual but couldn't help being curious.

"All my life. He's my cousin."

\* \* \* \* \* \* \* \* \* \*

The following week saw May and Fiona back at the gallery to find that Alex had hung the newly framed picture on one of the display boards. He greeted both women with a hug and kiss on each cheek. May didn't know what to make of him but Fiona laughed and punched him playfully. He put an arm round each of them and walked them through the gallery.

"What do you think?" he asked, standing back to admire the picture.

"Oh. How well it looks." May was amazed at the difference the frame made.

"It's great," Fiona said. "You've done a brilliant job, Alex."

"There's been quite a bit of interest since I hung it. I reckon I could have sold it several times over."

"Oh no!" May's hand went to her mouth, covering it in embarrassment.

"Why ever not? I told you, it's really good. Won't you tell me who the artist is, Fee and I'll get in touch to see if he or she would be interested in selling?"

"The artist is standing beside you," Fiona said quietly.

"Don't be daft. You can't draw like that," Alex snorted at the thought.

"Not me, you big idiot. May. It's May's work."

Alex's fair skin flushed to the roots of his hair. "I'm sorry. I didn't mean... I didn't think... I just assumed... Oh shit!"

May wasn't insulted by his implication that the drawings couldn't have been her own, and burst out laughing. "Just because I'm Chinese doesn't mean I can't draw. I can even read and write, you know." She continued to giggle for several minutes while Alex grinned back, ruefully. "And I'm really not interested in selling. Sorry, Alex."

"It's me who's sorry," Alex apologised. "But I'm not going to give up easily. I'll ask you again."

May shook her head, still smiling. "That would be up to you. But I think the answer would be the same. But tell me how much I owe you for the framing." She paid the ridiculously small amount Alex asked then he wrapped the picture carefully and carried it out to Fiona's car.

"There's a jazz band on at the pub on Saturday. Why don't the pair of you come? It'll be a good night. I might even buy you a drink," Alex offered.

"Now there's an offer I, for one, won't refuse. What do you think, May?" Fiona turned to her friend.

May only hesitated for a second or two. "That would be very nice. Yes, I'll come too."

"Excellent. See you both Saturday." Alex stood waving as Fiona drove off. He frowned as a blue Mercedes seemed to change its mind about driving into the gallery's car park and followed Fiona's muddy estate car back to the main road.

* * * * * * * * * *

May and Armstrong liked to walk in the fells as often as they could, now his leg was stronger. They talked a lot but May was still not ready to discuss what she should do next. She was happy – yes, she had accepted she could be happy – just taking life day by day. Her housekeeping and cooking skills were sufficient to satisfy even Mrs B's high standards, so there was no real reason for her to stay on at Ravendale Farm. Her life had settled down into a comfortable pattern. Until one day Armstrong forced the situation.

"There's a cottage for sale in Netherthwaite," Armstrong said casually as they walked along a well-trodden footpath. "I thought it would be just the job for you. Why don't we go and see it?"

May looked at him in surprise. "But I'm happy at the farm."

"That's as may be, but it's not your home. You need somewhere of your own, lass. So do I for that matter. I'm not going back to Tyneside, there's nothing for me there."

"There's nothing there for me either. Ravendale feels more like home than the Gosforth house ever did," May admitted.

"You can't stay at the farm for ever, though. It's Maggie and John's home, not yours nor mine," Armstrong said gently. "Come and look at this cottage, see what you think."

They walked on in silence, both deep in thought. Despite herself, May felt a sort of excitement begin to build inside. There was trepidation as well but she knew, had known all along, it would soon be time to move on, to take the next step in her life.

# PART THREE

## Chapter Twenty Three

"I don't know what's the matter with you." Mrs B sounded exasperated. "Isn't Ravendale Farm good enough for you?"

"Now, don't take it like that, woman. You know damn fine well she can't stay here forever." Armstrong was equally exasperated.

"Don't be angry, Mrs B. Please." May knew the older woman's attack was her own form of defence. "You know I've loved being here with you. I know I couldn't have coped without you. You've given me so much – a sense of worth I never knew before."

"Get away with you, lass. I've loved having you here. You're one of the family. You know that."

"Yes, I know it. But I've been here nearly nine months."

"Why don't you stay until Christmas, at least? We have a grand time then. The lads and their families all come for Christmas dinner."

"She'll be moved into the cottage and settled by then," Armstrong said. "But that doesn't mean she can't spend Christmas Day here with us, does it?"

Mrs B clattered dishes unnecessarily as she put them away. May would have spoken again, tried to make the older woman see she wasn't being abandoned, but she caught Armstrong's shake of the head and left it at that.

* * * * * * * * * *

The inquest into the accident that had killed the Lees, a young builder and a passer-by was a formality. May sat in the coroner's court flanked by Armstrong and Jenny. There was no evidence that suggested it hadn't been an unfortunate accident. The disappearance of the driver of the van that had caused the crash was put down to him fleeing the scene because he was in possession of a stolen vehicle.

Sam Castle had not been able to attend but he joined them later at the Scarlet Parakeet. May could see at once there was a marked difference in his attitude to Jenny. At first he had treated her with barely concealed impatience which had developed into friendly banter by the time they had come to Ravendale to visit. Now it seemed he could hardly take his eyes off her. Jenny, for her part, stole surreptitious glances at him when she thought no-one was watching. May followed Jenny into the kitchen using the excuse of helping tidy up.

"I think Sam likes you," she said with a smile.

"Oh aye?" Jenny replied nonchalantly.

"Yes, he does. And I think you like him too, don't you?"

"Oh, I would say it's a bit more than that."

"What do you mean, Jenny?"

"I think I'm in love with him, daft as it may seem. But I'm not exactly his type, am I?"

"What do you think his type is?"

"Someone older, more responsible, more serious. The very opposite of me, really." Jenny indicated at her riot of auburn hair escaping from a comb that was failing to hold it back, a colourfully patterned chunky sweater, swirling floral skirt and lace-up black boots.

"Is that what he said?"

"No, he said he's in love with me."

"Jenny, that's wonderful." May hugged her friend. "Don't you think it's wonderful?"

"I would if I believed it. But how can he be? I'm an art student and detective inspectors don't fall in love with art students."

"I don't think Sam would lie about a thing like that, do you?" May asked her friend.

"I don't know. I want to believe it, but..." Jenny looked at May, tears in her eyes.

"But what?"

"I'm afraid of gettin' hurt."

May took Jenny's hands in hers and looked her in the eyes. "Life is too short, too precious, not to take happiness when you can. Don't you think I'm right?"

"Perhaps," Jenny reluctantly agreed, sniffing back her tears.

"For sure," May persisted.

"OK, then. Shall I give it a go?" She sounded hopeful.

"Yes, Jenny. Give it a go."

"Come on then, let's get back. Them men have been on their own too long, they're bound to be talkin' about football. If I'm to make

anythin' out of him it won't be by lettin' him think about football."
Jenny laughed, her high-spirits renewed.

\* \* \* \* \* \* \* \* \* \*

Sam and Armstrong weren't talking about football. Sam was asking if there'd been any more sightings of David Wang or his sons in Cumbria.

"Not that I can be sure of. I'd have let you know if I had. I've seen a blue Mercedes about a few times, though."

"Has May said anything?"

"No. I don't think she's noticed and I didn't want to alarm her by asking, you know?"

"Right, leave it at that then. They've been very quiet recently – the Wangs. Too quiet. It makes me more suspicious than reassured." Sam leaned back, running a hand through his hair in frustration. "If only I could get something on them."

"You will, lad. Eventually they'll make a mistake."

"I hope you're right, Jim. I really do. Keep an eye open, though." Sam saw May and Jenny coming back and changed the subject. "What's all this about a cottage? I hear May's moving soon."

Armstrong laughed. "'Soon' seems to be a relative term as far as buying a house goes. It'll be at least a couple of months yet, won't it May?" He drew her into the conversation."

"I had hoped I'd be in for Christmas but that doesn't seem possible, now. Mrs B is pleased, though, isn't she James?"

"Aye. She's never happier than when she's got someone to take care of."

"How about the house here?" Sam asked.

"That sale is going through smoothly enough," Armstrong told him. "Arthur Mawson is handling it all for May. He's a godsend, he really is. May's got a meeting with him in," Armstrong consulted his watch, "in half an hour. We'd better be moving."

They said their goodbyes with promises that Jenny and Sam would come to see the cottage as soon as May moved in.

\* \* \* \* \* \* \* \* \* \*

Arthur Mawson seated May in the usual shabby chair.

Armstrong had gone to collect Jonathan's car. It had been serviced and was waiting at the garage.

"Now the inquest is over, perhaps you will turn your mind to other things?" Mr Mawson began. "My nephew, Tom, told me about the conversation he had with you over your inheriting Forster Shipping. Have you had any further thoughts about it?"

"I don't want it. I have realised the responsibility is too much for me. But all the time I am worrying about it and remembering the faith Adam had in me. So I don't feel I can sell it either. I am very confused." May admitted her deep misgivings.

"Very well, my dear. I see your problem. There is something I have been mulling over since I heard from Tom. I may have a solution for you."

May sat up and looked hopefully at the solicitor. "What is it? Will it keep the company running as Adam wished?"

"Yes, I believe it would. It involves me breaking a confidence, though." Arthur Mawson drew a deep breath. "Adam confided certain things in me many years ago. I have never had occasion, until now, to take them into consideration. I feel it would resolve the situation perfectly. But, at the moment, I cannot go into details. There are other people involved and I must look into it further. Would you bear with me for a little while, my dear?"

"Of course, Mr Mawson. But I don't want to put you into a difficult position." May was concerned she was causing him trouble he could do without.

"Not at all. I'll be in touch with you again and I'll tell you then what I propose. In the meantime you will have your hands full moving house."

May left the office wondering what on earth Mr Mawson had in mind. As she stepped outside she heard a car horn. She turned to see the green Mini drive up, a grinning Armstrong at the wheel. She felt a momentary pang as she remembered the last time she'd seen this car. Jonathan had been driving it. She put it deliberately out of her mind and jumped in. Armstrong roared off, heading for Cumbria and home.

\* \* \* \* \* \* \* \* \* \*

Christmas came and went, as did New Year. The move to

Fellbeck Cottage was accomplished without hitch on the last day of January. Mrs B oversaw everything, helped May to unpack, arranged furniture, then re-arranged it. She had decided to take credit for the whole idea of May's purchase of the cottage, even insisting it was her suggestion.

"It's high time you stood on your own feet. I can't be running around after you all the time, you know," she had told May. Armstrong grinned at his sister, pleased that she had come to accept the move.

"Aye, well. I daresay she'll have to manage," he commented wryly.

The cottage was at the end of a row of three whitewashed miners' cottages built early in the eighteenth century. The mines had long disappeared, leaving hardly a trace on the landscape. The cottages had been improved and extended over the years and provided comfortable homes. The one in the centre was occupied occasionally by a couple who lived and worked in Manchester. The one at the other end housed Jack, an old chap who had once worked in the sawmill in the next village. It was his pride to keep the tiny front gardens of all three cottages in immaculate order. He'd already talked to May about it and received her wholehearted permission to carry on. So far she didn't know the first thing about gardening, she told him ruefully. Jack said he'd be happy to show her the basics any time she wanted. His own back garden was given over to growing vegetables and fruit, most of which he gave away. There were a couple of dozen or so other houses in the village, as well as a pub and a small church which served the surrounding area.

May had had misgivings, of course, about buying the cottage. "What if the people in the village don't like me?" she asked Mrs B.

"Don't be daft. Why wouldn't they like you?"

May looked uncomfortable but went on. "Because I'm different."

"Everyone's different." Mrs B seemed determined not to understand what May meant.

"But I'm more different. Maybe they won't like me because I'm foreign."

Mrs B let out a mirthless laugh. "Lass, they thought I was foreign when I first came here and I was only born in the next county. They'll get used to you soon enough. It's more the folks with holiday homes that the locals object to."

"Do you really think I'm doing the right thing? Maybe I should go back to China."

"Do you want to go back to China?" Mrs B asked, a worried look crossing her face.

"No. I want to stay here," May said.

"Well, then. Stay." Mrs B planted a motherly kiss on May's forehead and went off to put the kettle on which was her answer to everything.

Fellbeck Cottage was larger than it looked from the outside, with a cosy kitchen which had a conservatory attached and a light, airy sitting room. There were three good-sized bedrooms, one of which had its own bathroom, much to May's delight. She and Armstrong had driven many miles around to salerooms and antique shops to find furniture to fit May's new home. She'd had unsolicited advice from everyone, but in the end she chose the things she liked best, whether they matched each other or not. In the end the cottage had a strange harmony of style that was neither antique nor modern. May loved it.

Netherthwaite didn't quite know what to make of the young woman moving into it. The gossips had a field day, of course. A young Chinese woman living alone in an isolated community – where did her money come from? Did she have a secret lover who had set her up in the cottage? Did she have a job? If not, why? Mrs B caught wind of the talk and let the truth be known. May wasn't unaware of the pitying glances she received at first, but her arrival was a nine-day-wonder and before long no-one treated her as anything different from themselves, passing the time of day whenever they met or waving as May buzzed past in the green Mini-Cooper that had once been her husband's.

Before May knew it, it was the first anniversary of the accident. She went alone to the little church on the lakeshore and found peace there as she had before. She'd hung the picture Alex had framed in her bedroom and that gave her comfort, too. She was able to accept all that had happened and that her life had changed forever. A new life had begun where she would make her own decisions and determine for herself the direction it would take.

Jack, from the end cottage, came over whenever he saw May out in her garden. He told her it would soon be time to start to mow the grass and offered to lend her a mower until she could get one of her own. As they talked he pointed out the birds that flew in and out of the garden, looking for grubs and insects. May laughed at the antics of the bluetits as they hung upside-down in the tree branches.

"What you want is some feeders," he told her. "D'you know what they are?" Jack was priding himself on instructing May in the art of being a countrywoman. "I'll get you some and the right sort of feed to put in them. They'll attract all sorts of birds. It'll be grand for you to watch from that summerhouse thing you've got there." He waved his hand at the conservatory. And so May began to take an interest in the garden.

Regular visitors came to and went from Fellbeck Cottage. Fiona popped in several times a week; she never passed without stopping for a quick coffee or a chat. Mrs B bustled in and out, assuring herself that all was well. Alex called in occasionally, too.

Armstrong had also moved out of Ravendale Farm. He had rented a small bungalow in Netherthwaite. He'd seen the 'To Let' sign as he visited May. He still had his own misgivings about May living alone, especially with the problem of the Wangs still unresolved. He didn't say anything, of course, but living nearby he could keep an eye on her without it being obvious. He was away for the day when the dark blue Mercedes drew up outside Fellbeck Cottage.

May was in the kitchen ironing cothes that had blown dry on the washing line strung across the garden, when the doorbell rang. It hardly ever rang: everyone came to the back door – the kitchen door. Wondering who on earth it could be, May went to answer it.

"Good afternoon, May. I hope I find you well. I was passing close by and I thought it would be polite to call in and enquire about my old friend's daughter-in-law." David Wang's dry voice grated on May's nerves. She wanted to slam the door in his face but ingrained politeness overcame the impulse.

"That is very kind of you, Uncle. I am well," she managed to reply in an even voice.

"I would deem it a great honour if you would be so kind as to offer an old man a cup of tea. My throat gets so dry, you know." He stepped over the threshold and May could do nothing but step aside and let him in. He looked at her with a question in his eyes and May directed him into the sitting room where a log fire burned in the grate.

"This is very comfortable. You have made a nice home here."

"Thank you. Please sit down and I will make tea for you." Annoyed at the intrusion May hurried through to the kitchen and quickly made a pot of tea. She added a plate of homemade biscuits to the tray and carried it into the room where her unwelcome guest sat blithely content in the chair by the fire. She poured a cup and handed it to the old man wondering how on earth he knew where she lived.

As if reading her mind he said, "I have made it my business, as an old family friend would, of course, to reassure myself of your wellbeing. I see you are well settled here in these beautiful surroundings. That must mean you do not intend to continue Adam's business interests."

May wanted to tell David Wang to mind his own business, but instead she said, "That is correct, Uncle."

"I would be happy, more than happy, to do you the service of seeing the shipping business is well run. I would ensure it was continued in the same way as Adam and Jonathan would have wished."

"You are very kind indeed, Uncle. But I do not need to trouble you."

"No trouble at all. I am a sentimental old man, you see, and I would even, to save you any worry you understand, be prepared to make you a very reasonable offer for the business."

So that's what he wants, May thought: he wants the Forster Shipping Company. Well he's not going to get it. She smiled.

"How thoughtful you are, Uncle. My poor father-in-law would have been very gratified to know you are still looking after his interests."

David Wang nodded solemnly, assured of success, but May continued.

"But I have no intention of selling or in any way disposing of Forster Shipping."

"You, a mere girl, cannot run a company like that." A sneer had crept into his voice despite his attempts to be urbane.

"I thank you for your interest and offer, but please don't concern yourself on my behalf."

David Wang put down his cup and rose stiffly to his feet. "Don't be too hasty to make a decision over this matter, my dear. My offer is made kindly. Shipping is not a comfortable business for a woman. There are all sorts of risks and dangers. Please consider this carefully and I'm sure you will come to the right decision. For everyone's sake, especially your own."

After he left May sat with her arms wrapped around her body, shaking with the implied threat of David Wang's words. Why was he so desperate to get his hands on the shipping company? Was it such a lucrative business that the Chinaman couldn't resist it? A knock at the back door made May start, then Alex Martin's voice called out, "Is anyone there? May? Are you there?"

They'd been out together several times: sightseeing, to the cinema, to the coast to walk by the sea. Alex had put his arm round her shoulders, casually like he had the first time they met. They'd held hands as they walked on the sandy seashore. He'd even kissed her lightly when he brought her home from the cinema.

May breathed a sigh of relief at the sound of his voice. "I'm here, Alex. Come in."

"God! There's a cold wind out there. How about a hot drink?" He looked at May's pale face. "Are you all right? You look a bit peaky."

May laughed in relief. "What a greeting. Yes, Alex, I'm fine. I'll put the kettle on. How about a scone or a piece of chocolate cake?"

"You've said the magic words, sweetheart. I'd do anything for a bit of chocolate cake: walk over hot coals, fight a dragon, buy a pint for old Jim Armstrong."

May sliced a thick wedge of cake and put it in front of Alex. He took hold of her by the shoulders and placed a hearty kiss on her lips. "That's my girl." He kissed her again and this time May put her arms around him and kissed him back.

## Chapter Twenty Four

After Alex had gone May sat at the kitchen table gazing out of the window over the garden, now alive with spring flowers. Daffodils danced in the light breeze that still held a distant memory of winter and catkins hung from the hazel trees in the hedge. Chaffinches and sparrows pecked about on the ground, bluetits and great tits hung from the nut feeders Jack had brought for them. She enjoyed watching their antics and, when something she didn't recognise arrived in the garden, she looked it up in the bird book Fiona had bought for her.

May didn't quite know what to make of her feelings for Alex. No-one had ever kissed her like that; had made her feel like that. It was as though she had discovered something new – strange and new – that had to be handled carefully in case it got broken. But now it seemed their relationship had taken on a deeper meaning, for May at least.

She'd been shaken by the intensity of her feelings when Alex had kissed her and confused when, afterwards, the world appeared to be the same as before. Alex hadn't seemed to notice and proceeded to drink his tea and eat the chocolate cake May had given him, with great enjoyment.

"You'll find your way into my heart with baking like that." He picked at the crumbs remaining on the plate. "In fact, I think you've found your way already." His eyes twinkled as he looked at her.

I wonder if he knows how good-looking he is, May thought, or how it makes me feel when he looks at me like that.

"What I really came for was to ask if you would do me the honour, Miss Lee, of accompanying me to what threatens to be a frightfully boring family party? It's on Sunday next week at my parents' home. Say you'll come. Please."

"When you ask me so nicely, it's impossible for me to refuse." May smiled. "Thank you, Alex, I would love to come. But you do realise I'm Mrs Lee?"

"You're married? Bloody hell! Fiona never mentioned anything about that. Where's your husband? Have you left him or what?"

"No, he left me, actually."

"Well, he's a bloody fool, if I may say so."

"He died," May said quietly.

"Ah, God. May, I'm so sorry. I didn't know."

"There was no need for you to know."

"Perhaps not, but I think I need to know, now."

May looked at Alex's face, into his eyes, trying to assess what his feeling might be. She continued, "There was an accident. A van hit his car. He was killed and so was his mother."

Alex took the two steps that separated him from May and took her in his arms.

"Our son was killed, too." May's voice threatened to break.

"Oh, love. Please, don't cry." Alex held her close then bent to kiss each eye as if to stem any tears.

"No, I won't. I think I must have cried all the tears I have. But I have a new life now and new friends. I'm happy."

"Good girl. Maybe, some day you'll tell me more."

"Maybe," May agreed.

"Look, love. I hate to do it, but I've got to go. How about getting together later?"

"I'm sorry, Alex, I can't. Not tonight."

"Oh well. Not to worry. Till Sunday week, then, but I'll phone you before then."

"Yes, please do. Goodbye, Alex"

May watched Alex walk down the path, get into his car and drive off. Thoughtfully she went back into the house and closed the door behind her.

* * * * * * * * * *

Armstrong cooked them a supper of Cumberland sausage and baked potatoes at the bungalow that night. He'd washed it down with beer but May, still unused to alcohol, had settled for lemonade. He listened grimly as May told him about David Wang's visit and his implied threats.

"I don't know why he wants the business so badly, James. Do you?"

He looked thoughtfully out of his window towards the village where May's cottage was. "Some people just want everything they can grab. And he was always jealous of Mr Lee."

"Do you think it's just that?"

"I don't know, lass. I really don't know. But if the old bugger thinks he can scare you into anything he's got another think coming, hasn't he? And he'll have me to deal with, too." He looked at May seriously. "You mustn't have anything more to do with him. If he, or either of his sons, comes back just you let me know. Ring me and I'll be right round. I'm not having him upsetting you like this." Armstrong turned back into the room and bent to throw a log onto the fire, poking it with unnecessary violence. He sat down in the chair he always favoured where he could either watch the television or look out of the window at the comings and goings.

May changed the subject, trying to divert Armstrong from the dark mood that had descended when she told him about that afternoon's visit from David Wang. "He'd just gone when Alex Martin came."

"Oh aye?"

"He's asked me to a family party on Sunday. Do you know his parents?"

"Yes, I know them right enough. Well, know of them, that is. We don't exactly move in the same social circle."

"What do you mean, James?"

"They might employ the likes of me, but I don't suppose they'd invite me to dine with them."

"But Alex is Fiona's cousin. Her father is a very nice, ordinary man."

"Aye, he is. But his wife, Fiona's mother... Well, I don't like to speak ill of the dead, and I didn't know the woman, but from what I've heard seems she was a bit of a snooty one. She was a Pennington-Martin – that's Alex's family name, though he's dropped the double-barrel bit. Fiona's mother and Alex's father were sister and brother."

May was now a bit worried about going to the party but Armstrong calmed her fears.

"Don't worry, lass. You'll be fine. How could you not be, a grand lass like you? Look, if you've any doubts about what to wear or anything, ask Fiona. She'll likely be going anyway."

"I will, James. Thank you."

After May left, Armstrong picked up the phone and dialled the number printed on a business card he had pinned to the noticeboard hanging in the kitchen.

\* \* \* \* \* \* \* \* \* \*

Jenny leapt out of the car almost before it had drawn to a stop and flung herself into May's arms before holding her at arms-length and looking into her face.

"My, you do look well. And happy, an' all."

May laughed at her friend's enthusiastic greeting. "Yes, I'm well and happy, too. How about you?"

"Brilliant," Jenny told her then called back towards the man getting out of the car. "Well, are you comin' in or what?"

"I'm coming if you'll give me a minute to lock up." Sam Castle grinned at Jenny's feigned impatience. "Hello May. How are you?"

"Very well, thank you, Sam. Come on inside out of this wind."

"If you don't mind, I'll let you two catch up on all the gossip for a while. I'll have a walk down to see Jim Armstrong. I'll fetch him back and we'll go out for lunch. How's that?"

"Sounds wonderful. See you soon."

Sam waved back at the pair, but they were already deep in conversation. He shrugged and smiled to himself, walking the few hundred yards to Armstrong's bungalow. Sam could see the older man pottering about in the garden as he approached.

"Morning, Jim. A grand morning for gardening, isn't it?"

"Sam! Great to see you, man. Come in, come in."

"How's it been? Got the place all ship-shape have you?"

"Oh aye. I can fill me time in, no bother – with a garden this big as well as keeping an eye on the lass." Armstrong led the way into the bungalow. Sam stood at the picture window and looked out across the village in the valley. Smoke rose lazily from the cottage chimneys.

"So, he's been here, then?" he asked.

"Aye. Shook her up a bit, I can tell you." Armstrong related the conversation May had had with David Wang. The younger man looked thoughtful.

"There's nothing there I can do anything about. He didn't actually make any threat, not explicitly."

"But it was there, nonetheless," Armstrong insisted.

"I don't doubt it. Not for a minute." Sam thought for a while.

"So, it's the shipping company he's after. That makes sense. Do you know what May intends to do with it?"

"No," Armstrong replied. "I only know she's not going to sell. The solicitor told her he has some sort of proposition that'll keep it going, but I don't know what it is."

"We'll just have to watch and wait, then."

"Aye, lad, we will."

"Come on then." Jenny was beside herself with impatience. "Have you slept with Alex yet?"

"Jenny!"

"I'm sorry. But he's so drop-dead gorgeous I'd have trouble keepin' my hands off him if it was me. Not that I would, though. Not now I've got Sam," she rushed to reassure May.

"You are impossible." May couldn't help but laugh. "And no, I haven't. And before you ask, I'm not going to."

"What? I thought you fancied the pants off him."

"I do. And that's why I can't."

"I don't understand, May. Why not?"

"Because of the golden dragon," May eventually said.

"What the bleedin' hell has that to do with anythin'?"

"I care for Alex too much to risk bringing misfortune to him."

"Oh May. You can't really believe that." Jenny sounded exasperated.

"I can and I do. Everything went wrong when I lost it," May insisted.

"But nothing bad has happened since, has it?"

May didn't want to admit she felt stifled by the huge legacy Adam had left and that David Wang was threatening her to get part of it. If she still had the golden dragon none of this would be happening she was sure. She was beginning to realise she just couldn't risk loving Alex – for his sake. A set look come across May's face.

"Is there nothin' I can say to convince you that it's superstition, pure and simple?" Jenny asked. The reasonable tone of voice failed to disguise her frustration. May opened her mouth to reply but the sound of men's voices interrupted the conversation and nothing more was said.

Jenny hugged May as she was leaving that evening.

"Grab happiness with both hands, that's what you told me," she whispered.

"I can't, Jenny. Not when it could bring disaster."

\* \* \* \* \* \* \* \* \*

Alex shook his head in disbelief, a look of deep hurt in his eyes. "I don't understand. I thought we were getting along so well." It was the day after the party.

"I'm sorry, Alex. It isn't what I want." May kept a note of determination in her voice.

"Was it my parents? Did they upset you in any way?"

"No, not at all. They were very kind." Armstrong's tentative warning had not been necessary. May had been worried they would perhaps be prejudiced against her but they had been charming and welcoming. The party hadn't been the dull affair Alex had predicted. Far from it.

\* \* \* \* \* \* \* \* \*

The house was imposing, set in terraced gardens overlooking Lake Windermere. The land stretched down to the waterside where a jetty reached out into the lake. After dinner Alex had taken May for a walk in the moonlit gardens. It was the most romantic setting she could have ever imagined. It seemed unreal it was so perfect. When Alex had kissed her, all May wanted to do was lie down in the soft grass and make love to him. But he had taken it no further and May wasn't confident enough to take the initiative. She had felt a surge of disappointment when he drew away. Surely she couldn't have attracted another man like Jonathan who, though caring in some ways, didn't want a physical relationship. Was she so unattractive to men?

"I want you, May," Alex had whispered, seeming to sense May's disappointment. "But not here. I want you in my bed all night. I want to wake up in the morning and see your face on the pillow beside me."

Oh, Alex, she thought. So do I. If only you knew how much. A flush of passion stained May's cheeks. She was aware of it and was thankful for the dark. They had walked hand in hand back up to the house, May's emotions in turmoil.

\* \* \* \* \* \* \* \* \*

"What is it then? What's wrong?" Alex persisted, hurt in his eyes at May's rejection the next day.

"I don't want to talk about it any more. I'm sorry, Alex, I can't see you again." But in her heart she cried out to him: It's not true. Stay. Please stay.

"I'm sorry you feel like that. More sorry than you could ever know." Alex walked out of the cottage and drove away without looking back. As he went May's resolve crumpled and she almost ran to call him back. Instead she sat at the kitchen table, put her head down and wept.

\* \* \* \* \* \* \* \* \*

May threw herself into redecorating the cottage. She painted walls and varnished woodwork. She washed curtains that didn't need it and vacuumed carpets until they were nearly threadbare. Armstrong watched her and wondered what had happened with Alex Martin. May never mentioned him and Armstrong, respecting her reticence, didn't ask. Without comment or complaint he moved furniture, fetched and carried, and watched over her in the weeks that followed the Pennington-Martins' party.

"What do you want to do with these boxes from the Newcastle house?" he asked as he eyed the sealed cardboard packing cases he had been working around all day.

"I suppose I'll have to unpack them sometime."

"Do you want to make a start now?"

"No. I can't think there's anything in there I need. What do the labels say?"

Armstrong peered at the printed inventory labels stuck to the top of each box. "This one says it contains your clothes and personal items. This has files and paperwork from Mr Lee's office."

"I'll sort through the clothes another day. As for the paperwork, I'll have to leave it. I don't know why it was sent – it's nothing to do with me." May was still reluctant to encounter anything that related to Adam's legacy.

"What about the contents of the safe?"

"Mr Mawson has them. I expect he'll send them when he's finished with them. Do you think the paint on the window is dry yet? I want to hang the curtains."

\* \* \* \* \* \* \* \* \* \*

Now the cottage was finished thoughts and tasks May had been trying to avoid began to force their way back to the front of her mind. Several weeks had passed since David Wang's visit. Twice her car had been overtaken by a dark Mercedes but she had told herself it wasn't an unusual car and had pushed her fears aside, refusing to let her imagination run away with her.

She thought of Alex often and missed his presence in her life with an intensity that astonished her. She'd never expected to fall in love. She now freely admitted the fact to herself. It wasn't something she'd even thought about. She'd hoped to grow to love Jonathan and that he would love her, but romantic, heart-stopping passion was never going to be part of it. But then she'd met Alex and that was exactly what she'd felt. Perhaps I shouldn't have sent him away so soon, she thought, torturing herself. Perhaps we could have been lovers. At least that would have left me something to remember, something to cherish on all the lonely nights ahead. But that would have been dishonourable, she knew, letting Alex think there could be a future when she knew there could not. May sighed, realising she had to stop thinking like this. She had behaved correctly in ending things when she had; the threats David Wang had made to her must not be allowed to affect Alex.

May pulled her thoughts back from what might have been to what she was going to do from now on. First, she had to contact Mr Mawson and try to resolve the problem of the shipping company. Then she had to get a job. May realised she couldn't go on like this from year to year. She didn't need to earn a living but she wanted to do something. But what? She'd had this same conversation with Jenny a couple of years or so ago before going to college. She'd almost completed her studies before it had all gone wrong, perhaps she should finish them and see what opportunities presented themselves.

Determining to see Mr Mawson as soon as she could arrange it

May reached for the phone to call him and jumped in surprise as it rang. It was Fiona.

"Is it safe to come to Fellbeck Cottage again? Is all the painting done?"

"Hello, Fiona. Yes it is. You must come soon. I've missed you."

"I've missed you too, but I'm a disaster when it comes to decorating. Dad says I'm the only person in the world who can put paint on back-to-front. I thought it was better to stay out of the way."

May laughed at the typically dramatic way Fiona spoke. "Well, it is safe for you to return. When can you come?" May thought about how similar Fiona and Jenny were: outgoing and fun. Neither were afraid to speak their minds. How different from me, she thought. I wish I could be more like them.

"How about ten minutes?" Fiona suggested. "I'm just going out on a call up the valley road and I want to ask a favour of you."

Fiona breezed in a short while later carrying a cardboard box with holes punctured in it. A scrabbling noise came from inside.

"What on earth do you have?" May asked, half afraid Fiona might be bringing a kitten or puppy. She'd expressed the opinion several times that May should have a pet of some sort; May wasn't so sure.

"An owl. A barn owl to be exact."

"But why are you bringing it to me?"

"That's where the favour comes in. On the way here I spotted this beauty lying at the side of the road. It let me pick it up and I managed to give it a quick once-over. I couldn't find any damage but there must be something wrong or I couldn't have got anywhere near. It's my guess it was hit by a vehicle and it's in shock, perhaps bruised."

"Oh, poor thing. But I still don't see…"

"There's a chap – other side of Cockermouth – who takes in sick and injured birds. He specialises in owls as it happens. If you haven't anything else to do I'd be eternally grateful if you could take it over to him. I'd do it myself but I've got a list of calls longer than your arm."

"Of course I will. Where exactly is it?" May, truth to tell, was at a loose end and was grateful for something to do.

Fiona's directions were comprehensive and May easily found her way to Brow Cross. The small community consisted entirely of two rows of miners' cottages flanking the quiet road that had once led to a coal mine. The mine had closed many years ago and the spoil heaps it had created had been grassed-over and taken back into the country landscape. May found the house and knocked on the door. She asked the woman who answered for Kevin Graham, the name Fiona had given her.

"He's round the back." The woman shut the door in May's face leaving her standing on the doorstep.

May looked around wondering what to do now. Go round the back, she supposed. The woman hadn't seemed inclined to summon Kevin Graham – her husband maybe? May walked to the end of the row of cottages and found a lane leading round behind. There were garages there and some parked cars. She returned for her car and drove round, counting the back gates as she went. She needn't have bothered because it soon became obvious which one belonged to the man she was looking for.

All the houses had long, narrow back gardens, most of them with a shed or garage. There were those that took pride in their small patch of land, with immaculate pocket-handkerchief lawns edged with flowers, or vegetable gardens just beginning to grow for the new season. One, however, had only the narrowest of paths leading between high cages constructed of wire netting on flimsy-looking wooden frames. May could see most of them contained birds: owls in the main. A man was in one of them holding, what looked to May like a bunch of brown speckled feathers. She called out.

"Hello. Are you Mr Graham?" He made no sign he had heard so May called again, louder.

The man turned and said in a low, quiet voice, "Yes, I'm Kevin Graham and I'm not deaf. There's no need to shout: you'll scare the birds. What do you want?" He was older than May had expected. If the woman who had answered the door had been his wife she was considerably younger than him. Maybe she was his daughter. He pushed his cap up out of his eyes and went back to stroking the head of the bird he was holding. He looked down at it saying, almost to himself, "Poor little bugger'll be dead within the hour. Peppered with shotgun pellets. What a waste."

"Oh no," May said sadly. "Can't you do anything for it?"

"Don't you think I would if I could?" The voice was gruff and not particularly friendly. May was contrite.

"I'm sorry. I didn't think."

"That's the trouble with most people: they don't think. Anyway, what do you want?" he asked again.

May told him and during the telling the injured sparrowhawk died. Kevin laid it gently on a bench inside a cage with a deep sigh. He looked a bit like a bird himself, small and slight with pointed features and sharp, bright eyes. Never still.

"Come on, then. Let's see what you've fetched me."

## Chapter Twenty Five

May drove towards Newcastle in the early summer sunshine, thinking about the day before. She'd stayed at Kevin's bird sanctuary for nearly three hours, fascinated by the work he did there. She was amazed that anyone could devote so much time and attention to wild birds. It was not part of the culture in China to have pets or to care for wildlife. She remembered one of the stories she'd been told by her mother about how, many years before she was born, Mao Tse Tung blamed birds for eating precious grain. It became everyone's duty to make enough noise to scare the birds, to stop them resting until they died, exhausted. What madness, she thought as she drove along. May wondered what Kevin would have said had she told him.

She'd rung Fiona to say her owl was expected to make a full recovery. Kevin would let her know when it was ready to be released. Then there was the phone call to Jenny to ask if she could put May up the next night. May almost laughed out loud when she remembered the conversation.

"Aye, of course," Jenny agreed. "But, look, I can't talk just now. You'll never guess…"

"What?" May asked wondering what on earth Jenny was going to tell her.

"I'm on me way out to a football match. Newcastle United, would you believe?"

"Jenny, I'd believe anything if it was you. But why? I thought you didn't like football."

"I don't. As for the why – it's because Sam has asked me to go with him. I'm that fed up of him goin' on about it I thought I'd better see what all the fuss is about. Anyway, I've got to rush or I'll be late. See you tomorrow. Ta ra."

May could hardy wait to hear all about Jenny's night out. But now she was on her way to meet with Mr Mawson.

\* \* \* \* \* \* \* \* \* \*

"It's good of you to come all this way," Arthur Mawson said as he seated May in his office. Tea had been called for and poured and May held the fine bone china cup and saucer as the solicitor made small talk. She wished he would hurry and get to the point. Now that there seemed a solution to her misgivings she wanted to get it settled quickly.

"Are you still of the same mind, my dear, regarding Forster Shipping Company? You don't want to sell." May nodded. He continued, "I have a proposal that could very well solve your problems in that regard. It could prove a very satisfactory outcome for all concerned." He paused, hands steepled in front of him, elbows on the desk, fingertips touching his lips. He was quiet for such a long time May wondered if he'd dropped off to sleep. She waited.

"Adam had another son."

May gasped, her black eyes widening in surprise. If she'd still been holding the cup and saucer she thought she might have dropped them. She couldn't think how to respond to this piece of extraordinary information.

"He was an illegitimate son, of course; the result of a passing affaire. Adam didn't even know about the child until well after he'd married Angela. No-one, apart from myself, knew of the child's existence. The boy himself did not, does not, know who his father was. Over the years, Adam kept a watch over him, saw to his education and wellbeing, even gave him a position in the company. But don't think he benefited from favouritism," he reassured May. "Everything he has achieved he earned – Adam wasn't foolish enough to employ someone who did not merit the job. He was the Chartering Superintendent in Adam's day, and a very good one at that. You may recognise his name: Simon Stanley, the acting General Manager since Jonathan's death. This is the person, I am sure, who would be the one to safeguard the future of the company." Arthur Mawson finished his speech and sat back in his chair pushing his spectacles back up his nose from the precarious position they had achieved as he was talking. He waited for May's response.

Throughout she had listened quietly to the revelations delivered in Mr Mawson's typical matter-of-fact manner. Thoughts and feelings were colliding in her head. She hardly knew what to say or think. But it was all so simple, really, so ridiculously, perfectly simple. No wonder she had felt it was so wrong for her to inherit.

There was another heir, one who was eminently suitable for the task.

"Would he be willing to take it on do you think?" May asked. "Who will tell him; ask him?"

"If it is your wish, I will telephone him now and ask him to come to the office. He may be able to come today."

"Yes. Please do." May was eager to meet this secret son of Adam Lee: the man who, she hoped, would take a great load from her shoulders.

"But, May," Arthur Mawson said warningly. "I need you to understand what I have told you is in the strictest confidence. If Adam had wished Simon to know he was his father he would have either told him himself or left instructions for me to do so. He did not."

"But how will you explain? What will you tell him?" May was disconcerted that Simon wasn't to be told what she felt was his right to know: who his father was.

"Only that Adam had the highest regard for him. That he saw great promise in him."

"I think you should tell him everything," May insisted.

"Listen to me, May," Arthur Mawson said sharply. "It took me a great deal of heart-searching to reveal this to you, and I only did it for a very good reason."

May nodded and looked down at her hands clasped tightly on her lap. "Very well, Mr Mawson. I will respect your wishes and what you believe were Adam's."

Arthur Mawson's phone conversation was brief. "He can be here by half past two," he told May. "Would you care to join me for lunch and we can talk a little more."

If May was expecting to meet a man who resembled Adam Lee she was to be disappointed. Nothing about his appearance betrayed their relationship. He was of medium height, and a little overweight. His light brown hair was thinning to premature baldness. He was smartly dressed in a dark business suit and well-groomed. Arthur Mawson introduced them.

"May, this is Simon Stanley; Simon, this is May Lee."

Simon's handshake was firm and warm, as was his smile. "I'm very pleased to meet you at last," he told May.

"Please sit down, Simon." Arthur Mawson indicated the chairs in

209

front of his large, untidy desk. In a crisp, businesslike manner he made the younger man the offer he and May had discussed. Simon kept his feelings pretty much to himself but the solicitor could see he was deeply affected by what he was hearing and the fact that Adam Lee had had such faith in him. He asked a few thoughtful questions and received Arthur Mawson's well prepared answers. It seemed there was little the solicitor hadn't anticipated even as far as Simon wishing for a little time to consider the proposal of himself permanently running the company.

"You must take as much time as you need, Simon," Mr Mawson told him. "You have much to consider."

"If I sleep on it I'm sure I'll have come to a decision by tomorrow. Could we meet again then?"

"That would be quite in order. Two thirty again?"

"Yes. That would be fine with me."

"Very well." Arthur Mawson shook Simon's hand as the younger man rose from his seat. "Until tomorrow."

"May I use your phone?" May asked Arthur Mawson after Simon had left. "I need to make arrangements to meet with the friend I'm staying with tonight. Jenny – you remember her?"

"Indeed I do," he laughed "A very singular young woman!" May wasn't sure what he meant but assumed, from his tone, it was good.

The receptionist at the gallery where Jenny now worked told May that Jenny hadn't come in today. May couldn't help but wonder if the football match had been too much for her friend and she needed a day off to get over it. May decided she'd make her way to the Scarlet Parakeet and see how her friend was feeling. Perhaps she wouldn't want to go out tonight. She thanked Mr Mawson and left promising to come back tomorrow afternoon.

May stepped outside the solicitor's office into a sharp rain shower. She was debating with herself whether to make a dash for the coffee bar across the street to shelter for a while or brave the rain and return to her car which was parked several streets away. She didn't notice the long, dark blue car until its front door swung open and David Wang stepped out, unfurling a large umbrella.

"May! How unexpected to meet you here. Are you well? This rain is most unpleasant. Come, shelter under my umbrella – it's big enough for two." All May wanted to do was get away but, again, good manners overcame her distaste.

"Thank you, Uncle."

The rain came down harder and a sudden squall threatened to blow the umbrella inside-out. May gasped as the wind swirled around, taking her breath away. People scurried past to shelter in doorways or inside shops. May's skirt was flapping wetly around her legs and her shoes were already soaked through.

"We're getting very wet. Come and sit in the car until the rain has passed," David Wang invited. He took her arm in a surprisingly strong grip for such a frail-looking man and May found herself in the back seat of the Mercedes before she could protest. "There now. That's much better." David Wang got in beside her. He took his hat off and shook the raindrops onto the floor. The driver did not turn round but sat stolidly, looking forward.

"You have been to see your solicitor." It was a statement rather than a question. "Are you ready to instruct him to attend to the purchase of Forster Shipping by myself?"

"Uncle, you must recall I told you I did not intend selling the company." May spoke firmly. David Wang appeared to consider her words.

"You did indeed. Yes, I do recall. You did tell me that." He sighed, looking out of the window at the rain-drenched street and the people hurrying along, eager to get out of the wet. "But perhaps you have had time to reconsider."

"No, I do not believe I will change my mind. My father-in-law's company will stay within his family." May feared she had revealed too much but David Wang did not appear to realise what she had said.

"I must insist you reconsider." His voice had taken on a hard edge quite different from his usual avuncular tone.

"No. That is not possible," May insisted.

"I think you will find it is possible and in your best interests, and those of your friend."

"What do you mean? What friend? This has nothing to do with anyone else." May was becoming angry that the old man would not take 'no' for an answer. "I am not prepared to discuss this matter any further." May reached for the door handle but found her wrist imprisoned in David Wang's wiry hand. May tried to pull away but found she could not.

"Please, stay a while. It's still raining very hard. You wouldn't want to catch a chill."

"No thank you. I'll be quite all right."

"It was raining last night, too," David Wang continued ignoring May's wish to leave. "The football match was nearly cancelled. It would have been such a pity with the other team coming all the way from Greece. We have a private box at St James's Park, you know. My sons love to support their team." To anyone else listening it would seem David Wang's mind was wandering. At first that was what May thought. "United won last night. But it was a pity about the trouble."

"What trouble?" May asked, struggling to keep her voice even while a crawling fear began to insinuate itself.

"It appeared to be the other team's supporters. It's the Greek temperament – so wild. They made something of a nuisance of themselves. I'm sorry to say that several people were injured."

"Oh," May gasped despite her efforts to stay calm. "I hope they weren't seriously hurt." She attempted to keep up the conversational tone David Wang had adopted and tried to take what he was saying at face value and not let her imagination run away.

"I believe some had to be taken to hospital. I hope there were none of your friends there. It's always the innocent bystanders that suffer, don't you find?" He released his grip on May's wrist. Pain struck as the blood rushed back but she was determined not to give him the satisfaction of rubbing her arm where it felt the circulation had been cut off for some time. "But, look, it's stopped raining a little." David Wang glanced out of the window and turned to smile at May. "I won't keep you from your shopping. Please take a little more time to reconsider my offer. You won't find me ungenerous. I'm sure we can come to an amicable arrangement. Here is my number. Please telephone me later."

May took the proffered card and got out of the car. It drove off, tyres swishing on the wet road.

There was a public phone in the coffee bar where May dashed for refuge and she punched in Jenny's home number with trembling fingers. Kate MacLeod answered.

"Jenny's still at work, May. She won't be back for a couple of hours yet. I'll give her what for, though, not letting me know she wasn't coming home last night after the football match. Why don't you come round, though, and we can have a bit of a gossip just the two of us?"

"Thank you, Mrs MacLeod. I'll see you later." May was trying hard to push the panic away. She took her notebook out and found another number.

"DI Castle. How can I help you?" It was Sam himself answering, thank God.

"Hello, Sam. It's May Lee."

"May! It's good to hear from you. How are you?"

"I'm fine thank you, Sam. Have you seen Jenny today? I'm trying to get in touch with her."

"No. She'll be at work still. I haven't seen her since we left the football match. There was a bit of trouble and I had to leave her to make her own way home. There'll be hell to pay when I do see her, that's for sure. You know how she is." Sam laughed fondly, not seeming to mind in the least that he'd bear the brunt of Jenny's temper.

"Oh no! Oh no!"

"Come on, May. She's not that bad. I know it's all a big act."

"Sam, listen," May almost shouted. "She's not at work and she's not been home. I need to see you Sam. I need to tell you…"

"Where are you, May?" Sam's voice was abrupt. May told him where she was. "I'll be there in a few minutes. Don't move." May's knees felt weak with relief and she almost collapsed into the nearest chair.

Sam's face was devoid of expression as May told him about her conversation with David Wang. He appeared detached, professional, as though they were discussing somebody neither of them knew.

"Come on." Sam steered May out of the coffee bar and into his car. "I'm taking you to my flat and you'll stay there until I come for you. Do you understand?" May said nothing. Sam took her by the shoulders and gave her a little shake. "Do you understand, May?"

"Yes. But what about Jenny's mother? What are you going to say to her?"

Sam said nothing while he started the car and pulled out from the parking place into the stream of traffic. "You leave all that to me. I don't want you to go out or to make any phone calls. Trust me, May. I'll move heaven and earth to find her and God help anyone who gets in my way.

* * * * * * * * * *

May heard Jenny's voice before she came into the room accompanied by Sam Castle. May ran over and looked at her friend in horror. A large red bruise covered most of one cheek and an eye was colouring nicely.

"You're hurt, Jenny, and it's all my fault. I'm so sorry." May was almost in tears at the thought of what might have happened. It's me, she thought. I've caused this with my bad luck. May couldn't begin to forgive herself for bringing this trouble to her friend. How could I have been so careless, so stupid, to lose the golden dragon? If only…

Jenny hugged May. "It's nothin' – nothin' compared to what Sam did to the ugly sod that did it," she said with delicious malice.

"Are you sure you're all right?" May asked. "But what happened?"

"If noise is any indication of wellbeing, she's very well indeed," Sam put in with a grim smile on his face, seeming to ignore May's question. "I could do with a stiff drink, but I'll make do with a strong cup of tea and then I'll get you two home."

Pleased to have something to do at last May disappeared into the kitchen to reappear a few minutes later with three mugs and a pot of tea as well as milk and sugar balanced on a tray. Sam poured the tea and added milk and a liberal helping of sugar. He handed them a mug each and insisted they drink.

May sipped and grimaced at the hot, sweet liquid. She put the mug back onto the tray. "I don't take sugar, sorry."

"It's good for shock," Sam told her. "Drink some of it, at least. You too, Jenny." They sipped obediently.

"Oh God! What's me Mam goin' to say?" Realisation hit Jenny. It was well after midnight the second night she hadn't been home. "She'll be mad as all hell. She'll kill me."

"I've already talked to her, love. I gave her an expurgated version and you're right. She is mad as all hell – with me."

"Is someone going to tell me what's happened?" May asked. Sam and Jenny weren't listening. "Tell me what's happened." May shouted above their voices. It was such an unusual thing for May to even raise her voice that they were both immediately shocked into silence.

"Look, it's going to be a long story, I can tell. Let's get you both into the car and home, then you can talk all night. OK? As you can see, May, Jenny is fine. The Wangs – both brothers and father – are in custody."

May let out a breath she didn't realise she'd been holding. Were the Wangs really out of the way? She tried to relax but the hours she'd sat alone in Sam's flat imagining all sorts of things had taken their toll.

"Are you sure?" she asked Sam the foolish question.

"Yes, I am sure," he told May. "I was there, remember?" he reminded her gently. "Come on, the pair of you. Home time."

Sam came in to face Kate MacLeod's relieved anger. His phone call to her earlier in the evening had reassured her that she'd have Jenny back with her soon. He'd omitted telling her the full story, of course. But eventually she'd have to know and May doubted his ability to come out of that confrontation unscathed. He turned back to May and Jenny.

"I'll call for you at nine in the morning. I'm sorry but I'll have to get you both to make full statements. It's going to take most of the morning." He kissed both Kate and May on the cheek but enjoyed a lingering kiss on the lips with Jenny. "Try not to get into any more trouble until then." Jenny seemed about to protest but he silenced her with another kiss and left, grinning.

After he'd gone the three women stared at each other in silence then all started talking at once. Kate held up her hands.

"That's enough, you two. Get yourselves to bed. We'll talk about this tomorrow. You're safe, that's all that matters for now."

But Jenny and May, in the darkness of Jenny's room, talked well into the small hours.

\* \* \* \* \* \* \* \* \* \*

Sam was right. Taking the statements did take up the entire next morning. There was only time to grab a sandwich before May's meeting with Mr Mawson and Simon. The skies were still grey and water-laden, threatening more rain as May arrived for the all-important meeting with Simon Stanley. The more she thought about it the more she was convinced it was the right thing to do – that Simon take over the company. She had to be assured, though, it would be run as Adam would have wished as far as was practical or possible. She opened the outside door and walked up the lino-clad stairs to the first floor. Simon was already there, waiting. He stood and greeted her. It seemed Arthur Mawson had heard May arrive as he peered round his office door and bid them come in.

It took some time before May had finished telling about the Wangs, and the police suspecting that they had wanted the company for criminal purposes: smuggling the most likely. Arthur Mawson was very concerned that Jenny had been in danger and May had been put under such pressure, but she assured him it was all over now. David Wang and his two sons had been arrested and charged with kidnapping. Other charges would undoubtedly follow as the police made further investigations into their dealings.

Having reassured himself May felt up to continuing with today's meeting, Mr Mawson asked, "Well, Simon, have you made a decision?" He leaned forward across his desk, eager to hear what the younger man had to say.

"First of all, I must ask May if she still wants to go ahead with this. May, are you sure you want me to take over the company?"

"Yes, Simon, but I must know you will run in accordance with Adam's principles and vision. Can you promise me that?"

"Yes, I can and will. He was a shrewd businessman. I learned so much from him. I often wondered why he took such pains with me when I was just another employee." May glanced uncomfortably at the solicitor. Simon paused for a moment just missing the silent exchange and again spoke directly to May. "I have concerns of my own, though. Will you be taking any part in the running of the business or will it be left entirely to me?"

May looked confused. "It won't be anything to do with me when the company belongs to you."

"What? I don't understand what you mean."

"The company will be yours, Simon. You will be the owner. What use would it be to me, or me to it for that matter?"

"Wait a moment, May," Arthur Mawson interrupted. "Where did this scheme come from? This wasn't what we discussed."

"But that's what I thought you meant. For Simon to take over the company."

"Yes, but as Chief Executive not owner. I cannot allow this, really I cannot." Arthur Mawson took his glasses off and rubbed the bridge of his nose before putting them back on again to sit more securely before gravity would inevitably pull them down again. "With all respect to you, Simon, Adam wished May to be involved." He turned back to May. "I cannot let you give away Adam's company, even to Adam's protégé."

"As I understand it, Mr Mawson, it is my company now." May spoke in an assertive voice the old lawyer had never heard her use before. "But I will be guided by your advice. What is it you suggest?"

If Arthur Mawson was startled to see this new side of May he kept it well hidden. "We'll need to seek expert financial advice on this which I cannot give. But, in a nutshell, I want to suggest to both of you that Simon be placed in overall control of the company with a salary commensurate with the responsibilities involved. Perhaps a profit-sharing scheme can be worked out and, if you are still insistent on Simon owning part of the company, May, some sort of share-option might be a possibility. This is just a tentative suggestion, though. We must consider all the implications and, of course and most important, you must agree, Simon."

"In principle, yes, I do agree." Simon nodded. "But I would never have accepted outright ownership. I may have been Mr Lee's protégé but I certainly wasn't his heir." He laughed humourlessly at such an outrageous thought. "He wanted you to have an interest in the company, May: he made you a trustee. I know he could never have imagined this scenario but circumstances have decreed otherwise. I will run the company as close to his own vision as I can. The profit will provide you with an income – a very good one if I do my job right."

Mr Mawson looked at Simon Stanley with approval. "Well said, Simon. What about you, May?"

"I respect your advice. Yes, I agree." Though she wished with all her heart that Simon was, indeed, Adam's heir.

"Good, good," Arthur Mawson said rubbing his hands together in satisfaction at the outcome. "I'll set the wheels in motion. I'll call you both into the office again in due course. I couldn't be more delighted. We should be having champagne but would a cup of tea and a biscuit do?"

May and Simon agreed it would and, toasting each other with tea, they began the pleasant job of getting to know one another.

## Chapter Twenty Six

The next day in May's kitchen with the sun pouring through the windows highlighting the jug of tulips sitting on the windowsill, she told Armstrong matter-of-factly about the confrontation with David Wang and his arrest. Several times during the telling he jumped up from his chair and strode around the room, May waiting until he had control over his feelings before continuing. She repeated Jenny's colourful account.

\* \* \* \* \* \* \* \* \* \*

Sam had called at the flat above the café to pick Jenny up. Seeing him with a black and white scarf wound round his neck and a black and white striped shirt on sent Jenny into delighted giggles. She tucked her arm into his and they made their way to St James's Park.

It was an important European Cup tie and the crowds flocked through the gates, Jenny and Sam among them. The air was tense with excitement as the preparations for play got underway, music and announcements booming out, floodlights making the pitch brighter than day. Cheers, blaring air-horns and chants greeted the home team as they ran on; catcalls and boos rose above the visitors' supporters' shouts for their team.

The atmosphere was electric and had Jenny on her feet shouting for the 'Magpies', totally involved with the cut and thrust of the game. She was almost deafened at the noise of the crowd as, all too soon it seemed to her, the whistle blew for the end of the match. It was a draw. Then she found herself and Sam carried along with the still chanting crowds belching out of the stadium into the night.

Jenny was jumping with excitement as Sam led her through the surging crush with his arm firmly around her shoulders. He tried to steer them to the side of the road where they could catch their breath before heading down to the Metro station. Sam smiled at her.

"I take it you enjoyed the match?"

"I never thought it would be so excitin'," she croaked. "It's that different from watchin' it on the telly. Can we go again next time?"

Sam laughed. "So the 'toon army' have another recruit, do they?"

Jenny's reply was drowned by the shouts of a group of black and white clad lads pushing past them. Sam was about to say something else when he was cut off by the noise of some sort of disturbance behind them. Even Jenny could tell it was far from the good-natured banter between the rival teams. He drew her on, faster down the street, away from whatever was going on. He didn't want her to be involved in what sounded to be an unpleasant confrontation.

Then, fighting against the tide of homegoing fans, Sam could make out the yellow coats of two policemen. As they ran past he could hear the radio of one of them crackling and a voice shouting from it, "Officer down. Officer down." The rest of the message was lost as the two policemen ran on, pushing and shoving as they went.

Sam grabbed hold of Jenny's shoulders, turning her to face him. "I've got to go," he shouted. "There's trouble. We're nearly at the Metro station. Get yourself on the train and get home. Can you do that?"

"Yes. But…"

"No buts, love. I've got to go. Take care." Sam kissed Jenny and pushed her firmly on her way towards the station. He turned and ran off after the uniformed policemen, following their bobbing yellow jackets without a backward glance.

Jenny was nearly at the station when she felt an arm go round her shoulders. She looked up smiling, expecting to see Sam had returned from a false alarm. All she had time to see was a bald head on top of shoulders the size of a wrestler's before she was clamped in a bear-like grip and bundled into the back of a van. Before she knew what was happening something that felt like a rough sheet and smelled of stale sweat was thrown over her head. Jenny began to struggle in fright, kicking and thrashing about. She felt her foot connect with something soft and heard a grunt. It might have been followed by swearing but she didn't understand the words. The tone, though, was unmistakeable. Good, she'd done the bastard some harm.

The blow that knocked Jenny out could have been the kick of a donkey or a boulder falling from a great height. It was, in fact, the punch of a twenty stone Chinaman but Jenny didn't know it. The first thing she was aware of as she regained consciousness was that she was still wrapped in the evil-smelling sheet. She tried to move but found she couldn't as her arms and her legs seemed tied together. As she began to become aware of the sounds around her Jenny got the impression she was in some sort of large space. She must have been taken out of the van. But where was she and why the hell?

Footsteps sounded and more talking. Jenny could make out at least three voices. It wasn't a language she recognised with certainty but she thought it was probably Chinese. She'd heard May speak a little of it and the cadence was similar. God, her head hurt. The pain and dizziness made her retch, bringing up a only sour dribble. She thought she must have groaned and dreaded drawing attention to the fact that she was conscious, but the conversation went on regardless. Then footsteps retreated and there was only silence and darkness.

Eventually Jenny could make out there were noises far in the distance: engines of some sort or machinery working. Was it dark because it was still night, or was it because she was shut in an unlit room? How long had she been here? Had it been only a few minutes, or hours? She let out a muffled sob and closed her eyes.

Jenny thought, despite the painful stiffness that was creeping into her arms and back, that she must have dozed. She became aware that there was a lifting of the darkness, through the cloth that still covered her, when she opened her eyes. She reasoned she must be in a room with a window and that it was morning.

Footsteps approached from a distance, echoing as if in a large space. I'm not in a room, Jenny thought. Maybe an abandoned warehouse or store. Was it one of her captors coming or, Jenny's heart leapt with hope, someone who would rescue her? The roughness of the way the man – it was definitely a man – handled her dashed any hopes. He hauled her up to sit in a chair. Jenny was so stiff and disoriented she fell off, banging her already aching head on the floor. She rolled herself into a ball and began to sob. She was picked up again and put back in the chair, arms holding her in place until it seemed she was able to sit up for herself. The footsteps retreated but Jenny thought the man hadn't gone away. She felt he was still there somewhere, watching her.

What the hell was going on? What did these people want? They must want her for something or else she would have been let go. Was it some sicko who was going to rape or murder her – or both? Then, rather than succumb to more tears of self-pity, Jenny began to scream. She yelled and cursed and tried to stand up. She felt herself pushed back and what must have been a hand clamped over her face, sending the revolting cloth into her mouth. After a time the hand loosened and again Jenny began to yell. Again she was silenced. Whoever it was had made his point for the next time she was released Jenny remained still and quiet and after a time the footsteps retreated. She was hungry, thirsty, exhausted and, she hated to admit it even to herself, very frightened.

In the hours that followed Jenny began to develop a sensitivity to the sounds around her, trying to interpret them: a constant distant hum – traffic on a busy road; clickety-clacking – definitely trains; engines approaching and retreating – lorries passing by, perhaps; occasionally other feet approached and the newcomer held a whispered conversation with her jailer then left. Then, when Jenny felt the overwhelming urge to begin to scream again, so great was the tension that had been building over the day, other sounds came: tyres screeching on tarmac; heavy blows on metal; a rush of fresh air; pounding feet and loud voices. A woman's voice spoke to her, asking if she was all right, had she been harmed.

Then Jenny was released from the horrible cloth and the ropes that held it round her. She gulped in the sweetness of the air and saw Sam striding towards her.

"My God, Jenny." Instead of taking her in his arms as Jenny was expecting, he gripped her shoulders and turned her towards the light. "The bastards hurt you." He looked her up and down, inspecting her for more damage. "What did they do to you? For pity's sake, what did they do?"

"I think one of them must have hit me and they tied me up." She put a hand up to shade her eyes – the brightness hurt them. She winced as her fingers touched the bruise blooming there. Her shoulder felt sore and stiff, too.

"Is that all? Jenny, you must tell me. Is that all?"

"Is that not enough?" Jenny could see the agonised expression on Sam's face. Her voice softened. "No, Sam, they didn't do anythin' else. But who are they? What did they want me for?"

"Come on, love." Sam put his arm gently around Jenny and led her towards the warehouse door.

Jenny saw two Chinese men in handcuffs being led towards the open back doors of a large van. "That's him! That's the bugger that grabbed me."

Before the policeman leading First Son Wang was aware of what was happening, Sam Castle had stepped up and punched the Chinaman low in the belly. He doubled up in agony. Then Mike Atkinson was pulling Sam away.

"Sir!" He didn't blame Sam for what he'd done, but he couldn't let it happen again. "Sam!"

Sam seemed to come to his senses for he released his hands from angry fists and turned his back on the prisoner.

"Get him out of here," Mike told the startled policeman. "Nothing happened, understand?"

"I don't know what you mean, sarge," the policeman said blandly. "I think Mr Wang must have tripped or something."

When Mike turned back towards his boss, Sam was getting into his car with Jenny. He drove off with exaggerated care, nodding his thanks to Mike as he passed him.

* * * * * * * * * *

Armstrong let out a long sigh as May finished the retelling. "Well the police have got them at last. Let's hope you hear no more of them. And Jenny? How did she take it?" he asked.

"I think she was badly scared but she was putting on a brave face for Sam's sake. I would never have forgiven myself if anything bad had happened to her." May was still deeply shaken by the whole affair but, like Jenny, was determined not to make a fuss about it.

"And Simon Stanley." May had told Armstrong about the agreement they had reached. "I always liked that lad. There was something about him out of the ordinary, I thought." May had told Armstrong the truth. "But who'd have guessed he was Mr Adam's son? I knew he thought a lot of him but I never ever suspected anything like that. I'm glad he's willing to take on the responsibility of the company. It must be a load off your mind, lass."

"Yes, James, it is. But I don't know why Adam didn't mention him in his will. He should have left the company to Simon if he didn't think Jonathan was capable of running it."

"He wanted Bobby to have it. It was his heritage from his great-grandfather, Sir Robert," Armstrong said quietly.

May sighed and said nothing. It all seemed so long ago, so far in the past as to be only a distant memory, yet at the same time she could still feel the warmth of her child in her arms, his breath on her cheek.

It seemed as if Armstrong sensed what May was feeling for he put his arm round her shoulders and hugged her. "Aye, well," was all he said.

With an effort May put all these thoughts away and remembered the box that was still in the car. "Mr Mawson gave me the things from Adam's safe. Will you help me to go through them, James?"

"I don't know. There'll be personal stuff there I expect – private things, like."

"There can be nothing I wouldn't want you to know about. Please?"

"I'll fetch it then, and we'll do it now. OK?"

Armstrong carried the heavy box into the cottage kitchen and sat it on the table. He stood back as May unsealed the lid and looked inside. On the top were five thick soft-backed notebooks filled with Adam Lee's small, neat writing. They appeared to be journals of some sort. May leafed through and read bits at random. She found they mostly concerned business meetings but there was one that related the details of a social event, right down to what Angela had worn:

*Annual Chamber of Commerce dinner tonight. Angela wore the diamond necklace and a pale blue silk dress. She looked beautiful. I am a very lucky man. Chairman of Kings Shipbuilders wants a meeting. Wonder what that is about?*

May thumbed through a few more pages until Jonathan's name seemed to jump out at her. She read:

*Jonathan admitted he owes several thousand pounds (he wouldn't say exactly) to Tony Lyons the bookmaker. He's a fool to keep betting on the horses. Should I pay this debt as I have the previous ones? Remember to speak to SS re new charter to Poland.*

May closed the book feeling almost embarrassed, as if she had eavesdropped on a private conversation. She remembered Adam telling her Jonathan gambled. She wondered whether he had paid Tony Lyons what was owed.

"I remember him writing in these books." Armstrong picked up one of the journals and looked at the dates printed on the spine. "I'll put them onto the bookshelf in the sitting room, shall I?" Armstrong asked. "You'll likely want to read them through sometime."

"Oh, I don't know whether that would be right. They seem to be Adam's diaries."

"Maybe one day, then."

"Maybe." May was unsure if she wanted to invade her father-in-law's privacy. She realised they would make fascinating reading, though, and provide an insight into the man. And maybe about Jonathan. Adam had tried to tell her things she hadn't understood at the time – hadn't wanted to understand she now acknowledged to herself.

She went back to the box as Armstrong stacked the journals on a shelf and took out a folder where loose papers had been carefully filed. Inside were birth, marriage and death certificates going back over many years. She put them to one side – they would be interesting to look at some time, too. Then she had a thought and picked them up again, leafing quickly through until she came to a copy certificate of Simon Stanley's birth. There was no father mentioned. How sad, May thought, for both Simon and Adam. But it proved Adam's interest in his firstborn son.

In the bottom of the box was Angela's jewellery case. May lifted it out.

"Miss Angela had some lovely things," Armstrong said, coming back into the room seeing what May had found. "They'll be very valuable I should think."

May was loath to open it but she slowly lifted the lid. Inside were other, smaller, boxes containing, May guessed, Angela's necklaces, bracelets and rings. She opened the smallest box and inside found the emerald ring Angela always wore, together with her wedding ring. They must have been removed from her body after the accident. May snapped the box shut unwilling to stir the memories they evoked. She wondered what she would do with it all. She would have to decide sometime soon.

May was about to close the jewellery case lid when a padded envelope caught her eye. She lifted it out and read the writing on it: 'Items from Mrs May Lee's room.' She tipped the contents out onto the kitchen table. There was the blue box containing the pearl earrings Adam had given her. She'd last worn them for his funeral then put them away; she had worn simple gold studs ever since. The red leather ring-box would hold the diamond engagement ring

Jonathan had given her in Hong Sing what seemed like a lifetime ago. She opened the box.

"It's a beautiful ring," Armstrong said taking the box from May and holding it up to the window for the sun's rays to send sparks from the diamonds. "Why don't you wear it? It's a shame for it to be shut away."

May hesitated for a moment before reaching out and taking it from the box. She slipped it onto her finger alongside the narrow gold wedding-band.

"It is a lovely ring. I will wear it and remember Jonathan." She turned back to the table to pick up a small manilla envelope – the kind that bills come in. There was writing on the front: *'Dear Mrs Lee, The person packing your things came across this in your son's bed, caught in the sheets. Kind regards, Jane Evans (Mr Mawson's secretary).'*

Puzzled, May lifted the lightly sealed flap and emptied the contents into her hand. She looked down at what lay there. The world around her receded into greyness and she heard a rushing sound in her head, like a river flowing swiftly over rocks. A wave of nausea welled up from somewhere deep inside as her legs lost the power to support her. She collapsed onto a chair, put her head on the table and began to cry with deep, wracking sobs.

"Good God, lass. What is it?" Armstrong was beside her in two long strides. "Are you ill?" Gently he lifted her head and eased her back from the table. He brushed the hair back to see her face contorted in agony, her black eyes flowing with tears and ringed in red. She did not seem to see him.

"May, what is it? Can't you tell me?" Armstrong lifted her hands to cradle them in his own to try to give her some sort of comfort. They were both curled into tight fists, but from one a thin trickle of blood stained the pale skin.

"You've hurt yourself. Here now, lass, let's have a look. I'll bathe it for you and you'll be right as rain." Carefully he peeled back May's fingers. A broken chain slid out and coiled itself, like a serpent, on the stone flags of the kitchen floor. He hardly noticed it as all his attention was taken by something gold embedded in the soft flesh of her palm. Ever so gently, he eased it out, sucking in his breath with shock as he recognised it: the golden dragon.

Armstrong scanned the words of explanation written on the envelope, tears springing into his own eyes. Practicality returned and he reached into a drawer for a clean cloth and soaked it with water to dab May's hand. The puncture mark wasn't deep and had already stopped bleeding but May seemed to be stuck in some sort of limbo. Not knowing what else to do he brewed two strong mugs of tea. He took a deep swallow of his before offering the other to May. She took it in unsteady hands and, for the second time in as many days, shuddered at the sickly sweet taste.

Either the tea or the pain from her hand brought May back from wherever her mind had temporarily retreated. She took a huge, unsteady breath. "Where is it?" she asked. Armstrong placed the golden dragon gently in the palm of her uninjured hand. "Bobby had it," she told him. "Bobby had it all the time." May looked up at Armstrong.

"Aye, it seems he did. It always fascinated him, didn't it?"

"That night, the last night, he made me tell him the story. He wouldn't let me go until I had." May remembered the little boy's favourite trick of catching hold of the charm as it dangled from the chain around his mother's neck. He would hang on to it until she relented and told him how his grandmother in China and her mother before had hidden it from their husbands and the marauding Red Guards. "The chain must have broken and I didn't notice." May remembered her frantic search of the house when she had discovered the golden dragon was missing. "I looked all round his room. I couldn't find it." She raised her head in shock. "But why did Bobby die when the dragon, our good fortune, wasn't lost? Why did they all die, James?"

"It was never the dragon, lass. Now was it?" Armstrong asked softly. "How could it be?" May began to protest but he silenced her. "Oh aye. I know you believed in all that superstition, but that's all it was – superstition: a belief in this thing's supernatural powers that couldn't be real. I'll tell you something I've kept to meself until now." He stood up and began to pace up and down the small room. "It was them Wangs. That's who caused the accident right enough. Sam knew, but there was no proof – nothing to tie them in." He went back and knelt in front of May. "We'll likely never know for one hundred percent sure, but Sam and me – we're as sure as can be."

It took a long time to sink into May's uncomprehending mind. She hadn't lost the golden dragon at all. The accident wasn't her fault – good fortune, in the form of the amulet, hadn't deserted them – it was outside forces: those wielded by David Wang. David Wang had murdered her family!

The horror of it made May feel as though she was going to vomit, but she swallowed the bile and vowed to herself she would do everything in her power to see him pay for what he'd done. His treachery, instead of weakening her as he had wanted, strengthened her. She felt the vitality that had been drained from her begin to flow back. Bobby, Jonathan and Angela were dead; gone from her forever. May felt the last frail thread that had tied her to them dissolve and free her. For the first time she truly accepted what fate had decreed.

She leant down and picked the broken chain from the floor and put it, with the golden dragon, back into the envelope. "I'm going to take this to be mended. Come on, James, let's get the rest of this lot tidied up."

Armstrong, who had been watching as May struggled to come to terms with her discovery, straightened his shoulders. "Aye, we'd better get it done. What have you got in the fridge? I'll make us something nice for supper."

## Chapter Twenty Seven

A knock on May's kitchen door was followed by Fiona cheerfully calling out, "Get the kettle on, I'm parched."

"Come in, Fiona. I'm pleased to see you. I was going to telephone you. Have you heard anything from Kevin Graham about the owl?" May asked as she filled the electric kettle and switched it on. She spooned coffee grounds into a cafetiere and waited for the water to boil.

"That's the main purpose of the visit. He tried to get in touch with you yesterday and the day before but couldn't, so he phoned me. The owl's ready to be released."

The kettle switched itself off with a click as the water boiled. May waited a few seconds before pouring hot water onto the coffee grounds. She reached into a cupboard for two mugs and took the milk-jug out of the fridge.

"That's good news." May began to pour the coffee. "When?"

Fiona added milk then mooched around the kitchen looking for something to eat. She found three slices of sponge cake in a tin. "Can I have a piece of cake?" May nodded. "Do you want some?" Fiona asked. May said she did and Fiona put two slices of May's homemade cake onto a plate and brought it to the table. She sat down and began to devour the cake with every sign of deep enjoyment.

"Kevin said the sooner the owl is released the better. This evening would be good. Is that OK with you? You must be there, too." Fiona looked around the tidy, homely kitchen. She marvelled that May who, by her own admission, had not been at all domesticated until the last couple of years, had created such a lovely home. It was somewhere Fiona always felt comfortable and welcome.

"I'm all yours this evening. I said I'd go to Ravendale Farm this afternoon. It's ages since I saw Mrs B. They've been busy since lambing."

Fiona laughed. "Yes, I know. You're becoming quite the country-girl, aren't you? Right. I'll call for you about fiveish. We'll pick up Kevin and the owl, drive back to where I found it, release it and drive Kevin back. Does that fit in with your busy social life?"

"Aye. Grand." May imitated the local accent, making quite a good job of it apart from not quite being able to roll the 'r', laughing as her friend grimaced.

\* \* \* \* \* \* \* \* \* \*

May got out of her Mini in the yard at Ravendale. The sun was warm here where there was shelter from the wind. Three large, sleek lambs came bounding over, leaping and butting each other as they vied for her attention. May pushed her way past them and into the kitchen.

"Make sure you shut the door or the terrible trio will be in here begging for their feed," Mrs B shouted.

"Hello, Mrs B," May called out. "It's me."

"May," said Mrs B, coming over and enfolding May in her arms. "It's such a long time since we saw you." She held May away and looked her up and down. "Well, you look fine, I must say."

"I'm very well, thank you."

"Our Jim told us about you finding that dragon necklace thing and that you were right upset, too."

"Yes, I was, but I'm all right now."

Mrs B was putting a flask and a plastic box of what looked like buttered scones, into a bag. "I've got to take John and the lad some bait, to put them on till they get their dinner. They're still out in the top pasture. Fancy a walk? You can tell me all the gossip."

A walk out in the fresh air was just what May needed. Last night she had lain awake in her bed as memories and regrets chased each other through her head. She'd watched the three-quarter moon as it travelled across the sky to hide behind the fells, before eventually falling into a light sleep. She realised she'd sent Alex away needlessly and denied herself the chance of a little happiness. But the thought of his being hurt in some way had been too much for her to bear. The fact that she herself had hurt him hadn't crossed her mind. Now she realised it had all been for nothing. Before sleep overtook her, May decided she must go to see Alex, apologise to him and ask for another chance. She unburdened herself to Mrs B.

"Well! That's quite a story. The sooner you go to see that lad the better. That's what I think."

"That's what I think, too. I'll go tomorrow," May said.

\* \* \* \* \* \* \* \* \* \*

Fiona pulled her car into the side of the road. She got out followed by May and Kevin Graham. "This is about where I found the owl," she told Kevin.

"Aye, best to release him in his own territory." He went to the car-boot and carefully opened the box that sat inside. He took the owl in gentle hands, one gloved to protect him from the strong, killing talons. He stroked the creature's pale feathers. He's a lovely bird, Mrs Vet, just young." He held the owl out to Fiona. "Do you want to release him?"

"Will you do it? You're the expert. Anyway, you've got the glove on," Fiona pointed out with a grin.

Kevin looked up and down the road then listened for any traffic, tilting his head from side to side, which reminded May even more of a bird. The evening was silent, the light fading fast. He lifted his arms and opened his hands. The owl stretched out its wings then seemed to float into the air. It rose into the sky then flew silently into the woodland, vanishing like a ghost among the trees. Kevin sighed in satisfaction. "It's great seeing them go like that. It's a privilege, you know, helping them, getting them back to health. We've done all we can here. You'll be ready for the off, Mrs Vet. Come on, get me home. My supper'll be ready soon." He climbed back into the car, Fiona and May following.

"Next time anyone brings me a bird that needs nursed back to health I'll send it to you," Fiona told him as she pulled the car back onto the road and accelerated away.

"Not much point doing that, Mrs Vet. I won't be able to take it," Kevin told her gruffly.

"Why's that?"

"The neighbours have started complaining. And the daughter-in-law's expecting and she wants somewhere for the bairn to play. I can't say I blame her, really. The garden's not a suitable place to keep so many birds. I've agreed to move them off, a.s.a.p."

"That's too bad. I'm sorry." Fiona was sympathetic.

"Aye, so am I. It was something that grew out of nothing, you see. One injured bird led to two and then a dozen and so on. It's become an eyesore, I've got to admit."

"Where will you put them?" May asked.

"Your guess is as good as mine."

"Can't you put out an appeal – get someone to house them for you?" Fiona said.

"I could, but who'd want to take on the responsibility? It's a damn shame, though."

"If you could find somewhere else, would you still carry on?" May asked.

"Of course I would, but it's a big 'if'. It's the cost you see. All the money I've got, as well as what's donated, goes on food. I can't afford to pay the sort of rent someone would want in this area."

"I'll keep an eye out when I'm on my rounds and ask about if you like. I'll let you know if I hear anything," Fiona offered.

"That'll be just the job. You can pull in here," Kevin said as they neared a pub. "That's my lad's car. He can buy me a pint and give me a lift home. Ta-ra, lasses. See ya sometime." Kevin got out and strolled over to the pub's back door and disappeared inside. Fiona turned the car round then headed back towards Netherthwaite. She drove in silence for a few miles.

Eventually May said, "It's not like you to be so quiet. Is there anything the matter?"

"No, I'm just thinking about what Kevin said. D'you know, I've an idea where he could move the birds to if we could get permission. There are some redundant farm buildings and a tumble-down cottage along with a couple of fields."

"Where is it? Do you know who owns it?" May's interest was sparked.

"It's up behind Laurel Bank where my aunt and uncle live. They own it. It hasn't been used for years. I used to play there with my cousins."

"Do you think they would allow Kevin to keep his birds there?"

"I don't know, but there's no harm in asking, is there? Trouble is," Fiona said as she braked to a stop outside Fellbeck Cottage, "I'm up to the eyebrows with work for the next few days. I couldn't spare any time until next week. I don't suppose you'd be interested in contacting them, would you?" she asked hopefully.

"Well..." May was doubtful about her abilities of persuasion. It wasn't something she knew a great deal about apart from watching the blue tits that came to the feeder in the garden and the blackbird that sang so sweetly in the branches of the hawthorn. If these people asked questions she wasn't in the least qualified to answer them. "I suppose I could make enquiries. Ask if they would consider such a project." Suddenly May made up her mind. For quite some time she'd been trying to think what she could do; she didn't want to waste her days in idleness. Helping Kevin Graham set up a new site for his bird sanctuary, if he agreed to accept her help, promised to be very interesting. "Yes. Yes, I will do it. Give me their name and the phone number and I'll ring them tomorrow."

"But you know them already," Fiona told May. "They are Alex's parents, Andrew and Caroline Pennington-Martin." Fiona scrabbled in the glove-box for pencil and paper then wrote down a telephone number. She didn't notice, in the dark, May's look of consternation. "They'll be delighted to hear from you, I'm sure. Have you seen much of Alex recently? I haven't spoken to him for ages."

"Er, no, I haven't."

"Well then, maybe you'll kill two birds with one stone." Fiona let out a peal of laughter. "An unfortunate choice of words, in the circumstances, but you know what I mean."

May got out of the car and Fiona drove off, still giggling at her inadvertent joke.

\* \* \* \* \* \* \* \* \* \*

The next morning May phoned Andrew Pennington-Martin and asked if she could come to see him. He seemed, as Fiona had predicted, pleased to hear from her, and asked her to come over that afternoon. But first, May wanted to see Alex. She drove over to the gallery at Beckthwaite trying to think what she would say to him.

The morning was bright and clear and already warming into what promised to be a glorious day. Flowers bloomed in the hedgerows and birds sang songs to their mates. A delicate haze of green covered the larch trees on the fellside above Beckthwaite. May drove slowly, drinking in the beauty all around.

She'd taken her time getting ready, trying on and discarding several outfits: jeans and sweater – too casual; black trousers and shirt – too smart; red straight skirt – too bright. In the end she chose a flower-sprigged dress in soft lilacs and greens and threw a jersey over her shoulders in case it got cold. Her long, black hair had been cut short, feathered to frame her face in a very flattering style. A touch of pale pink lipstick was the only cosmetic she allowed herself. She looked in the mirror and almost went to change back into jeans again. What was she doing, dressing to please a man: to attract a man, if she was honest with herself?

The gallery was quiet with only one or two people strolling round. May asked the receptionist for Alex. The girl looked at her unsmilingly, seeming to sum up May's appearance and finding it wanting.

"He's not here."

May was disappointed but tried not to let it show. "Do you know when he will be back?"

"No," the girl replied, curt to the point of rudeness. She returned her attention to the papers on her desk, dismissing May. May sighed to herself in disappointment as she walked slowly back to the car. She looked out over the valley towards Ravendale Farm, remembering the first day she had met Alex and how he stood beside her on the balcony enjoying the view.

A movement in the lower part of the garden caught May's eye. It was Alex, on his knees, fingers in the soil rooting out weeds from the flowerbed. May stood, watching him, willing him to look up and come to her. He didn't seem to sense her presence and carried on with his task. Hesitantly May walked towards him.

"Hello, Alex."

Alex hadn't heard her approach, hadn't had time to assume a look of indifference and May saw his eyes light up at the sight of her. Quickly, he changed his expression to one of polite interest.

"Oh, it's you, May. What brings you here on this lovely morning?"

"I came to see you," May said softly.

"I would have thought I'd be the last person you'd come looking for. You made that perfectly clear the last time we met."

"I'm sorry."

"No, it's me who's sorry. Sorry for wasting my time with you." He resumed his weed-pulling.

"I was wrong: wrong to send you away like that." Alex didn't respond to the tentative apology. "You don't understand..." This wasn't going how May had planned. This wasn't the conversation she had rehearsed in her head. Alex jumped up putting his muddy hands on his hips and looked at her with disdain.

"Oh, I understand perfectly, May. You made it very clear. There was no room for misunderstanding."

"But it's different now."

"What's different? I'm the same person as the one you didn't want. You can't come here all misty-eyed and sweet and expect me to come running like a lap-dog. It just isn't going to happen."

"But…"

"But nothing. Go away, I'm busy." Alex picked up the bucket he'd filled with weeds and strode away to dump it in the compost heap.

Hurt and disappointment bit into May's heart. The exact hurt and disappointment she'd inflicted on Alex only a few weeks ago she realised. What had she done? How could she have? She wanted to go after him, make him listen, make him understand why she had sent him away, but she could see now: his pain was still too raw. But she was determined she wouldn't give up so easily. She'd wait for an opportunity when he would be willing to listen.

* * * * * * * * * *

"Come in, come in. How lovely to see you." The welcome from Andrew Pennington-Martin couldn't have been more different than the one she'd received from his son. "My wife is visiting our daughter in Carlisle, I'm afraid, so it's only myself here today. Come and sit on the terrace, it's lovely out there."

They sat on rattan chairs, the soft cushions worn and shabby after many years' use. Andrew poured glasses of homemade lemonade and sat back enjoying the view across the lake. Bees hummed in the purple flowers dripping from the gnarled branches of a venerable wisteria which must have climbed up the side of the house for generations. They chatted easily about Andrew's daughter, Hazel and her children, about how May was settling into the cottage, about the Bells at Ravendale Farm.

"Mr Pennington-Martin…" May began.

"Please call me Andrew. Pennington-Martin is such a mouthful," he said, laughing.

"Thank you. Andrew – Fiona suggested I came to see you."

"Ah, Fiona. Wonderful girl."

"Yes, she's a very good friend. It's about what she calls 'the old farm'."

"The old farm?" Andrew frowned, trying to think where she meant.

"Fiona said she used to play there with her cousins," May explained.

Andrew's face cleared as he recalled the place. "Oh, did she now. A bunch of young rascals they were, roaming the countryside from dawn to dusk. Yes, I know where you mean. But what about it? It's a wreck of a place, has been for years."

May explained about Kevin Graham and the bird sanctuary. Andrew listened, nodding from time to time with interest. As May feared, he asked her things she couldn't answer, but she promised she could find out and let him know.

"It would be better if this Graham chap could come over to have a look at the place himself and give me the chance to get the measure of the man. If it was only a question of him moving his birds up here, I don't think there'd be a problem – I'd even let him have it at a very reasonable rent, assuming we hit it off. Yes?"

"That would be marvellous."

"But hold your horses, there's a bit more to it than that. As I said, the place is in a dreadful state. It would take a great deal of time and money to get it up and running, to say nothing about planning permission as well as some sort of approval from the RSPB or whoever has to rubber-stamp these things."

"I will ask Kevin about getting permission to keep his birds there and my solicitor will know about everything else."

"The finance?" Andrew reminded her. "The cost will be enormous. Do you know of anyone willing to invest in such a project? I'm afraid I wouldn't be able to help."

"I think I do." May smiled to herself knowing that at last she could put some of her legacy to good use. "I think I know someone."

"Jolly good. Fetch Graham over and I'll take you both to see the old farm. By the way, it's called Nether Grange."

May took her leave, promising to come back soon, excitement at the new venture acting as a balm on her wounded heart.

\* \* \* \* \* \* \* \* \*

Kevin Graham listened carefully as May told him about Nether Grange. He was standing in front of a rickety cage that held three young jackdaws who hopped around cawing and peering at the two people, their grey-feathered heads tipping from one side to another as if they understood what was being said.

"Aye. I'll come and look at the spot, right enough – tell his lordship."

"I don't think he's a lordship, Kevin," May said.

"I know that, but he's as good as, I reckon. The big trouble is the money. Where's that to come from? I've only got a pension and that doesn't stretch very far. From what you say it's going to take a lot of cash to get the place up and running. Me and me lad can do a fair amount of the work and he's got a mate that's a good builder." Kevin was trying not to get excited at the thought of having a new place for the bird sanctuary, it might yet fall through, but already he was talking practicalities.

"I think I know where the money will come from," May told him.

"And where might that be? The Emperor of China?"

"China doesn't have an emperor any more," May said, missing the irony in Kevin's voice. "The person I am thinking of may wish to remain anom... amon... anny..." May was having problems with pronunciation and Kevin laughed.

"Anonymous?" he suggested.

"Yes. That. And I'd very much like to help, too. Will you let me? And teach me about birds?"

"If you can see to the paperwork and do the running around arranging this, that and the next thing, that would be spot-on. And as for birds – love for wild creatures has to come from inside, from the heart. Do you think you have it?"

"I don't know," May had to admit. "When I was growing up we ate any wild animals and birds we could find. We kept chickens which I quite liked, and pigs which scared me."

Kevin shrugged. "At least it's a start, but don't go eating any, will you?"

May couldn't help but laugh at his expression and shook her head.

## Chapter Twenty Eight

"I think you're jumping into this too quickly. Give yourself time to think about it a bit more," Armstrong said. He let out a long piercing whistle and a dog, which seemed to have little control over his long legs, came bounding over to him. "Stay close, Finn. Good lad." The dog responded by putting his wet nose against his master's hand and licking it wetly. "Give over, you daft beggar." But he smiled at the show of affection and stroked the young dog's head. His coat resembled steel-wool but was soft and warm beneath the man's square hand.

Finn was a recently acquired pet for Armstrong. Tess, the collie at Ravendale Farm, had had an illicit romance with, they suspected, a greyhound and had, in due course, produced two long-nosed, long-legged puppies. One had found a home immediately but the other was sickly and failed to thrive. Mrs B had lavished all her care on him and gradually he began to grow but he would always be small. She had persuaded her brother to take him on and he had somewhat reluctantly agreed. Finn proved to have very winning ways and Armstrong had taken to the young dog.

May and Armstrong walked on along the rough path beside a beck, the clear green waters flowing noisily over its stony bed. An arched packhorse bridge carried them over the beck and onto the open fellside. Finn trotted ahead, exploring every hump and hollow but always keeping an eye on his two companions. Armstrong paused to catch his breath after the steep climb. He looked back up the valley to the shimmering blue of Derwentwater.

It was early June and the air was still fresh, yet to feel the humid heat of full summer. The greens, painting the trees, hedges, fields and fells, were soft and delicate. White daisies speckled the pasture and already, in the stone-walled fields, grasses had grown long enough to sway in the light breeze. It was a perfect day for walking in the fells.

"What about here for our picnic," May suggested pointing to two flat boulders. Armstrong shrugged off the rucksack that held their lunch. They sat in companionable silence enjoying their sandwiches, the view, and Finn's antics. Armstrong came back to the subject of the bird sanctuary.

"Do you really think it's your sort of thing?"

"It's as much my sort of thing as anything else," May said. She was still feeling wounded by the news Fiona had given her the day before: Alex had given up his jobs at the gallery and gone away.

"I don't know what happened with you two," Fiona said. "I thought you were getting on so well – you both seemed happy when you were with each other. Then... finito."

"It was my fault. I sent him away," May told her miserably.

"But why? Was it too soon after Jonathan?"

"No, it wasn't that." Then the whole thing came tumbling out. When she told Fiona how Alex had turned her down when she went to see him after the golden dragon had turned up Fiona snorted in disgust.

"He always was stubborn. He'd cut his nose off to spite his face."

"I can be stubborn too," May said. "I'm not going to give up so easily. One day I'll get him to listen to me. Perhaps he'll change his mind when I tell him I sent him away because I was afraid for him."

Fiona sighed. "I don't think he has any plans to come back."

"Where has he gone? Do you know."

"Yes, didn't I say? He's gone to stay with his grandmother in the south of France. She retired there when her husband died and Alex's father took over the estate."

"Oh," May said, the taste of disappointment bitter in her mouth.

"Don't give up, though. You'll think of something.

What that 'something' could be, she had yet to discover. May turned her attention back to the present.

Armstrong poured coffee from a Thermos flask and handed it to May. She sipped thoughtfully bringing her mind back to their conversation. "The bird sanctuary does seem to be a very worthwhile project. I was very impressed with the way Kevin cares for them." May's voice became more animated as she talked. "I would never have believed anyone could care so much about wild creatures. It wasn't something I was brought up to think about."

"Oh, I'm not saying it isn't worthwhile." Armstrong threw a piece of biscuit to the dog. "All I'm saying is: are you really interested? It's a hell of a big thing to take on, you know. Once you start you can't suddenly give up. People will be depending on you."

"I am interested, James. I've been doing a lot of reading: finding out about other similar projects. And I don't propose to get involved with the birds myself, you know. Kevin's been trying to teach me about them but I know I'll never have a fraction of the knowledge he has. No, any work I do will be administration, I think. I've got an appointment with Tom Watson tomorrow. I'll see what he advises."

"Right. Just don't go doing anything you might regret."

"I won't. And I'll tell you what he says." May stood up and stretched.

Armstrong staggered to his feet, rubbing his bad leg that had stiffened as they sat. "Come on. Let's get on, then. My backside's gone to sleep sitting on this rock. Finn! Here, lad!"

* * * * * * * * * *

Tom Watson shook his head emphatically. "No. I must advise you most strongly against this."

"But..." May began.

Tom held up his hand. "I've listened to you May. Please hear me out." He waited a second or two before continuing, "There are several reasons I say this. First, and most important: you must not spend what promises to be a huge amount of money on property that belongs to someone else."

"But..." Tom's look silenced May. He reminded her of a particularly bossy teacher she'd had at school.

"Next: even if this scheme did get off the ground, what would happen if, and when, Kevin Graham cannot continue to look after the birds? And there are other obstacles piling up for you to overcome; I know there are stringent laws about protected species for a start."

"I've been doing some research on similar projects in other parts of the country. I know it would be possible to set something up here."

"But there's the question of ownership of the property. You say the present owner, Mr Pennington-Martin, is prepared to rent to you at a very low rate." May nodded. "But what if the situation changes? What if he sells? What will your position be then? You, of all people, must realise the consequences of the unforeseen."

May hesitated. "Maybe he would sell to me."

"Why would he want to do that? What's in it for him?"

"He seemed very interested when I talked to him about it. He said he'd loved birdwatching when he was a boy." Tom Watson looked sceptical. May continued, "I could ask him, see what he thinks."

"Why don't you do that? If he agrees, and you are still determined to go ahead, then I will advise you how to proceed. If he turns you down..." Tom shook his head. "There will be other places, far more suitable than this one appears to be."

May rose to leave. "Thank you for your help. I will be in touch again, soon." The steel of determination had hardened in her veins. She would see this through, whatever she had to do to achieve it. She had money, and money, she had learned from her father-in-law, was power.

Before she left Carlisle, May went to a little jewellery workshop Mrs B had told her about. When she handed the jeweller the golden dragon and its broken chain he murmured in admiration. "This is very unusual. Chinese, isn't it?"

"Yes. It was given to me by my mother. It has been in my family for many years. The chain broke and I thought I'd lost it."

The man examined it closely through the loupe he somehow held clenched in front of one eye. "Wear and tear," he pronounced. "One of the links has worn through. There are several more worn dangerously thin, too. You were very lucky not to have lost it. You need a new chain."

May chose a more sturdy one from the selection in the shop and the jeweller threaded it through the loop of the dragon's tail, again examining it to ensure it wasn't too worn. May left the shop, once more wearing her precious pendant. Even though she now acknowledged it held no mystical power, May felt renewed and protected with it round her neck, feeling its familiar presence against her skin.

Suddenly, she had a thought and turned, re-entering the shop, the bell jingling to announce her presence.

"Anything wrong, Miss?" the jeweller asked at May's reappearance.

"No. I just had a question I thought you might be able to help me with."

"I'll help you if I can, of course."

"I have some jewellery I want to sell. Do you know how I'd go about it?" May asked.

"That depends," he said. "What is it?"

"Some things that belonged to my mother-in-law," May replied, somewhat hesitantly. She wasn't sure yet whether it was something she really wanted to do.

"Why don't you bring them in," the man suggested. "I often break up old jewellery to make new pieces."

"Oh, I couldn't do that!" May was horrified at the thought of Angela's lovely things being torn apart.

"What exactly do you have?" he asked.

May went on to describe a spectacular necklace with unusual rectangular-cut diamonds she'd once seen Angela wear and had admired, and an emerald and diamond pedant she also remembered. The man suggested May take the collection to an auction house; they'd be able to value the pieces and advise May where best to sell them. May thanked him and left the shop.

* * * * * * * * * *

"Buy Nether Grange?" Andrew Pennington-Martin's deep, fruity voice boomed out. "Well, I never!"

"That is how my solicitor advised me to proceed," May said, bending the truth a little.

Alex's father peered at her, assessing her seriousness. "Can you afford it?"

"I don't know how much you're asking," May replied steadily.

"I didn't say I was selling," Andrew said, a twinkle appearing in his eye.

"I will pay whatever a fair valuation puts on the farm."

"Oh will you, now?" Andrew was amused and impressed by this young Chinese woman. "And if – I stress if – I decide to let you persuade me to sell, what assurance do I have that you will not develop the place into holiday homes and sell to people with more money than sense or taste?" Andrew asked as though he was laying the final trump card. He leaned forward, resting his arms across his thighs to hear her answer. May was at a loss for words. But, giving it some thought, she felt he had a valid point, and said so.

They were in the library at Laurel Bank which Andrew used as his office. From where she sat May could see her little car parked on the gravel beside the front door. They sat on high-backed leather armchairs, worn soft by many years' use, either side of the fire, unlit this warm day. A coffee pot and two chunky mugs sat on the low coffee table between them. Andrew sat up and poured the strong, fragrant coffee. He offered May a mug, taking the other and drinking with relish. He sat back and crossed his legs.

"Enough of this business talk. Let me speak as a friend. What I would advise you to do is to set up a trust of some sort and let the trust purchase the farm."

"You'll sell it to me? May asked eagerly.

"No, not to you personally. I will sell to the trust."

May beamed and, before she could consider what she was doing, jumped up and kissed Andrew firmly on his whiskery cheek. He laughed delightedly.

* * * * * * * * * *

The next months were an agony of applications, proposals, negotiations and interminable waiting. May filled some of the empty hours with her sketchbook, drawing scenes around Netherthwaite including several of her own cottage. She didn't, now, feel compelled to put the little boy in the blue dungarees and the red jersey into the composition.

## Chapter Twenty Nine

One quiet afternoon May picked up one of Adam's journals from the bookshelf in the sitting room. In the weeks since she'd found them she'd thought about them many times, wondering if they held secrets or just so much trivia. Well, she told herself, there is only one way to find out. So, settled in a garden chair in the dappled shade of a silver birch tree, May opened the first book.

Over the following days May discovered Adam's growing unease about Jonathan; how he discovered his son's addiction to gambling and his disturbing preference for young men and how Adam had kept it all from Angela. Adam's heartbreak that he would never be a grandfather was written about; his growing disillusionment in Jonathan's conduct; his fear it would bring dishonour on his family.

Adam had agonised over whether he should tell Simon he was his father; set him up as his heir. Always Simon was referred to as SS, but now May knew who Adam had meant.

Then May read how Adam had blackmailed – there was no other word for it – Jonathan into marrying; how she had been chosen, cold-bloodedly, as the perfect bride. Anger as well as sadness filled May as she discovered the true reasons for her being brought to England, for being taken away from her parents and the path of life she had been happily following in China.

Then her name began to appear in the entries. Adam wrote of his growing regard for her and his joy in having the grandson he had once been certain he would never have. Again, Jonathan's failure to live up to his promises to give up his gambling had disappointed his father.

It took some time before the implications of what she had read sunk in. It wasn't that Jonathan didn't want her, that there was something wrong with her to drive him away from loving her. It was that Jonathan didn't want any woman. How must he have felt having to make love to her on their wedding night, fulfilling the unwelcome duty he must make his body perform? And how fortuitous, for him, she became pregnant so quickly.

She wasn't unlovable – which was what she had come to believe.

It wasn't something in her that Jonathan had shied away from. Just because he wasn't capable of loving her didn't mean no-one could love her. Once again May found herself mourning Jonathan; mourning the man he was never allowed to be.

She remembered how life had been back in the market town close to where she had been raised. She could picture the scene when the market was in full swing. For the first time in a long time she missed the noise, smells and colour of her homeland.

\* \* \* \* \* \* \* \* \* \*

Hong Sing on market day was bustling: vendors shouting the quality of their wares, customers elbowing each other aside to get to the best bargains.

The air was thick with the humid heat of summer. The smells of rotting vegetables, fresh dung from pigs and poultry, the sharp tang of blood dripping from sides of beef and pig meat, and the fragrant scent of freshly cooking noodles and rice, mingled to hang over the market place. Flies buzzed and swarmed in green metallic sheets on the dung and the meat and were snapped at by the hens, ducks and geese crowded into their bamboo cages, always on the lookout for a tasty morsel, blissfully unaware that death awaited them before the end of the day.

The noise was unbelievable as shouts and cries from the market folk drawing attention to their wares rose above the chattering and laughing crowds thronging the market place. Stalls were crowded in rows, each one huddled against the next, proximity not necessarily bringing good fellowship. There were farmers selling pigs which would be weighed on the great scales, their cost being calculated by weight. The beasts grunted and resisted as they were driven unwillingly onto the scales by the pig-men when they got a customer. Surrounding them was a sea of dung and urine. Next door was the sweet potato seller and in front of her was the vegetable woman. Further along the row the meat stall owner cut great chunks, or small ones, from the carcasses hanging from hooks on the frame around his concrete counter, as his customers required. Nearby were cages of chickens, so closely packed at the start of the day that they could hardly move. As the day wore on and more were sold, the ones left had room to fight and peck each other. In one cage were geese that the children made a game of teasing so the creatures would crane their necks between the bamboo bars and hiss threateningly. Then there were baskets heaped with rice and nuts next to the fresh noodle-stand where customers consumed bowls of steaming noodles or rice, sitting on the narrowest of wooden slats.

Both men and women wore similar baggy grey cotton trousers, most of them rolled up to the knees in the hot weather, but the blouses the women wore bloomed like a garden of exotic flowers in colours that were as loud as the crowds.

At the end of the day unsold goods were packed away in their baskets and taken home again on their carrying poles.

* * * * * * * * * *

It seemed to May like a scene from another existence. It was another existence. It was in the past, a picture preserved forever in a corner of her mind. May sighed, but not sadly, as for the last time she locked the memory of Jonathan and their short, ill-starred marriage in the deepest reaches of her heart knowing now, finally, the whole truth.

## Chapter Thirty

The Nether Grange Wildlife Trust was established with Andrew Pennington-Martin as one of its trustees. Kevin Graham accepted, without asking any questions, the story of the anonymous investor from Newcastle. May suggested inviting Simon Stanley to be one of the other trustees. Kevin, of course, deduced that this was the secret investor. May was more than happy to continue to let him think it.

Gradually, with a great deal of hard labour, the ground was cleared and levelled and Kevin and his son, Sid, began to erect the cages in which the birds would be kept. Concrete walkways were laid, the noisy motor of the concrete mixer providing an ever-present background din to all proceedings. A small mechanical digger was hired to dig trenches for new drainage to be put in and an electric power cable to be laid underground. Andrew had suggested the old cottage be renovated to provide living accommodation for Kevin. An office was included as well as storerooms, food preparation rooms and a treatment room for sick and injured birds. Kevin declared that he must have died and gone to heaven. It far exceeded any dreams he had dared have.

When Armstrong saw May so determined and excited he relented. He did all he could to support and encourage her when bureaucracy threatened to undermine all the plans. Most days he and Finn could be found at Nether Grange, lending a hand somewhere or other. He couldn't help but be impressed by the way May took advice, honed and improved the suggestions made. He thought asking Simon Stanley to be a trustee was a master stroke. It also meant May was still connected to the shipping company, as well as maintaining the last remaining link with Adam Lee.

* * * * * * * * * *

In December the work slowed to a standstill. Since November they had been battling against wet conditions and now the freezing temperatures made it impossible to continue. With Christmas on the horizon Kevin suggested they call a complete halt until the festive season was over. He had a grandson now and wanted to spend a little time with the baby. His daughter-in-law had been more relaxed since she had learned she would soon have Kevin and his birds off her hands. May thought Kevin was looking tired. Seeing to the renovations as well as looking after his birds was taking its toll. It would do him good to slow down for a little while.

May was at home kicking her heels when Fiona called and suggested a night out. May said she wasn't sure she wanted to socialise.

"You can't shut yourself away forever, May. You're a young woman, act like one." Fiona sounded exasperated.

"You're right." May could see Fiona had a point. "I would be happy to go out with you."

"How about tomorrow? It's the practice's Christmas party. Please come."

"I'd like that. It'll be nice to see your father again. And everyone else, of course."

"Right. It's a date. Seven thirty at the Cumbrian Hotel in town. Don't be late or we'll start without you," Fiona joked and May laughed at her friend's high spirits. They hadn't seen each other for over a month and it would be good to meet up.

The foyer of the hotel was milling with people taking off coats and gloves and calling greetings to others as they came in, faces bright from the cold. May had chosen to wear black silk trousers and a long red tunic embroidered with black thread. The golden dragon round her neck reflected the multi-coloured lights hung on the large Christmas tree just inside the entrance. May touched the dragon, unconsciously seeking the confidence it always gave her.

"May! Over here. May!" Fiona's voice rose above the hubbub and May wove her way towards her. Fiona kissed May's cheek. "Wow. Look at you. You should dress up more often." Without giving May time to return the compliment she introduced the people she was with. "I'm sure you remember Rob, our partner at the surgery. And this is Will and Kathryn."

Before they'd had time to exchange no more than the customary pleasantries Fiona was leading the way into the bar. "Grab a table, you lot, and I'll see to the drinks.

The evening was noisy and fun and May enjoyed herself enormously. She'd never experienced anything quite like it. Before they sat down to eat Kathryn excused herself and joined another group. Until then, May had assumed she and Will were together. May looked at Fiona with a question in her eyes, realising she had been set up with a date for the evening. In reply Fiona just raised her eyebrows and grinned. May let herself relax and enjoy the party.

Next morning Fiona rang May. "So, how did it go with the gorgeous Will?" she asked without preliminaries.

"Whatever do you mean, Fiona?" May replied with a question of her own.

"You know. I saw you leave together."

"He saw me to my car, and I came home."

"Alone?" Fiona asked.

"Alone," May replied. "You weren't matchmaking by any chance, were you?"

"The thought never crossed my mind," Fiona said innocently.

"He asked for my phone number and he said he'd ring."

"I suppose that's something, then. But now I've got you in the partying mood, what about New Year's Eve? Have you anything arranged?"

"Jenny and Sam are coming over. There's a 'do' at the village hall and they thought New Year's Eve at a 'country bash' would be a laugh – that's how Jenny put it, at least."

"Sounds fun. Got room for me and Rob?"

"Mrs B still has some tickets left, I know. I'll get two for you."

"Jolly good show. Have to rush now, talk to you soon." Fiona was gone before May could make any comment.

Christmas Day, as usual, was spent at Ravendale Farm with all of the Bells and James Armstrong. It was a dull, murky day, never seeming to get completely daylight. The farmhouse, in contrast, was awash with Christmas lights, decorations, food, laughter and gifts, hugs and kisses under the mistletoe: Robin and Tom Bell made the most of May unknowingly standing underneath it to the amusement of their families. She blushed deeply as they kissed her thoroughly then laughed with the rest of them when Mrs B pointed out to her the white-berried wreath hanging from the beam.

Less than a week later the New Year's Eve dance was in full swing. May looked around at the faces of all her friends: Mrs B presided over the buffet table along with other ladies of the WI, John Bell with his sons and their wives filled a large table near the stage where a local band played. Fiona and Rob were dancing. For the very first time, May realised how close they'd become. She'd thought they were only friends, partners in the veterinary practice, but she could see it was far more than that now. James Armstrong and Sam were deep in conversation. Jenny regaled May with stories about the museum art gallery where she worked on restoration projects. Life as a wife and mother in Newcastle seemed, to May, like a hundred years ago and China and her parents and childhood friends a million miles away.

May sat in happy harmony with her friends, laughing at Jenny's comments. Then she saw Alex. He came in with a girl; May recognised her as the receptionist at the gallery where once Alex had worked. She'd been very rude when May had gone there to see him. Alex didn't see her. He put his arm round the girl's waist and led her to a table with some vacant seats then went to the bar.

He was on his way back with the drinks when he saw May. His eyes widened and his step faltered. He regained his composure, nodded to her in acknowledgement then turned his back as he sat down. Jenny talked on and May must have given her satisfactory answers for she didn't seem to notice anything was wrong, but May's heart was thudding. The unexpected surge of joy she'd felt when she saw Alex had been quenched when she realised he was with someone else.

Then the music went from modern to traditional and suddenly everyone was on the dance floor. They danced in pairs, fours; in circles and in lines. Children and adults, old and young alike joining in. May was taken along, caught up in the contagious excitement, led through the moves, whirled this way and that, changed partners in a dance that left her breathless: Robin Bell's exuberance, James Armstrong's solidity, Will Bentley's closeness – May hadn't even realised he was here, Sam Castle's steadiness. Then it was Alex Martin holding her, swinging her around. May wondered if he felt the electricity sparking between them as she did. The noise of the crowd seemed to fade. Colours became brighter. The music slowed as May whirled around in Alex's arms. Then it was over and the band struck up another tune. The girl Alex had come with was there, linking her arm through his and dragging him away to dance with her. Will was taking May's arm, leading her back to the table.

No-one else seemed to notice the world had changed in the last few minutes; they danced, chatted, laughed, ate and drank as though nothing had happened. May had to make an effort to join in the conversation, a greater effort not to turn her head and stare, like a fool, at Alex Martin. Then Fiona was saying something May didn't quite catch.

"...married in August." There was a great cheer from round the table.

"What?" May asked. "What was that, I didn't hear?"

"She's gettin' married," Jenny said. "Fiona and Rob are gettin' married in August."

In genuine surprise and pleasure, May went to hug her friend and congratulate Rob. "I didn't realise," she began.

"No, neither did we till recently," Fiona said. Rob kissed her soundly and everyone laughed in delight, including May. This wonderful news had succeeded in dulling the sharpness of her reawakened feelings for Alex.

A fanfare announced the count-down to midnight. Then the hall rang with cheers as balloons cascaded down and party-poppers sent streamers flying. There were hugs, kisses, "Happy New Year" called out from one to another. Will took May in his arms and kissed her. Caught up in the fever of the moment, May kissed him back. Turning from Will to the motherly embrace of Mrs B, May saw Alex watching her. He turned away to take his companion in his arms and kiss her with a passion that caught May's breath.

Some days later, Fiona told May that Alex had gone back to France.

# Chapter Thirty One

Almost before the place was finished, Kevin made the move to Nether Grange. He declared he didn't need working central heating yet – it was nearly summer, after all. The kitchen wasn't finished either, but he was content to use a camping stove if he wanted a hot meal. Kevin's main problem was the lack of transport so was very grateful when 'His Lordship' donated an old Landrover.

Angela's jewellery had proved to be worth far more than May could have imagined. The valuer had been very impressed by the collection, enthusing particularly over the necklace of baguette-cut diamonds along with a matching bracelet May had discovered in with other things. The auction house had put the collection into one of their major sales in London and the bidding had been high for the unique pieces. The diamond necklace and bracelet, in particular, attracted some high bidders and it had gone, for an exorbitant sum in May's judgement, to the United States. The proceeds financed the entire renovation of the old farmhouse. All May kept were Angela's emerald engagement ring and her wedding ring. She wondered what Angela would have thought about it all.

Work went on in fits and starts. Each stage of development was inspected and either passed or suggestions made for modifications. At times it was a struggle to comply with the maze of almost incomprehensible regulations. Despite this, gradually each part was completed and the day came when Kevin started moving the birds to their new home.

May consciously stayed in the background, careful not to let herself become synonymous with the centre. It was Kevin's project; as far as anyone knew he was its driving force. May acknowledged that he really was – she saw herself as merely a helper in getting it started.

Then it was finished. A little more than a year since the outset the centre was up and running; the workmen had left, the mud was covered with new grass, the drive was tarmaced and fenced. The old farmhouse was unrecognisable: the tumbled mess of masonry had been re-assembled and renovated.

Kevin decided on a grand opening. He talked his ideas over with

His Lordship who suggested inviting all those who had helped in the achievement as well as the local papers and television. At first Kevin wasn't too sure about appearing in front of the television cameras but Andrew's bluff heartiness soon convinced him. May set about organising it.

"I'd like to invite His Lordship to officially open the place," Kevin said one day. "What do you think, May?"

"I think it would be very appropriate. Will you ask him?"

"Would you ask him, lass? You seem to have a way with him. He wouldn't turn you down – he's very fond of you, you know."

"And I'm very fond of him. If it wasn't for His Lordship," increasingly May found herself calling Andrew by his honorary title, "there wouldn't be the Nether Grange Wildlife Trust. Yes, I'll ask him."

"You don't think Mr Stanley will be upset not being asked, do you?" Kevin said, concerned for the feelings of the man who, he imagined, was the main benefactor.

"I don't think he will mind at all," May said with a smile.

Andrew was delighted to accept. He confided in May, "This will be my last official duty as 'Lord of the Manor' as it were."

"What do you mean, Andrew?" May asked.

"It means, my dear, that I'm retiring." Andrew put a finger to his lips in warning. "Don't go blabbing about it though. I want to go quietly, don't want a fuss or anything. Folks will think I'm just going on holiday to my mother's in France but Caro and I plan to stay there permanently. Alex will return instead of me and step into my shoes here. It's time the boy took some responsibility and didn't go jaunting around the world."

"But…" May began, unsure how to respond to this piece of news. Alex was coming back. Coming back to stay and run the estate in his father's place. She hadn't seen him since the New Year's Eve party. Had he seen her kissing Will? What would he think of her if he had? Andrew looked at her in amusement at her apparent confusion. "I'll miss you," May finished lamely.

Andrew patted her on the arm. "And I'll miss you, too, my dear. But, like I said," he reminded her, "say nothing." He winked and tapped the side of his prominent nose with a stubby index finger. "Come on. Let's plan my speech."

\* \* \* \* \* \* \* \* \* \*

The opening was a great success and, as promised, Andrew Pennington-Martin did the honours. Part of the opening ceremony included the planting of a tree in front of the main building which was accomplished by Kevin and Andrew – it was a hawthorn. Andrew had explained its significance to May. She was deeply touched by the thought.

"It's to honour you and all you've accomplished," he said. "The hawthorn is also known as the may tree, you know. The usual colour of the blossom is white but – correct me if I'm wrong – I understand that to the Chinese this is the colour of death. So I've chosen one with red blossom, which I've been told is a lucky colour." May nodded at his explanation. Andrew hadn't finished. "The hawthorn is a prickly customer, not something anyone tangles with without coming off the worse for wear, and it's extremely tough, withstanding whatever the weather might be. And, very appropriate to this establishment," Andrew said looking around at the wire cages full of birds, "in the autumn and winter it provides an abundance of berries to feed the wild birds."

May was very moved by his words and leaned forward to kiss Andrew's cheek. "What a beautiful thought, but I never thought of myself as prickly or tough," she said ruefully.

"Oh, I mean it in the best possible way. I never meant to suggest you were prickly," Andrew said quickly. "It's just that I rather suspect under that very calm and serene exterior of yours is a spirit that is strong and determined. You're just the sort of woman young Alex needs." May stiffened at these last words. It was the first time Andrew had referred to her relationship with his son.

"Now, don't go all prickly on me," Andrew said with a grunt of a laugh. "I'll mind my own business and say no more on the subject."

That evening May sat with Armstrong after having supper together at the bungalow and watched the opening of the centre featured on the local television news. Finn sat curled up on the sofa, Armstrong beside him occasionally stroking the dog's soft ears.

Armstrong murmured in approval at Kevin's eloquence in front of the cameras. He'd done a first class job in publicising the place. Already donations were coming in with more promised and a training programme had been set up to allow a young man to join the team as Kevin's understudy.

The Pennington-Martins were leaving for France the next day. May had already said her goodbyes, sad to see them go. Alex would be returning in a week or so, certainly in time for Fiona's wedding. May wondered whether Andrew had told his son anything about her true depth of involvement in the sanctuary.

\* \* \* \* \* \* \* \* \* \*

The long summer days slid by with unexpected swiftness. Visitors thronged the streets of Keswick and the winding Lakeland roads were clogged with cars. One or two ventured up the narrow track to Nether Grange and were disappointed to find it was not a visitor attraction, but a working bird sanctuary.

"I'm going to look at the pros and cons of opening to the general public to show them what we do here," Kevin told May one day. "I think it might be a money-spinner and we could educate the kids, and their parents, on the bird-life of the area." From being a taciturn character, Kevin was turning into a remarkably astute and far-seeing manager as well as continuing the hands-on care that was his forte. "I'm going to put together some proposals for the next trustees' meeting. I wonder what Alec-what's-his-name will have to say. I don't suppose he'll be a patch on His Lordship."

Kevin had taken Andrew's departure to heart and May knew he missed the man's bluff joviality as much as she did. He hadn't transferred the honorary title to Alex but insisted on pretending he couldn't remember his name. May hadn't yet come face to face with Alex but she had seen him about now and then. She looked at the tree Kevin and Andrew had planted and which had become the centre's emblem, noticing how dark the leaves were becoming and the haw berries beginning to ripen. She was going to need all its toughness to overcome Alex's rejection. She was determined not to give up anyway.

"You get yourself off home and get some beauty sleep. It's Mrs Vet's wedding tomorrow and you want to look bright-eyed and bushy-tailed for that, don't you?" Kevin told May. "You've been looking a bit peaked for a few days. You've been doing too much in that office. Being indoors doesn't do a body any good at all, if you ask me."

May smiled automatically. True, she was looking forward to Fiona and Rob's wedding but the thought of being with Alex again was giving her butterflies. The afternoon was warm and drowsy and the thought of relaxing in the garden for a couple of hours held a definite appeal, so May relented and went home.

\* \* \* \* \* \* \* \* \* \*

The church was packed to capacity. Bells pealed, the organ played and a choir sang. It was the full traditional dream of a wedding. Fiona was wearing a long dress of cream silk. Her curls, as ever, were untameable and framed a face that today looked glowing rather than the usual weatherbeaten. Rob's three young nieces were bridesmaids. Rob himself wore a morning suit and a broad smile that remained in place all day. Will Bentley stood at his side as his best-man, competently handsome in his matching outfit.

May couldn't help but compare the religious ceremony to her own marriage which had involved nothing more than an anonymous clerk stamping official papers and had ended in a wreck of twisted metal. Tears sprang unexpectedly to May's eyes as she listened to promises made and saw rings exchanged. She glanced to the side to see Alex watching her. She looked away quickly, unwilling to let him see how affected the was by the service. She felt James Armstrong's presence at her side and was comforted by his nearness and the unassuming care and support he had always given her, right from the moment they first met at the airport. They'd come such a long way together, from his days as the Lees' general factotum to the paternal friend he was now.

The organ music swelled and bride and bridegroom walked back down the aisle, smiling and nodding to friends and relatives as they passed. Confetti and cheers saw the couple into the white limousine which whisked them away to the wedding breakfast at a country house hotel. Champagne for toasts, delicious food and hearty speeches followed. Cameras flashed as photo after photo was taken.

Gradually people began to drift out to the garden or to sit on the terrace after the tiered wedding cake had been cut and distributed to all. May was talking to Fiona's father in the shade of a parasol-covered table when Alex strolled up.

"It been a wonderful day, Uncle Charles. Rob's a lucky man."

"He is indeed, Alex. Come and sit and talk for a while." Charles Wrightson indicated a white painted wrought iron chair. Alex pulled it out from the table, its metal feet scraping on the stone of the terrace. He settled comfortably, leaning back and crossing one leg over the other, ankle resting on knee, obviously at ease and willing to while away the afternoon in conversation. May didn't quite know what to make of it. He'd seemed, to her, to have been avoiding being in her presence since he came back from his time in France. Uncle and nephew chatted easily, occasionally throwing a comment or question in May's direction. Then Charles was called for by a group of departing guests and he left Alex and May alone. They sat in silence, not seeming to know what to say to each other without the presence of a third party.

Then they both began to speak at once. "You first," Alex offered.

"No, please, I was only going to say it's warm," May said lamely.

"Yes, it is warm. A beautiful summer afternoon. You look lovely, May. Green suits you."

May wasn't expecting the compliment and blushed deeply. She looked away not knowing how to reply. It was true, she had dressed carefully, knowing the colour flattered her, in a green linen suit which matched perfectly the deep shade of Angela's emerald ring on her right hand. She still wore the narrow gold wedding-band and diamond ring Jonathan had given her on her left.

"Look at me, May," he asked. She slowly raised her eyes. "You're looking at a fool," Alex told her. "Why did I ever let you go? Why did I let you send me away? I should have fought to keep you. But no, I had to run away, hide and feel sorry for myself while pretending to have not a care in the world."

May's eyes widened at the admission, hardly daring to believe what she was hearing, hardly daring to hope. She looked away, over the smooth lawns, anywhere but at Alex.

"But I went to you, asked you to listen," she said at last. "You wouldn't let me explain."

"Then I'm an even bigger fool."

"Alex..." May began but was cut short by a bell ringing from the French-window. Charles Wrightson stepped out calling to anyone in earshot.

"They're going. Come on, everyone." People laughed and hurried round to the front of the hotel where Fiona and Rob were standing beside Rob's car which was decorated with streamers and daubed with lipstick saying, 'Just Married'. Alex and May followed the others.

"We can't talk now," Alex said. "Can we meet tomorrow?" Not giving May the chance to refuse he said, "I'll come round to your place at two o'clock. OK?"

"OK," May agreed, hope, at last, beginning to flower in her heart.

\* \* \* \* \* \* \* \* \* \*

The phone was ringing when Armstrong dropped May off at her front door. She rushed in, hoping it wouldn't stop before she got to it. Before she could give the customary greeting a distant voice said, "*Wei?*" May could make out a man's voice but there was a great deal of crackling and noise. "*Wei, wei?*" A Chinese voice. May replied in the same language.

"Hello. Who is it?"

"Xi Mei? Is that you?"

"Father?" It was the first time May had heard her father's voice over the telephone. She hadn't spoken to him since he saw her get on the train to begin her journey to England, years ago.

Thanks to the money May sent regularly to her parents, they had been able to buy a small house in the town of Hong Sing. She had paid for a telephone to be installed and called her mother regularly once a week. Her father would never answer its ring, nor make any calls himself.

"Yes, it's me." Usually the connection was good, could have been from next door, but now it echoed and faded, reminding May of the thousands of miles of land and ocean between.

"Father, what's wrong?" There had to be something wrong or he wouldn't have rung.

"It's your mother."

May's heart gave a lurch. "What's the matter? Where is she?" The reply was more crackling obliterating her father's voice. "What was that? I can't hear you."

"...very ill. She's in hospital. You must come home." Fu Gui sounded like an old man, beaten by life. "I don't know what to do. Come home." It might have been interference but May was sure she heard her father crying.

"I'm coming, Father. I'll get on the first flight I can. Tell Mother I'm coming." May put the phone down and immediately picked it up again. She called Armstrong; he was with her in minutes. While she packed a small case he made her travel arrangements.

An Air France flight was leaving from Manchester to Guangzhou late that same evening. Within an hour of speaking to her father, May was on the first stage of her journey to China. Why now, she asked herself. Why now? She had tried to ring Alex, tell him what was happening, but there was no reply. She was distraught that she would have to leave without speaking to him and explaining why she had to go away so suddenly, but Armstrong promised to phone him as soon as he got back from taking May to the airport. May hated not being able to tell Alex herself, but what could she do? She prayed Alex would understand, then she prayed for Lin Yong, her mother.

## Chapter Thirty Two

May found Fu Gui in a state nearing collapse. She was frightened by how old he seemed. His hair was grey and straggly, his baggy trousers were crumpled and stained and his shirt was buttoned up wrong. The smell coming off him suggested he had neither washed himself nor changed his clothes for some days. Grimy hands and stubbly chin confirmed he wasn't looking after himself.

The little house was in an equally squalid condition. The rooms May was sure Lin Yong kept clean and neat were turned upside-down with dirty dishes left everywhere.

"Where's Mother? How is she?" was May's greeting.

"Who's that?" Fu Gui peered short-sightedly at the figure standing in the doorway outlined against the light outside.

"It's me, Father. May... Xi Mei."

"Is it really you? You've come?"

"I'm here, now. But what about Mother?" May asked with growing concern that she was too late and Lin Yong was dead.

"She's in hospital. She needed an operation and now there's not enough money to pay for her to be looked after," Fu Gui almost whined.

The words tumbled out, May struggling to understand. She eventually learned that her father had had to pay in advance before the operation had gone ahead. May was alarmed: there should have been sufficient in the bank account that had been set up so May could send her parents money. But that was a different question, one that she didn't have time for now.

"Have a wash and get changed, Father, and we'll go to see Ma. I'm here now. I'll take care of everything."

The hospital was an ugly concrete block on the edge of town. It had been built since May had left but looked depressingly down at heel for a new building. The doors creaked alarmingly as she pushed them open. Inside it was surprisingly clean with white-painted walls and well-scrubbed tiled floors. May had expected the inside to be as awful as the outside. Obviously no thought had been given to making the place comfortable or welcoming for either patients or visitors, though. A glass-fronted office stood off to one side and May went to enquire for her mother. The directions to the ward were not particularly helpful, Fu Gui didn't seem to know the way either. Nevertheless May found it and was intercepted by a nurse who looked May and her father up and down as if assessing their cleanliness to enter her pristine domain.

"How is my mother? What is wrong with her?"

"She's had an operation to remove her appendix." Disapproval was written all over the woman's face. "You, her daughter, should know this." May let the comment pass. At one time she would have been defensive, tried to excuse her perceived shortcomings to the other woman.

"I'd like to see my mother, please."

Without further conversation the nurse led May and Fu Gui into a spartan ward with four beds. Only one was occupied, the others stood empty, mattresses bare. The first thing May noticed about her mother was her grey-streaked hair; there had been only one or two strands of grey last time May had seen her. Lin Yong's lined face was sallow and her hands, which lay on top of the sheet which was the only covering necessary in this hot, humid climate, were thin and mottled.

"Ma." May stepped to the bedside and took her mother's hand in her own. Lin Yong opened her eyes.

"Xi Mei! There was no need for you to come." Lin Yong's voice was as strong and musical as ever, belying her apparent frailness. She turned to her husband who was standing staring dejectedly at the floor. "I told you not to send for her." He gave no sign he had heard.

Footsteps crossing the floor made May look up. A doctor was coming over towards them. May met him half way across the room, offered her hand and said, "Hello, I'm May Lee, Lin Yong's daughter."

Her self-assured demeanour seemed to surprise the doctor, but he shook the offered hand and introduced himself. Under May's questioning the doctor told her that her mother had indeed had her appendix removed, but her condition had been serious. He shook his head.

"She is a stubborn country-woman. She should have seen a doctor long before she became so ill. She chose not to complain about the pain she was in and, as a consequence, suffered peritonitis. But you mustn't worry, she's well on the way to a good recovery. Will you be able to pay for her care here in the hospital?"

May wasn't really surprised at this question. She knew rural healthcare was in crisis. Most poor local people didn't have health insurance and payment was often demanded up-front for any treatment. It wasn't that the hospitals weren't there – many were very well equipped – the difficulty was people couldn't afford them. She was pleased that she could.

"That will not be a problem. I will pay for anything my mother needs. I would be grateful if you would see to it that she is well looked after until she is fit to come home."

Reassured that cash would be forthcoming, Lin Yong's care was guaranteed. May thanked the doctor and the nurse and left with the promise to return the next day. Fu Gui followed, his good spirits beginning to return now everything was being looked after.

Back at her parents' house May set about putting things in order while her father pottered in the garden. They still grew many of their own vegetables and even had a trio of hens scratching for worms and grubs in the loose earth. May managed to prepare a simple meal; her culinary skills were confined to English cooking.

At last she had time to catch her breath after the mad dash to get here and May's thoughts turned to Alex. What had he thought when James told him where she had gone? She desperately hoped he didn't think she had run away from him again. She needed to speak to him, reassure him that it wasn't the case. She was uncertain what day it was. What time was it? She worked out it would be about six in the morning back in England. That was far too early to ring. She'd give it another hour. Seven was still early, but at least it would mean Alex wouldn't have gone out. The next hour dragged.

"Hello. Laurel Bank."

"Alex." Just hearing his voice made May's legs shake and heart pound. It was something she'd never experienced before; almost a thrill of danger.

"May? Sweetheart, is that you?"

"Alex." She couldn't seem to say anything else.

"How are you? What about your mother?" His voice was full of concern.

"She'll be fine. I'm sorry I had to leave like that, without even being able to tell you, to explain."

"Jim Armstrong explained. I would have come with you, you know. You didn't have to..." A sudden burst of static made May jump and hold the phone away from her ear.

"Hello? Hello?"

"I'm still here, sweetheart, but I can hardly hear you. Do you know when you'll be back?"

"Maybe in two weeks, perhaps sooner." May knew she would leave as soon as her mother was home and a reliable woman brought in to look after her until she could manage on her own.

"Ring me. Let me know. Take care of yourself, sweetheart. Bye."

"Goodbye, Alex." May put the phone down gently and sighed. It was going to be all right. Alex understood.

Lin Yong understood, too, when May told her she was leaving so soon after she returned home to convalesce. "I have a life of my own in England, now. I need to go back to my own home, to my friends." May hadn't told her mother about Alex. It was too soon, this feeling was too new to be talked about. Fu Gui didn't understand. He said a daughter's place was to look after her parents if she had no husband or children.

May found out what had happened to the money that should have been in the bank: Fu Gui had had another of his many disagreements with Xiao Cheng, the Chief of Police. Another hefty fine had been paid. It didn't seem as though her father would ever learn not to antagonise the man. It hurt May to think of the worry it would always cause her mother.

Lin Yong touched the golden dragon May wore. "I'm very pleased to see you wearing this," she said.

May told her mother about thinking she had lost it and believing it was the cause of the deaths of Bobby, Jonathan and Angela.

"I should have realised it wasn't the dragon that caused it all. Come to think about it, it didn't bring you such good fortune, did it, Ma?"

Lin Yong looked away, saying nothing. May was horrified with herself that she had spoken to her mother in such a way. She changed the subject.

"I'm leaving tomorrow, Ma. I must go and pack." She left Lin Yong to her own thoughts.

\* \* \* \* \* \* \* \* \*

Hong Sing station was alive with noise and packed with people all seeming to be carrying on conversations at the tops of their voices. As the train drew in the crowd pushed and jostled, people dangerously close to the platform's edge, each one determined to be first to board and get a seat. If she wasn't to be pushed aside May had to join in the free-for-all. Despite her innate good manners she found it grimly satisfying to squirm in front of a big woman with a loud voice and win a seat beside a window. She waved to her father who was searching the faces of the crowds on the train. Just as it began to grind its was out of the station Fu Gui caught a glimpse of his daughter and waved back. She wondered how many years it would be before she saw either him or her mother again.

Three changes of train brought her into the city of Guangzhou late that afternoon. Her flight to England didn't leave until the next evening, but May had wanted to get there with plenty of time to spare. She didn't want to run the risk of being held up and missing the plane. As a rare treat, she had booked herself a room in one of the big hotels overlooking one of the city's waterways.

May hadn't become acclimatised to the hot and humid conditions of this part of southern China in the short time she had been back and appreciated the luxury of the air-conditioned room she was shown into. She put her small case on the bed and took out a light blouse and cotton skirt. The journey here had left her feeling sweaty and grimy and all she wanted, at this precise moment, was to have a shower and put on some clean clothes. That accomplished, she had time to relax, be by herself without any demands on her time and attention.

There were large sliding doors that opened out onto a balcony with a table and two chairs. She slid the doors apart and stepped outside into the cooling day. From the balcony she looked out over the Pearl River where the city's modern high-rise buildings towered above its tree-lined banks. May thought it was one of the most exciting city views she had ever seen, but was it because she was on her way back to Alex that she felt that way? She wished he was here to share it with.

Tomorrow she would go shopping, she decided. She was going to buy presents for everyone at home. Interesting or amusing little things. She smiled in happiness at the thought.

She waited until late evening before phoning Alex. Ignoring her protests he insisted he would be at Manchester to meet her from the long flight. She was longing to see him again.

"Goodnight, Alex. See you tomorrow. Or will it be the day after?" May laughed at her own confusion over days and time differences.

"Goodnight, sweetheart. I love you," Alex said softly.

May stood on the balcony for a long time looking at the lights that were strung along the bridges; the moving lights of water-craft; the street lights twinkling through the trees and reflecting in the moving waters of the Pearl River. This must be one of the most beautiful places in the world, she thought. This was where Alex had said, 'I love you.' No-one had ever said that to her before. She couldn't believe her good fortune; perhaps the golden dragon did have powers, after all.

* * * * * * * * * *

Alex and May were shyly restrained with each other. He was waiting in the crush of people clustered in the arrivals lounge at the airport. Just time for a fleeting kiss before Alex navigated them through the confusing corridors and walkways. Each looked the same as the previous one and May was amazed he managed to find his way to the car, then round the many-branching roads before finally getting onto the motorway that would lead them home. He stopped the car outside the front door of Fellbeck Cottage and delivered May into the care of the waiting James Armstrong.

"Tomorrow, May," Alex told her. "Come to see me tomorrow? Elevenish? We'll talk." May nodded in reply. "Sleep well, sweetheart," he said. She knew she would. She was home, now. Where she belonged. With the people she loved.

* * * * * * * * * *

May told him everything. Nothing was spared, not even the lack of physical intimacy with her husband. She wanted him to know everything, understand everything that had made her the person she was. They sat on the west terrace of Laurel Bank looking over the lovely gardens to the lake beyond. On the table between them were the remains of their lunch. Alex listened in silence, punctuated only occasionally by an encouraging word or a murmured one of sympathy. When it came to the inheritance he let out a thoughtful whistle. "That's quite a responsibility, sweetheart." He didn't seem to know what to say as she finished but he knelt at her side, put his arms around her and kissed her. She fervently hoped that all she had told him didn't make him change his mind about the way he said he felt about her.

"You're an amazing woman, May. Truly amazing. All you've been through. I don't know how I would have coped with half of it." Alex looked at her as if he would say more. Instead he grinned, got to his feet and pulled her up. "Let's go over to see Fiona and Rob. They're back from their honeymoon and I know Fiona can't wait to see you. I rang her yesterday to say you were home." May was grateful Alex said no more at present. He seemed to understand her need for a little time to recover, to push everything back into the past again, where it belonged.

They walked hand in hand to the car, each wrapped in their own thoughts but content just to be in the presence of the other.

* * * * * * * * * *

The long summer days shortened as fruits ripened in the hedgerows. Leaves turned to yellow and rust and bracken coloured the fellsides a glowing bronze. May's garden overflowed with chrysanthemums and dahlias, crocosmia and asters. Up at Nether Grange the birds either flourished with the care lavished on them or sadly died if Kevin couldn't coax them to live. At Ravendale Farm the hay making was done and the bales led in to be stored in the barn. The tups were put in with the ewes to ensure next spring's crop of lambs. Armstrong was never seen without Finn at his side as they walked the fells. His leg was almost as strong and sturdy again as it ever had been, though as the frosts came on he complained of pains in his knee. It became a standing joke that he could predict a frost more accurately than the weather-man. May and Alex took their time, got to know each other and grew closer each day.

On Christmas Day Alex was included in the Bells' festive celebrations at Ravendale and caused a furore when, in the middle of Christmas dinner, he stood up and clinked a spoon against his wineglass, calling for attention. All heads turned to him, eyes bright and curious. With much show of theatrical formality he asked May to marry him. There was much good-humoured shouted advice both pro and anti to both parties until Alex called a halt, raising his voice above the din.

In the hush that followed May said, "Yes," in a loud clear voice bringing cheers from everyone. Alex kissed her soundly and she responded by kissing him back to the great delight of all.

* * * * * * * * * *

May was a spring bride and went to her wedding in a wine-red dress on the arm of a proud James Armstrong who gave her away. The church was filled to overflowing with friends and family when May Lee became May Martin.

* * * * * * * * * *

Their first daughter, Pearl, was born the following March. The turn of the millennium. The year 2000. The Year of the Golden Dragon. Good fortune would surely smile on this child.

Printed in the United Kingdom by
Lightning Source UK Ltd., Milton Keynes
137347UK00001B/289/P